The Carnival of Ash

Tom Beckerlegge

First published 2022 by Solaris
an imprint of Rebellion Publishing Ltd,
Riverside House, Osney Mead,
Oxford, OX2 0ES, UK

www.solarisbooks.com

ISBN: 978-1-78618-500-6

10 9 8 7 6 5 4 3 2 1

A CIP catalogue record for this book is available from the
British Library.

Designed & typeset by Rebellion Publishing

Printed in Denmark

The Carnival of Ash

Tom Beckerlegge

SOLARIS

Contents

First Canto
The Five Deaths of Carlo Mazzoni

I. *An Auspicious Arrival*

THE RETREATING WINTER had left cypresses shivering in the graveyard beside the Church di San Felice. In the shadow of listing crosses, muddy hollows stagnated; angels slipped despairingly into a tangled sea of grass. Rows of headstones stood absent-minded, crumbling and clad in moss, their inscriptions weathered to the point of illegibility. Having already departed the world once, the graveyard's inhabitants now faced disappearing from memory altogether—a mouldering republic, on the verge of oblivion.

Presently, an old man came tramping through the forest of crosses. Wild-haired and stooped with age, he moved nevertheless with a light step, pulling behind him a small cart bearing a body wrapped in a sheet. An upended shovel jutted into the air above his shoulder. Upon arriving at his destination, an unmarked plot at the cemetery's eastern limits, he planted the shovel in the hard ground and began manhandling the corpse from the cart, only to discover—

to his surprise—that the hole he had laboured to dig the previous day was already occupied.

A young man lay at the bottom of the grave, his eyes closed and his arms folded across his chest, cradling a sheaf of parchment. He was unshaven and unkempt, his hose torn at the knee and his doublet motley with wine stains, dirt and what appeared to be dried blood. An ugly bruise flowered on his temple. Try as he might to affect the inert and indifferent air of the dead, the youth was visibly shivering in the cool morning. The gravedigger, whose name was Ercole, reached down with his shovel and nudged him in the leg. He twitched but did not open his eyes. Ercole straightened up.

"I confess that the ways and whims of the nobleman will forever remain a mystery to me," he said, his tone conversational, "but I'll wager there's softer beds to be found in the city."

"Leave me be, sir." A sombre whisper, floating up from the earth. "The only comfort I seek is darkness, silent and eternal."

"You would have me throw a blanket of soil over you?"

"Wield your shovel, sir," the young man said, his eyes still closed. "I am no more alive than the heap of flesh and bone inside that sheet."

The gravedigger looked down at the corpse by his feet. "You've a lot more to say than he has," he said.

"Then I will speak no more." He drew his papers tight to his chest. "This city is deaf to my words anyway."

"Ah. You are a poet."

At that, an eye opened. "What would you know about poetry?"

"Scant little, sir. I am but a humble gravedigger—my daily companions have few pretty words to offer me on our short journeys together. But this is Cadenza, home to a hundred poets, all of them solemn with heartbreak, their spirits bruised and buffeted by the violent affections of their art."

"Do not speak to me of broken hearts, as though I were some lovestruck maiden," the youth said bitterly. "You know nothing of the black deeds I have committed to leave myself here, my clothes torn and my reputation in ruins."

"I know that you would not be the first to find yourself nursing a sore head and regrets at the day's first light," Ercole tried. "The sun will still rise in the sky, the birds will not fall silent at your passage. Do not rush to make a decision that cannot be undone."

"Would that I could undo the previous night," came the groan, "then I would bound from this place and bid you good morning. But what is done is done, and here I must remain."

Ercole tugged thoughtfully on his ear. "This does present me with something of a problem," he said. "Seeing as I now have two dead men—a tanner, steeped in the odoriferous perfume of his trade; and a poet, cloaked in the dismay of a night gone awry—and only the one grave with which to accommodate them."

"A question of arithmetic. Do you see an abacus upon me?"

"Would you not wish a headstone for your final resting place, so that your family may find you?"

The young man shook his head. "I have brought eternal disgrace to my name," he said hoarsely. "I am not fit to bear it, even in death."

"And what house would this be, so brittle a construction that it trembles at a single night of mischief?"

"Mazzoni." He swallowed. "My name is Carlo Mazzoni."

Ercole's brow wrinkled. "Not a family I am familiar with."

"We left Cadenza twenty years past—I am the first of my line to return. I arrived two months ago, directly upon the day that Tommaso Cellini died."

"An auspicious arrival. A bookcase fell on him, so I hear."

"It was a tragedy," Carlo said. "He was a true poet."

"And a beloved ruler, yet what protection did mere reputation offer him, in the face of toppling furniture? I wonder what Tommaso would give, to be alive."

"I dreamt of walking beside him at the March of the Poets," Carlo murmured. "Two artists, step in step. Now I dream only of death."

"Only a young man would speak of death so lightly. You have not seen enough of life to know its value."

Carlo laughed incredulously. "You would accuse me of ingratitude?"

"The priest would contend that violence to oneself is an affront to God."

"And what would the gravedigger contend?"

Ercole considered the question. "The gravedigger tries to affront as few people as possible," he said finally, "especially those blessed with the all-seeing gaze of the omniscient. But—so far as he has seen—one corpse looks very much like another."

"In death, we all are brothers," Carlo proclaimed. "Let us speak no more. Pick up your shovel and give me my blanket."

A gust of wind blew through the cypress trees, rain upon

its breath. Ercole blew out his cheeks. Finally, with a shrug, he bent down and rolled the tanner's body over the edge of the grave. A cry of protest echoed around the cemetery.

"Hold, hold!" Carlo spluttered, wriggling out from beneath the stinking corpse. "Surely you cannot think to bury me with this stranger?"

"In death, we all are brothers," Ercole reminded him. "And if you had any idea how difficult it is to dig a grave in this weather, you would not ask such a foolish question. Stay if you will, but you will have to share your blanket, for now and all eternity."

He prised free a clump of earth with his shovel and flung it into the hole, his hair blowing in wild strands across his face. Raindrops peppered the headstones. The soil, too, fell without distinction, covering the dead and the living alike. Finally, a pale hand of surrender rose up from the grave. Shouldering arms, Ercole stood back as Carlo climbed awkwardly out of the ground. The poet's unruly brown curls were flecked with soil, the dark rings beneath his eyes only exaggerating the gauntness of his cheeks. A sour cloud of wine hung about him.

"Wisely done," said Ercole. He nodded at the sheets of parchment garlanding the tanner's body. "Though I think you may have forgotten something."

Carlo bowed his head. "The earth can have it," he said quietly. "I will leave it in the unlit halls of the dead and blind worms, where no eyes shall look upon it."

"A most sympathetic audience," the old man agreed brightly.

Once more, the shovel's bite rang out in the cool air.

Yet before Ercole could deliver its contents to the earth, Carlo made a strangled noise and leapt back into the hole. Gathering up the loose pages, he brushed the dirt from them and clambered to the surface, offering Ercole an apologetic look as he scrambled to his feet.

"Poets," the gravedigger said, with a shake of the head.

II. *City of Words*

TRADITION HAD IT, around the busy hearths and dining tables of the Mazzoni family, that their copy of *De Incendio Urbis* by the ancient poet Lucan had been one of the first volumes to enter Cadenza, back when the City of Words had been little more than a cluster of workshops and rude dwellings on the banks of the Adige River. The scroll, part of a library of epic poems and lost plays, had travelled the rutted paths from Venice in a cart belonging to a man named Angelo Uccello. How this august collection had come into Uccello's possession remained a matter for debate. Some named him a son of Alexandria, a direct descendent of the librarians of the Museaum; others claimed he was the son of a crazed Venetian nobleman, who had spirited away his family's books when his father had threatened to burn them; still others, more prosaically, declared him to be nothing more than a common thief. Uccello himself offered no comment on the subject. He remained an elusive figure, who commissioned no busts or paintings of his likeness in his lifetime, and in death bequeathed to the city the histories and lives of all manner of men, save himself.

So Cadenzans could only speculate as to why Uccello paused in their village, where fishing boats dozed on the river and ploughs etched their simple signature in the earth. He presented his scrolls before a local landowner, for whom the wisdoms of Athens and Rome meant little, and who wrinkled his nose at the cylinders of stale parchment. It was rumoured that Uccello averted dismissal only by thrusting upon his host a codex infused with the obscure magic of the Kabbalah, said to predict the hour of death of any man who would open it. Before the week was out, Ucello's volumes had been installed in a townhouse somewhere in the vicinity of the Old Market. He sought to add to his collection, sending agents to comb the catalogues of remote Alpine monasteries. Word of the assemblage of codices and tracts at the House of Uccello drew curious scholars from the universities of Bologna and Padua; in time, a second reading room opened on the other side of the river.

Just as Salerno, the Town of Hippocrates, was a font of medical knowledge, and the glassblowers on the Venetian island of Murano were acknowledged as the masters of their craft, so Cadenza became defined by its love of the written word. Noble families vied to build ever-grander libraries, complex networks of patronage extending down to the lowliest reading desk. The guild of the Folio was established to arrange and administer the flow of volumes around the city. Cadenza's eastern and western banks were christened the Recto and the Verso: upon the former, traders and scholars rubbed shoulders in the busy streets; upon the latter, well-to-do citizens built palaces by the Adige. A second bridge, the Ponte Nuovo, was built upriver from the Ponte Mercato to link the two banks. Imposing walls encompassed Cadenza like parentheses.

This period of prosperity and civic accord came to an abrupt end on the Feast Day of San Sebastiano, amid trembling floors and a tumultuous rain of masonry. A violent earthquake struck the city, felling towers and swallowing up the House of Uccello. Rescuers hastened to the library through clouds of choking dust but there was no sign of its founder. All that could be retrieved from the reading room before it slipped into the earth was a handful of damaged scrolls—including, so the Mazzonis maintained, Lucan's *De Incendio Urbis*.

In their grief and dismay, some Cadenzans saw the hand of divine judgement, a warning against the city's infatuation with its books. Stinging verses were nailed to doors, accusing the Folio of fattening themselves at the city's expense. Men marched through the streets beneath the banners of the wolf and the hawk. To staunch the threat of insurrection, the Folio proposed a new ruling council, the Seven, whose members would be decided by a popular vote every two years, and who would meet inside a new library to replace the House of Uccello. The Accademia was constructed on the Piazza della Rosa: a cathedral dedicated to the worship of books, its vast central chamber was surrounded by eight reading rooms, each topped with cupolas that nested in the shadow of the great dome.

The scrolls saved from the House of Uccello—carefully brushed free of dirt and dust—were the first to be re-housed in the new library. *De Incendio Urbis* was afforded pride of place on the shelves of the Mezzanino, a magnificent gallery that extended around the perimeter of the dome above the Accademia's main reading room. Here, beneath the gaze of studious cherubs leafing through winged volumes, it was promptly stolen by a librarian named Guido, who slipped the poem beneath his robe and walked calmly past the guards at the doors. Such an act risked banishment or even the loss of a hand: Guido, however, who prayed nightly in an inn by the Garden of Leaves to the Sword and the Cup, the Baton and the Coin—the four gods of cards—was inured to fortune's fickle winds. He sold the scroll to an unscrupulous dealer at the Old Market, who in turn sold it on (at a significant mark-up) to Duke Sandro Strozzi, a noted collector of rare volumes.

Arrived from Rome in the aftermath of an ugly dispute with Pope Boniface VIII, and wealthy beyond imagining, the Strozzi family had stamped their mark upon Cadenza's skyline with their palaces and libraries. They sought also to alter the architecture of its corridors of power, filling the Seven with allies and supporters. At the Strozzis' instigation, a new position of power was created, the Artifex, to sit at the Council's head—an office duly assumed, upon a unanimous council vote, by one Bartolomeo Strozzi, Duke Sandro's younger brother. In celebration of his coronation, Bartolomeo ordered the building of a Palazzo Nero directly opposite the Accademia on the Piazza della Rosa, symbolizing a new balance between Cadenza's libraries and the institutions of the state: and all of them subservient to the will of their new master.

De Incendio Urbis remained on the shelves of Duke Sandro's study for almost ten years before taking its leave in dramatic fashion, flying through an open window like a startled canary. It had been launched by Sandro's wife, the Duchess Alessandra, upon the discovery of a stash of letters from the celebrated ink maid Ginevra di Lecce detailing in explicit fashion an imagined coupling between the duke and his sister-in-law, Monna. A loud cry went up from the street below but Strozzi—whose head had been directly in the scroll's path before he had sought cover behind a divan—judged he had more pressing issues to attend to than the pursuit of his lost volume.

Had the beleaguered duke been able to go to the window, he would have seen the druggist Pandolfo sprawled out in the dirt, a bruise on his temple and the scroll resting innocently beside him on the ground. The unfortunate druggist, momentarily rendered senseless by the duchess's wrath, was helped to his feet, the scroll pressed into his uncomprehending hands. Returning to his shop on the Via Maggio, Pandolfo brusquely palmed it off on to a melancholy poet named Neri, who sought to ease his troubled nights with infusions of a sleeping draught of henbane, mulberry juice and lettuce. The gift—offered with such apparent disdain—was in fact a silent token of Pandolfo's love. Yet its contents proved a bitter poison for Neri. Driven to despair by the brilliance of Lucan's poetry, one night he took a walk across the Ponte Nuovo and vanished in the fog. Pandolfo's body was discovered three days later, black lipped and ghastly, dead by his own arts. *De Incendio Urbis* was clutched in his grasp: a sexton carefully pried the scroll free and tossed it into a chest, where it would lie forgotten for decades.

As Lucan's poem surrendered to darkness and obscurity,

the insalubrious neighbourhood north of the Via Maggio witnessed the arrival of men with strange tools, metal workers claiming the skills of type-founding and punch-cutting learnt in Cologne, Paris and Kraków. Cadenza's first press was established at the sign of the Heron, from whose generous bill came flooding forth all manner of books and pamphlets. No longer would the Folio have to send out its agents to procure volumes for its libraries' shelves. The Printing Quarter flourished, marching to the stamp and thrum of its presses while never quite shaking off its reputation for double-dealing and skullduggery. It was at the sign of the Cart that an apprentice punch-cutter produced a chest filled with dusty scrolls that he had discovered in his family's attic—scrolls purchased on the spot by Giacomo Mazzoni, a trader of growing prosperity.

At this time, the Palazzo Nero was newly occupied by Tommaso Cellini, a brash and brilliant young poet who had swept to power on a tide of public support. Under his command, Cadenza had embarked on a campaign of aggressive expansion, sealed not on the battlefield but the page, contracts and secured lines of credit snaking back to banking houses in Antwerp and London. The new Artifex became famous for his extravagant feasts and festivals, the centrepiece of which, the Carnival of Wit, was said to rival even Venice's orgies of extravagance. Raised aloft over the salty lagoons to the north-east of Cadenza, Venice had watched the rise of its provincial cousin with amused condescension, confident in the unsurpassable skills of the Aldine Press. Only once, during a dispute over contract writing, had skirmishes flared into open warfare, which had ended in a chastening defeat for Cadenza in the field at Rovigo—although there were those who also detected Venice's subtle influence behind the riots that engulfed the Printing Quarter that winter.

These were turbulent, uncertain times for the city. In the fourth year of Tommaso's reign, he survived an assassination attempt by Donato Pitti, head of one of the city's noble families. The Artifex reacted with characteristic speed and vigour, rounding up every last member of the Pitti bloodline and casting them onto bonfires in the middle of the Piazza di Pietra. Donato himself was tied face-down beneath a plank and dragged by an ass through the streets before his bloodied body was added to the flames. His palaces were torn down, reducing the once opulent neighbourhood in the south-eastern corner of the Recto to rubble and ash. Giacomo Mazzoni— who had had cause to do business with the Pittis and was, by nature, of a cautious disposition—judged it wise for his family to leave Cadenza, quietly packing up their possessions and heading for their countryside villa on the edge of Ferrara.

As a young boy, Giacomo's son Carlo had been fascinated by the story of the ancient poem in the family library, from where he was regularly chased for trying to free *De Incendio Urbis* from its protective glass case. While his elder brothers learned the ways of the family business, Carlo had been earmarked for the church—to which end, his father had engaged a tutor from Cadenza, a scholar persuaded away from the Accademia at no small cost. Frustrated by the limits of a provincial education, Carlo petitioned his father to be allowed to return to the city in which Giacomo had made his fortune.

To further his cause, he turned to Lucan's verse. In *De Incendio Urbis*, the poet had turned upon his former ally, the Emperor Nero, accusing him in crackling invective of starting the Great Fire of Rome. Inspired, Carlo began work on a poem of his own—though his effort, which he named in tribute *The City of Flames*, was devoted to Cadenza, and the efforts of Tommaso Cellini to shield the city from those who would put it to torch. Time and again, Carlo affirmed the Mazzonis' loyalty to the Artifex, devoting verses to lauding his name and deeds. Giacomo proudly declared the finished poem to be a work of genius, and it even drew grudging praise from Carlo's tutor.

Carlo's entrance into the church was delayed. Instead, several months after his twenty-first name day, he rode forth from his family estate for Cadenza. He carried on his person a letter from his father to Lorenzo Sardi—one of the city's foremost poets and an old acquaintance of Giacomo—and his own verse, its pages bound in cloth like a sacred relic. As he followed the Adige's meandering path through the countryside, Carlo entertained himself with idle dreams of his reception: of stages before packed squares, and salons hushed in awe; of wistful sighs and rapturous applause.

At the appearance of Cadenza's proud towers on the horizon, however, he quickly apprehended that something was wrong. There was a hubbub at the city gates, its walls alive with frantic activity. Bells reverberated in their chambers: their mouths round with surprise, a death upon their lips. Tommaso Cellini was no more.

* * *

III. *A Restless Temper*

CARLO STOOD AND watched, his teeth chattering with the cold, as Ercole filled the grave he had just vacated. The rain fell in insistent diagonals; rolling up *City of Flames*, he slipped the poem inside his doublet. His skull was a cage of pain, a crushing weight pressing down on his brow, nerves scraping against one another like shrill blades upon the whetstone. The smell of the luckless tanner lingered in his nostrils, threatening to rouse the dregs of wine sloshing about in his belly into open rebellion.

Yet what was pain but passing discomfort, when measured against the shame that had settled around Carlo's shoulders like an icy cloak? Befogged by wine, his mind retained only ugly glimpses of the previous evening, but in the whistling wind he heard echoes of the catcalls and jeers that had marked his exit from the Ridolfi salon. How he had come to find himself in this dank graveyard remained a mystery— Carlo could not bring himself to search his recollections further. It was as though he had been possessed by a demon, so violently and inexplicably had he behaved. Never again, he vowed, would a drop of wine pass his lips.

A metal clang made Carlo start. Ercole had tossed his shovel into the cart and was brushing the soil from his hands.

"That should do it," he said. "Come, let us remove ourselves from the rain's reproach. I'll not prise you from the grave only to lose you to a chill."

He whistled a jaunty air as he navigated his cart away through the puddles. Benumbed with cold, Carlo saw little option but to follow him. The angels on their plinths formed a disapproving gallery as he trudged by. Upon descending from the terrace, Ercole abruptly wheeled his cart off the path and ducked behind a statue, gesturing at Carlo to follow suit. Crouching beside him, through the rain Carlo spied a cloaked figure kneeling before a headstone.

"What are we doing?" he whispered, shivering.

Ercole ran a damp palm through his hair. "Paying our respects," he said. "You are gazing upon the magnificence that is Hypatia the ink maid."

"I have seen ink maids about the city," Carlo said—curious, despite himself. "But I have not heard the name Hypatia."

"You are so ignorant I could weep for you," Ercole murmured. "Of all those elemental creatures who serve the city's hearts with their pen, Hypatia is the most brilliant and elusive. She comes here, from time to time, to pay her respects at the tomb of Ginevra di Lecce."

Hyptia glanced back over her shoulder, as though feeling their gaze on her. Within the depths of her hood, Carlo caught a fleeting glimpse of a heart-shaped face, framed with dark ringlets of hair. At the sight of the two men watching her, Hypatia rose. Drawing her hood around her, she walked quickly away.

"Like a startled faun, she flees," breathed Ercole. "Yet, mark it well, she will return. Reason enough to stay alive, my boy."

Manhandling his cart back on to the flagstones, the gravedigger pressed on with renewed vigour. Above the soaring crosses, a high wall marked the cemetery's end—Ercole steered through the gate and tramped along a muddy, overgrown path lined with thorns. They crested a small rise.

Before them rose a crumbling church of blackened stone, listing upon its foundations, a round tower rising up at an uncertain angle. Sections of the roof had been torn away, leaving gaping holes between the slates. Birds nested in the tower's upper reaches.

"Behold, the Church di San Felice!" Ercole exclaimed, his face crinkling with delight. "It was held to be the finest on the Verso, in its day."

"That day would seem to be long passed," said Carlo.

"The church was struck by lightning five summers ago and burned beyond repair," the old man explained. "Now it stands empty, abandoned by parishioner and cleric alike. Yet life cannot continue without end, and the dead still need a place to rest. For now, I stand as custodian of the graveyard di San Felice, welcoming new occupants in the hope that a priest might appear to perform the holy ministrations. But as the city stands currently, in chaos and confusion…"

Ercole deposited his cart outside the entrance to the church and slipped inside. The cavernous nave had been stripped of altar and pews, its bare stone floor covered in dust and droppings. Cobweb tapestries shivered in the draughts. A set of wrought-iron steps spiralled up to the pulpit, where the lectern had been fashioned into a writing desk with the addition of a stool, parchment, pen and ink. Lighting a candle from a set by the door, Ercole headed in the opposite direction, towards a flight of stairs leading down to the cellar.

Carlo followed him down into a windowless chamber with blackened and scarred walls, the ceiling adorned with arcane chalk symbols. A bench was scattered with cracked glass vessels and misshapen tongs. Jars filled with murky liquids lined the shelves. A furnace had been installed in the corner of the room, its smoky breath laced with the unmistakable tang of gunpowder.

Carlo stared him about in wonder. "What manner of gravedigger are you, Ercole?"

"One possessed of a restless temper—a wayfarer, given to digressions and sudden enthusiasms that leave me unable to linger long in any one place," Ercole replied, picking up a beaker and tapping its contents. "I have broken bread with Englishmen and shared a Tartar's fire. I have roamed uncharted lands by sled and by dhow, dodging the snapping jaws of monsters undreamt by the bestiaries. I have encountered savages in the court of kings and nobility in peasant hovels. And just as I have learnt that a man's title offers little clue to his true nature, so I am compelled to find the true nature of matter, in all its forms and various transformations from one state to another."

"You speak of alchemy."

Ercole spun round and gripped Carlo by the arm. "Do not confuse me for some peddler of quackery, my words coated in worthless yellow lacquer. I speak of the science of transmutation, the search for a harmony both natural and perfect."

"Transform my misery into joy," Carlo said dourly, "and I will name you the greatest alchemist who ever lived."

Ercole filled a bowl of water from a pail. "Let us begin with the application of water to dirty flesh," he said. "Your night's misadventures have left a smell upon you that makes even my hardy nostrils recoil."

Carlo ruefully obeyed, carefully laying down his poem

before commencing to scrub himself clean. To his surprise, Ercole reappeared with a fresh doublet and hose, of finer quality and fit than Carlo's own, before proceeding to lay out beer and bread upon the table. The old man attacked the food with glee, but Carlo's stomach remained too tender to eat, the pungent waft of ale threatening to decant the contents of the previous night all over the floor. He stared mournfully into space.

Ercole took a deep swig from his tankard and smacked his lips.

"Sitting here as we do," he said thoughtfully, "in the depths of this ruined building, I am reminded of the works of Caesarius of Heisterbach. He wrote of an unchaste priest who hastened to ring his church bells to ward off an approaching storm, only to be struck by lightning, burning his robes and consuming certain intimate parts of his body as punishment for his sins."

Carlo grunted.

"My point being," the old man continued, "that if your transgressions truly require atonement, God knows where to find you. Do not punish yourself unduly in the meantime. Come, eat—the world is a happier place for a full belly."

"Are all the gravediggers of Cadenza so wise?"

Ercole shrugged. "Spend a day with a shovel in your hand," he said. "Picking up a pen will feel as no great labour."

"Then take me on as your apprentice, and I shall dig happily forever."

"This is no place for the young. Heed the words of an old man, Carlo: go home to your father. Better a son in disgrace, than no son at all."

"But when he learns what I have done, how I disgraced myself before Lorenzo Sardi…"

"Sardi? The Duelling Count?"

"I did not know about the feud until I arrived here," Carlo told him. "My father left Cadenza before it began. He wrote me a letter of introduction to give to Lorenzo."

"Let me see if I have your plan aright," Ercole said, brushing the crumbs from his beard. "You arrive at the count's door and proffer him this letter; he welcomes you like a long-lost son and at once demands to see your poem, sitting in raptures as you read it to him, earning instant acclaim and the promise of eternal literary renown."

Carlo reddened. "There is no need to mock me."

"It is your father who deserves upbraiding. He did not prepare you for the ways of the world." Ercole tore off a hunk of bread and took a bite. "So," he said, through a busy mouthful, "what did happen?"

IV. *Giddy Memorial*

IN THE FURORE engulfing Cadenza in the immediate aftermath of Tommaso Cellini's death, it had taken Carlo several hours to gain entrance to the city. He had to step smartly to avoid knocking into people as they staggered by, dizzy in their distress. Wails rained down from shuttered windows. On a townhouse balcony, a woman was dragged screaming from the balustrade; beneath an elevated passageway between two libraries, angry youths gathered to denounce the malign hand of Venice. The clamour of the bells reveberated around the streets.

Although Carlo's father had drawn him a map showing him the way to Lorenzo's palace, the city had changed greatly in the years since Giacomo Mazzoni's departure, and evening had fallen by the time Carlo entered the secluded square before the Palazzo di Sardi. He brushed himself down before knocking on the door, rehearsing the lines of introduction he had practised during the journey to Cadenza. Yet before he could even present his father's letter, the steward curtly informed him that Lorenzo was not at home and would not be expected any time soon. The door banged shut in Carlo's face.

He retreated to a fountain and slumped down beside it, blinking back tears of humiliation. His triumphant entrance into Cadenza was in danger of becoming a mockery. He was considering a second, more forceful essay on Lorenzo's palace when the door opened, and two men hurried away across the square. They were deep in conversation—at the mention of Lorenzo's name, Carlo's ears pricked up. He elected to go after them, heading through the streets and down a long alleyway to the river, where a broad stone bridge trailed off into the darkness over the Adige. Lorenzo's men headed north, making for a tavern where a crackling torch lit up the sign of the Ship. As Carlo neared the entrance, a glass shattered on the cobbles by his feet: he looked up, startled, and saw shadows moving on the roof. He ducked hastily inside the tavern.

The courtyard was a rolling and restless sea of shoulders, young men packed tightly around the open casks of wine, drowning their grief beneath waves of burgundy and claret. Under the influence of the grape, the atmosphere was exuberant and fragile in equal measure: a giddy memorial. As Carlo squeezed through the throng, through the vine-trailed columns he spied Lorenzo Sardi seated at a table beneath the arcades. He could identify the poet by the empty chairs and respectful space cleared around him; alone in the courtyard, Lorenzo had been given the luxury of room. Carlo tried to push his way towards him, and felt a hand against his chest. It belonged to an elegant young man dressed in sleeves of slashed crimson, curly dark hair spilling out from beneath his beret. A jewel glinted in his ear, a mocking half-smile on his lips. "Welcome, stranger!" he declared. "You have invited yourself into the house of Lorenzo Sardi, the great poet. He is in mourning for our dead ruler and does not wish to be disturbed. I would know your name, sir, before you take another step."

"I know well whose house this is," retorted Carlo. "I bring Lorenzo greetings from my father, Giacomo Mazzoni. I am his son, Carlo."

The young man stared at him. "And is Giacomo Mazzoni also a madman, who would endeavour to make an introduction on the day that Tommaso Cellini died?"

Carlo faltered. "I did not know about the Artifex. This is my first day in the city, I do not have a bed to sleep in. If Lorenzo will not see me, I do not know where—"

"My lord is the Duelling Count of Cadenza, not a German hostelier! Find rooms on your own account."

"Hold!" An imperious palm, raised aloft, stilled the tavern. Lorenzo Sardi sat back in his chair. His forehead was high and majestic, his prominent brows following narrowing diagonals towards the bridge of his nose, setting his eyes in an inquisitorial frame. Caught in the poet's intense gaze, Carlo felt himself being appraised and found wanting—an unsatisfactory manuscript, riddled with errors and infelicities.

"Let him pass, Raffaele," the count ordered. "You entered the city this day, young man?"

"I did, my lord," Carlo replied, approaching Lorenzo's table. "I bring a letter from my father, Giacomo Mazzoni, bearing his greetings."

"Why, it has been a quarter-century since I last heard the Mazzoni name."

Carlo bowed. "My father will be honoured you remember him."

"Naturally, I remember Giacomo, though many years have passed since we last had cause to speak. Remind me again why your father left Cadenza."

"There was unrest in the city. He feared for his family."

Lorenzo stroked his beard. "Unrest?"

"My lord..." Carlo faltered. "I am sure you remember. There was a plot... to poison Tommaso."

"I do indeed remember. The Pitti family. Donato Pitti and Giacomo Mazzoni were partners, were they not?"

At this revelation, so delicately imparted, a murmur ran through the crowd.

"In matters of trade only," Carlo said quickly. "My father was ever a loyal servant of Tommaso's, but he feared the Artifex might suspect his compliance in Donato's madness."

"A strange way to prove loyalty," Lorenzo mused. "To flee, in order to avoid having to give account for oneself."

"He could not be assured of a fair hearing, my lord. Armed gangs were roaming the streets looking for Pittis and anyone who associated with them. The city was blind with vengeance!"

"Much like tonight."

In the silence of the packed courtyard, Carlo realized that the bells had stopped ringing. Lorenzo took a sip of wine.

"At best," he said, "your family has a most unfortunate sense of timing. Two decades after turning tail following an assassination attempt, Giacomo sends his son back to the city upon the very day that Tommaso dies?"

"To make my name as a poet." Carlo held out his parchment. "I offer this as testament to my abilities. If you would only look at it…"

Lorenzo waved him away irritably. "I have no interest in your verses," he said. "To think that you can thrust your work beneath my nose at the mere mention of a name long-dismissed from my memory, I can only mark as brazen impudence. That is, unless this poem is but a mask for some darker errand."

"Of what are you accusing me, my lord? The bells were ringing before I entered the city!"

"You would name yourself a harbinger of death, rather than a villain outright."

Carlo could feel the ring of men about him draw closer. Fists tightened around goblets. He stared in disbelief at Lorenzo, who returned his gaze without blinking. Taking a deep breath, Carlo raised *City of Flames* into the air.

"Allow me to perform my work," he called out, "and the crowd can decide whether or not I am an imposter."

"A most diverting proposal," came an amused voice from behind him. "But the only verses heard tonight shall be Tommaso's, by order of Lorenzo. I fear they would be wasted upon you—come, let me show you the door."

Raffaele's grip was tight on Carlo's arm as he ushered him away through the glowering throng.

"What are you doing?" Carlo hissed.

"Saving your life," Raffaele muttered, through a forced smile. "The men in this tavern are reckless with grief and would like nothing more than a straw man on which to visit their wrath."

"Only because your master names me a traitor! Surely Lorenzo cannot think I had a hand in Tommaso's death!"

"It does not matter," he replied. "Either way, word of this exchange will soon be flying around the city. I advise you make for the countryside with all possible haste, and pray that the *becchini* do not come looking for you."

"Who?"

Raffaele shook his head incredulously. "I swear you come direct from the stage, a country innocent playing for laughs. The *becchini* are Tommaso's personal guard. They are known as gravediggers for good reason, and are not in the habit of taking chances."

Propelling Carlo through the tavern door, Raffaele gestured down the street.

"Here we must part," he said. "I wish you safe passage home."

Carlo jammed his boot in the door.

"A moment, please!" He could hear the desperation in his own voice. "You are a member of Lorenzo's circle, are you not? A poet, hoping to earn renown, just as I am!"

"You think us brothers-in-arms?" laughed Raffaele.

"There is more than this door standing between us, Carlo son of Giacomo."

"I see that now; I should not have come here," Carlo said quickly. "I seek to redeem the Mazzoni name, not muddy it further. What would my father say if I returned to him now, after a single day? I cannot leave the city until Lorenzo has heard my poem. If I have to recite it from atop a bonfire while the *becchini* stoke the flames, then so be it. In the meanwhile, do you not know of a place where I may stay?"

A glass flew down from the tavern rooftop, exploding on the cobblestones inches from Carlo's feet. Raffaele sighed.

"Follow the river south and you will come to a tavern at the sign of the Boar. Tell them I sent you." He gripped Carlo by the arm. "You understand the risk I am taking for you, should my master find out?"

"Upon my honour," Carlo vowed solemnly, "you shall not regret it."

V. *The Moon's Embrace*

NIGHTFALL MADE LITTLE impact on the ruined church's cellar, whose blackened and pockmarked walls lay sunken in perpetual gloom. Carlo lay on a bed of straw, his fingers laced behind his head as he gazed up at the chalk pentangles shivering on the ceiling. Liquids trembled inside phials; the furnace coughed ash through its grate. The entire cellar was reverberating to the stentorian snores coming from the chamber above, where Ercole lay dead to the world. The gravedigger cut a strange figure, at once earnest and comic, his flowery speech at odds with his earthy profession. Carlo had little doubt that his grand claims of wayfaring were an invention of fantasy, and his alchemical experiments hinted at a mind unhinged. Yet had Ercole not taken him into his home, offered him food and clothing, a place to rest his head? Carlo was not so lost to despair that he could not appreciate such generosity.

And yet. Torn clothes could be sewn up, cuts and bruises would scab over, but names and reputations could not be so easily repaired. The events at the Ridolfi salon had left Carlo's prospects in ruins—all that was left to him was a humiliating return to his father's estate to confess his misadventures. What struck Carlo was the sheer *unfairness* of it all, doomed as he had been by a single, malicious accident of timing. Had he but arrived in the city a day earlier, who knew how his tale might have unfolded? To simply return home like some forlorn tragedian seemed tantamount to cowardice: Carlo would not lie supine in the face of his misfortune.

Rolling off the straw, he snatched up his poem from the bench and strode out of the cellar. He emerged from the church into a cold and moonless night. In the graveyard, he soon came to regret not bringing a lamp with him, stubbing his toe on a loose flagstone as he stumbled swearing about the pitch-black tombs. When finally he escaped the labyrinthine pathways, there was a surprise waiting for him at the church gate. Ercole sat on the wall, his hair unruly with sleep and his skinny legs dangling in the air.

"I thought I left you dead to the world!" exclaimed Carlo. "What are you doing here?"

"Strange to tell," the gravedigger replied. "My dreams were

disturbed by the magician Agrippa, whom I encountered years ago at the house of Trithemius in Würzburg. He came before me holding a shimmering pool of quicksilver in his cupped hands, which he drank in a single gulp. Through silver lips, he whispered that he would share with me the secrets of the metals. At once awake and in the grip of sleep, I rose from my bed and followed him out into the graveyard—whereupon Agrippa's cloak turned into a raven and flew off into the night, leaving naught but a sulfurous pile of bones on the ground. I was pondering the meaning of this vision when you happened upon me. Come, sit beside me, and let us consider the matter together."

Carlo shook his head. "Grateful as I am for the hospitality you have shown me," he said, "I would rather walk on alone."

"A bold move, sir, and striking in its decisiveness," Ercole declared. "But—at the same time—one of questionable wisdom, if I might be permitted to say so. The new Artifex has entrusted the night-time streets to Swiss and German sellswords. Such men," he added meaningfully, "as are unlikely to appreciate the romantic whims of the poet."

"I do not set out on a whim," Carlo said stiffly.

"All the more reason for a companion, if only to provide a set of extra eyes to watch out for those who would impede you."

Carlo scratched his cheek. He could not deny that this part of the Verso was a mystery to him, and while marching on to the tip of a Swiss pike might offer an end to his despair, it seemed to lack a certain poetry.

"Very well," he said finally. "But you must swear to assist me in my designs."

Ercole hopped down from the wall and sank into a deep bow. They descended carefully through the Verso, eschewing the open expanses of the piazzas for obscure back alleys. At the river, the moon emerged from behind the clouds to greet them: a perfect silver coin, suspended high above the Ponte Nuovo.

"A pretty picture, is it not?" said Ercole. "I am reminded of the Chinese poet who drank so much rice wine that he fell in love with the moon's reflection in the river."

Carlo snorted. "A tall tale, even from your mouth."

"Which of us hasn't become enchanted by the charms of some luminous and unattainable beauty?" sighed Ercole, as they stepped out on to the empty bridge. "Alas, the Chinaman paid a higher price than heartbreak for his folly. When he reached out to embrace the moon, he fell out of his boat and drowned."

Carlo gave the old man a sidelong glance.

"Becoming slowly accustomed as I am, Ercole, to the ornate and Byzantine ways of your speech," he said coolly, "I suspect you try to tell me two stories: the first, of a drunken Chinese poet; and the second, a parable in which you would cast me as the foolish hero. If I have that aright, I would greatly appreciate it if you could momentarily staunch the flow of wisdom that pours unceasing from your mouth."

Ercole opened his mouth to object, then closed it with a nod. Along the bridge, the moonlight fell upon a statue of a dolorous-looking young man with a pen in his hand. Although Carlo had crossed the Ponte Nuovo many times he could not remember noticing the figure before, and in the night's ghostly air he could almost believe that it had appeared just for him: his sorrow made flesh.

"Here," he said. "This will do."

Tucking *The City of Flames* into his doublet, he scrambled up on to the balustrade and wrapped an arm around the statue. Ercole looked on with interest, his hands clasped behind his back. Carlo could feel the drop falling away beneath his feet, the suggestion of water rushing through the darkness below him. He swallowed. Keeping tight hold of the statue, he turned to face the slumbering rooftops, brandishing his poem with his free hand.

"Hear me, Cadenza!" he cried, above the churning river. "Heartless and haughty as you are, you would not deign to know my name, even as you slam your doors in my face. I will introduce myself now, upon the threshold of this world and the next, as Carlo Mazzoni, son of Giacomo! You denied him a voice to defend himself when you denounced him a traitor, even as you deny me the right to prove myself as a poet. So I commend myself and my poem to the watery depths, with this statue as my witness, so that this place shall forever be entwined with my name and the cruelty that led me to—"

Below him, there came a polite cough. Carlo twisted awkwardly around and glared down at Ercole. "Yes?"

The gravedigger held up his hands. "Forgive me, I am aware I promised to stay silent. Only..."

"Only what?"

He pointed at the statue. "You stand arm-in-arm with Fredino di Rossi, troubadour and son of Cadenza. Inspired by his love for a Venetian courtesan, he wrote the verse *Pulchra*, which he delivered to a packed square during the Carnival of Wit—only to flee the stage, when it was greeted with jeers and laughter."

"Truly, a tragic tale," Carlo snapped. "Why do you offer it now?"

"The statue commemorates the place where Fredino flung himself in the Adige afterwards."

"He jumped into the river?"

"From this very spot."

"And died?"

"In that regard, at least, he was successful."

Carlo paused. "Then I would not be the first to do so."

"Merely the latest in a long and honourable tradition," Ercole replied. "Rejected poets, jilted lovers, debtors and criminals... countless souls have followed Fredino's dive into the Adige. There are so many bodies tangled up at the bottom of that river that I fear the city would not even notice another addition to their ranks—heartless and haughty as she is."

Carlo's grip on the statue was slipping. He tried to shift position, only for his foot to go out from beneath him. Crying out, Carlo threw his arms around Fredino di Rossi, a single sheet of parchment fluttering from his grasp and spiralling down towards the water. He felt a steadying hand upon his arm.

"Come back to shore, gentle poet," Ercole said. "Spare the moon another death on her conscience."

His shoulders sagging in defeat, Carlo allowed the gravedigger to help him down from the statue. He peered over the bridge in vain for the page he had dropped.

"I should throw the whole poem in the river and have done with it," he said miserably. "What purpose does it serve, other than to remind me of my humiliation?"

"You have not yet heard the end to my story," Ercole told him. "*Pulchra* is now widely regarded as Fredino di Rossi's masterpiece. Every woman of breeding in the city owns a copy. Why not give history a chance to make up its own mind?"

The old man gave Carlo a sympathetic pat on the back and guided him away from the parapet. They walked back together towards the Verso, leaving Fredino di Rossi to resume his moonlight vigil alone.

VI. *The Shade of Cicero*

CARLO AWOKE TO find that the worst of his wine-sickness had abated, although his head still pounded—whether a stubborn legacy of his overindulgence, or a by-product of the cellar's alchemical fug, it was impossible to say. His appetite, however, had returned, and he gratefully shared a breakfast of beer and bread with Ercole. During the course of their meal, he agreed to accompany the old man on a journey to the Recto.

They took the cart with them, pushing it across the squares as children scampered around its wheels and took turns to climb aboard. A stiff wind was coming in off the Adige, animating the pennants above the Palazzo Monti by the riverfront. On the Ponte Nuovo, Carlo and Fredino di Rossi agreed to look the other way, making no mention of their encounter only hours earlier. When a flock of gulls convened a noisy council above their heads, Ercole broke off and scampered to the back of the cart, reaching inside for a steel helmet. Carlo watched with bewilderment as the old man clamped the barbute down over his head, peering warily up at the gulls from through the 'Y'-shaped face opening.

"As protection from bird droppings goes," Carlo remarked, "the helmet might be viewed as an excessive precaution."

"Hah!" scoffed Ercole. "You think that dung is the worst thing that can fall from the skies? Wait until the tortoises start raining down, and then we'll see who is dressed appropriately."

He rapped his knuckles against the barbute. Carlo stared at him.

"You are mad," he said finally.

"And you betray yourself with your own ignorance," Ercole retorted, hunching over at a swooping gull. "Have you never heard of the death of Aeschylus? An eagle dropped a tortoise on his bald head, mistaking it for a rock."

"I see no eagles in the sky. And you are not bald."

"Nor my wits so dulled as to escape the true meaning of the message. A tortoise falling from the sky, as though the world tipped upside down; a church admonished by a fork of lightning; the great Tommaso Cellini, buried beneath his own bookcase. What do these things all have in common? They come delivered to us from the aether: first and greatest of the elements—mortal heaven, breath of the gods, incorruptible and sublime! Beyond fire and earth, water and air, aether is the essence of the celestial vaults. It is because of the aether that the poet sharpens his pen, and the artist wets his brush— inspiration is its true gift, albeit one unknowable in its form and manner of imparting."

"And painful besides, when hard shells are involved," Carlo replied, with a straight face.

Ercole gave him a reproachful look. "I once saw Agrippa stand before the Elector of Saxony and conjure up the shade of Cicero from the aether," he said. "I wonder what manner of sardonic remarks you would have addressed to *him*, had you been standing beside me."

He kept on his barbute long after they had left the bridge, blind to the stares and quizzical gazes it attracted. As they entered the Old Market, Carlo's pulse quickened, aware of the possibility that one of Lorenzo's men might be examining the fine inks and writing tools on display in the stalls. Thankfully, Ercole skirted around the edge of the square, before descending a series of narrow sloping alleyways that heralded the beginning of the Printing Quarter. The light took on a murky quality, the slam of a distant press reverberating around the walls. In his brief time in Cadenza, Carlo had heard lurid stories of the perils that lurked beyond the signs of the Cart and the Heron—of robberies nonchalantly conducted in broad daylight; of complicated confidence tricks and seductions; of forged certificates that turned criminals into men of qualification and standing; of bodies left bleeding in the shadow of churches. Yet Ercole appeared unconcerned by the quarter's reputation, smiling brightly up at the balconies and ruffling the hair of ragamuffins as they raced past him. Bouncing the cart down a series of steps, they emerged into a tight, shaded square. A solitary pine contorted its trunk in the vain hope of reaching sunlight. Beneath the sign of the Marble Trout, Ercole stopped at the entrance to a cellar.

"It is an unhappy sight that awaits us at the bottom of these stairs," he warned Carlo. "A scholar lies dead in these quarters."

"I did not think you were taking me to perform for the Artifex."

"Had that been our aim," Ercole conceded, "I would have likely left the cart behind."

He ducked through the doorway and went down the steps. The cellar was cold and musty, patches of moss sprouting between the stonework on the walls. A writing desk was set below the solitary window. There was little else by way of comfort or adornment. A door guarded the way to another room, presumably a bedchamber; the hearth was filled with ashes and torn pieces of parchment. Before it lay the body of a man of advancing years, face-down on the flagstones, his skin the same colour as his grey scholar's robes. Sucking in through his teeth, Ercole knelt down beside the corpse.

"How did he die?" asked Carlo, hanging back by the steps.

"Hard to say," Ercole said. "I see no wounds upon the skin, nor any sign of violence."

Carlo glanced over at the hearth, and back to the empty writing desk. "He threw his work in the fire," he said. "I would name his killer Despair."

"Another lost masterpiece," Ercole said, with a shake of the head—whether in wry humour, or genuine sadness, Carlo could not quite tell.

As the old man examined the scholar's remains, Carlo became aware of a scrabbling sound from behind the door. He went to push it open, and was nearly bowled off his feet by a black hound as it sprang free. Laughing with surprise, Carlo dropped to his knees and greeted the dog, scratching it behind the ears.

"What are you doing here, boy?" he said.

The hound trailed a slobbering tongue down his cheek.

"I have a dog like you back home," Carlo told him, grinning. "He is just as foolish as you are, though half the size."

Ercole straightened up, a suspicious expression on his face.

"You will not greet our new friend?" said Carlo.

"Agrippa had a dog," the gravedigger said darkly. "He called it Monsieur. The two of them were more like lovers than master and pet. They shared the dining table and the bed alike; it was said that the dog was a demon in disguise."

"Come now, Ercole!" chuckled Carlo, ruffling the dog's ears. "Does this silly fellow look like a demon to you?"

"All dogs are Monsieur to me," he insisted. "Leave him be and help me with this body."

Carlo patted the dog on the head and went over to Ercole, who had taken the scholar by the arms. Together they hauled the body up the steps and loaded it into the cart, carefully tucking its limbs inside the wooden slats. The dog followed them outside, watching them curiously from the step.

"Be off with you now," Carlo said fondly.

The hound cocked his head to one side, its eyes wide with incomprehension. Carlo glanced across at Ercole.

"Do you suppose that he could come with us? His master is gone, and I fear this dog is too good-natured to survive on the street."

Ercole didn't reply. He was staring across the square at the gnarled stone pine, where two men stood watching them from the shadows. Differing greatly in height but identical in the tattered aspect of their dress, they stood either side of an empty cart.

"Time to go," Ercole said abruptly.

"Why the hurry?" asked Carlo. "Do you know those men?"

"By name and reputation. Suffice to say, there is more than one type of gravedigger at work in this city."

He picked up the cart's handles and began hurriedly pushing it back towards the alley, the scholar's body rolling around inside. Beneath the stone pine, the shorter of the two men leaned in towards his companion and murmured up into his ear. Neither of them moved. Casting a final glance back at the pair, Carlo hastened to catch up with Ercole—all the while hissing and shooing away the scholar's black dog as it loped happily after him.

VII. *Quicksilver and Sulphur*

RETURNED TO SAN Felice, Carlo and Ercole dug the scholar's grave in silence. The old man showed no inclination to discuss what had occurred in the Printing Quarter, his mood soured by the continued presence of the hound, who had resisted all attempts to turn him away and now crouched watchfully by his dead master's body. The corpse had been divested of his robe and was now garbed in a plain smock—Ercole buried him without ceremony, tossing his shovel into the cart beside the folded gown and wheeling it away without waiting to see if Carlo followed. The dog remained by the graveside, its head resting forlornly on its paws. Carlo took a seat on the muddy ground beside it. Picturing the heartbroken scholar sprawled across the floor, his work destroyed in the grate, he sighed and took his poem out of his doublet.

"These works of ours do not make for happy labour," he told the hound, scratching its ears. "Perhaps you have it aright, you seem contented enough living a life without words. Would I be happier with a stick between my teeth than with a pen in my hand?"

With a loud bark of assent, the dog snatched the pages frm Carlo's hand and went bounding away through the tombs. Carlo sprang to his feet and gave chase, shouting at the top of his lungs. The dog scampered down through the terraces, its paws slipping on the worn flagstones. With an oath, Carlo vaulted over the balustrade and raced through the trees, hurdling headstones as he pursued the small black blur. Crashing through a thicket, he came out into a clearing and skidded to a halt.

By a graveside bench, Hypatia crouched down beside the black hound, stroking the back of its head. The dog had laid the poem at her feet and was panting happily up at her. Before, Carlo had caught only a distant glimpse of the ink maid; now he reeled back, as though struck by a physical blow. In a city where ladies dyed their hair blonde and lightened their skin with applications of vinegar and egg, Hypatia's olive complexion and tumbling black curls seemed more than merely exotic, but a statement of outright defiance. Beneath her cloak she wore a gown of embroidered crimson, which gathered tightly about her waist before plunging in luxurious waves of fabric towards the ground. A coral necklace, her only adornment, rested above the laced bodice. In her eyes, a startling shade of hazel, Carlo saw wariness. It was this gravity, the suggestion of sorrow, which lent Hypatia a luminous and unworldly quality—shimmering quicksilver, the moon in the night sky.

"What is his name?" she asked.

"I call him… Monsieur," Carlo replied hesitantly. "Forgive us for intruding upon you."

"It is of no matter," she replied, as the dog nuzzled her fingers. "I am not quite sure what you are disturbing. If it is a conversation, then it is a one-sided affair."

"This is the grave of Ginevra di Lecce?" asked Carlo.

Hypatia nodded. "In her day, she was said to be the finest writer in the city." She gestured at the plain headstone. "Not that you would know, to look at her now. Nor does a single of her letters survive."

"Even in a city of libraries?"

"Our correspondences are not the kind that people wish to share," Hypatia told him, smiling unexpectedly. "They contain the heart's deepest secrets and innermost desires."

"All the more reason to preserve them."

"A worthy sentiment." She picked up his poem and handed it back to him. "You are a writer?"

"A poet. At least, in aspiration, if not yet renown."

"Renown." Hypatia wrinkled her nose. "A dubious honour."

"You have accrued no small amount of it."

"And yet how many people have actually laid eyes on my letters? You will not find any of my works in the libraries either."

"The acclaim means nothing to you?"

"I do not write for accolades. To try and write, with cheering and applause echoing inside my head… I should find it distracting."

"Is it vanity, then, that I should wish people to hear my work? That they might admire it?"

"If it is a sin, then it is a common one among poets," she replied. "But would it truly be so terrible to write something of worth that only you could see?"

"You would have me become an ink maid," Carlo said morosely.

She laughed. "I think not," Hypatia said. "The passions of a poet burn hot and bright, and would eclipse those of the people you would seek to become."

Carlo blushed. "I fear my heart is an open book to you," he said. "I will leave before it betrays me further. My lady."

He retreated with a stiff bow, dragging Monsieur from the clearing by the scruff of the neck. The clouds' grey reign relented; for the first time that day, Carlo felt the sun's warmth on the back of his neck. At the gate, he released Monsieur and shooed him away, smiling as the dog galloped off through the long grass.

Inside the ruined church, the air remained wintry. A waft of foul-smelling smoke greeted Carlo as he went down into the cellar, to find the furnace letting out sooty belches. Ercole held aloft a phial, intently examining its contents.

"I trust you left the hound outside," he said, without turning around.

"For a man of a singularly bright disposition," Carlo remarked, "the mere sight of a dog seems to trouble you more than a flock of birds overhead. Were you bitten as a child?"

"It is not the past I worry about, but the future. Mark my words, that creature is a bad omen."

"Then, quickly, pass me some iron!" Carlo jested. "I will touch it and ward off the evil spirits."

"You might want to, before opening that," Ercole said, nodding at a letter on the bench. "A stable boy came from the Recto to deliver it to you."

At the sight of the wax seal, Carlo's smile faded. He broke open the letter and began to read. He barely finished a sentence before tossing it to one side, his head in his hands. Ercole laid down his phial.

"Unhappy tidings, I take it," he said.

"It is from my father," said Carlo, his words muffled behind his palms. He looked up to the ceiling and let out a groan. "Lorenzo has sent him word of what happened at the Ridolfi salon. I have been ordered home at once."

"Your secret has been revealed," Ercole said. "Painful as it might seem, perhaps better to face the consequences now, than torment yourself in private for eternity."

"I would rather private torment than public disgrace— especially where my father is concerned. How did they find me here?"

"The stable boy said he was directed by a lordly young fellow at the Boar tavern."

"Raffaele." Carlo punched his fist into his palm. "I should have guessed." Springing to his feet, he began pacing up and down. "Lorenzo... my father... Raffaele... they all would have me slink home with my tail between my legs," he declared. "If they wish me gone, then so be it. But I will not creep from sight, meek as a mouse."

Ercole raised a quizzical eyebrow. "What do you propose?"

Carlo clutched 'The City of Flames' in his fist. "If they will paint me a villain, then a villain I shall become—violent and shameless as Nero." He looked down at the dead scholar's robes, folded neatly over a chair. "I will burn the city down around me."

VIII. *The Road to Macedonia*

BY LONG-STANDING TRADITION, the benches of the Piazza della Rosa were reserved for oratory: stone pulpits well-worn by the tread of restless feet. Snatches of verse and obscure screeds washed over Carlo as he strode across the square, careful not to trip over the voluminous folds of his scholar's robes. On opposing sides of the piazza, the grand palaces of the Accademia and the Palazzo Nero confronted one another like a pair of clenched fists. An ornate fountain spurted ink into the air—three pools of black silk arranged in a trefoil, in the centre of which rose a statue of the muse Calliope, naked and majestic as Venus upon a scallop shell. Clutching a roll of parchment to her chest, she gazed toward the Accademia, flecks of ink dappling her smooth flesh.

"Carlo, wait!"

He turned to see Ercole, red-faced and wheezing, waving his hand frantically.

"Have you not heard my pleas to stop?" the old man demanded indignantly. "I have been chasing you halfway across Cadenza!"

"You would have been better served husbanding your breath," Carlo told him. "Do not tell me again to rethink my plans or rhapsodize over the works of Fredino di Rossi. This time I will not be deterred."

"Then leave your poem here to be picked over by the birds

and go home to make amends with your father. Save yourself this unnecessary theatre."

"No," said Carlo, quietly but firmly. "You did not hear the jeers that greeted me at Ridolfi's salon… they ring in my ears, without end."

"The tragedian Euripides was so wounded by the barbs and lampoons of the comics that he fled to Macedonia," Ercole said. "I'd venture your father's estate is closer."

"Then by all means, make the journey yourself and give him my regards. You are the wayfarer, are you not?"

The gravedigger shook his head. "I knew giving you those robes was a bad idea," he said.

"As though they were yours to give!" Carlo laughed incredulously. "I wonder how many keepsakes you have prised free from cold hands. Where did that fine helmet of yours come from—did you win it on some distant battlefield upon your Odyssean travels? Or did it magic itself from the aether, tumbling down from the sky like a shiny grey turtle?"

"It is a meagre gratitude you offer me," sniffed Ercole, "to ask for my assistance, only to damn me when I provide it. You may be happy to consign precious objects to the dirt, but I will not leave iron to rust and gems to tarnish, linen and fine silk to rot."

"A pretty excuse for grave robbery, if ever I heard one."

The pigeons strutting around the fountain took to the air in alarm as Carlo marched through them towards the Accademia. Clouds were scudding around the library's great dome; at the entrance, grey-gowned scholars flocked beneath the guards' crossed pikes. Carlo affected an air of lofty indifference as he passed through them, even as his step quickened nervously.

Ercole, assuming the role of an unlikely scholar's attendant, gave the guard a familiar nod. The pikeman stared suspiciously back at him. Abandoning all attempts at subterfuge, Carlo hastened on through the atrium, trying to melt into the sober ranks of scholars as they filed along the corridor. Fragments of wisdom and erudition decorated conversations like shining mosaic pieces. Carlo waited for a guard's hand to clamp down upon his shoulder, but to his amazement he was allowed to go on unchallenged until, through an archway, he could see a vast reading room gradually unfolding before him. At the threshold, Carlo stopped and circled slowly around, the breath catching in his throat.

He had entered a circular hall of dizzying proportions, light pouring down through the generous windows of the Mezzanino and painting afresh in golden hues the friezes that ringed the gallery. Scholars bustled up and down the levels, pausing to stand aside for librarians wheeling wooden carts laden with volumes. Steepling bookcases cast the shadow of ancient standing stones across the tiles—thousands upon thousands of volumes arranged in a collection so vast that it seemed to the awestruck Carlo that before him was gathered the entirety of human knowledge, from the wars of the Scythians to the inner workings of the bumblebee. Buried somewhere in the obscure reaches of the Accademia, he felt certain, lay clues to all the mysteries of the universe, answers to every question that man might pose.

"Incredible!" breathed Carlo. "Have you ever seen a library like it?"

"I have not," Ercole said, with a shrug. "Then again, this is the first one I have ever stepped inside."

Carlo gave him a sidelong glance. "You jest."

"Do you see any books upon my shelves?" He tapped his temple. "My head is my library."

"And a disorderly and maddening institution that must be," Carlo retorted. "With aisles turning back upon themselves, and books standing on their heads and running back to front."

"And yet everything within reach, exactly as I left it," the gravedigger replied evenly. "Shall we stand here all day, admiring the view?"

"Let us seek out my old friend Raffaele," Carlo said, craning his neck above the throng. "I believe he favours the light in the East Reading Room."

Antechambers were situated at regular intervals around the reading room, each entrance flanked by statues of thinkers and scholars. Carlo crossed the hall and passed through the doorway into the adjoining chamber, where the scholars were arranged in studious rows among the bookcases. He spied Raffaele almost at once, standing at a lectern by the window. Carlo crept soundlessly up behind him and tapped the poet on the shoulder. Raffaele jumped.

"Carlo!" he exclaimed. "What are you doing here?"

"I thought I could turn the page for you while you read."

"Where did you get that robe? You are no more a scholar than I am Suleiman the Magnificent!"

"Would that I could call a Turk friend, rather than a poet," Carlo shot back. "Suleiman would not have abandoned me in a freezing grave."

"A freezing grave *you* had crawled into of your own volition, having led *me* a merry dance across Cadenza. What would you have had me do: nestle down beside you to keep you warm?"

"At the very least, keep my location a secret. I know that my father's letter reached me under your direction. Did you tell Lorenzo also?"

"You left me no choice!" Raffaele exclaimed. "He was *this* close to expelling me from his circle after your antics at Ridolfi's. Be thankful it was merely a letter to your father Lorenzo signed, rather than a petition for your arrest."

"Either way," Carlo said stubbornly, "my life is ended."

"Don't be so dramatic. You have taken a match to your immediate prospects, it is true, but all may not be lost. Allow the dust to settle and unhappy memories to fade. Above all, cease these histrionic public displays and leave here now, before Lorenzo sees you!"

Carlo replied by reaching inside his robe and pulling out *City of Flames*. Scattering the poem about his feet, he took out a flint and knife.

"What fresh madness is this?" Raffaele hissed. "You brought fire into the Accademia? The guards will run you through!"

"Then hush your tongue." To Carlo's surprise, it was Ercole who replied. "Else I will ensure they think us three comrades-in-arms when they come running."

Raffaele scratched his head. "Carlo, who is this gnome?"

"Why, Ercole is no gnome!" Carlo declared grandly. "He is a wayfarer who has travelled the world!"

"And a fairer dandy I have yet to encounter, for all my traverses of the Earth's circumferences," added Ercole, looking Raffaele up and down. "The Tartars would think you a woman."

"You have *both* lost your minds," the poet declared. "I will not stand here while you burn the library down."

"Fear not, friend!" There was a note of wild hilarity in Carlo's voice. "Nothing of any value will be lost—merely the clumsy verses of a poetaster. Your master will be delighted!"

He struck the flint against the knife with a flourish, sending sparks raining down over his poem. The weathered parchment needed little encouragement, its edges catching eagerly and beginning to glow.

"Hold!" a voice cried out.

Pens paused; turning pages froze in the air. Lorenzo Sardi stood in the reading room doorway, a trembling finger pointed straight at Carlo. The count's face had turned a furious shade of puce. At the sight of the smouldering parchment, there were gasps and exclamations of horror—as Carlo went to strike the flint again, Raffaele lunged forward and knocked it from his hands. Tripping over his robe, Carlo went sprawling to the floor in a shower of sparks. He felt a warm sensation about his elbow.

"Your sleeve, Carlo!" Ercole warned.

Carlo sprang to his feet, frantically flapping his sleeve as smoke rose from his arm. Raffaele backed away.

"Summon the guards!" Lorenzo shouted. "There is a madman loose inside this place!"

The library stirred to his call. Urgent cries ignited the aisles and stairs, galleries rumbling with heavy footfalls. The scholars of the East Reading Room rose as one to show their displeasure, aiming boos and catcalls at Carlo. He felt Ercole's hand on his shoulder.

"Time to go, I think."

"But my poem!"

Rolling his eyes, the gravedigger stamped out the burning parchment and snatched it from the ground. Guards were converging on the chamber from all directions: Carlo joined Ercole in haring for the exit, almost bowling Lorenzo off his feet on his way out. The great poet stared after them, a statue of incandescent indignation.

IX. *A Succinct Reply*

THOUGH THEIR INITIAL encounter in the courtyard at the sign of the Ship had been an awkward one, in the weeks that followed there had grown between Carlo and Raffaele a certain amity, if not outright friendship. Raffaele clearly relished dispensing wisdom to his younger companion, while also seizing every opportunity to expound upon the assorted cruelties and deficiencies of character of his vaunted master. But Carlo had troubles of his own: hard as he pressed Raffaele, he seemed no closer to a fresh audience with Lorenzo Sardi, and his funds were running low. The prospect of an inglorious return to the family estate was looming ever closer.

The two poets had been glumly sharing a cup of wine at the sign of the Boar when word arrived that Tommaso Cellini's successor had been chosen. The announcement of the name Cosimo Petrucci, a mid-level Folio bureaucrat, was greeted with bewilderment and anger by the tavern's patrons, who for the large part had never heard of him. Carlo and Raffaele spent the remainder of the afternoon exchanging sardonic toasts to the new Artifex, their spirits lifting with every cup. When Raffaele let slip that he was to visit the Ridolfi salon that evening Carlo at once vowed to accompany him, donning his best doublet and slipping *City of Flames* inside it before marching forth from the Boar.

They went through the streets in high spirits, exchanging quips and jests and play-fighting beneath the archways. Outside Ridolfi's salon, the sound of voices floated down from the balcony; laughter, light and knowing. Upon the stairs, Carlo slipped, giggling drunkenly as he landed upon his backside. Raffaele quickly hauled him to his feet but the damage had been done: the attendant at the salon entrance shook his head as they approached. Raffaele stepped between them and whispered in the man's ear. If coins changed hands, then it was done so subtly Carlo missed it. All he knew was that the doors were opening, and he was stepping across the threshold.

"This far only can I bring you," Raffaele warned him, as they entered. "I cannot risk Lorenzo seeing us together. Heed my words—do not approach him tonight!"

"Fear not, faithful Virgil," Carlo replied gaily, slapping him on the back. "You may leave me at this circle of Hell in good faith. No Mazzoni will trouble your master."

He strode off before Raffaele could call him back. Throughout the lavish apartments, Ridolfi's guests had divided themselves into small circles around the halls and at the divans; upon the stage, a musician played the viol. Through the fronds of a fern, Carlo spied Lorenzo Sardi, deep in conversation with Salvatore Ridolfi himself, and an ink maid dressed in a brilliant white cloak dappled with inky spots. The talk, naturally, was of Cosimo Petrucci. Cadenza's new ruler was an enigma to the denizens of the salon, his lineage unknown and no works bearing his name to be found inside the libraries. What had the Seven been thinking, to have handed the keys to the Palazzo Nero to a man of no account?

Without Raffaele, Carlo had to make his own introductions, yet he soon discovered that Ridolfi's guests had formed tight rings of association that offered no easy entrance to a stranger. He lingered at the fringes of conversations, seeking a chance to interject, but each time he opened his mouth someone else spoke to cut him off, or the talk moved on in a different direction. Disconsolate, Carlo retreated to an empty divan and sought company in his wine glass.

It was around this point that he began to lose stretches of time, black tesserae appearing in the evening's mosaic. He remembered treading on a courtesan's foot, earning himself a volley of abuse, and the viol player shooing him away as he called out jovially for a country air; from across the room, Raffaele shot him a warning glance. Carlo ignored it. Buoyed by drink, he found the courage to interpose himself into a discussion, holding forth to a French troubadour and a librarian from the Bibliotheca Niccoló. His words came in a rush, joyous and profound, yet even in his enthusiasm he could sense his companions' polite sufferance, bordering on unease. Was Carlo's accent really so rustic to their ears, could they smell soil on his breath? He took a moody swig of wine.

"Upon my eyes, I had thought it was you."

It was Lorenzo. The poet nodded at the troubadour, who

swept into a graceful bow. The librarian flushed. Lorenzo offered Carlo no greeting. Turning to the others, he spread out his palms.

"Time was, entrance to the Ridolfi salon was reserved for poets of renown," he intoned. "Perhaps, with Tommaso dead, this is the best we can hope for."

"Poetry did not die with Tommaso Cellini," Carlo said quickly.

"I did not expect a Mazzoni to weep for our beloved ruler."

"You judge our family wrong, my lord. Perhaps if you had read my poem, you would be assured of our fealty to both Tommaso and Cadenza."

"It is not I you need to convince," Lorenzo replied meaningfully. "Though the *becchini* are not known for their love of verse."

"I would deliver my poem to any ears that would listen," Carlo declared. "It is inspired by a work of the poet Lucan— the copy in my father's library was brought to Cadenza by Angelo Uccello himself."

There was a momentary pause, and then the circle burst into laughter.

"I meant no jest!" Carlo protested. "Why do you laugh?"

"Why, half the books in the Old Market were first brought to Cadenza by Angelo Uccello!" Lorenzo exclaimed. "His cart must have been the size of a Portuguese carrack, so laden was it with volumes."

"It is the easiest claim for a charlatan to make," the Frenchman added airily. "It being almost impossible to prove otherwise."

"Do you call me a charlatan, sir?" Carlo demanded.

He glared at the troubadour, aware—even in his drunken ire—of the figure of Raffaele hastening, aghast, across the salon towards him.

"You mistake your surroundings for a Printing Quarter tavern," Lorenzo mused. "The apartments of Signore Ridolfi are a haven of the mind, a celebration of the written word. They are no place for hot tempers."

"Then let us celebrate the written word," Carlo shot back, pulling out the parchment from his doublet. "I brought my verse with me in the hope our paths might cross."

"My lord," Raffaele broke in breathlessly, "do not—"

Lorenzo held up a finger, silencing him. He accepted the poem, smoothing down the wrinkled pages and holding them up for examination. Carlo held his breath. The viol player finished his song with a flourish; across the room, a quip was greeted with a peal of laughter and applause. Around Lorenzo, the silence was absolute. The count read on, his expression offering no clue to his thoughts.

"As I suspected," he declared finally, handing back the parchment.

"My lord?" Carlo inquired.

Shooting an icy stare at Raffaele, who blanched, Lorenzo turned to leave. Carlo caught his elbow.

"Spare not my feelings!" he said, reddening. "I would know your thoughts upon my work."

Lorenzo let out a sigh. "You would insist on my judgment. Very well. Your verse is clumsy and childish, the vain overreaching of a poetaster. You compound this sin with your intrusion inside these halls, mouth flapping and addled with drink, heedless to the grave insult that your very presence represents. The Mazzoni have already fled Cadenza once, Carlo, son of Giacomo. I would advise you to do so again, before brazenness and stupidity are added to treachery in the annals of your family's transgressions."

The troubadour winced theatrically; a nervous smile crossed the librarian's face. Carlo's cheeks grew hot. Honour demanded that he reply, that he not swallow this insult in silence. Yet now—when he needed them the most—the words had deserted him. He had no witty riposte, no stinging putdown, no triumphant rebuttal: only a surfacing fury, the poison of his soul these weeks past. The humiliations and dashed dreams that had marked his time in Cadenza, the slights upon his family name, and now this mocking dismissal, this lordly disdain... he felt it, hot and sour inside his throat, his mouth burning and his tongue black with bile. Carlo's reply flew from his mouth, succinct and irreversible: a gob of phlegm, deposited in a foaming arc directly into the face of Lorenzo Sardi.

A terrible hush came over the room. The count's cheek glistened in the candlelight.

And then uproar.

Lorenzo's men sprang forward, setting about Carlo with fists and feet. He lashed out blindly, only to feel a hand on his collar, pulling him away. Someone threw wine in his face. Hisses and catcalls echoed around the salon as Raffaele dragged him grimly toward the doors, whereupon a boot connected with Carlo's backside, propelling him outside. He went stumbling down the steps, collapsing in a heap at the bottom. A glass arrowed down after him, narrowly missing his head. Struggling to his feet, Carlo turned and cursed the furious crowd gathering at the door, even as Raffaele wrestled him away down the street into the night.

X. *The Little Key*

THE POETS OF the Piazza della Rosa broke off from their recitals as Carlo sprinted by, his robe hoicked up around his knees, dragging the stumbling Ercole along in his wake. Behind them, the guards of the Accademia gave spirited chase, red-faced and cursing. Calliope averted her gaze as they bundled past her plinth. Afraid to cast a glance over his shoulder, Carlo had no way of knowing that the weight of the guards' armour had begun to tell, and that their pace was slowing—upon reaching the edge of the square, he dragged Ercole through the alleys until the gravedigger collapsed into a gasping bundle on the floor, clutching Carlo's singed poem to his chest.

It was a quiet and dispirited duo who trudged back to the Verso. At the Church di San Felice, the exhausted Ercole went to rest in his chamber; in the cellar, Carlo sank into a brooding stupor, confronting his reflection in the glass jars. Clouds of dust drifted though the sepulchral gloom. Suddenly, seized by some unspoken resolution, he leapt up and grabbed his poem. His footfalls echoed around the church as he climbed the dropping-splattered steps of the round-tower. With every turn, the scratch and squawk of roosting birds grew louder. Nests were visible in the exposed rafters, glimpses of sky through the holes in the tower roof. Carlo went through into an attic room and locked the door behind him. At the window, he hurled the key out over the cemetery, watching with satisfaction as it drew a silver line through the air before vanishing into the bushes. He settled down on the floor and waited.

The sun was dipping behind the tombs when Carlo heard footsteps on the stairs. The door handle rattled.

"Carlo?" Ercole called out. "Are you in there?"

"Leave me be."

"I was about to sit down for supper. Do not make an old man eat alone."

"I have eaten my last meal," Carlo declared. "And taken my last drink. I have retired from this world and will not leave this room again."

"I see." Ercole's voice hardened. "I had hoped that your brush with fire would have shown you the error of this self-piteous crusade."

"Perhaps you should furnish me with another of your fables, to show me the error of my ways," Carlo shot back. "Or allow me to take a turn. What of the librarian Eratosthenes, who abandoned himself to despair when his eyes failed him? Would you have shown him the same contempt you show me?"

"Eratosthenes was an old man," came the reply. "Without hope of improving his condition. You are a young man, albeit one hobbled by his own foolishness."

"Do not talk to me of *hope*," Carlo said bitterly. "The doors to the Accademia are forever closed to me, just like those of the Ridolfi salon. I cannot even walk the streets for fear of running into Lorenzo's men. Would you have me hide out in this graveyard for the rest of my life? I would rather commend myself to the air."

There was a long pause. "As you wish," Ercole said finally. "I have wasted enough words trying to make you see the sense of this. If death you are resolved upon, then death you shall have. But allow me one final wisdom: you see yourself a tragic hero, Count Ugolino imprisoned in the Muda. Yet this is a cell of your own devising. When you reach the other side, do not expect a sympathetic ear from those shades on whom you are so crassly intent upon intruding."

The old man departed, his peeved footsteps fading away down the church tower. Carlo huddled beneath his cloak as the attic slid into gloom. Only now did he come to regret that he had brought neither blanket nor straw to lie on. Would they have signalled such a weakness in his resolve? Even as he lay starving, surely Eratosthenes had not punished himself further by lying out on bare floorboards. Hunger gnawed a hollow in the pit of Carlo's stomach. The moon rose in the window; down in the graveyard, a dog began to howl. Monsieur? It was impossible to tell in the darkness.

The combination of discomfort, hunger and the hound's cries kept Carlo awake for much of the night before exhaustion claimed him just before the dawn. Morning, when it arrived, was damp and grey. Carlo got to his feet stiffly, kneading a painful crick in his neck. He went to the window and gazed dolefully out over the headstones. Through the trees, he caught sight of a cloaked figure walking swiftly across one of the terraces. Carlo did not need Hypatia's hood to fall to know her; even on so brief an acquaintance, the ink maid's bewitching presence was familiar to him. "Reason enough to stay alive," Ercole had named her—and even now, Carlo found his heart beating faster in his chest. He willed her to stop, to turn and spy him in the tower window. But her name died on his lips as Hypatia walked down the terrace and disappeared behind the trees that shrouded the grave of Ginevra di Lecce.

A sharp gust of wind sliced through the attic, rousing Carlo's poem from the floor and scattering it about the chamber. He went scrambling after it, gathering up the pages. His recent misadventures had left their mark upon the parchment, which was stained with mud and river spray, the edges blackened by fire. Certain words had been obscured, some lost forever. Carefully smoothing out the pages, Carlo settled down on the floor and began to read.

An hour passed. Carlo did not move, his brow furrowed in thought. Occasionally he turned back to check an earlier page. Then, letting out a cry of triumph, he sprang to his feet and began to pace the room, muttering to himself—the same lines over and again, shifting and transforming by small degrees, a word here and there, lines growing and flowering. Eventually Carlo stopped and looked around the chamber, clicking his tongue with frustration at the absence of pen and ink. He hammered on the door with his fists.

"Ercole! Ercole!"

The commotion loosed a cloud of dust from the rafters, bringing forth squawks of protest from the roosting birds.

"Carlo?"

From the other side of the door, a voice.

"Ercole!" Carlo cried. "I wasn't sure you would come."

"I will not leave you while you have sense left in your head, though it seeps from you like sand in an hourglass. Have you reconsidered?"

"You were right," said Carlo. "I have been a fool. And that is not all. Lorenzo was right also—my poem is clumsy and naïve, the work of a child." He took a deep breath. "But I think I know how I can improve it. I have new lines; better lines!"

"Which will count for naught, if they remain only inside your head," Ercole told him. "You know that there is parchment, pen and ink downstairs at the lectern."

"Then you will help me get out of here?"

"That depends. Do you swear upon your honour to cease this senseless campaign against your own person?"

"I swear it."

"Then I will happily set you free. Where is the key?"

Carlo turned and looked out of the window. He scratched his cheek.

"I threw it away," he said.

"Where?"

"I don't know! Into the graveyard somewhere."

"So how do you propose I open the door?"

"I thought there might be another key."

"Why would I need another key? The one I had worked perfectly well."

"Ercole!"

"All right, all right. Can you put your shoulder to it?"

Carlo sized up the door. He shook his head. "My shoulder would break before it did."

Ercole hurried away down the stairs, leaving Carlo to wait impatiently, repeating his new lines to himself to prevent them slipping from his grasp. After what seemed like an age, the gravedigger returned. Glass clinked against glass.

"Where have you been?" Carlo called out.

"Where do you think?" exclaimed Ercole. "Plucking inspiration from the aether. Why use a key of iron, when one fashioned from sulphur and saltpetre will open any door it touches?"

Carlo backed hastily away from the door. "Are you sure this key is safe, Ercole?"

"I have tried it once before, in Ulm. It is a matter of judgement and degree." He paused. "You might want to stand back."

Before Carlo could take a step, a great hand lifted him from his feet and hurled him against the wall. The door buckled and flew open, shaking birds from their rooftop nests into the sky. Carlo's skull sang. Through billowing clouds of smoke, he caught the gleam of a silver helmet: Ercole's head popped into the room, his eyes wide with delight. The old man danced a little jig as Carlo picked himself up and shook his head clear. There was a loud crash as the door gave way, toppling from its hinges to land face-first on the floor. Carlo's coughs turned to laughter—he grabbed the startled gravedigger and kissed him fiercely on both cheeks. Snatching up his parchment, he marched back through the smoking portal: Count Ugolino restored to liberty, Eratosthenes renewed.

XI. *The Clear Sky of Heaven*

CARLO HURRIED DOWN from the tower to the lectern in the nave, where he began scribbling furiously upon the fresh paper. Absorbed in his writing, he gave no thought to his stomach, and Ercole had to physically drag him away to eat supper. Only with the first mouthful of food, did Carlo remember how long it been since he had eaten. As he eagerly attacked a platter of cold meat and beer, Ercole rooted through the shelves, pulling down dusty alchemical concoctions stoppered in glass beakers: wines, pungent and heady. They sat late into the night, offering toasts to Hypatia and to Fredino di Matteo, to Tommaso Cellini, even Lorenzo Sardi himself. At one point, there may have been singing. Optimism—that elusive, vital sap—surged through Carlo's veins. His poem was not the herald of genius he had imagined it to be, but with work, it could perhaps be fashioned into something he could present without fear of mockery. He had surely embarrassed himself, yet a man need not die from embarrassment. Apologies could be offered. Time would act as a salve. What did a young man's foolishness matter, in the grand scheme of time's passage? Carlo raised his glass with Ercole, and toasted the future.

Then came the morning.

As he stirred on the cellar floor, Carlo's first thought was to question whether he had succeeded in his quest for death after all. But surely death could not be this painful. His head was besieged by a hellish cacophony: a furious drumming that threatened to shatter his temples like fine china. As he sat up with a groan, his stomach lurched violently—crawling across the floor, Carlo was abruptly and conclusively sick into a wooden pail. He wiped his mouth on the back of his hand, tears in his eyes. In the reflection of an empty phial, he saw that he was wearing Ercole's barbute. He lifted it off his head and threw it to one side, flinching at the metallic clang the helmet made against the flagstones.

The noise was not enough to rouse Ercole, who lay face down at the bench, a pool of saliva by his mouth. The gravedigger muttered something in his sleep and loudly broke wind. As the sulphuric fug ripened, Carlo forced himself to his feet, skirting around exuberant exclamations of smashed glass on his way to the stairs. Halfway up the steps, he had to pause, at once struggling for breath and fearful that he would be sick again. He consoled himself by imagining a series of cruel and inventive punishments to visit upon Ercole, by way of retribution for pressing his poisonous concoctions upon him.

At length, Carlo reached the nave, to find sunlight flooding in through the open door. A joyous bark greeted his appearance: there, in the middle of the chamber, was Monsieur. The hound was turning in excited circles, tongue lolling from its mouth, frolicking upon a bed of torn parchment.

Slowly, painfully, Carlo turned his gaze up to the lectern. There was no sign of his poem on the desk. He let out a small squeak of horror. Stumbling over to Monsieur, Carlo sank to his knees and placed his head in his hands. His verses lay all about him, savaged beyond recognition. Only now—too late—could he unpick the truth of the scene he had encountered inside the Printing Quarter cellar: the manuscript destroyed in the hearth, the dog shut behind the door, the heartbroken scholar lying dead on the floor...

Monsieur loped over to Carlo and dropped a shred of parchment before him, panting happily. He stared at the dog balefully. Gauging the change in mood, Monsieur opted to make his exit—Carlo ran after it, yelling at the top of his lungs. At the gate, he hurled a stone after the rapidly retreating hound, missing it by a distance as it bounded away through the gravestones and chipping a piece off an angel's wing.

Behind Carlo, came the sound of wheezing laughter. He stalked back to the church to find Ercole leaning against the doorway, helpless with merriment.

"Bumpkin that I am, bereft of your great learning," Carlo said coldly, "I fail to see the humour in what has just occurred."

"Then you have the soul of a counting-house clerk," chuckled Ercole.

"The dog destroyed my poem!"

"I did try to warn you. Follow it around for a day or so. You will see your poem again, in one form or another."

Swearing loudly, Carlo launched another stone in the direction of the departed hound.

"After all that I have endured," he muttered, through clenched teeth. "At the very threshold of despair, when all seems lost, I find a small chink of light, a glimpse of hope. Yet even that is taken from me."

"And does that not give you pause to wonder why?" enquired Ercole. "You offered up your poem to each of the elements in turn—to earth, water, fire and air—only to be rejected. But then there is aether, quixotic and divine; provider of inspiration and light, of falling tortoises and hounds ascending. You made no gift of your verse to the aether, yet it took it from you anyway. Why?"

"My head is pounding, and my soul is in tatters. I have no appetite for riddles."

Ercole gave him a meaningful look. "Perhaps it would have you write something better."

Marching Carlo back inside the church, the old man bullied him up the lectern steps, kicking scraps of paper from their path. He pressed Carlo down onto the stool.

"What am I to do here?" said Carlo.

"Why, write of course!"

"Have you lost your mind? My poem is no more! You would have me magic up a new one on the spot?"

"What is aether, but the clear sky of heaven?" Ercole laid a fresh piece of parchment in front of Carlo and patted his hand. "Fill it with stars," he said.

Second Canto
The Letter O

I. *The Silent Tower*

IT WAS THE bells that woke her, a chiming tide breaking across the city. Vittoria stirred, drowsy and dry-mouthed. She was not, by habit, an early riser: most of her work was composed at night, her pen casting a slanting shadow across the page. Pulling her sheets over her head, she burrowed down into her bed, fleeing the daylight. But the path back to her dreams was lost, a thread that unravelled even as she reached out to grasp it.

Finally she conceded defeat, sitting up and drawing the sheets around her shoulders. Come summer, Vittoria would fling open the shutters and invite the night inside her chamber to leave its glistening breath on her skin. But now the room was cold, the fire turned to ash in the hearth and a bitter draught knifing through the drapes. Vittoria's skin rippled with gooseflesh as she ventured out an arm towards the chair beside her bed. She snatched up the white robe lying across the seat and wrapped it around herself.

The garment, fashioned in the east from finest silk, had been a present from a correspondent. As a rule, Vittoria did not accept such gifts. But the robe, with the sheer softness of its touch, had caught her in a moment of weakness. Instead of sending it back, Vittoria had composed a short, discreet note of thanks—which she had, after a brief deliberation, torn up.

She rose, the tiles offering chaste kisses upon the soles of her feet, and slipped through the drapes out onto the balcony. From here, atop a bell tower on the brow of the Via Liguria, she could look out across the whole of Cadenza. A thick mist had created a second city high above the first, the upper reaches of the libraries transformed into imposing cliffs, cupolas into rolling hills—islands in an ocean of white. Birds arced and wheeled above vague shorelines. In the face of the bells' clamour, the belfry directly above Vittoria offered only a rusty silence; her tower had lost its voice many years ago. She stared, shivering, down through the clouds.

From inside the tower, came a brief knock at the door; she stepped down from the balcony and admitted Andrea. Vittoria's attendant was a tall man with thin, greying hair that reached down to his shoulders, covering a crimson birthmark on the left-hand side of his face. Years in the service of the Giodarno family had transferred upon Andrea a certain patrician-like dignity, which neither his reduced circumstances nor his position in Vittoria's employ could erode. He handed her a cup of hot water and placed a bundle of letters on her writing desk. With a flicker of irritation, she caught his quick glance over her unfinished correspondences.

"Did you write last night?" he asked—although already, he knew the answer.

She blew upon the cup's surface. "A little."

"More letters arrived today."

"So I see."

"Is there anything else I can bring for you?"

Vittoria shook her head.

"Then I will draw your bath." He bowed.

It was ludicrous in a way, to impose such formality upon this ruined house inside the Printing Quarter, where forgers stamped the page with deceits and footpads plied their trade under the cover of the slamming presses. Yet Andrea would have it no other way. Every morning, he insisted on hauling steaming pails of water up from the kitchen hearth for Vittoria's bath. As the years went by, she began to worry that he might slip and hurt himself on the stairs, but Vittoria knew that the mere suggestion he should stop would cause Andrea mortal offence. Their relationship was built on a solid understanding of matters that would remain unspoken: certain affairs of the past, the very things that had drawn them together, were never openly acknowledged.

As her bath filled, Vittoria occupied herself by glancing over the day's new letters. Andrea withdrew without a sound. Warm fingers of steam beckoned her through the doorway to her bath—kneeling beside the tub, she traced a finger across the surface, disturbing her reflection. The robe slipped from Vittoria's shoulders with a silken whisper. She removed her shift and stepped gracefully into the bath, her skin tingling as she lowered herself into the piping-hot water. A small sigh escaped her lips. She closed her eyes and lay absolutely still, luxuriating in the heat's caress. Water spilled out over the rim of the tub, splashing the worn tiles.

Vittoria lingered in her bath until it cooled, only reluctantly climbing out to dry her dripping hair. The silk gown was returned to the back of the chair. Having dressed, she busied herself with small, long-neglected chores, trying to ignore the half-finished letters waiting on her writing desk. Vittoria was in the middle of a message to Fabrizio Groto, a librarian at the Bibliotheca Marciano—written, as requested, in the guise of the Chief Librarian's daughter, a pretty young thing with whom Groto had fallen hopelessly in love. At last settling into her chair, Vittoria cast an eye over her work:

"...and only now, dearest Fabrizio, dare I recount to you the dream which keeps returning to me. I am sitting in the library, late at night. On the desk before me lies a book. It is filled with your words, telling me how you desire me, and explaining in great detail the ways in which you would make love to me. Almost without realizing it, as I read on, I find myself unhooking, unbuttoning and untying myself from the heavy garments that suffocate me. With every sentence, I submit more of my bare flesh to the statues' deathless gaze. So lost am I to passion at your words, I am scarcely aware of the scholars around me ceasing their work. Wrinkled necks crane in my direction; forgotten worms stir beneath robes. Emboldened by my shameless display, and the lateness of the hour, the old men crowd around me, reaching out with yellowed fingernails to paw at my breasts.

At the very moment they threaten to overwhelm me, the reading room echoes to the sound of your

footsteps. Gnashing their teeth with frustration, the
scholars retreat, ceding to your claim over me. They
can only watch as you pick me up and lay me down
on the desk, the wood cold and smooth against my
back. I turn to water; with one swift movement you
free yourself from your drawstrings and suddenly I am
filled with you, my cries shattering the silence into a
thousand pieces..."

Thus far had Vittoria—known to all but a handful of
Cadenza's citizens as the ink maid Hypatia—come the
previous evening, before giving up. It had felt as though she
was wading through ink, wrestling with sentences as cold
and ugly as eels. All she needed, she told herself briskly, was
one good day. A bold thought, a pleasing phrase... how
many hundreds of such letters had she written, these past
years?

II. *Courtesans of the Quill*

THE TALE OF Eleanora Conti had been handed down through
generations of Cadenza's womenfolk, an heirloom passed
in whispers from bed to bed long after the last candle had
been extinguished. During the first Carnival of Wit in the
reign of Bartolomeo Strozzi, Eleanora had climbed out of
her bedroom window one night to visit a notorious salon.
Within moments of her gaining entrance, the impetuous
young noblewoman had been swept up in a melee between
rival factions of poets—a Venetian soldier named Beppe
had stepped in, knocking a drunken brawler to the ground

and escorting Eleanora to safety. They did not leave each other's side that night, and embarked on a series of secret assignations that continued long after Carnival's end.

But even as the lovers exchanged fierce protestations of devotion, events in Venice were to dash their hopes of marriage. The blind Doge Enrico Dandolo, ruler of the floating city, knelt before the altar inside the Church of San Marco and took the cross upon his cloth crown, declaring war on the infidels of the Holy Land. Beppe had little choice but to return home to join the regiments—though not before vowing that, should he survive the campaign, he would wed Eleanora on his return. She pledged in turn to keep faithful vigil until that day arrived. Deaf to her family's cautions about the casual promises and inconstancy of fighting men, she retired to a tower in her family's palace overlooking the East Gate and waited for her love to return to her.

Two years passed. Eleanora prayed from sunrise to sunset, at once desperate for news and terrified of the tidings it might bring. She tore open letters and listened numbly as her servants recounted the rumours circulating the Old Market—of the eastward plough of Venice's warships, the fall of Zara, and the siege and sack of Constantinople; the looting and the killing, the brutal untethering of the bronze horses of Saint Mark from the Hippodrome. Just as Eleanora was beginning to lose hope, a breathless page ran up the tower with a letter. Beppe had survived the slaughter and was returned to Italy. True to his word, the honourable soldier was headed for Cadenza, stopping along the way at the hillside town of Schio to seek out a noted silversmith to fashion a ring for Eleanora.

The day after his arrival, plague swept through Schio's narrow streets, striking down both the silversmith and Beppe, who died in agony in a makeshift pesthouse outside the town walls.

When word reached Eleanora's tower, her horrified scream dragged iron nails across the rooftops, bringing the Via Maggio to a standstill. Thalia Conti raced to her daughter's chamber just in time to pull her back from the window—it took three people to hold down Eleanora, who hissed and spat as though possessed. Tied to her bed for her own safety, she sank abruptly into a melancholy stupor from which neither entreaty nor medical infusion could rouse her.

Weeks passed before Eleanora stirred. When finally her speech returned, the first words from her lips were a request for pen and ink. From her bed, she began to write—letter upon letter, inconsolable, impossible pleas, all addressed to Beppe. Weeks became months. Her family tried in vain to prise her from her room with bribes and threats, even bringing up suitors to try and win her heart anew. But Eleanora would not be moved. She died a maiden ten years later, having penned almost a thousand letters to her lost love. Her correspondences were locked away in the Conti family vaults, a now-legendary byword for fidelity and love.

Within six months of Eleanora's death, three self-proclaimed 'ink maids' had set up shop in Cadenza, offering their services to the city: courtesans of the quill, who invited letters from lovelorn men and women with the promise that their innermost desires could be voiced and satisfied in kind. One delighted correspondents with her boldness and salacious wit; another with her demure acquiescence.

The third revelled in a lewdness that earned her both an ardent following and disdain within the more discerning salons. Over time, the ink maids and their successors came to occupy a singular place in Cadenzan society, fêted and frowned upon in equal measure.

Vittoria Giodarno gave little thought to her standing in the city. Those who had seen her work proclaimed her to be the pre-eminent ink maid of her time—the finest, perhaps, since Ginevra di Lecce. Yet such plaudits meant nothing to Vittoria. Not once had she sought entry to a salon, nor petitioned to have work published. She had rejected the supple blandishments of the patron Orsini, who had sought to inveigle himself into her acquaintance by requesting messages of a most intimate and unusual nature. It was said that Tommaso Cellini himself had considered inviting Vittoria to the Palazzo Nero, only to decide against it, mindful of the popular disapproval that consorting with such a woman might attract. Even Vittoria's mother viewed her as little more than a common *puttana*, while her father had not spoken a word to her since a hot summer's day eleven years earlier.

So she wrote only for herself, and her small network of correspondents with their secret, forbidden loves: the cloth merchant's wife and the notary's son; the scribe and his hard-hearted master; the noblewoman who walked down a certain street once a month just to catch a glimpse of a muscular smith at work on the anvil. The grand passions of the everyday could still take Vittoria by surprise. Now, in the shadows of the bookcases she had fashioned for Fabrizio Groto, she tried to flesh out her vision: the mewls and grumbles of the withered scholars as they competed for a view, their hot breath visible in the air, the wooden desk scratching her buttocks as she wrapped her legs around the librarian...

Vittoria let out a sigh and pushed the letter away from her. The library felt no closer, no more real, than her lost dreams of the morning. Casting glumly about the room in hope of inspiration, she saw that one of her messages had fallen down the side of her desk. She reached down and picked it up. The note, composed in an elegant hand and left unsigned, was short and to the point:

I would like to watch you write. The Ponte Nuovo, at dusk.

Vittoria frowned. Rising from her desk, she left her chamber and went down the stairs, stepping carefully around the sections of crumbling stonework. Andrea was standing at the kitchen hearth, addressing a bubbling pot. He frowned when she put the letter before him.

"What is this?" he asked.

"I was going to ask you the same question. Did you see who delivered it?"

Andrea shook his head. "I did not. Nor was there anything untoward when I emptied the *tambura*."

"You are certain?" pressed Vittoria.

"It is hardly the first strange message you have received," he told her, handing the note back. "Throw it on the fire as you did the others."

She nodded. "Thank you, Andrea."

He grunted and returned to his pot. Her attendant, Vittoria knew, approved of her work no more than her parents did, though he would die before ever saying so. She returned to her rooms and tossed the anonymous note into the hearth. Andrea was right, of course. Vittoria's reputation ensured that the *tambura* attached to her door had to swallow all kind of sour mouthfuls: obscenities and misspelled threats, offers of salvation, promises of damnation. The letter she *should* be concentrating on was lying on the desk before her. She read it once more, her brow wrinkling in concentration. It would suffice as it stood, she judged—all it required was a final flourish. Vittoria let her mind drift, trying to locate a place of perfect stillness.

An errant shaft of sunlight nosed its way through the gap in the drapes, falling hot and bright across her face. Her bedchamber melted away. She could hear the soft whickering of horses, the lazy flick of their tails. Straw prickled against her back. A small constellation of knotholes, each bursting with brilliant sunlight.

Vittoria stared at the unfinished line.

III. *The Round Room*

STONE IMPS MANNED the parapets of the Ponte Nuovo: priapic watchmen who leered at Vittoria as they tasted the air with their tongues. Night was falling, lights glimmering in the distant windows of the Accademia. Ordinarily, Vittoria would ask Andrea to accompany her if she were travelling after dark, but tonight she had slipped out without a word. She knew that anyone encountering her in this lonely spot would think her a woman of the streets; already, she had received one unwelcome offer from a gang of rowdy apprentices. At her back, the Adige spilled and churned through the gloom. Closing her eyes, she fancied she could feel the stone bridge tremble at the river's surge through its arches.

A low whicker cut through the darkness—startled, Vittoria looked up to see a carriage pull up on the bridge. It bore no coat of arms, offering no clue as to the identity of its owner. Gathering up the hem of her gown, Vittoria crossed the bridge and called up to the coachman, who sat motionless in his seat, muffled beneath a heavy cloak. He nodded at the carriage door. Vittoria reached out hesitantly to open it. There was no one inside; a letter bearing her name was waiting for her on the seat. She took a last glance back at the city slipping into night and climbed into the carriage.

Vittoria had barely taken a seat before the vehicle lurched forward, bolting across the Ponte Nuovo towards the Verso. She opened the letter, a blindfold falling into her lap. It was accompanied by another terse message.

When the carriage stops, put this on.

Vittoria fingered the blindfold thoughtfully. In the course of her work, she had come to learn the intimate secrets of some of the most important figures in Cadenza. Some might have mistaken this for power, but she was well aware of the dangers that came with such knowledge—Vittoria was not, by nature, a reckless woman. Yet here she was, willingly entrusting herself to the care of a stranger without a face or a name, with no idea as to why they had sought her out. She reached over to the window and tried to pull aside the curtain, only to find that it had been nailed into place. So far as she could tell, they had left the river behind and were travelling up into the steep reaches of the Verso. A long way from home. What would Andrea say, if he could see her now?

Halfway up a hill, the carriage slowed and rolled to a stop. Taking a deep breath, Vittoria slipped the blindfold over her head and pulled it down over her eyes.

For a long time, nothing happened. She forced herself not to move, hands clasped in her lap, aware of the quick, shallow breaths inside her chest. Finally, she heard the carriage door open, could not help but tense as a cool hand reached out and grasped hers. The driver, or someone else? Vittoria allowed herself to be guided down from the carriage. She felt firm ground beneath her feet; four steps, and then a door creaked open. A hand guided hers to a thin cord running along the wall and, with a slight push in the small of her back, indicated that she should follow it. She went on alone, an icy draught playing around her ankles. Her foot banged into something—Vittoria cried out, gripping the cord to prevent herself from falling over. Ruefully, she realized that she had reached a flight of steps. There appeared nothing to stop her from lifting up the blindfold, yet she had no intention of doing so: she would not allow herself to be cowed by this exaggerated secrecy. These stairs were nothing compared to the tight and treacherous spiral inside her tower, and there she had no thread to guide her. She followed the cord to the top of the steps, and along another passage to a door.

Grasping blindly for the handle, she twisted it and felt the door give way before her. She let go of the cord and walked slowly across the threshold.

Vittoria lifted up the blindfold.

She was standing inside a perfectly round room, a single dark window set into the wall. The floor and walls were bare, the only furniture a chair and writing desk placed in the centre of the chamber. A pair of red candles had been entrusted with the room's illumination, casting light over the paper and ink on the desk, carefully positioned beside a glass and bottle of wine. Whatever she had been expecting—and there had been time enough in the carriage and the lonely hallways to conjure some nightmarish propositions—it had not been this.

Placing the blindfold down on the desk, Vittoria went over to the window and cupped her hands against the glass. She could make out nothing of the chamber beyond. Beneath the window, an iron grille was set into the wall, designed in the shape of a perfect letter 'O'. Vittoria reached out to trace a finger around the metalwork. At a loud slam, she snatched back her hand. The sound reverberated around the curved walls. Opening the grille, she saw that it contained a rolled-up piece of paper, which presumably had been fed through an identical grille at the back of the drawer. From inside the darkened room.

She took out the note.

Welcome, Hypatia. I am glad you came.

Vittoria glanced up into the glass. "You have the advantage

of me, sir," she called out. "You call me by name, without offering your own."

The grille banged once more, signalling the depositing of another note in the drawer.

You may call me Zanni.

"Is that so?" The scheming servant Zanni was a popular character in the summer plays at the Garden of Leaves. More games. "If you would be my faithful and cunning attendant, come out of the darkness and present yourself."

For now, I must serve you from the shadows.

"A pretty offer, but I already have an attendant. I need no others; I am no lady."

I do not propose to run your bath and scrub your clothes.

"A servant who would pick and choose their duties. Should you not come running to *my* summons?"

As you said—you are no lady.

The notes were written in an educated, fluent hand. Whoever Zanni truly was, it was clear that this chamber had been fashioned for this exact purpose, the furtherance of this mysterious communication. It would have required time, and a good deal of money. Vittoria had not been brought here on a whim.

It was not a reassuring thought.

"You have gone to great effort, Zanni," she called out, adopting a playful tone, "to swap notes with me. A less naïve woman might wonder as to your true intentions."

You are the least naïve woman in the city. And yet you came anyway. Why is that, do you suppose?

That question, she chose not to answer. "I am an ink maid; I trust you know what that means. The only thing of mine that can be bought is my pen."

Do you see a bag of coins on the desk?

"I see the tools of my trade. You would have me work for free?"

I would have you write a letter for your own desire, not for anyone else's.

Butterflies whirled and fluttered inside Vittoria's chest. Were Andrea here, she knew, he would be urging her to leave this strange house at once. But if she tried to flee, did she risk angering the man on the other side of the glass? Vittoria poured herself a glass of wine and took a sip, the possibility only belatedly occurring to her that it might have been drugged. What on earth was she *doing* here?

The grille rattled.

There is nothing to fear here, truly. The door is unlocked—

you may leave when you wish. I seek only to bring you happiness.

"Yet in this, I fear I may disappoint you, Zanni," she replied. "I am an empty vessel, who serves only as a conduit for the passions of others. I have no desires; I have not loved."

I do not believe you.

Vittoria laughed. "You presume too much, my servant. You may tidy my papers and clean my shelves, but the contents of my heart are not open to your inspection."
The reply came back swiftly.

I know more about you than you think, Vittoria.

She took a quick sip of wine. Here now was a prick of danger, pressing sharp against her skin. Zanni knew her name. It should not have been possible: the Giodarno estates lay many miles from Cadenza, and her father had suppressed all mention of his eldest daughter's name in the wake of their brutal falling-out. How many in the city knew her true identity?
Folding her arms, she looked directly into the black window. "I should like to leave now."
The Round Room fell silent. Vittoria held her breath.

As you wish.

She went over to the door and found, as Zanni had

promised, that it was unlocked. A corridor stretched out before her. Yet upon the threshold, Vittoria paused—going back to the writing desk, she retrieved the blindfold and slipped it down over her eyes before continuing on her way, trusting the cord to lead back through the blind passageways of Zanni's house to the street outside, where a carriage was waiting to take her home.

IV. *Maddelina*

IT WAS THE last Sunday of the month. As was her custom, Vittoria made the short walk through the Printing Quarter to the river. Bands of young men were sunning themselves on the Ponte Nuovo, wolfishly eyeing the passing ladies and exchanging lewd pleasantries with the whores who offered themselves from the shadows beneath the bankside arches. Among the families taking the air, one young woman stood alone, impatiently surveying the crowds. Maddelina Giodarno was almost ten years Vittoria's junior, and a head taller: fair-skinned and striking in appearance—handsome rather than beautiful, perhaps, her features too strong for some men's tastes; her manner too impatient, her tongue too sharp. She retained the manners of the countryside like pieces of straw tangled in her hair. Maddelina had followed her elder sister to Cadenza six months earlier, taking one of the rooms at the palace of their uncle Baldassare upon the Verso. Ostensibly, this situation had been approved with the intention of finding her a husband. However, the younger Giodarno displayed no greater appetite for marriage than her sister, and had set about deterring potential suitors with gusto. Their mother would be despairing, Vittoria was certain, at the prospect of both daughters becoming spinsters.

She was grateful for Maddi's company that day, in the aftermath of her visit to the Round Room. Vittoria had sensed Zanni's disappointment at her request to leave—yet could she not own to the same emotion, having embarked upon such a mysterious journey, only to reach an impasse so quickly? Satisfaction had been denied to them both. But for Zanni, it would surely be no difficult matter to find another woman to fulfil his desires. At that very moment, did another ink maid inch blindfolded through his house? And did Vittoria not feel a twinge of jealousy, at the thought?

Maddelina caught sight of her sister and waved eagerly. The two sisters walked arm-in-arm north along the riverside. Vittoria had learned to avoid the city's parks and piazzas, seeking out its quieter paths and side-streets. Though she shunned the traditional ink maid's cloak—white with black blotches, as made famous by Filiberta Giustini—Vittoria's notoriety made it hard for her to pass unnoticed. She walked a gauntlet of reddening faces and conspiratorial smiles, stares and insults, spit glistening on the ground before her. For all their boldness on the page, the sight of Hypatia in person could cause her correspondents to lose all composure. Once, upon encountering Countess Gondi in the Garden of Leaves—a most respectable lady, whom Vittoria had privately promised, in the guise of a friend's niece, to insert her tongue between her legs and lick her until she screamed with ecstasy—the horrified lady had fainted into a dead swoon, causing consternation among her retinue. Vittoria never heard from her again. She wondered how long it had taken the countess to work up the courage to write to her; whether she had kept the solitary letter she had received or cast it into the fire. It seemed such scant reward, for so great a leap of trust.

"Well?" Maddelina asked, her eyes bright and eager. "Do you have them?"

"I'm not sure about this, Maddi," Vittoria said slowly. "I would be happier if I knew what you wanted them for."

"But I told you, I can't!" Maddelina twined her fingers around her sister's, a pleading note in her voice. "I'm only borrowing them for a couple of days, and I *swear* that they will come to no harm. You know that you can trust me."

As it happened, Vittoria didn't trust her sister in the slightest—Maddelina was too impetuous, too prone to sudden fashions and enthusiasms. Vittoria suspected that once her letters had served their purpose, they would be either mislaid or abandoned to moths and mildew on some dusty shelf. She had brought a handful of copies of her earliest letters, sent to long-forgotten correspondents. The only names were those of ghosts. It was still, she knew, a betrayal. But she had never been able to refuse Maddelina.

She drew out three letters tied with a black ribbon and handed them to her sister. Maddelina seized them gleefully.

"Thank you, Vita!" she said. "You will not regret it, I swear."

"I hope not, little sister."

An off-key warble stopped them in their tracks. Looking up beyond the sign of the Ship, Vittoria saw a boy standing atop the tavern roof, his hands clasped over his heart as he serenaded her, roared on by his unseen companions beyond the eaves. She blushed, bowing her head. Maddelina winced dramatically and covered her ears.

"Can we not take *one* walk about this city without some love-drunk buffoon trying to woo you?" she exclaimed, as Vittoria's troubadour hit a particularly jarring note. "I swear, you will be an old crone without a tooth in your head and still the men will be lining up bearing gifts and sonnets of their undying devotion."

"And still, I will be alone."

Her sister rolled her eyes. "You are astonishing," she said. "The most beautiful woman in the city and one of its greatest writers, who could have any man she chooses. And yet you talk as though you were some wrinkled maid, bedecked with cobwebs!"

"I am not a young woman anymore. Not like you."

"It is not me the men gaze at, slack-jawed and drooling, as we walk by," Maddelina retorted. "Old maid or not."

Vittoria drew her arm back through her own. "Come now, Maddi. Would you really have me believe you have not a single admirer?"

She was rewarded with a slight flush of embarrassment. "There is… someone," Maddelina admitted. "Although I cannot truly say how much he admires me."

"He leaves you unsure on the matter? Where are *his* sonnets of undying devotion?"

"I'm not sure the poetry of love comes naturally to him. On the page, at least."

"Maddi! Mother would be horrified."

"Which is why I have no intention of telling her,"

Maddelina laughed. "Do not worry about me, old crone! We cannot all turn our backs on love."

Across the Adige, the washerwomen of the Verso were attending to their laundry, knotting the damp bedsheets into balls and pounding them against the rocks. Vittoria shaded her eyes against the sun as she watched them.

"I have Andrea and my letters," she murmured. "That is enough for me."

A shadow crossed Maddelina's face. "There is something else," she said. "I was not sure... if I should..."

She lapsed into silence.

"Ah," Vittoria said finally. "Father."

"He is an old man, now," Maddelina told her. "He grows more frail with each passing day. If you have any hope of ever seeing him again, you will need to act soon."

"And do you act as his messenger in this regard? Or is my name still forbidden to be spoken in his hearing?"

"Vita, you know how difficult it has been—"

"I thought as much. I will not waste my time seeking an audience."

She threw her hands up in the air. "What would you have me say? I know you are hurt, and Father also. But are your wounds really too deep to even *try* and have them heal?"

"Father is hurt?" Vittoria said quietly. "I will match him, bruise for bruise."

Her sister nodded and fell quiet, staring down at the letters she had been given. By unspoken agreement, at the next junction they turned back for the Ponte Nuovo. The gaiety had gone from Maddelina's voice as they parted farewell, replaced by something complicated by regret.

V. *A Place of Complete Disdain*

SEVERAL DAYS LATER, Vittoria received a letter from one of her most loyal and long-standing correspondents, a man who had risen to a position of no small importance within the city. This fact was in no way apparent from the tone of his letter, in which he begged Hypatia's forgiveness for his intrusion in an abject and pitiable manner, declaring himself her most ardent admirer and begging for a few gentle words of love. Vittoria's desk had grown cluttered with unanswered letters, yet here, finally, was a request she could not ignore. She forced herself to sit down and take up her pen. Andrea appeared at her door with a bowl of broth, and could barely contain his delight when Vittoria shooed him away.

Rereading her correspondent's letter, Vittoria pictured him before her on his knees, snivelling and wiping his nose on his sleeve. She reluctantly granted him attention, searching out a place not of anger, but of complete disdain. He was nothing, less even than a man: a dog trailing after her on its leash, slack-jawed and panting, lips wet with saliva as it begged for scraps from her hand. For a time, the only sound inside the bedchamber was the brisk scratch of Vittoria's pen.

> *Three days hence I will permit you to accompany me on a walk through the Old Market. You will follow two paces behind me upon your knees with your mouth wide open, and anything I choose to place upon your tongue you will swallow.*

Two sentences, nothing more. There could be no spoiling him. Vittoria returned her pen to the pot and folded up the note. She had no idea how long it had taken. When the words came easily, surging forth from her pen on to the page, it was as though she were submerged in the ocean depths, beyond the reach of time itself. Feeling somewhat brighter for having finished a message, Vittoria turned to her other letters. She *still* hadn't finished her reply to the librarian Fabrizio Groto, but it required only a line or so, and then two of her correspondents would be satisfied. Who knew how many she could please before the day was out?

At the sound of raised voices, Vittoria's pen paused. She rose and went out onto the balcony. In the street below, Andrea had accosted an urchin by the *tambura* on the tower door—he made a grab for his collar, but the boy twisted out of reach, laughing as he scampered away to safety. Shaking his head, Andrea unlocked the wooden box and took out a letter. Vittoria watched with growing curiosity as her attendant glanced up and down the street before slipping the note inside his jerkin.

She returned to her desk only to discover that the words, so obliging at hand only minutes earlier, had vanished again. An hour passed without a knock on her door. Vittoria went in search of Andrea and found him composing a letter of his own. He looked up as she watched him from the doorway.

"My lady? Is something wrong?"

"I was expecting a letter before the end of the day. Have you checked the *tambura* this afternoon?"

Andrea dipped his pen in the inkpot. "It is empty, as far as I am aware."

"Forgive me," Vittoria said, laughing lightly, "I must have been dreaming. For I felt sure I saw you chase a boy away from the tower and hide the message he delivered upon your person."

"A strange vision, to be sure," he murmured.

"Andrea?"

Carefully laying down his pen, he opened the desk drawer and took out a note. Bearing—as she had suspected—her name, rendered in Zanni's unmistakeable hand.

"It is difficult to reply to letters, as you keep insisting I must," she said, "if you hide them from me."

"It would not be the first harmful message I have kept from you," he replied evenly.

Vittoria folded her arms. "And why would you think it harmful?"

"My lady, do you really think you can bid leave to the tower for an entire night without my knowing?"

Not wishing to reply, she broke open the seal.

I would like to see you write again. The North Gate, at dusk.

Cursing Andrea under her breath, Vittoria rushed upstairs to her chambers. She changed into a gown of midnight blue and tied up her hair with a leather cord, barely glancing at the looking-glass before making for the stairs—leaving her latest letter, so swiftly and scrupulously addressed, lying forgotten on the desk.

VI. *The Letter O*

THE NORTH GATE was closing as Vittoria hurried towards it, earthy curses filling the air as a wool trader struggled to direct his belligerent livestock out into the countryside. For a moment, she feared she had arrived too late, only to catch sight of Zanni's carriage waiting by the side of the road, the horses standing to attention. She called out a greeting to the coachman, but he did not acknowledge her. There was nothing else to do but climb inside—where she found, as before, the curtains fastened securely over the windows, and a blindfold on the seat.

This time, Vittoria resolved to plot the carriage's path through Cadenza, trying to keep track of the streets they took. She was sure that they crossed no bridge—if pressed, she would have said they had travelled east towards the Piazza della Signora, the exact opposite direction to last time. Now that she had the chance to compose herself, Vittoria's predominant emotion was irritation, directed at three different persons: at Andrea, for presuming to interfere in her private correspondences and causing her to arrive flustered and out of breath; at Zanni, for presuming to send another imperious summons; and—lastly and most keenly—at herself, for allowing these men such sway over her affairs.

The journey was shorter than the previous one, and she was surprised when the carriage pulled up. Vittoria slipped on the blindfold, and upon the opening of the door was guided down from the vehicle and over to a doorway. Passing through the entrance, her hand reached out to find the guiding cord attached to the wall. She followed it along a long, straight corridor—no steps this time—until she reached a door, which swung open at her touch. Vittoria took off her blindfold. And blinked with surprise.

She was back in the Round Room.

It could not be the same room, of course. There was no way the carriage could have ferried her back to the Verso without her noticing, and the journey through this house had been completely different to her last. And yet everything here was as before: the bricked-up hearth and the writing desk and chair, the blackened window set into bare walls, above an iron grille in the shape of a perfect 'O'. Even the red candles on the desk had been set in exactly the same position. They bowed their heads as Vittoria walked by. Smooth sheets of vellum parchment were arranged on the desk, beside a pen and fresh pot of ink.

The grille rattled.

I was beginning to think you would not come.

"I had business requiring my attention," Vittoria replied levelly, trailing a finger across the top sheet of paper. "Believe it or not, you are not my only correspondent." She gestured around the walls. "I feel as though I am reliving a dream. Is this the same room in a different house? A different room in the same house?"

It is always the same room.

"So you say. Then again, I cannot even be sure that you are the same man as before."

Or even that I am a man.

Vittoria laughed. "No, you are truly no man, Zanni. What kind of man would skulk so in the shadows, fearful of a woman's gaze? You would wear mystery like a cloak around your shoulders, yet all I see is a little boy, cowering in the darkness."

There was a long pause before the reply came.

You know the power that names and faces hold, the way that truth can intrude on desire. Why else would you have the city call you Hypatia, and not Vittoria Giordano?

"That is the second time that you have turned my name upon me like a weapon," Vittoria replied tartly. "I should like to know how you have become so acquainted with it."

I knew the girl you used to be. What happened on your father's estate. Marco.

Vittoria flushed. "I do not know a Marco."

Was it really so long ago? Or did he mean that little to you?

With a furious cry, she ripped up Zanni's note and hurled it at the glass. Vittoria snatched up her shawl and was marching for the door when the grille banged behind her. Taking a deep, steadying breath, she walked back and reached inside its metal mouth.

I am sorry. An unworthy suggestion.

"I grow tired of these games," Vittoria told him. "You present yourself as some kind of intimate acquaintance, yet all I hear is a gossip's flapping tongue."

How many gossips have read your letters with their own eyes? I know the passion that burns through you, though you fight to deny it.

"And how did you come to see these letters? You cannot pass yourself off as one of my correspondents, Zanni. I would not forget your handwriting."

They were not written to me. But I have read them, regardless.

Vittoria groaned inwardly. Only now did it occur to her that she had entrusted, just days earlier, some of her private letters to her sister. Feckless, flighty Maddelina, who was entangled in a relationship with a man she would not name. What on earth had Maddi been thinking, sharing Vittoria's correspondences?
"You had no right, Zanni."

I know this. I am here to make amends.

"By leading me upon this dance?"

By persuading you to write a letter in your own name.

To Marco.

She hesitated. "To Marco? And tell him what?"

Whatever you desire.

Followed quickly by another message:

Please, take a seat. Fill your glass. I wish only to serve you.

Vittoria slumped down at the desk. She felt dizzy, overwhelmed. Zanni's notes were scattered across the floor of the Round Room. When had someone last spoken of Marco to her? Memories, stirred up like dust clouds, swirled through her mind. The darkest of shadows. As she stared down at the blank page before her, Vittoria fancied she could hear the soft whickering of horses. Knotholes bursting with sunlight; the prickle of straw on skin...

She dipped her pen in the inkpot.

VII. *Whip and Whim*

THE NEXT MORNING, Vittoria awoke in her chamber to find a letter from Fabrizio Groto waiting for her. The incensed librarian demanded to know why he had received no message from her, shrilly declaring Hypatia to be little more than a swindler and a prostitute. She replied with an abrupt termination of their agreement, enclosing the money he had sent her and the ashes of his final encounter with the Chief

Librarian's daughter. Groto would not be her only unhappy correspondent right now; a point Andrea was quick to reinforce. Two sentences were all that she had managed to compose in a fortnight, and even they remained on her desk. Yet still her pen lay idle.

It had been different inside the Round Room. Vittoria had stayed until dawn, opening her heart to a ghost: hesitantly at first, but with growing urgency, until the chamber had grown warm and she had tossed her shawl to one side, filling pages with breathless sentences. Zanni had spoken of desire, but no words of love or tenderness touched the vellum—rather a stream of thoughts that dipped in and out of coherency, almost violent in their insistency. As she wrote, Vittoria could feel Zanni's gaze on her bare neck and shoulders. He offered no comment upon her efforts, the grille remaining tight-lipped. When finally it offered up a new message, it was to warn her that the sun was about to rise. Vittoria allowed herself a single read-through of her letter and then fed it to the dying candles, watching the paper brown and curl and burn away to ash. Then she replaced her blindfold.

Now, with the morning, she felt empty, the night's euphoria given way to nagging questions and doubts. Foremost of these was how Zanni could know about Marco. There was no mention of him in the letters she had given Maddelina—nor in any she had written, for that matter. Vittoria could not believe that her sister would betray her by openly sharing the tragedy that had befallen her, but, in a careless moment, might something have slipped loose? She sent a series of urgent notes to her uncle's palace but received no reply. There seemed little option but to set out for the Verso herself.

Vittoria felt stripped bare as she crossed the city squares, her colour rising at the casual glances of passers-by. It was as though a leash had been fastened tight around her throat, leaving her subject to the whip and whim of a man without a face. She waited outside the gates of her uncle's house for hours, craning her neck up at the balconies for a glimpse of Maddelina. But there was no sign of her. Perhaps she had returned to the Giodarno estate; perhaps their father's health had worsened.

Unwilling to return to the tower and her stack of unanswered letters, Vittoria lingered on the Verso, resting by the graveside of Ginevra di Lecce at the Church di San Felice. At the other end of the row, the gravedigger and his young companion were manhandling a cart along the uneven paths—catching sight of Vittoria, the poet blushed and stumbled, nearly tipping the contents on the ground. He was little more than a boy, really, a bubbling pot of awkward and unguarded passions. Yet that, in itself, was not without charm. Vittoria had told Zanni that she had no desires. It was her life's truth: a fire that had been brutally extinguished, a heart filled with cold ash. "Old crone," Maddelina had called her teasingly. Was it too late to change, were such a transformation even possible? Vittoria watched the boy hurriedly right the cart and continue on his way, the gravedigger chiding him as they disappeared among the gravestones.

It was growing dark by the time Vittoria returned to the tower on the Via Liguria. Rooks perched atop the seized-up bells; the staircase was wreathed in shadow. Finding the *tambura* empty and no new messages on her desk, she headed to the cellar and slid a bottle of wine from the rack.

Andrea was waiting outside his quarters as she climbed the steps. Raising her nose in the air, Vittoria marched past him up to her bedchamber and firmly closed the door behind her.

VIII. *Paper Birds*

SHE WOKE LATE to find her room in disarray. Letters were scattered across the floor, where her gown lay discarded beside an empty wine bottle. At some point in the evening, Vittoria had changed into her white silk robe: as she sat up, she saw that it was now covered in splatters of ink. She let out a groan, working her aching temples with blackened fingertips. Andrea had pointedly left her morning cup of lemon water on her bedside chair—Vittoria took the drink and scurried back to bed, taking a couple of sips before gratefully tumbling back into unconsciousness.

Some time later, the brisk parting of the drapes announced her attendant's return. Sunlight burrowed its way beneath Vittoria's eyelids.

"Leave me be, Andrea," she groaned. "I will not write today."

"Nor did you yesterday, nor the day before that," he replied, a disapproving silhouette by her bedside. "There are people waiting for your letters across Cadenza."

"Let them wait," Vittoria said. "Does an empty belly not make a meal more welcome, or a dry mouth a drink? Is anticipation not sweeter than the reality?"

"Rhetoric. Save it for your correspondents, it is wasted on me."

Vittoria pulled her pillow over her face. "Must I satisfy the entire city?"

"You did not accept money from the entire city," Andrea countered, "on the understanding that you would write to them. Only these people here."

"And have I not given them faithful service, all these years? How many hundreds of letters have I written, how many fantasies have I presented for their pleasure? I have given them so many *words*—could not one of them have summoned the courage to act upon their own desires, and allow me some respite?"

"You know better than anyone the folly of acting upon certain desires," Andrea replied evenly. "That is what makes what you do important."

"Do not suddenly pretend you find my work important. You have always disapproved of what I do, just like Father. You judge me for it."

Andrea drew himself up proudly.

"Never in my life have I judged you," he said.

"Yet look at you now!" laughed Vittoria. "So majestic with pride, so delighted to have cause to scold your errant charge!"

"I do not deny that I am concerned for you," Andrea replied. "I see you heading out into the night on unknown assignations, and each time you return I see a change in you. You scorn your work; but worse, I see a festering contempt for the people for whom you once cared."

Vittoria rose angrily from her bed, deliberately careless as she adjusted her gown. At the glimpse of her exposed skin, Andrea flushed.

"Which letter would you have me write, then?" she inquired acidly. "To whose care should I tend today: the cuckold who wishes to spy on his wife coupling with their lodger, or the poet who dreams of a cloud of cherubs urinating over him? Perhaps I could furnish them with a fresh image: a loyal servant attending to his fallen mistress, eagerly waiting for the moment her courtesan's mouth covers his quill with her filthy lips?"

Her words landed on Andrea like a physical blow: he took a step backwards, bright spots of colour appearing in his cheeks. He opened his mouth and closed it again. Finally, with stiff formality, he held out a small bundle of parchment.

"These are the correspondences in most urgent need of your attention, my lady," he managed.

Vittoria snatched the letters from Andrea's hands with a shriek of frustration, running out onto the balcony and hurling them over the balustrade. A flock of paper birds took flight, dipping and fluttering on the wind as they spiralled slowly into the city, alighting upon church roofs and tangling up in tree branches, speckling the streets with profanity and smut and shame.

When the last letter had disappeared from view, Vittoria took a steadying breath and turned back from the balcony. Her chamber stood empty; Andrea had gone.

IX. *Brusque Meeting*

SHE DRESSED AT once, wrestling back into her dirty gown and hurrying down the stairs without so much as a glance towards Andrea's quarters. Let him attend to her messages if they mattered that much to him. Spitting rain greeted Vittoria as she stepped outside; she slammed the door behind her and marched away down the hill, treading one of her own scattered letters into the mud as she went.

There was a giddy edge to her anger. She had no idea where she was going or what she would do, living from second to second like a mayfly in the dying afternoon sun. Beautiful, selfish, perfect freedom! As she continued down the hill, a monk in the white robes of the Dominicans stopped and stared at her—Vittoria blew him a kiss, laughing with delight as he blushed and hurried on his way. She wandered through the Printing Quarter, following a circuitous and contradictory path. In a secluded church square, she stopped to watch children chase one another around the flagstones, laughing and bickering, in the thrall of some arcane game whose rules Vittoria had no hope of understanding. An old man resting beside her on the bench shared his almonds with her, an offer she gratefully accepted. Almost a day had passed since she had last eaten. Clouds were drawing in overhead, bringing an unnatural evening down over the square; voices rang out from upper-floor balconies, calling the children inside. Vittoria bid farewell to the old man and selected an alley at random to walk down, skirting beneath the dripping eaves as the rain began to fall.

She came out by the riverfront, where the Via Fiume intersected with the Ponte Nuovo. The storm was directly overhead, the river roiling beneath a black and violent sky. Vittoria felt the first prickle of doubt—she ought at least to have brought a cloak. Her gown was already sodden, and she could not bear the thought of returning to the tower in a state of bedraggled defeat. Andrea would never let her hear the end of it. Shielding her eyes from the rain, Vittoria looked up and down the deserted riverfront. Finally, in desperation, she stepped quickly through the puddles and went down the steps leading beneath the Ponte Nuovo.

There was shelter here, at least, from the downpour, if not the wind, which pursued the shivering Vittoria under the arches. Wiping damp curls from her eyes, she peered through the gloom. The arch was adorned with white chalk markings: tallies of numbers, arranged in rows and accompanied by notes scrawled in an indecipherable hand. It looked like the work of a stargazer, driven to madness by the unknowable mysteries of the heavens. As Vittoria gazed up in wonder, there came a shout from the next arch. She crept over to the abutment, stones sharp through her shoes, and peered around the corner.

There, at the river's edge, a man and a woman were conjoined in the shadows, his face lost to darkness, hers obscured by long, unruly tresses. Skirts hoicked up around her waist, she bent forward with a hand resting against the wall to steady herself: palm flat, fingers spread out across the stone like a starfish. The man's breeches were around his ankles, his hands tight about the woman's waist as he thrust himself inside of her. Feet slipped on wet stones; grunts and ragged breaths elbowing for room.

Vittoria shrank back against the stonework, her breath tightening in her chest. The man grabbed a fistful of hair and pulled the woman's head up, offering Vittoria a glimpse of her face, her mouth set somewhere between a grimace and a half-smile of defiance, brow wet with sweat and throat muscles taut. She slapped the man's hand away, twisting around to spit a curse over her shoulder. Yet still they remained locked together, entangled and drenched in spray as the rain lashed down on the bridge.

The woman cried out as the man drove faster and harder inside her, his thighs making a fleshy slap against her backside. Vittoria could feel the colour rising in her cheeks, a burning sensation across her chest. She was stripped raw. How hollow, by comparison, her letters seemed! Here now, before her, was truth, neither love nor kindness nor gentleness; nothing more than a transaction, conducted with white knuckles and gritted teeth. Yet could Vittoria not deny a certain thrill at its urgency—its discomfort, even? That even now, upon this dreary afternoon, at the conclusion of lonely stairwells and in gloomy cellars across the city, there were such burning needs and desires that demanded satisfaction. As she watched the man and woman collide against one another, the brusque meeting of sexes, Vittoria's fingers inched beneath her rain-sodden gown.

"Lost, my lady?"

Vittoria whirled round, her face scarlet, to find a young woman eyeing her with amusement.

"I am no lady," Vittoria said quickly. "I was taking shelter from the rain."

The girl looked her up and down. She was painfully thin, wrists jutting out from a gown she had long outgrown: a brittle tatterdemalion with a red weal visible, like a brand, on her shoulder blade.

"You wouldn't be the first," she said idly. "Many's the

man who's taken a wrong turning in bad weather and found himself beneath the arches. I've seen them on a bright summer's afternoon, too; dazzled by the sun's glare, I suppose. Women are a rarer sight, and ladies rarest of all. But I've seen them." The girl advanced upon Vittoria, who retreated until she felt stone at her back. "Come Carnival time, they come creeping down here with their fancy masks, fair shaking with excitement at the thought of getting something stiff inside them; so come-drunk, they forget to even ask for payment. What is the point of all that money, those fine gowns and jewellery, if you have to come down here to get fucked by some stinking tanner who's drunk his weight in wine?"

Vittoria swallowed. The wind howled in over the water as the shouts gathered pace through the next arch. The girl's lips hovered close to Vittoria's ear, wine upon her breath. She took Vittoria's hand in her own and examined the ink-stained fingers.

"These aren't working hands, however much you dirty them," she said. "But then a pretty face can get you more than a purse of coins, if you know how to use it."

Without taking her eyes from Vittoria, the girl took her index finger in her mouth and sucked upon it. Vittoria felt dizzy—should she cry out, or scream for help? With a sudden, sharp movement, the girl pressed her up against the wall and wedged a knee between her legs. A small gasp escaped Vittoria; she leant her head back against the stone and closed her eyes, helpless to stop the girl from guiding her own finger beneath her gown and finding the softness inside her. From the other side of the abutment, the furious smack of flesh on flesh; a man's ragged cries. At the girl's urging,

Vittoria abandoned herself to the storm, a raincloud made flesh, a furious torrent of desire. Just as she felt herself ready to explode, the grip on her wrist vanished. She opened her eyes.

"If you want any more you'll have to pay for it, my lady," the girl said, with an impudent grin. "I was told only to give you this."

Her heartbeat pounding in her ears, Vittoria only dimly registered a note being slipped into her hand.

Time to write again.

Through the archway came an exchange of sharp words, a contemptuous shower of coins across the pebbles. The tatterdemalion stepped back with a mocking approximation of a curtsey. Stumbling past her, cheeks hot with humiliation, Vittoria ran out from beneath the archway and looked up through the stinging rain.

And saw, with a shiver of recognition, a carriage waiting for her at the top of the bridge.

X. *The Prickle of Straw*

THE HORSES GALLOPED along the pitted and pockmarked lane, their hooves splashing through deep puddles. They had passed through the North Gate hours ago, the city walls long since lost to the night. Inside the carriage, Vittoria sat shivering in her clothes, her teeth chattering and her brow burning up. This time there had been no blindfold waiting for her on the seat, nor were there curtains pinned over the windows. Yet still she travelled blindly, without any idea as to her destination. Darkness devoured the fields beyond the glass. The carriage let out a violent hiccup as it hit a rut, jolting Vittoria from her seat. She picked herself up on her hands and knees, cursing herself for the impulsiveness that had brought her to this point.

As the carriage struggled along the path, a hunting lodge appeared, on the fringes of a dense wood. Hounds barked greetings from their kennels as the vehicle came to a halt. Vittoria made a vain attempt to address her dishevelled appearance before throwing up her hands with exasperation. It was enough that she had made this journey; she would not prettify herself for whoever waited for her inside. She stepped down to find that the coachman had disappeared. Steam rose in great clouds from the horses' flanks as they panted and nickered. The night sky seemed impossibly dark and vast. Vittoria walked slowly towards the lodge, the mud sucking at her shoes. The hounds redoubled their gruff chorus.

She had prepared herself for another Round Room, but inside the lodge there was neither darkened window nor iron grille. The floor was covered in animal pelts; a fire burned in the hearth. Upon the wall, an oval looking-glass inlaid with pearls offered Vittoria an unwelcome reminder of her tousled hair and mud-splattered clothes. She went over to the fire and crouched down to warm her palms over the crackling logs. Behind her, a floorboard creaked. Liquid glugged into a glass.

"Wine?" a man's voice inquired.

Vittoria straightened up.

"A drink of any kind would be most welcome," she said stiffly. "It has been a long and uncomfortable journey."

"My apologies. I wanted to ensure we would not be disturbed."

"You could not find more suitable quarters inside Cadenza? I assumed you had a hundred Round Rooms within the city, each with its own bedazzled maiden inside."

"A delectable proposition, but alas, no. This lodge belongs to Lazzaro Negri, august member of the Seven, who will no doubt be most aggrieved to learn that he has had guests. He is not a man known for his generosity."

Only then did she turn around. There, sat behind a writing desk, was Zanni. His face was hidden behind a black and gold mask bearing the arched eyebrows and elongated nose of the cunning servant, a profile that would be visible on every street when the Carnival of Wit began the next week. Of middling height and middling years, Zanni offered only small clues to his true identity: shoulder-length black hair, long, delicate fingers—musician's fingers—that toyed with his wine glass. She had anticipated the idle drawl of a nobleman, but there was a rustic edge to his accent that seemed somehow at odds with the cultivated author of the Round Room notes.

Assuming, of course, that they had been the work of the same person.

"How did you find me?" Vittoria demanded. "Were you following me?"

"I am your most solicitous servant, am I not? My man informs me he found you beneath the Ponte Nuovo. What on earth could have driven you to such iniquitous quarters, I wonder?"

"I was sheltering from the rain."

"And that was the only roof open to you in the whole of the city? Huddled beneath the arches with the whores?"

"There are many who would claim me no better than a whore."

"The ladies of the Ponte Nuovo are not known for their poetry."

"They have more pressing demands on their time."

Beneath his mask, Zanni's mouth curved into a smile.

"I did not envy the women I saw down there," Vittoria told him.

"I did not think that you would."

"Yet you would have me explain myself to you."

"I am curious, nothing more."

"For all I know," she said accusingly, "you arranged the whole thing."

Zanni spread out his hands. "I cannot make rain fall from the sky, Vittoria."

She turned back to the fire with a snort, folding her arms.

"You are angry with me," he said.

"Let us say that I have had my fill of surprises for one day," she replied. "Do not mistake me for a marionette who will dance at the merest twitch of your fingers. Why did you bring me here?"

"To write another letter."

"I have laid down my pen. I have written enough."

"Then tonight I will be your scribe," he said. "Tell me about Marco."

"I thought it a story you knew well."

"I would hear it from your lips."

Vittoria sighed. "Zanni, I do not know what my sister has told you, but she is a foolish girl, barely more than a child, and she—"

"You sister has told me nothing."

"Play your games with me if you will, but leave Maddi be!"

"Upon my life, Vittoria, we have not exchanged a single word! Truly, my only interest is you."

"My most solicitous servant," she said, sourly.

The fire spat and snapped in the hearth. Zanni went to the cupboard and pulled out a wooden box. He brought it over to Vittoria.

"I wish neither to anger nor offend you," he said, his tone softer. "Say the word, and my man will drive you back to Cadenza."

"The city gates have closed for the night."

"They will open for me."

At the look in his eyes, she bit back a retort. "And if I stay?"

From within the box, he drew out a phial filled with black liquid and poured it into a cup.

"This comes from the East," he said, "by way of Venice. Drink it. It will bring you ease."

Vittoria stared down into the swirling water. A note she could have ignored. A blindfold she could have removed. A room she did not have to enter. She had been given so many chances to turn back. Without taking her eyes from Zanni, she raised the cup to her lips and drank. A bitter taste filled her mouth. Nodding with satisfaction, he took the cup from her and returned to the writing desk. He briskly dipped his pen in the inkpot.

"Please," he said, gesturing towards the divan near the fire. "You will be more comfortable there."

She lay down on the divan.

"Tell me about Marco," he said.

"You know who Marco is."

"A lover."

"A dead lover. You would have me write to a ghost." She laughed humourlessly. "Like Eleanora Conti and faithful Beppe."

Zanni leaned forward, his eyes serious. "Tell me Marco's story."

Vittoria shook her head. "You ask too much. Have I not shown you enough already?"

"You have barely shown me anything at all."

She could feel the fire's warmth spreading up from her toes, melting away her irritation. Outside, the hounds had fallen silent. The crackle of flames and the whistling wind. Vittoria laid her head against the rest.

"When I was younger, I liked to ride," she said softly. "There was a stable at the edge of my father's estate, I would walk there across the fields. It was summer, the day almost violent with heat. I remember the sun beating down on the parched grass, the glare off the lake so bright it hurt my eyes. My head was pounding but I was too stubborn to turn back. Inside the stables, it was scarcely cooler, the baked air rich with the horses' earthy smell. I sought a shady corner, where I found a pail of water drawn fresh from the well. I knelt beside it and splashed my face. My gown felt so tight around my chest I could barely breathe. I slipped my shoulders free from its restraint and wrung a rag out over the back of my neck, gasping at the water's cold kiss against my skin. All this time, I had thought that I was alone, but at a whicker of warning from the stalls I looked up to see Marco at the window, watching me.

"Of all the boys who worked on the estate, his name alone I knew: for secretly I had watched from the terrace as he laboured in the fields, dark-haired and serious; this honest work more stirring to me than any fine words and courtly manners. At night, I summoned him to my dreams, where he came before me as a servant no longer. Had he followed me to the stables, or had our paths crossed by chance? I never found out. To gaze upon me so boldly would have earned him a beating from the steward, and had I screamed or shouted at Marco to go away—had I uttered a single word— he would have fled, I am sure of it. But I did not want him to go away. I did not want him to stop looking at me."

Zanni looked up from the page. "So what did you do?"

The soft whickering of the horses. The prickle of straw against her back. Knotholes filled with brilliant sunlight.

"I offered myself to him," Vittoria said dreamily. "Button by button, with trembling fingers. I freed myself from my gown, so heavy upon me, until it fell at my feet. Only now, can I marvel at the bravery of it. I was so afraid that he might laugh! But Marco did not laugh. He stood motionless, betraying no emotion as I lifted my shift over my head to stand naked before him, the water droplets glinting on my burning skin. I do not know how long we stood there, gazing at one another. Finally, he came inside the stables. His hand brushed through my hair and traced a path down my neck to my breast. I had not thought he might be gentle."

The words came tumbling from her mouth, sprung stays upon a gown. Zanni's pen scratched urgently across the page.

"Our mouths met, and at the press of Marco's lips against mine, I felt a sudden urgency, pulling at his shirt so that I could feel his skin against my own. We sank into the straw and I freed the stiff stalk from his breeches to guide him inside me. What did I know, of the act of love itself? Nothing, and yet its rhythms came as naturally to me as a childhood melody.

"We moved in time together, our bodies tessellating, slippery with sweat. My passion built into a growing fury, my fingernails scoring his broad back. I bit his lip, and Marco pulled away suddenly. Shifting to his knees, he dragged me by the hips towards him and raised my legs high above my head. This time, when he entered, a key turned in a lock somewhere deep inside me, and though he had asked for my silence I could not obey him. I filled that small wooden building with my cries until the rafters shivered and the horses bucked and stamped their hooves. I heard Marco's breaths, louder and faster in my ear, and then he let out a great exclamation, his shudder passing through his body into my own, and as he melted inside me I felt my own release, that sent me arrowing, empty and alone, to a place of perfect stillness.

"For a long time, afterwards, we did not move, the pair of us breathless and drenched in each other's sweat. Finally, Marco rolled away." Vittoria closed her eyes. "It was then I saw the silhouette of my father in the stable doorway."

Zanni paused, his pen quivering in mid-air. "Your father."

Vittoria nodded. "I do not know how long he had stood there. What he had witnessed. I remember screaming, something shattering inside of my chest. My father dragged me naked from the stables and across the estate, knocking my hands away when I tried to cover myself. When we reached the house, he took me down into the cellar and beat me. At one point, I remember thinking that he was going to kill me, so fiercely did the blows land. I must have blacked out, because suddenly he was gone, and I was alone. The door was locked. It was dark and the floor was very cold. I still had Marco's smell on my skin, but I had no water to wash it off, nor any rags to wipe myself. Even in the very depths of the house, I could hear my mother crying.

"I don't know how long they left me down there. My sister later told me that my father had vowed to horsewhip anyone who tried to help me. When finally he relented, it was Andrea who came for me. I remember the cellar door opening, the painfulness of the light around his silhouette. I shied away but he came forward so gently, a blanket in his hands. He wrapped me up and carried me to my room, where he had run a steaming hot bath." Tears glistened in Vittoria's eyes. "The kindness of it—my heart broke a second time. Andrea shushed me and told me that everything was going to be all right. He knew otherwise, of course, but what else could he say? I stayed in my room until the bruises healed. When I felt strong enough, I left in the middle of the night, resolved to travel to Cadenza alone. Then, at the gates to the estate, I saw Andrea waiting for me...

"I never dared ask what happened to Marco, but I heard

that he had been dismissed from my father's service in disgrace. I was young enough and foolish enough to believe it. Years later, Andrea told me the truth. My father had Marco killed, his privates severed and fed to the dogs. He was such a beautiful boy; he did not deserve such a fate."

"What crime was committed here, truly?" said Zanni.

"I had never spoken a single word to him," Vittoria said faintly. "Nor he to me. When I reached Cadenza, I wrote him letters in a disguised hand, but by then it was already too late. I do not know what happened to them."

"I do," Zanni told her. He laid down his pen. "Your father intercepted them. And gave them to me."

Sunk in the black water's numb embrace, Vittoria heard the words only distantly. She frowned. "You have my letters... to Marco? But how could you know my father?"

Zanni sighed. "I too worked on the Giodarno estates, Vittoria," he said finally. "Although my name and face would mean nothing to you—no one watched me labour in the fields. I loved you, then; all the boys did, I think. But you only had eyes for Marco. He knew that you favoured him above the rest and confided to me of his plan to seduce you, unaware of the heat of my own passions. I said nothing, but jealousy ran like a poison through me. Your father gave me your letters as a reward—you see, it was I who directed him to the stables that afternoon."

She gasped. "Zanni!"

"In my wrath, it did not occur to me that you might also be disgraced. When I heard about the humiliation that your father had inflicted upon you, it was like a dagger in my breast. I read the letters you had sent Marco and tried to pretend that it was me you addressed, me who you loved and desired. But it was a lie I could never believe. I resolved that I would seek to redress the damage I had wrought, no matter how long it took me. I have spent the last ten years making my fortune, through fair means and foul, in that hope."

"My most solicitous servant," she said, softly this time.

A chair leg scraped across the floor. Zanni came to sit beside her on the divan. Vittoria reached out and traced a finger around the eyeholes of his mask.

"I should hate you," she said.

"You would have every right."

"One single, solitary afternoon of pleasure. Ten years of shame. It does not seem fair."

"Then perhaps you should stop punishing yourself."

The room was melting into the fire. Zanni's mask flickered and shimmered, his features changing with each second. He laughed and grimaced and leered and wept, at once friend and foe; servant and master.

"If you tried to take me now," Vittoria murmured. "I would not stop you."

"I know," he said.

XI. *Love Letters*

VITTORIA AWOKE WITH a start. In the darkness, it took time for the world to take shape around her, the familiar outlines of her bedchamber slowly asserting themselves. She lay entangled in the sheets, her skin covered in a film of sweat and her head pounding; she remembered nothing of the journey back to Cadenza, nor any of the hours that had followed the end of her tale. Rolling over with a groan, Vittoria fell back asleep at once.

It was light when she opened her eyes again. Judging by the bright blue shard of sky visible through the balcony curtains, the day was well underway, but there was no cup of hot lemon water steaming by her bedside, and no knock came at her door. In the silence, she was confronted by the awful possibility that Andrea might have left her. Then she remembered it was Sunday. He would be at church. Vittoria pictured him sitting in the pews, straight-backed and tight-lipped with disapproval.

So long as he did not leave her. So long as he would forgive her.

Perhaps it was the after-effects of the black drink Zanni had given her, but Vittoria's mouth was sour with disappointment. She had unburdened herself of her innermost secrets yet felt no lightness of release, only a dull fog. What was it that she required of him? Or was it more what he required of her—her forgiveness for his betrayal, and its brutal consequences. She had learnt everything and nothing about Zanni, and the man behind the scheming servant's mask. A stable hand with the means to construct the Round Room, and the impudence to take Lazzaro Negri's hunting lodge as his own. He claimed to have read her letters to Marco but had not offered to return them. Indeed, she had only his word that he had burned the record of her confession last night. Did Zanni truly want freedom for her? Or did he seek to stoke her desires, only to satisfy his own?

One thing was certain—she would not lie in bed like

Eleanora Conti, waiting dutifully for a satisfaction that would never come. Vittoria reached for her ink-stained robe. Perhaps if she could finish a letter or two, Andrea might accept that as a peace offering. The air's chill bite had softened; soon spring would take root inside the bell tower, warmth flowering in the corners of her room.

As she sat up in bed and wriggled into her robe, Vittoria paused. Upon her upper right thigh there was a patch of reddened, tender flesh. Slowly pulling up her shift, inch by inch, she saw with mounting excitement the letters inked across her flesh, in the same elegant hand that had corresponded with her in the Round Room. A single sentence, eight simple words, which she heard her own voice recounting as though in a dream:

When I was younger, I liked to ride.

As she traced the words across her skin with her fingernail, following the letters' loops and jags, Vittoria felt her heartbeat quicken and the breath tighten in her throat. Her shame, delicately rendered on her leg at Zanni's design. A creeping warmth spread through her body; a bucket of molten gold drawn up from a deep well.

Across the city, bells began to ring.

Third Canto
The Lions of Libya

I. *A Straight Face*

HOWLS OF LAUGHTER swept across the terrace, hot gusts of a sirocco wind. Every year, the patron Orsini marked the beginning of the Carnival of Wit with a feast in the grounds of his estate upon the Verso, serving his guests sumptuous and exhausting courses of oysters and plover, chicken with pomegranate, fennel, onion salad and honeyed walnuts. Full-bellied and refreshed with wine, the audience retired to benches arranged along the terrace, which looked out across a small lagoon to an island where a wooden stage had been erected. Torches punched crackling holes in the darkness, the moon a large white circle balancing on the upper branches of the trees.

On the stage, a man sat at a desk, gazing off into the distance with a faraway expression on his face. Paper littered the floor by his feet. Clearly, he was labouring over a work of great importance—twice, now, his wife had appeared in the bedroom doorway at the top of the stairs and beseeched him to join her; twice, she had been waved away. Now, as the writer sighed and crossed out a line, a trapdoor flew open in the floor behind him, and a grinning devil crept out onto the stage. The fiend was dressed all in red, its grotesque face topped with a pair of horns. To the delight of the audience, he capered behind the unwitting writer, cutting a merry path up the bedroom steps. When the door opened and the wife peered out, the devil dropped to one knee and lasciviously stroked the length of its spikes. The wife took one look at her husband and yanked the fiend into the bedroom, slamming the door shut behind them as the crowd exploded with laughter.

Alone among the packed terrace, one man remained expressionless. Lorenzo Sardi shifted in his seat, his bladder uncomfortably heavy with wine. With his fifth decade of life had come mounting small indignities: joints that stiffened and seized in hard chairs; ears that struggled to catch all but the loudest noises, their sharpness perhaps dulled by the thick hairs now sprouting from their interior; and—most troubling of all—the dead-ends and oubliettes inside the once-secure fortress of his mind. These concerns were only thrown into sharper relief by the youthfulness of Lorenzo's companions, the aspiring poets who comprised his *fideli*. As far as Lorenzo was concerned, a sorrier collection of mimics and peddlers of empty flattery it would have been hard to find, but a Cadenzan poet without such a coterie was considered no poet at all. And within the House of Orsini, appearances were everything. The patron's feast was considered one of the highlights of the Carnival, invitations proffered only to the city's most prominent or promising artists. From his vantage point, Lorenzo could see Orsini in the middle of the front row, dabbing at his mouth with a handkerchief, his gold rings glistening with chicken grease.

Piercing shrieks of desire erupted from behind the bedroom door, carrying across the lagoon to the chortling audience. Yet the writer was too absorbed to notice. He rose from his desk and paced the front of the stage, strewing the water with rejected parchment. At his back, the devil's leering face re-emerged from behind the bedroom door to a chorus of cheers. It extended a red claw and beckoned down to the trapdoor, which spewed forth a line of eager suitors: more leering devils; mincing fops and gallants stumbling over their swords; and then—to boos and catcalls—a host of Venetians, instantly recognizable by their flowing blond locks. As they headed one-by-one up to the bedroom, the wife resumed her ecstatic chorus. Finally, her husband turned around: the screams died out at once, suitors melting behind the furniture. Tapping his cheek thoughtfully, the writer turned back to his work.

The audience was now writhing and convulsing as though caught in the grip of some terrible fever. Hands clutched at sides and spit flew. The lady beside Lorenzo was sobbing with laughter; in the row behind them, a nobleman had guffawed himself into a coughing fit, his companion hurriedly slapping him on the back as he turned purple. Was it possible, Lorenzo wondered idly, to die from laughter?

Better that, than from a burst bladder—Lorenzo would have given his eye teeth for a piss. Clenching his jaw, he willed the play to its conclusion. After what felt like an interminable delay, this arrived when the writer rejected his wife for a third time and she replied by shoving him into the lagoon, while behind them the devils and the Venetians danced a giddy reel together. The actors took their bow, soaking up the applause—the devil sweeping off his mask, the wife his woman's wig, while the writer doffed his sodden cap to the crowd. Lorenzo's *fideli* turned to him expectantly.

"A most entertaining spectacle," Lorenzo said, at last.

The *fideli* chirruped in agreement.

"Orsini has surpassed himself this year."

"A light blade, but a keen edge."

"Its victim will certainly feel its blow land. A bold choice of target, do you not think?"

"Just imagine the look on the poet Rinaldi's face," spluttered Paolo, the son of one of Lorenzo's distant cousins, "when he hears that he is being mocked!"

Lorenzo turned on him in disbelief. "You thought the writer was *Rinaldi*?"

The colour drained from Paolo's face. "B-but, maestro, who else could he be? I hear that Rinaldi has not written a single line in twenty years."

"I heard he died twenty years ago," piped up Francesco, an unfortunate-looking youth with skin pitted by acne.

"Is that not the same thing?" Raffaele replied archly. He was the cleverest and least talentless of the *fideli*—and therefore the one Lorenzo despised the most.

"Rinaldi's *Song of Summer* was dedicated to Orsini!" Lorenzo exclaimed. "You think he would host a play that mocks his greatest protégé?"

Paolo's face fell. "But if it was not Rinaldi," he said, "then who—?"

"Why, it was Cosimo, our new Artifex, of course!" Raffaele exclaimed, laughing. "Waiting for inspiration to strike."

"But Cosimo does not have a wife," said Paolo, bewildered.

Lorenzo massaged his brow. "Of *course* he has no wife," he said. "But as Artifex, he is married to Cadenza. We are his wife, one and all."

"And while he ignores us, the devil lets the Venetians in," Raffaele explained.

Paolo scratched his head. "So with Cosimo in charge..."

"...we're fucked," Francesco finished.

"His reign is barely begun, and already Cosimo is a laughing stock," Lorenzo murmured disapprovingly. "Tommaso would never have permitted such liberties."

"Should comedy not be free from the threat of reprimand?" Raffaele inquired, with an attempt at artlessness.

"Not if it, in turn, threatens something more important than comedy," Lorenzo replied firmly. "Without respect, how can a man hope to rule?"

"What does a playwright care whether or not his ruler is strong?"

"Why, nothing at all. Yet tell me this, Raffaele—what great comedies did the Visigoths produce?"

Raffaele hesitated.

"Name me but the one," Lorenzo declared, "and I will have Orsini stage it in your honour next year."

He rose from the bench stiffly, which he judged added a decisive flourish to his rhetorical thrust, whilst also providing some much-needed relief from the pressure on his bladder. If he didn't piss soon he was going to rupture something. The stage had emptied, leaving the audience to drift amicably into the night. Orsini was deep in conversation with Salvatore Ridolfi, his mouth in conspiratorial proximity to his ear.

A firework went off with a deafening bang above Lorenzo's head, colour dappling the startled sky. He felt his leg run hot. Several tiers below him, a commotion had broken out: his ears ringing, Lorenzo was aware of heads turning and looking up towards him. The *fideli* were talking animatedly amongst one another, their voices lost beneath the clatter of the fireworks. He angrily shook off Paolo as the young man tugged at his sleeve.

The crowds around Lorenzo parted, offering him a glimpse of a man walking off the terrace—an imposing figure with an ermine-lined cloak wrapped around his broad shoulders, a full head taller than his own circle of *fideli*. A large paw rested protectively on the shoulder of the young woman beside him. Sensing Lorenzo's gaze upon him, the man stopped and looked up towards him. Their eyes met.

Erupting stars peppered and punctured the night. In between explosions, Lorenzo could hear voices calling out his name. Then the *fideli* were flocking protectively around him, ushering Lorenzo away in the opposite direction.

> All of Cadenza knows the Bear,
> By his pungent trail through our streets:
> Noses are pinched, breaths withheld
> 'Gainst the musky fug he secretes.
> Long after the Bear has shuffled on,
> His odour lingers in the air
> Unwelcome and as hard to shift,
> As a ball of shit, matted in arse hair.

II. *A History of Vitriol*

THERE HAD BEEN a time when the Duelling Counts of Cadenza had been the most amicable of friends. A pair of young noblemen with poetic ambitions, Lorenzo Sardi and Borso Cardano made for an unlikely match—the one, earnest and sharp of feature; the other, a laconic, tousle-haired giant of a man. Yet the Owl and the Bear never seemed happier than in each other's company and could often be seen in the wineshops and salons, bickering good-naturedly over the merits of one writer or another.

In the fourth year of the reign of Tommaso Cellini, a Sunday morning in early spring found the two friends lying idly beside a stream inside the Garden of Leaves. They said little, the excesses of the previous night weighing heavily on them. Borso's heavy breaths gave way to rattling snores, his broad chest rising and falling. Lulled by the trickling brook and the soft grass beneath his back, Lorenzo felt his own eyes grow heavy. However, just as sleep threatened to claim him, he was struck by a vision that made him sit bolt upright.

Though it would quickly become a delirious two-word rhapsody to his ears, at that moment the name Lucia Pitti was unknown to Lorenzo. She appeared to him without warning or preamble—an angel, hesitant and glorious, stepping across the bridge upon her mother's arm. Fair-skinned, Lucia was a delicate, bewitching beauty who carried herself with a bashfulness that bordered on the awkward. She tucked a stray lock of hair behind her ear, her head tilted towards the ground. Lorenzo's cheeks grew hot, his heart pounding against his ribcage, demanding to be set free. As their eyes met, Lucia hesitated, offering him an uncertain smile as her mother drew her closer. Lorenzo waited until they had passed by and shook Borso awake. Ignoring the Bear's startled grumbles, he hauled his friend to his feet and set off in pursuit of Lucia's silhouette as it flitted in and out of the trees, stumbling over roots and burrows like Actaeon with Diana's hounds on his heels. Each time they drew near to the two women, Lorenzo faltered, unable to countenance what he might say to such a vision. Before he could think up a suitable introduction, Lucia and her mother had proceeded along the paths to the garden gates, and were gone.

Love visited itself on Lorenzo like a sickness. His chest ached every time he thought of Lucia; at night, his dreams tormented him with fleeting visions of her beauty. On the occasions when Lorenzo happened upon her in the park or the salon, words abandoned him, leaving him silent and crimson-faced. Yet Lucia treated him with such unfailing kindness that it only served to fuel his ardour, leaving Lorenzo unable to think or speak of anything else. At last, goaded by his friends' taunts—save Borso, who elected to keep his own counsel—Lorenzo summoned the courage to declare his love. On the eve of the Carnival of Wit, he wrote Lucia a passionate letter in which he offered himself to her completely, promising devotion and tender companionship until his dying breath.

And was swiftly rejected, with impeccable courtesy and unexpected firmness.

The heartbroken Lorenzo stumbled through the city's festooned streets in a daze, Lucia's reply stinging the pocket over his heart. Every laugh, every jest, seemed aimed squarely at his own misfortune: a fool crowned for Carnival's amusement. He fled Cadenza for his family's hunting lodge, where he drank himself into a stupor and harangued the stars. Cruel, pernicious love—why had Lucia shown him such kindness, if not to encourage his hopes?

As Lorenzo pondered both the unfairness of life and the malicious caprices of the female character, back in the city Lucia's father, Donato Pitti, held a lavish dinner to celebrate his name day. Towards the end of the meal, he attempted— unsuccessfully—to poison the guest of honour, Tommaso Cellini.

Even now, a quarter of a century later, Lorenzo could not begin to comprehend it: what manner of vanity and thwarted ambition could drive a man to such a senseless act? Donato's madness had condemned his entire family. The *becchini* waded into the carnival crowds to round them up, tearing the masks from their faces and dragging them from their dancing partners. Word of Lucia's arrest pierced Lorenzo like a shard of ice through the heart. He wrote Tommaso an urgent letter, pleading with him to spare her. It remained, by some distance, the bravest and the most reckless act of his life. In reply, the Artifex icily informed Lorenzo that his prayers had been granted: a phial of hemlock had been smuggled into Lucia's cell in the dungeons beneath the Palazzo Nero, delivering her from justice before the torturers could begin their work.

Upon reading Tommaso's message, an abject wail rose up from inside Lorenzo. His hands shook violently; he crumpled, sobbing, to the floor. Only later, numb with drink, did he find the second letter enclosed alongside the first. Recovered by the Artifex's agents from Lucia's possessions inside the Palazzo Pitti, it contained a dire warning of the dangerous and malign character of a certain Lorenzo Sardi—a man whose bland appearance, according to the letter's author, concealed a dire temper and a weakness for wine and whores. And every word composed in the hand of Lorenzo's faithful friend, Borso Cardano.

The hunting dogs cowered in their kennels as Lorenzo visited his rage upon the lodge, smashing glasses and hurling volumes of poetry into the fire. He rode back to the city in defiance of the darkness, heedless of footpads and wolves, bitter lines on his lips as he swigged from a wineskin. The Muses rode beside him that night, mothers of inspiration, nine spectral figures dressed all in black. Doleful Melpomene wept for his loss, while Erato sang a song of yearning; Calliope urged Lorenzo to take vengeance against Borso, whispering lines of caustic verse into his ear. With the Muses' aid, Lorenzo's poem was finished as the city walls came into view; before the day was out, *The Bear's False Tongue* had been copied and distributed throughout Cadenza.

Had Lorenzo harboured any doubts about the authorship of Lucia's letter, Borso's reply served to dispel them. *The Owl's Hoot* was a vicious broadside, its blows aimed squarely at Lorenzo's tenderest regions, the weaknesses to which he had owned to his friend after a glass of wine too many. And prepared at such speed—reaching the taverns within hours! How else could Borso have pulled it off, had he not prepared for just such an eventuality?

In the wake of the Pittis' failed assassination, a feverish bloodlust had gripped Cadenza. Impromptu mobs dragged men from their homes and set about them with sticks and cudgels. The stench of burnt flesh hung in clouds over the piazzas. Stirred by the poets' inflammatory verses, *fideli* flocked to Lorenzo and Borso's banners. Rival gangs exchanged insults in the street, scuffles degenerating into running battles. On the eve of the Feast of St Anthony, two opposing factions ran into one another inside the Accademia. Scholars ducked behind lecterns as books flew across the aisles; in the ensuing melee, Borso's nephew caught a boot to the head and died.

Set-tos in the street were one thing—a brawl inside Cadenza's main library, quite another. Lorenzo and Borso were abruptly summoned to the Palazzo Nero, where Tommaso told them in no uncertain terms that any more violence would see both men follow the Pittis onto a bonfire. With a truce out of the question, the warring poets elected to divide up the city between them: Borso took the southern reaches of the Recto around his palace, and the corresponding area on the other side of the Adige, while Lorenzo claimed the north. On Saturday mornings, Lorenzo could be observed deep in thought on the benches of the Parco Durazzo; at the same hour, Borso prowled the Garden of Leaves. The Owl picked through his meals beneath the sign of the Ship, while the Bear ate at the Black Lion. The Bibliotheca Niccoló counted Borso as its most eminent patron; the largest private reading room in the Bibliotheca Marciano was reserved for Lorenzo. They had to share the Accademia, apportioning visitation rights on alternate days.

If the hope had been that distance and the passage of time would act as a salve on the poets' wounds, it was to be disappointed. From the writing desks of their respective fortresses, Lorenzo and Borso fired salvos out across the rooftops, trading accusations of ugliness and impotence, alopecia and halitosis, body odour and buggery, greed and miserliness, cowardice and treachery, envy and enfeeblement, incest and bestiality, rude table manners, unnatural methods of masturbation and clumsy use of metre. Neither willing to cede the final word, every fresh insult only served to bind them more tightly together. The Owl and the Bear were fashioned anew, as the Duelling Counts of Cadenza.

In the quarter-century that had followed their grudging demarcation of the city, the poets had crossed paths only twice: the first time, during the celebrations to mark twenty years of Tommaso's rule, the presence of armed guards lining the procession route had dissuaded any thoughts of confrontation; at the second—the funeral of the revered madrigal writer Doffo di Cello—basic propriety had played a similarly civilizing role.

Now, amid fireworks and farce, there had been a third encounter.

III. *Muzzle and Guncotton*

ROUSED BY THE sun's merry fist beating against his bedchamber window, Lorenzo forced open his eyelids. His skull was filled with broken glass, his mouth stuffed with stale cloth. As he looked blearily around his chamber, he was confronted by the sight of his robe cast over the back of a chair, an accusatory stain running from groin to knee. He had the fireworks to thank for that. Could Orsini not have warned his guests before unleashing his rockets? It was supposed to be a feast, not the last days of the Siege of Rhodes.

Only then, did the memory of Borso on the terrace return to him. So many years had passed since he had last laid eyes upon his bitter rival that Lorenzo had almost forgotten what Borso actually looked like—a parchment ghost clad in stinging verse, rustling through the dark corners of his imagination. The Bear was an old man now, Lorenzo thought to himself; a thought that would have given him greater satisfaction, had he not been aware that the Owl was getting no younger either.

He rose slowly from his bed, a creaking shipwreck dredged from the ocean floor. A fresh jug of water was waiting for him on the side; he poured it into the basin and washed himself before donning a fresh robe. Every movement only seemed to intensify the crushing weight on his temples. In his youth, Lorenzo had stayed awake for the Carnival's entirety, imperiously rejecting sleep to drink and feast for days on end. Now the excesses of a single night had left him craving a period of private recuperation. But that was out of the question this day. It was the Carnival of Wit: his *fideli* would be expecting him.

At the threshold of his bedchamber, Lorenzo knelt down to inspect the floor, wincing as the shards inside his head scraped against one another. The tiles were covered in red splatters, which he judged to be wine rather than blood; with relief, even if the mere thought of the grape made his stomach lurch. He followed the trail of spilt alcohol—weaving and messy, the unsteady footsteps of Bacchus—through the corridors of his palace to his study. The surface of his writing desk was sticky to the touch, red circles visible on the parchment where Lorenzo's flagon had drunkenly kissed them. Tutting, he peeled off the top sheet. A frown creased his brow. The page beneath had been covered in angry scribbles, obscuring the verses beneath almost completely.

In the doorway, his attendant Guilio announced himself with a cough. Hurriedly slipping the defaced poem inside the desk, Lorenzo turned around and instructed him to ready the litter. He fled the palace soon afterwards, sinking down behind the carriage's drawn curtains and massaging his temples as he tried to piece together the previous evening. Upon leaving the House of Orsini, he had continued to drink with the *fideli* in a wineshop off the Piazza della Rosa, but he remembered little of his journey home, and nothing that could explain his actions in the study. It made no sense: Lorenzo had been working on the *Denunciation* since before Tommaso Cellini's death and had bullishly proclaimed that it would prove the decisive blow in his duel with Borso. Gone were the juvenile insults and insinuations, replaced by a measured, statesmanlike tone that made the poem's charges all the more devastating. How deep in his cups must Lorenzo have been, to vandalize his best work yet?

The litter continued east until it reached the banks of the Adige, whereupon it turned north along the Via Fiume and stopped outside a tavern. The sign of the Ship may have hung above the entrance, but all Cadenza knew it as the Arsenale. Here, just as the shipbuilders of Venice bent their backs to the labours of warfare, so Lorenzo and his acolytes prepared for their feints and sorties against the enemy, their pen points trained like bombard muzzles, ink furious as boiling pitch.

Lorenzo stepped down from the litter and ducked through the doorway, crossing an open courtyard where vines wound tangled spirals around the columns. The Muses stood watch over the tavern, nine sylphlike statues rendered in flawless alabaster bearing the instruments of inspiration: pens, tablets and the lyre. Beneath the welcome shade of the arcades, a set of steps led up to the roof terrace, where Lorenzo found his *fideli* sunning themselves on the benches. A wine jug was being passed back and forth in defiance of the early hour. At the sight of his master, Raffaele rose hastily from his seat.

"God give you good morning, my lord," he said, with a low bow. "I trust you slept well?"

"During Carnival?" he replied coolly. "This is no time to lie dead to the world. I spent the night at my desk."

"The *Denunciation*?" Francesco sat up. "It is finished?"

Lorenzo pictured his poem, bleeding wine and ink over the desk.

"Work progresses," he said.

"After last night, the city is more eager to hear from you than ever," Raffaele said ingratiatingly. "Your encounter with Borso is already the talk of the Carnival."

"Any word on what the damned Bear was doing there?" said Francesco. "Borso declines Orsini's invitation every year. That's why *we* go!"

"I heard his niece begged him," another youth replied—Lorenzo vaguely recognized his face, but could not summon his name. "You know Borso treats her as though she was his own. He cannot refuse her anything."

"Fiametta?" Raffaele said slyly. "Does she not dine well enough at home?"

Snickering laughter greeted his remark.

"Feasting Fiametta!" declared the nameless youth—Nicola, Lorenzo decided—raising his glass. "The only girl in Cadenza whose heart can be won with a recipe rather than a love poem."

"Who would rather a cake than a jewel for her name day."

"I would give her a pastry encrusted with diamonds," another proclaimed extravagantly, "if only to slap that great rump of hers!"

"Then better a comb with long teeth," Francesco suggested. "I hear her arse is hairier than Borso's."

"Hold your tongue!" Lorenzo said sharply.

Francesco blinked. "My lord?"

"What kind of infantile quarrel do you mark this for? The matter between myself and Borso is one of *honour*. An innocent woman died; a friendship was callously traduced. Fiametta has already suffered the loss of a brother on account of our hostilities. Must she also be subject to your witless barbs?"

Francesco went crimson and looked down into his glass. As the rooftop fell quiet, Lorenzo irritably raised his hand up against the sun's glare. Would nothing ease the din inside his head?

"My lord! My lord!"

The sound of footsteps clattering through the courtyard sent the *fideli* scrambling to the edge of the terrace. Paolo came sprinting up the steps, a piece of paper clutched in his fist. He tripped over the final stair and sprawled headlong across the terrace, to mocking cheers from his companions. Before Paolo could pick himself up, a mischievous gust of wind snatched the paper from his grasp—he gave chase, a hapless goatherd stumbling over tufts and hillocks, snatching it at the roof's edge with a headlong dive. Raffaele burst out laughing, only to hurriedly feign a coughing fit at Lorenzo's glare.

"Cease this horseplay at once!" Lorenzo snapped at Paolo. "Must you profane the quiet halls of morning with your entrance, ill-timed and clad in idiot thunder?"

"Forgive me, my lord," he panted. "A new verse from Borso has been circulating the city since dawn. I thought you would wish to see it."

"Already?" said Raffaele. He glanced at Lorenzo. "It seems you were not the only one at your desk last night. And the Bear has finished his poem."

"It is easy to write quickly when the words are of no consequence," Lorenzo replied loftily. "And you were mistaken in thinking I had any interest in whatever phlegm-soaked egestion Borso has coughed up on the page."

He shooed Paolo away when the youth tried to place the poem before him. The rest of the *fideli* could not resist, affecting an air of casual disinterest even as they crowded around it. Lorenzo gazed out over the river, trying very hard to ignore the muttered oaths and sucking-in of breath.

There was a long silence.

"You are wise not to read this, my lord," Raffaele offered finally. "It is a silly rhyme of no consequence. A child would be embarrassed to have written it."

"Would that Borso had a child's dignity," Lorenzo murmured. "I could have laid down my pen two decades ago."

"Silly rhyme or otherwise, it cannot go unanswered," said Francesco, striking his fist into his palm. "What shall we do, my lord?"

Downriver from the Ponte Nuovo, a single boat was tacking across the water, its sail billowing in the fresh breeze. The *fideli*'s eyes turned as one to Lorenzo. He sat back in his chair and steepled his fingers together.

"For now," he said, "I believe I shall take a glass of wine."

> *The Owl has fallen quiet of late,*
> *Beak shut tighter than its purse.*
> *Once-sharp talons, now too enfeebled,*
> *To scratch out a line of verse.*
> *The Bear resolved to climb its tree,*
> *And was surprised to learn,*
> *When face-to-face, the bold bird's feathers*
> *Took a yellow turn.*
> *Its dire threats upon the page*
> *Empty as a courtesan's kiss,*
> *the Owl took off into the night,*
> *With flapping wings,*
>   *and a shower of hot piss.*

IV. *A Distance of Twenty Paces*

O BLESSED GRAPE, sweet restorer! Bestower of happiness and wisdom! What manner of glorious elixir was it, that such small, judicious sips could deliver a man from the depths of woe? Lorenzo's spirits had returned, exuberant and fierce, the lingering unease in his belly the only reminder of prior excesses and regrets. Coarse songs rang out along the terrace at the sign of the Ship. The *fideli* were a glass filled dangerously to the brim, an unruly chorus impatient to avenge Borso's latest insult. They were but children, Lorenzo reflected, restless and impulsive. The *Denunciation* would serve as his reply, but only when it was ready. After twenty years, what did a few more days matter? Must he respond to every jibe, every needle prick?

He took his leave of the Arsenale midway through the afternoon, turning down all offers of company. Carnival would bring the *fideli* back within his orbit soon enough. Selecting a hawk from the collection of masks by the tavern door, Lorenzo strode out into the city. Cadenza's libraries would be locked for three days and three nights until the celebrations' end, the streets given over to throngs of brightly costumed revellers: knights of check and motley, adorned with beaks, whiskers and plumes. He had barely walked the length of the street before catching the eye of a dark-haired beauty in a cat's mask, who responded to his deep bow by trailing her hand up his thigh as she sashayed away down an alley. How little it took to change a person's nature, Lorenzo reflected—a mere mask could make a satyr of a burgher, and bring strangers together to couple in doorways in broad daylight.

Yet, for all its fleeting indulgences of the flesh, the Carnival of Wit was primarily a celebration of the mind and the written word. Not for Cadenza, Venice's horse races and human pyramids, their bitter neighbourhood scuffles over this or that canal bridge. The fiercest competition here centred around the salons, whose doors remained open throughout the Carnival—if not to everyone. Should a young poet manage to talk his way inside, a bold quip or stinging put-down could announce his arrival; a humiliating rebuff at the entrance, on the other hand, signalled another year of anonymity. Bribes and blackmail were commonplace, and who knew what graver crimes had taken place in the obscure reaches of the queues?

Away from the salons, troupes of actors staged plays in the city's parks and gardens, while poets nervously presented themselves before the unruly crowds on the Piazza di Pietra, offering up their works in the hopes of winning a laurel wreath from the judges. Lorenzo had claimed two such prizes in his youth, both with Bear-baiting verses. Borso himself was notable for his absence during Carnival. Never comfortable in crowds, he even eschewed the festivities' grand climax, the March of the Poets, when the city's writers walked arm-in-arm through the streets to bask in the cheers of their fellow citizens. Though it had almost certainly saved further bloodshed between their circles, Borso's stance struck Lorenzo as precious—that of an anchorite, squatting atop a pillar of his own churlishness.

He followed the crowds down to the Old Market, lured on by the aroma of roasting chestnuts. Jugglers tossed coloured balls into the air in time to the lively stamp of the band. High above the flagstones, a line had been drawn taut across the sky. A rope-walker saluted the throng as he prepared to step across it. Much was as it had been the previous year—yet, as he stepped about the busy square, Lorenzo could not help but note the absence of open wine casks, the thin garlands about the loggia. It had been said that Cosimo Petrucci did not share his predecessor's enthusiasm for the Carnival of Wit. Tommaso was renowned for leaving the Artifex's float empty during the March of the Poets, preferring to walk among his fellow writers. Lorenzo himself had been honoured to fall in step alongside Tommaso on more than one occasion, exchanging a few careful words. The Muses knew he had been given cause to fear the man—to hate him, even—but at moments such as those, carried aloft with his ruler upon their city's swelling acclaim, Lorenzo's personal concerns seemed trifling and petty.

This year, Cosimo Petrucci would presumably take his seat on the float: he was no writer.

Above the square, the rope-walker feigned a misstep, earning screams of horrified delight as he wobbled violently on the line. Lorenzo left the acrobat to his mock dance with death and followed the sound of laughter to an alley sloping down towards the river, where a small crowd had gathered around a blue-and-white-striped booth. The puppet show was one of the small joys of Carnival—to Lorenzo's mind, its robust humour provided a truer mirror of popular sentiment than the ornate verses of the Piazza di Pietra. He stood at the back of the audience, craning his neck to catch a glimpse of the show. A puppet with a squeaking voice was delivering a flowery verse to the audience, reading from a tiny piece of paper clasped in his carved hands. He was interrupted by the appearance of a second puppet, near twice his size, who shook his fist and startled the first with his booming voice.

Behind his mask, Lorenzo's eyes narrowed.

To growing mirth, the two marionettes began to enact the solemn rituals of the duel. Neither puppet carried a sword: instead, at some unspecified signal, they turned their backs on each other and bent over, lifting up their robes to reveal their wooden backsides. Wet rasps echoed around the booth, to hoots of laughter. The two puppets took turns to fart at one another, each hurling insults at the other as their buttocks rattled with the force of their flatulent missiles.

Only then, did Lorenzo notice the sign above the puppet booth: *The Duelling Counts of Cadenza*. As the audience broke into applause, he adjusted the hawk mask on his face and walked swiftly away.

V. *Some Small Place of Envy*

LORENZO'S HUMOUR—ALWAYS prone toward the melancholic when he was in his cups—had taken a sudden black turn. His footsteps led him to the river, where he watched the gaily decorated fishing boats bob on the current. He had come regularly to this spot in the weeks after Lucia's death, alone and after dark, the Adige rippling invitingly at his feet. Her ghost was always at its closest come Carnival, a shadow hovering at the edge of the torchlight: a reminder of that which could not be replaced. Lorenzo had never married. He had been left with neither family nor any true friend to speak of—his *fideli* were his closest companions. And, for them, Lucia Pitti was little more than a myth, a few lines of extravagant admiration in half-forgotten poems.

A sudden peal of bells startled the birds into flight. Across Cadenza, church towers had burst into song, the clanking foot soldiers of Mercury bearing fresh tidings for the city. Turning his back on the river, Lorenzo fought his way through the busy alleys towards the Piazza di Pietra. He emerged to find it plunged into chaos, poets battling valiantly with the din as their audience stared up at the bells. As Lorenzo had anticipated, his *fideli* had grown restless at the sign of the Ship and had adjoined to their habitual benches in the southeast corner of the square. They were set for the hunt, masked to the last man as hounds, greeting their master's return with theatrical barks. Peppered with questions as to the bells and their significance, Lorenzo—who could feel his headache returning—announced that he would consider the matter all the better with a glass in his hand. They adjourned to a wineshop in the shadow of the Accademia, where Lorenzo stood by the window and watched the clamour build outside. He drank quickly, barely tasting his wine. Presently, he became aware of someone standing at his shoulder.

"What do you think is happening, my lord?" Raffaele asked.

"Who knows what Fate intends for this city?" Lorenzo replied, with a humourless laugh. "Perhaps Venice comes a-knocking, or Tommaso's nephews return with an army at their back. Perhaps some unfortunate accident has befallen Cosimo, as it did his predecessor. Perhaps the city will be returned to the stewardship of a true artist."

"Bold words, my lord," Raffaele murmured. "Perhaps better saved for private chambers, where you can be sure you have the ears of friends."

Lorenzo squinted at him. "And what manner of man would that make me, Raffaele, to be your friend?" he inquired sourly. "Should I also try to burn down a library, or spit in a man's face?"

"Carlo Mazzoni was no friend of mine," he replied quickly. "Had I known that he was capable of such desperate acts, I would never have invited him to the Ridolfi salon."

"Yet despite this colossal error in judgement, still you presume to watch my words for me! Do you think I have need for a translator, so incapable am I of framing the thoughts of my own mind? You are so keen to see my *Denunciation* in print, perhaps you should finish it for me. My clumsy labours must be a source of great frustration for you."

"I would not dare to even compare my talents to yours," Raffaele said, reddening. "You are my teacher and my master. I urge caution only as your humble servant."

Lorenzo snorted and drained his glass.

The tavern door banged open to reveal Francesco, his hound mask pushed up over his hair. The street behind him was in uproar. "It's off!" he cried. "There are decrees going up around the city—Cosimo has cancelled the March of the Poets!"

"What?" Lorenzo roared. "He would not dare!"

"He says it is an expense Cadenza cannot afford."

"What matter the expense? It is the March of the Poets!"

"This will not come to pass," Raffaele declared. "The Folio will not allow it."

"They have already consented," Francesco countered. "With regret."

Howls of dismay greeted this announcement. Lorenzo sat

down, shaking his head with disbelief. What on earth was Cosimo thinking? This was not vanity—the March was a show of strength, of independence. No other place in the world bestowed such an honour on its writers; not for nothing, was Cadenza known as the City of Words. Never before had the question of *cost* intruded upon the festivities. Did the Artifex really care for his coffers so much? Or did his decision come instead from some small place of envy over the garlands and acclaim that Lorenzo and his peers would receive?

He knocked away a hand as it tried to refill his glass. The noise was fading around him—he could feel the weight shifting inside his skull, the passageways of his mind growing crowded and insistent, a city rising in rebellion; less a headache than a growing pressure, demanding his attention. On the table before him, he saw his *Denunciation*, damned by dismissive swathes of ink. *In vino veritas*. For too long, Lorenzo had been doing battle with a paper phantom. It was time for him to set aside his petty feud and take up his pen in the name of the city.

He would write a new *Denunciation*. Against Cosimo Petrucci, the Artifex himself.

VI. *Midnight Retributions*

INVECTIVE POURED DOWN from the balconies like a summer shower, drumming on the roof of Lorenzo's litter as it battled through the streets. This, here, was the voice of the city, united in furious condemnation. Caught up in the protests, the carriage rocked violently in the throng, fists beating against its side as Lorenzo's attendants shouted and cursed. He felt light-headed, dizzy with wine and his own daring.

Upon finally arriving at his palace, Lorenzo was out of the litter before it touched the ground. He hastened up to his study, sweeping poems from the desk and reaching for a fresh piece of parchment. The shape of his verses, framed in advance by the people's cries, came to him instantly. Lorenzo wrote without pause, barely noticing the sun setting, only reaching to light a candle when his words began to disappear into the darkness. The Muses had returned to his side—Urania stood by the window in a cloak of stars, her eyes upon the night sky, while Terpsichore strummed her lyre and Clio read aloud of Cadenza's past glories from a book upon her lap. As the lines mounted, Lorenzo fought to rein in his excitement, terrified that his inspiration might betray him at the last.

The night had reached its ashen epilogue by the time he laid down his pen. As he cast a weary eye over his new *Denunciation*, Lorenzo was put in mind of a blood-red rose, its thorns dipped in vitriol. In its savage exposure of Cosimo, the man who had dared to stop the poets of Cadenza in their tracks, the poem also served as a lament to the Artifex who had previously walked alongside them. The hairs on Lorenzo's arms prickled as he read. This was more than mere censure, little less than a call to arms.

He was aware of a certain irony at work here. The composition of such a piece would have been unthinkable under Tommaso Cellini, who, for all the exquisiteness of his verse and tender sentiments of his sonnets, had not ruled with fine words alone. The brutal reprisals against the Pitti family bore testament to his ruthlessness. All Cadenza had heard the tales of the *becchini* and their midnight retributions: the torsi tangled up in the reeds at the bottom of the Adige, the tongueless corpses rotting in shallow trenches beyond the city walls. On Tommaso's orders, the libraries had been fitted with *tambura*, locked wooden boxes with a circular mouth, into which citizens could place anonymous accusations against those who had questioned their ruler. The Artifex had understood—as only a writer could—how dangerous words could really be. Yet one of Cosimo's first acts, after kicking the *becchini* out of the Palazzo Nero, had been to order the *tambura* stripped from the library walls. He gave his citizens licence to write mocking plays, inviting their contempt. What punishment need Lorenzo fear for his verse—a dressing down in the Palazzo Nero, a night or two in a cold cell? He would welcome it. If anything, some form of admonishment from the city's authorities would only lend weight to his words.

A slow warmth crept over Lorenzo as he locked his *Denunciation* away in his desk. Borso could do as he pleased—let the Bear trail his paw through the sewer and smear it across the page. Lorenzo had his mind set on higher things.

VII. *The Count Commands*

LOCATED ON THE top floor of a sprawling palace beside the Bibliotheca Niccoló, the salon of the Countess di Contarini was reputed to be one of the most dazzling rooms in all Cadenza, as inaccessible and stocked with treasures as a Medici vault. The countess's late husband had belonged to one of the great Venetian houses; an adventurer, the influence of his Moorish exploits could be detected in the quatrefoil windows and elegantly tiled courtyards of his palace. A circular tower built around a spiral staircase ran up the side of the building, adorned with roundels of red porphyry. Stone lions crouched watchfully on the loggias.

Once a year, infused with carnival spirit, the countess opened her salon doors for a ball notable for its refinement and respectability. As he watched couples sketch stately circles beneath the friezes, Lorenzo raised a hand up beneath his boar mask and stifled a yawn. He had allowed himself only a couple of hours' rest before returning to his desk, where he was gratified to discover that his latest work had lost none of its lustre for the morning's light. Having made a few minor adjustments, Lorenzo had returned the *Denunciation* to the drawer. He could not simply hammer it to the doors to the Palazzo Nero; publication would require careful consideration.

Ideally, at that point Lorenzo would have retired in triumph to his bed, but there was no question of his offending the Countess di Contarini—to his mind, one of the most gracious and admirable women to be found in all Europe. After a prolonged administration to the demands of his guts, which were rowdy with wine after two days of carousing, Lorenzo proceeded to squeeze himself into his finest doublet and hose. As he dressed, his man Giulio informed him of the previous night's events. The cancelling of the March of the Poets had stirred up trouble across Cadenza, leading the Artifex to threaten sending forth his mercenaries to restore order. Giulio thought further clashes inevitable. When Lorenzo's litter left the palace, the streets were shrouded in an eerie atmosphere. Empty casks lay on their sides, the piazzas strewn with charred garlands. The Carnival of Wit was withering on the vine.

Even in the rarefied heights of the Palazzo di Contarini, a note of uncertainty prevailed. The countess looked on from her seat—alone in the room, she refused to cover her face. She was accompanied by a rotund figure in a rich blue gown and peacock mask, whom Lorenzo identified, with a slight shudder of distaste, as Diambra Albertini. Encountering her at a salon the previous autumn, he had judged Diambra both ignorant and inexplicably vain, a barrel filled with corked wine.

At a sudden commotion, a frown troubled the countess's wrinkled face. Following her gaze, Lorenzo's heart sank at the sight of his *fideli* stumbling through the entrance to the hall. Their costumes dishevelled and torn, lips reddened with wine, they swaggered across the dancing floor, laughing and wrestling with one another. A mischievous elbow sent Paolo crashing into one of the dancers—as he stammered an apology, Lorenzo angrily beckoned his *fideli* over.

"What are you doing?" he hissed. "Did I not impress upon you all the need for decorum in this most respectable of houses? Were my words too delicate for your peasant ears, that they would have been more usefully rendered through the cuff of my hand across your head, or the toe of my boot up your arse?"

Francesco held up his hands. "Upon our word, my lord, we were not sure whether this ball would even take place. Since Cosimo called off the March of the Poets, we resolved to squeeze the last grape dry."

"And milk every teat we could lay our hands on!" added another—Giovanni?—to laughter.

A full day and night at play, and they didn't even have the decency to look tired. Lorenzo would have happily wished them all into a long and irreversible slumber.

"I see," he said coolly. "It may interest you to learn that, whilst you have been drinking and whoring, your master has been hard at work."

It was Raffaele—always quickest on the uptake—who saw it first. "You have finished it," he said. "The *Denunciation*. It is ready."

Lorenzo nodded majestically. The *fideli* let out a rousing cheer, raising their glasses in a toast.

"Long live Lorenzo!"

"Death to the Bear!"

"Let us hear it, my lord!"

"The stage, the stage!"

Lorenzo offered them an enigmatic smile. Were he to inform his *fideli* of his change of subject, the news would likely be greeted with dismay. They would try and talk him out of it, offer up well-meaning words on the perils of criticizing the Artifex. Lorenzo couldn't even rule out one of the cunning snakes trying to alert the Palazzo Nero in advance, in order to absolve themselves from any ensuing repercussions. It was a good job that Cosimo had removed the *tambura* from the libraries...

The idea, as unexpected as it was satisfying, caused him to laugh aloud. Drawing his startled companions closer around him, Lorenzo explained what he needed.

A slow smile spread across Raffaele's face. "My lord!" he said admiringly.

Francesco clapped his hands together. "A masterstroke!"

"What's a *tambura*?"

As one, they turned and stared at Paolo.

"You have been in a library, haven't you, Paolo?" Raffaele inquired.

"Of course!"

"Then do you not remember the large wooden boxes that graced their walls under the reign of our previous ruler? They allowed the noble citizens of Cadenza to rat on each other to Tommaso's *becchini*."

"Oh, the *tambura*!" Paolo paused. "But if Cosimo took them down, what would we want with them?"

"Consider it for a moment," Francesco said patiently. "What has Lorenzo been working on?"

"Why, a *Denunciation*..."

"So what would be the most fitting way to deliver it to the city?"

A cautious smile crept across Paolo's face. "I see it!"

"Do you, though?"

"I believe so!"

He was buried beneath a flurry of hearty slaps on the back. Behind their masks, the *fideli* may have fancied themselves cunning and subtle—foxes rather than hounds—yet they could not hide their true nature from Lorenzo: bewildered Paolo, prisoner of his own stupidity; Raffaele, so clever and self-satisfied, forever calculating his next move; love-starved Francesco, unable to keep his eyes from the bounteous bosom of Diambra Albertini. Such was the calibre of man that Lorenzo had drawn around him.

He gestured at the table before him. "Why is my glass empty?" he exclaimed. "Surely the least a lord can expect from his loyal followers is a drink come Carnival time?"

"My lord, the March of the Poets has been cancelled," Paolo replied hesitantly. "Carnival is over."

"It is still Carnival," Lorenzo said obstinately.

"But the Artifex—"

"*I do not care what Cosimo Petrucci says!*" he roared, hammering his fist on the table. "The Carnival of Wit is for writers; he has even less claim over it than he does the Palazzo Nero. Let him sit at his desk and keep his coins company—out here, in the city, where men labour and sweat, in the taverns and the salons, where they chase dreams and inspiration, we shall celebrate as our fathers and forefathers did, with a pen in one hand and a glass in the other!"

Almost to his surprise, Lorenzo found that he was on his feet, his voice echoing around the chamber. A growing roar greeted his words: not just his *fideli*, but the entire salon rising to acclaim him. At the neighbouring table, the Countess di Contarini bestowed upon him an approving nod. Could anyone doubt the power of Lorenzo's words? He would rouse the entire city to action, until the piazzas trembled to the defiant march of feet.

"I am Lorenzo Sardi, Duelling Count of Cadenza, lord of my *fideli* and the doughty warriors of the Arsenale!" he roared, to deafening cheers. "Carnival continues—I *command* it!"

VIII. *Nether-mouth*

EVEN BEFORE HE opened his eyes, Lorenzo knew that something was terribly wrong.

He lay sprawled on his belly, a cool draught playing across his bared buttocks. His head was pounding and there was a crippling pain in his gut. Rolling over with a groan, Lorenzo found his hose around his ankles, his fine doublet nowhere to be seen. A mask was stuck to his face—he grabbed at it clumsily and yanked it off, only to find himself staring at a battered array of peacock feathers.

"About time," a voice said icily.

Lorenzo could barely bring himself to turn around. There, on the bed behind him, bare breasts erupting from her rumpled gown, sat Diambra Albertini. Her eyes were small and cold.

"Bad enough that I have to endure a night of your snores and stinking wind," she said, "than you lie dead to the world through the morning, keeping me waiting for my reward."

His mind befogged by wine, Lorenzo could not comprehend the nightmare to which he had awoken. He reached down to haul up his hose, only to elicit an excruciating clench amid his lower regions, his nether-mouth threatening to burp its stinking contents over the floor. Ignoring his small squeak of distress, Diambra turned over on to her hands and knees and began hitching up her skirts.

"Come now, be quick about it," she rapped, without turning around. "We have wasted enough time as it is."

"Forgive me, my lady," he said weakly. "I fear I must take my leave of you."

"And leave me empty and dry?" she retorted. "You promised to make me groan with pleasure with your silver tongue. Come, poet, dip your quill in my inkpot and give it a stir."

"A most tempting offer. Alas, I must demur."

Diambra snorted with contempt. "I knew I should have brought the young pup home with me instead. Speeches are all well and good for the salon, Lorenzo, but the bedchamber demands deeds, not words." She briskly rearranged her gown. "My one chance of pleasure, thrown away. I should have listened to my husband. How many times has he warned me to stay away from poets?"

Lorenzo froze. "You have a husband?"

"Naturally. He gives me licence to seek my own amusement come Carnival, while he does the same. Provided my bed is empty come morning, we speak no more about it."

The drapes, still drawn across the balcony, were dyed a golden shade of orange. Lorenzo ran his tongue across his lips.

"The sun has most certainly risen," he said.

"Why else would I want you to be quick about it?"

He began inching towards the bedchamber door, aware that a headlong flight might be taken as provocation. Where in the name of the Lord was his doublet? Outside the gates to this infernal chamber, did some three-headed hellhound chew on its fine stitching?

"Alas, my lady speaks the truth," he said, playing for time, "I am indeed a poet, and as such unworthy of your munificent charms. I have laboured long into the night on a poem of no small importance and find myself utterly spent.

The Muses are the most demanding mistresses to which a man can dedicate himself." He smiled weakly. "There are nine of them, after all."

"It is a long wait until next Carnival, poet." There was a dangerous edge to Diambra's voice.

"Perhaps in the meantime, your husband can tend to your... inkpot?"

"Hah! Borso was right about you all along. How did he describe your manhood? 'Soft and small as a melted candle.'"

"*The Owl's Bare Nest*," Lorenzo said automatically. "One of his lazier efforts, I would say, and not at all—"

Somewhere within the house, a door slammed.

"My husband returns!" Diambra cried. "Like a gallant, in my hour of need!"

Lorenzo made a placatory gesture. "Please, my lady," he whispered. "This is a most delicate situation. If you could keep your voice—"

"Up here!" she screamed.

He winced, her shrill cry slicing through his skull. Answering footsteps came stomping up the stairs.

"One way or another, you'll stain my sheets, poet," Diambra vowed. "I'll not be denied my satisfaction."

Lorenzo stared at the door as it shivered in time to the heavy tread in the corridor. At the rattle of the handle, he snatched up Diambra's peacock mask and scuttled out on to the balcony. The drop down to the street below was a forbidding one, but a growled oath encouraged him to swing a tentative leg over the rail. At an accusatory shriek from Diambra— may her vocal chords rot, and Cupid sew her nether-mouth shut—Lorenzo took a deep breath and let himself go.

He felt a tug upon his hose, a ripping of material. The ground came rushing up to meet him. He landed on his side, punching the air from his lungs and leaving him in a wheezing heap on the floor. The street exploded with laughter. As Lorenzo levered himself up, wiping the mud from his face, he realized that his hose had snagged on the rail, tearing the leg and exposing a sizeable flap of his buttocks to the world.

There was no time to look to his dignity, unless he wished to suffer a beating to add to his injuries. Adjusting his ripped hose to best cover his parts, Lorenzo fitted the peacock mask over his face and hobbled away down the street, bare-chested and bent-double in agony, his cheeks burning at the curses pursuing him from Diambra's balcony and the screams and roars of the watching crowd, delighted to be presented with such unexpected entertainment.

IX. *A Boozy Poet of the Dark Archways*

AT THE END of a snaking corridor deep in the guts of the Arsenale, a door banged shut, followed moments later by a loud gasp of triumph. Lorenzo squatted in the corner of the cellar privy, hose around his ankles, a blissful smile on his face as his bowels galloped forth beneath him. Let the heralds blow on their discordant bugles, let the muddy battlefield churn beneath the thundering hordes! The air thickened and ripened around him in a foul, intoxicating brew: the smell of victory.

He had run a gauntlet of mockery all the way from Diambra's lair to the Arsenale, clad in nothing but torn hose and a peacock's mask, gritting his teeth for fear he might start shitting in the street like some elderly ass. Even now, above the strangled exaltations of his gut, Lorenzo could hear the city's derision echoing in his ears. Of all the noises that the human mouth could expel, was there anything less pleasing to the ear than laughter? The snigger and tittle, smug chortle and sly giggle, celebration of all that was empty-headed and trivial. Rather the wet-lipped sonnets of his nether-mouth, than the farmyard's honk and idiot's bray.

Lorenzo lingered in the privy until he was sure his guts were empty, secretly wallowing in the stink he had created. He occupied himself by reading the messages scrawled across the wall. *Wine, why do you punish me so?* asked one, plaintively. *Paolo has a goat's cock,* disclosed another. And below that: *Welcome to the House of Borso. Shit well, Fiametta needs feeding.* Shaking his head, Lorenzo cleaned himself up and made his way back up through the levels of the tavern. His *fideli* were taking cover from a passing shower beneath the arcade. Lorenzo strode regally across the courtyard and tossed his peacock mask on their table.

"Fetch me a fresh robe," he ordered. "And be quick about it."

The *fideli* stared at their master. Paolo's mouth fell open. Even Raffaele, usually so quick, so glib, was rendered speechless. Finally, one of their companions—Lorenzo could not even guess his name—sprang to his feet and ran for the door. There was a power of sorts here: Lorenzo stood before his youthful circle near-naked, haggard and hungover, with the loamy perfume of excrement hanging around him in clouds, *and they did not dare mock him.*

"Thanks be!" Raffaele managed. "We were worried, my lord."

"As you well should have been," Lorenzo replied. "I was trapped all night in the wily clutches of a succubus. Only with the morning was I able to escape."

Did he imagine it, or did Raffaele's mouth twitch? He elected to let it pass.

"I would have gladly escorted the Lady Diambra home," Francesco said. "But you insisted, my lord."

"An act of gallantry for which I was ill rewarded," Lorenzo told him firmly. "My only comfort is that I awoke in time to deny her full satisfaction."

The ugly youth folded his arms, a stony expression on his face. Lorenzo suddenly recalled Francesco gazing at Diambra back at the salon—could it really be that he was *jealous*?

"Enough of the inconsequences of the flesh," he said abruptly. "We are poets, are we not? Let us speak of poetry. How go the preparations for my *Denunciation*?"

"We have located the *tambura* that Cosimo removed from the libraries," Raffaele told him, in a low voice. "Come nightfall, we will go forth and nail them to doors across the city."

"It will not be the only denunciation heard before Carnival's end," warned Francesco. "I heard Diambra's son is a close companion of one of Borso's *fideli*. Mark my words, there will be a fresh poem pinned to the door of the Accademia before the day is out."

"Let him write!" Lorenzo declared scornfully. "Let the Bear take his pen in his clumsy paw; I care not. You think I fear the sting of Diambra's scorpion tail?"

At his words, he felt the poison fog lift unexpectedly from his head. Blinking in astonishment, Lorenzo watched as the statues of the Muses came alive, stone limbs softening into supple curves. One-by-one, they stepped down from their plinths and arranged themselves around the courtyard, reclining on chairs and leaning against the columns, somehow untouched by the rain. Clad in diaphanous robes, with laurel sprigs entwined around tumbling locks of hair and expressions of idle amusement on their faces, they spoke not a word, nor did the *fideli* give any sign that they had witnessed the wondrous creatures. The Muses had appeared for Lorenzo alone.

A sculpted nail plucked at the string of a discarded lyre. A quill brushed an alabaster cheek. And then words—urgent and unbidden, tessellating perfectly inside Lorenzo's head. Throwing out his arm, he cried:

> "Mercy, gentlemen! A hand if you please,
> A suckling pig, basted in its own grease,
> Is too much meat for one man to dine alone.
> This lady's mouth, coarse from a diet of leper balls,
> Is now a twin with the two dank maws
> Beneath her skirts, in tangles of hair o'ergrown:
> Each too large to satisfy, unless interred
> With a cock in one hole and a bull in the other,
> And a pastry to staunch the third."

Lorenzo delivered his verse as though in a dream, the words floating out of his mouth without thought, joyous and light. When the echo of the final line had died away, he opened his eyes to find the rainy courtyard echoing to the sound of whistles and applause. Paolo rocked back and forth with laughter, tears running down his cheeks, while Raffaele led the rest—bar the scowling Francesco—to their feet to acclaim their master. The Muses returned to their plinths, their smooth faces betraying no emotion. Lorenzo sketched out a deep bow and sat down at the table.

"Again, again, my lord!"

He raised a modest hand. "That will suffice for now, I think."

"We must celebrate!" Raffaele cried out. "A glass of wine, my lord?"

Having voided his bowels and vented his spleen, Lorenzo was starting to feel a little better about the world. Yet the merest waft of the grape's sweet odour was enough to rouse his stomach into fresh rebellion, a sour tide rushing into his mouth. Oh, treacherous, ageing frame, oh, creeping infirmity!

Raffaele waited. "My lord?"

"A small one," Lorenzo said finally. "And bring me water to go with it."

X. *Cloaca Maxima*

COME NIGHTFALL, A new host crept forth into the city, masked figures bounding and pirouetting through the puddles. They hurled stones at the windows of the Accademia and daubed insults on the Well of Calliope, taunting the patrons of the Ridolfi Salon and placing a motley hat on the statue of

Doffo di Cello. As Lorenzo went swiftly through the streets, wrapped in a hooded cloak and a lion's mask over his face, he felt drunk on the heady spirit of recklessness. *Here* was a carnival, enacted by the sprites of discord and misrule—may the marionette wires dance, and Cosimo's purse-strings snap.

All afternoon, the Arsenale had rung with guffaws and crude songs, the ripe glug of wine. The *fideli* took turns leaping on the table to perform Lorenzo's lampooning verse against Diambra Albertini, which one of them had copied down in a shameless attempt to find favour. As he watched his followers dissolve into helpless laughter, Lorenzo could not help but acknowledge the power of his art. If he could reduce his audience to tears with this mere bagatelle, what manner of reaction awaited his *Denunciation*? Lorenzo had entrusted Raffaele with the recovery of his latest work from his study drawer, while Francesco was charged with overseeing the copying. Paolo and the others were to post the finished verse into the *tambura*, before carrying them forth to be nailed to doors across Cadenza. Only now, at the last, would they begin to comprehend the scale of Lorenzo's ambition. The *tambura* were more than vessels—they were a ring of explosives, powerful enough to make the Palazzo Nero shake.

Any other night, Lorenzo would have stayed to oversee the copying, and his announcement that he was leaving the Arsenale was greeted with dismay. The *fideli* pleaded with him to reconsider, fearing for his safety in the restless alleys. But he would not be dissuaded. Every Carnival for the last twenty years, Lorenzo had stepped abroad on the eve of the March of the Poets. He would not stay home this night if the city were wreathed in flames. Such a prospect felt closer that evening than any he could remember, with citizens in open rebellion. As he skirted the edges of the Piazza della Rosa, Lorenzo heard orders barked in a foreign tongue, and saw iron gleaming in the torchlight through the gates of the Palazzo Nero. Cosimo's mercenaries were preparing to march forth.

He pressed onwards, following an intricate route of shortcuts and side alleys through the city. When the wavering pines of the Garden of Leaves came into view, he ignored the locked gates and walked round to the eastern wall, where a crumbling section of stonework provided entrance into the park after nightfall. Scrambling up through the gap, Lorenzo caught his cloak on a tree branch and slipped, scraping his knee. The bravado that had carried him through the city was beginning to ebb. He waited to catch his breath before following the gently sloping paths through the garden, the scent of jasmine carrying on the breeze. The bridge where he had first laid eyes upon Lucia soon came into view—where he and Borso had once dozed by the riverbank, a stage had been erected. Cypresses cast their shadow across the empty boards. On the bridge, Lorenzo slumped against the rail, swallowing a sob of grief.

A stone came flying out of the darkness, hitting him hard on the shoulder.

Startled, Lorenzo looked out across the stream. A troupe of masked figures had sprung from the darkness to occupy the stage, coarse laughter echoing around the twilit park. A second missile sang past Lorenzo's ear; suddenly, the air was alive with stones. He turned and fled, shielding his head with his arms. Boots thundered across the bridge as his assailants gave chase. Lorenzo stumbled down into the stream, gasping at the icy water's grip on his ankles. He ran splashing along the shallow course, following its turns through the trees. Beneath the park walls, the stream fed into a gated sewer. His nostrils caught a heady waft of excreta. Reaching the tunnel's mouth, Lorenzo saw that the gate had already been wrenched open. He dived inside.

At once, he was assailed by the stench of the city's innards, scooped out and deposited in the noisome passage. Clamping his fingers over his nose, Lorenzo forced himself to press deeper, praying that the stink would drive back his pursuers. The shouts grew dim behind him; eventually, he judged himself safe enough to stop. He leaned back against the wall and tore off his mask, his expression one of pure misery. Was this to be how he would pay his respects to the love of his life—huddled in a sewer, smeared with excrement and terrified for his life?

"Lorenzo."

He jumped, slipping on a patch of night soil and landing with a loud splash on his backside. A huge hand reached out from the gloom and grabbed Lorenzo's own, hauling him to his feet.

"Borso?!" spluttered Lorenzo, snatching his hand free. "What in the name of God are you doing here?"

"The same as you, I would imagine," Borso replied. He too was dressed in black, with a mask pushed up over his brow: a lion, to match Lorenzo's own. "It has been twenty-five years since she was taken from us, has it not? I had half-expected to see you in the Garden; the mob came as more of a surprise. Are you hurt?"

Lorenzo shook his head. "I ran when the first stone hit me. '*With flapping wings, and a shower of hot piss.*'"

"Ah." Borso scratched his greying beard. "Those were not my words, though the city would have it otherwise. In truth, I barely even saw you at Orsini's. My eyes are not what they were."

"Then who, pray, was the author of the poem defaming me?"

He shrugged his great shoulders. "Does it matter? One of my *fideli*, I should imagine. Sometimes I wonder whether this feud means more to them than it does to me."

"I do not have to wonder on that score," Lorenzo replied. "I know it for a fact. I seem to have saddled myself with some of the most craven and worthless young men in Cadenza. Were we also so... venal?"

"An old man's question."

"We are old."

Over the course of a quarter-century, Lorenzo had imagined countless verbal duels with Borso, mapping out in satisfying detail the feints and counters leading to his decisive victory, rendering the Bear speechless and red-faced with embarrassment. Yet no encounter had he imagined thus, wet and stinking in the darkness, futilely trying to brush the turds from his cloak. As he examined Borso now, what struck Lorenzo was the very absence of feeling. There was no fury, only the cold remains of a long-dead fire. He looked back towards the sewer entrance.

"Do you think it safe to go outside yet?"

"Until the Artifex's men restore order, probably not," said Borso.

Lorenzo laughed contemptuously. "The Artifex's men? Swiss and German sellswords, you mean. Cosimo Petrucci cannot count on the loyalty of his own citizens."

"If his citizens cannot be counted on to be loyal, what choice is left to him?"

"Come now, Borso! You may be no lover of Carnival, but even you cannot think he was right to cancel the March of the Poets."

"I would wager Cosimo knows more about the city's finances than I. Such a decision was never going to be popular—why make it, if not absolutely necessary? And what, truly, has been lost?"

"What has been *lost*? You would so quickly sacrifice centuries of tradition?"

"The poets walk through the city. The people get drunk." Borso shrugged. "There have been greater sacrifices."

Lorenzo could not believe his ears. He searched for a suitably biting reply but the best he could summon was a strangled harrumph as he pushed past Borso. Where were his feints and counters now?

"Where are you going?" Borso called out.

"By all means, stay here if you want," Lorenzo replied. "But this must lead somewhere, and I'll not spend all night hiding in a shitpipe waiting for Cosimo Petrucci to rescue me."

A sigh echoed around the sewer, and the Bear came wading after him. The fetid night thickened. Lorenzo had to concentrate on every footfall, pulling up his cloak for fear that the rats swarming around their feet might try to climb it. At one notably loud squeak, Borso kicked out a large boot, nearly slipping over in the process. He cursed.

"I am a fool for ever listening to you," he muttered. "Ten paces from fresh air and freedom, yet thanks to you we are now condemned to wade this river of Hades."

"Then you must hope it is not Cocytus," Lorenzo shot back, "else you will find yourself buried to the neck with all the other traitors."

"I would prefer the Lethe," growled Borso. "Oblivion would be a small price to pay, to forget that I had met you."

"Then perhaps you would find peace in the fires of Phlegethon. Pray, take your rhymes with you into the flames."

"Your indignant squawking is even more unmanly in the flesh than it is on the page. Say what you must say and have done, poet."

"I have nothing more to say to you."

"Say it, damn you!" roared the Bear.

"*Why*, Borso?" Lorenzo's voice echoed plaintively around the sewer. He needed no Muses now, the words—so long submerged—surging up from the very depths of his soul. "Why did you write to Lucia and besmirch my name so? You were supposed to be my friend!"

Borso held his gaze steadily. "And so I remained," he replied, "though I loved Lucia with an ardour I have never felt before or since. I held my tongue as you pressed your suit, though I stayed awake at nights despairing at the thought of my best friend and my beloved marrying. And how did you repay me? With *The Bear's False Tongue*. I wrote no letter to Lucia, Lorenzo—the only name besmirched was mine, and by your own hand."

"Liar." Lorenzo's voice was flat and hard. "I saw your

letter to her with my own eyes, Tommaso sent it to me. Do you not think I would recognize your hand?"

"Do *you* not think the Artifex capable of forging my hand?" countered Borso. "Deny it to the grave if you must, but I wrote Lucia no letter defaming you."

"But why would Tommaso lie?"

"Think, Lorenzo! The woman we both loved had just died at his hands; better that we were set at odds than united in our grief against him. We were powerful, once."

"Powerful enough to bring down the Artifex?"

"Did Tommaso ever strike you as a man willing to take chances?"

"A strong ruler does what is required for the good of his city."

Borso snorted. "You will defend him to the last. Very well."

He stomped away down the sewer.

"If this is true," Lorenzo called out after him, "why did you not say anything to me?"

The Bear splashed to a halt. "You were not the only one grieving for Lucia," he said, without turning around. "Nor the only one wounded by the slights of a friend. Anger was all that kept me from leaping from the Mezzanino of the Accademia."

"And me from diving into the Adige," Lorenzo admitted ruefully. "Do you think, if you had declared yourself for Lucia, she would have accepted you?"

Sewage slopped against the side of the tunnel as Borso considered the question.

"I had no more claim to her affections than you did," he said finally, with a shake of the head. "She would not have approved of our quarrel, I think."

"No," Lorenzo conceded. "Perhaps not."

They pressed on through the stink together, too weary now to speak. A growing roar alerted them to the tunnel's end, glimmers of light visible in the darkness ahead. They came out by the banks of the Adige at the southern edge of the Recto. It seemed that Cosimo's mercenaries had restored order, the city sunk in sullen acquiescence. Isolated cries interrupted the night.

There were no apologies, no acknowledgements of past mistakes nor mentions of a truce, but as the Owl and the Bear parted company and turned towards their respective territories, caked in the filthy outpourings of their fellow citizens, Lorenzo caught an abrupt nod of the head from his great enemy, and was surprised to find himself respond in kind.

XI. *Denunciation*

HAVING SAFELY NAVIGATED the streets back to his palace, Lorenzo removed his reeking clothes and collapsed into bed, whereupon he fell instantly asleep. He awoke to find his head surprisingly clear, his bowels unknotted and the terrible pressure on his bladder abated. Throwing open the shutters, he hummed a melody as he washed in his basin. The night had provided surprise and revelation in equal measure. Could it be that he and Borso had been at war for all these years over a misunderstanding—or some malicious artifice, even? By daylight the notion seemed a fanciful one, though Lorenzo might have wished it so, and he could not countenance Borso's assertion that it was Tommaso who lay behind their rift. The act did not bear the Artifex's bullish signature; rather, the cowardly connivance of some council underling. But then the Bear had never liked Tommaso. Lorenzo allowed himself a smile at the thought of Borso at his desk that morning, brow furrowing as he read the *Denunciation*. They would see who squawked indignantly.

Over a light breakfast, Lorenzo resolved to forego the litter and walk on foot to the Arsenale—at least one poet would march forth that day. But he would wear no mask. Today, of all days, Lorenzo wanted the city to know him. Rarely had he stepped out into the city with such anticipation, such delicious apprehension. Even the empty streets could not dampen his spirits. Outside the Bibliotheca Niccoló, Lorenzo glimpsed a knot of people gathered by its locked doors. Faint laughter carried on the breeze. For once, it appeared, his *fideli* had not let him down.

As he continued his triumphant passage through Cadenza, Lorenzo entertained himself with notions of the welcome awaiting inside the Arsenale—the garlands and cheers, a mighty throng gathered to sing his name. Upon ducking beneath the sign of the Ship, however, he found the courtyard deserted. Peering through the columns, Lorenzo spied Paolo asleep in a chair, his feet propped up on the table and his head tipped back. The youth started when Lorenzo cleared his throat, hastily righting the chair as it threatened to topple over.

"Forgive me, my lord," he said, rubbing his face. "It has been a long night."

"A short night during Carnival is no night at all. You followed my orders?"

"To the letter," Paolo replied confidently. "We filled the *tambura* with copies of your poem and nailed them to the door of every library and tavern in Cadenza. Already, the city talks of nothing else."

Lorenzo drew himself up grandly. "You have read the work?"

Paolo nodded enthusiastically. "Of course, my lord!"

"I know you may have been surprised by its contents; frightened, even, by its boldness. But the people cannot fail to see the truth of my words. Even if he had the pride and the courage to seek redress, the Artifex will not harm you. I will not permit it."

"Thank you, my lord!" He blinked. "Why would the Artifex wish to harm me?"

"On account of my *Denunciation*, of course."

"I see. But why would that concern him?"

Lorenzo massaged his brow. "Paolo, stunted and slovenly as your wits may be, even you cannot have read my verse without failing to discern its target."

"I *thought* I had," the youth said hesitantly. "I know I was wrong about Rinaldi at Orsini's, but the title seemed clear. Unless..." He frowned. "I see it! 'Tis like players on the stage, only this time it is Cosimo disguised as a woman!"

"Like players on the stage? A woman?" Lorenzo grabbed hold of Paolo and dragged him to his feet. "What did you put in the *tambura*?" he hissed.

A squeak escaped the youth's lips. "We did as you ordered, my lord, I swear it!"

Lorenzo was already hurrying out of the Arsenale. He marched down the Via Fiume, Paolo stumbling in his wake, towards the tavern by the bridge. There he found Raffaele and Francesco, amid a chortling crowd gathered around a *tambura*. He barged his way over to them and snatched a piece of parchment from Raffaele's hands.

"What is this?" Lorenzo snapped. "Where is my poem?"

"It is as you see before you, my lord!" Raffaele said hastily. "I took it from your writing desk as ordered."

"And I copied it, word for word," Francesco added. "And delivered it to Paolo to place inside the *tambura*."

And yet this was not the *Denunciation*. It bore instead the title, *Ode to Fiametta*. Almost against his will, Lorenzo started reading.

Mercy, gentlemen! A hand if you please...

It could not be.

A suckling pig, basted in its own grease...

Gales of laughter swirled around Lorenzo. He closed his eyes.

"I did not write this," he said hoarsely.

"But, my lord," stuttered Paolo, "We all heard you at the Arsenale, just yesterday morning..."

"I was talking about Diambra Albertini, not Borso's niece! Do you know what this means?"

A cock in one hole, a bull in another...

Raffaele, Francesco and Paolo gazed back at him: three masks of innocent incomprehension. It would only have taken one of them to double-cross him, motivated by malicious calculation, vengeance, or sheer stupidity. Was it possible that they were in cahoots, banding together to thwart their master? Or could this have been the work of another of the *fideli*, one of the nameless faces that blurred into the next?

And a pastry to staunch the third.

Word was spreading through the throng that the poem's author stood among them. A cheer went up for the Duelling Count of Cadenza.

"Tell me, Raffaele," Lorenzo said tightly. "Were I to return now to my study, would I find *any* sign of the verse I had intended you to deliver, a righteous unmasking of the usurper Cosimo Petrucci? Or has it vanished completely?"

"I cannot say, my lord," Raffaele murmured dutifully. "But if that was your original intention, this… misunderstanding may yet turn out to your advantage."

Lorenzo had to fight the urge to lace his fingers around the young man's neck and squeeze until Raffaele turned blue. "How, exactly?"

"There is no way Cosimo could have allowed such a poem to stand unpunished. You would have almost certainly been imprisoned, perhaps even killed. You said it yourself at Orsinis's—without respect, how can a man hope to rule?"

"*Those* lines you remember faithfully."

"Look around you!" urged Raffaele. "Do you think the city would be alive with such joy, had it discovered an assault on its leader inside the *tambura*? Is it truly so unworthy to make people laugh?"

A shoving match broke out around the tavern entrance, a pair of apprentices grabbing handfuls of each other's robes. Goaded by the crowd, they began to scuffle. Tearing the *tambura* from the wall, the larger of the two boys whirled around and crowned his opponent with it. The second apprentice reeled away as though drunk, the shattered remnants of the wooden box still upon his shoulders.

Francesco gleefully punched Paolo in the shoulder. "There's no way Borso can let this stand," he cried. "This means war!"

As he stared down at his words—blessed and most precious gift from the Muses—Lorenzo felt his shoulders begin to shake. He threw back his head and roared with laughter, even as the tears rolled down his cheeks.

Fourth Canto
The Palace of Ink

I. *Nightfall*

OCCUPYING AN ALCOVE set into the left-hand wall of his office, the bookcase maintained a troubling presence in the corner of Cosimo Petrucci's eye as he looked out from behind his desk. The stern layers of shelving had been carved from a walnut so dark that it verged upon black; the side panels were adorned with carved imps, who poked out impudent tongues as they dug their claws into the wood. Ornate crenellations ran along the top of the bookcase, lending it the suggestion of a castle's ramparts, or some kind of portal.

"My lord?"

Cosimo looked across at Pietro, who instinctively scuttled a half-pace back. Years in the service of Tommaso Cellini had reduced the Master of the Scrolls to a wheedling minion, forever flinching from some anticipated blow or rebuke.

"Forgive me," Pietro stammered. "Only the Venetians…"

"Quite," said Cosimo, waving his hand. "Continue."

"We have received word from Worms—Andrea Gritti has

175

signed the treaty. The war between Venice and the Emperor is at an end."

Cosimo frowned. "I thought Gritti was a warrior."

"He is," Pietro replied. "And he knows an unwinnable battle when he sees one. The power of France is waning; Charles's fist tightens around their throat. For 200,000 ducats, Gritti has bought Venice peace and control of all of her territories. It may well prove a bargain, especially as she can now refocus all her energies on commerce and coin."

"How have our friends taken the news?"

"As yet, without comment. But I would not be surprised if emissaries from Venice are not already headed to Florence, Rome and Milan, bearing fresh overtures from their contract writers and the House of Aldus."

Cosimo tapped his fingers together. "And the Venetians themselves? What say their diplomats?"

"Ha!" A bark of derision went up from the divan, where Cosimo's nephew Cesare lounged. The burly youth had one leg propped on the cushions while the other trailed down to the floor, ensuring his crotch was presented in Pietro's direction— less a trusted advisor, than an idle rogue lolling in a rowboat.

"Yes, nephew?" said Cosimo.

"All Venetians are diplomats," Cesare remarked, with a careless wave of his goblet. "You'll have more luck trying to find a drop of the Doge's piss in one of their canals than a Venetian who'll own to his true purpose. What do we care what their contract writers do?"

"Because if they take business from *our* contract writers, it will cost the city money," Cosimo explained patiently. "Money we can ill afford to lose."

"You sound like a counting-house clerk."

"That is what responsible government often sounds like. Do you think I *wanted* to cancel the March of the Poets?"

"That was a mistake," Cesare averred. "All it did was piss everyone off and make us look weak."

"So what would you have had me do, nephew—drain our coffers dry, in order for our citizens to drink themselves senseless and rut and scuffle in the street? How, pray, would we pay for anything once the headaches had cleared?"

He shrugged. "The same as we always do. Take it from whoever will give it to us."

"Do you know how much this city owes the banker Agostino alone? Fifty thousand florins! Is his seat in the Star Chamber not enough, that we should empower and embolden him with every mounting obligation?"

"Agostino cannot convince his own wife to share his bed! You think the city will swoon at his feet?"

"A city's heart can be softer than a woman's," Cosimo replied. "And perhaps in time, you will learn that its accounts cannot be refilled as easily as your wine glass."

Night was falling outside the Palazzo Nero, the city's rooftops losing their certainty in the encroaching gloom. Cesare grunted and took another swig of wine. No doubt he was girding himself for another evening's swagger through the streets of Cadenza with his accomplices, smashing windows and picking fights with the *fideli*. Cosimo would have gladly swapped Cesare with any number of men for his inner circle, but he had little option other than to keep his nephew close— if only for fear of what trouble Cesare might cause, if left to his own devices.

A cough broke the silence.

"I hesitate to trouble my lord with further matters," Pietro said, "but I fear the Venetians are not our only cause for concern. We still have no word of the whereabouts of Tommaso's nephews, or any sense as to their intentions. Were Alessandro or Galeotto Cellini to return to Cadenza at the head of an army, I worry that some of our citizens would flock to their banner. Their uncle was a much-beloved man."

"Their uncle was an abomination," Cosimo said quietly.

The word hung in the air.

"And all Cadenza rejoiced when you replaced him," Pietro replied hurriedly, eliciting a sardonic grin from Cesare. "Rest assured that we have agents in the great cities looking for Alessandro and Galeotto. If they dare to make a move against us, we will know of it."

"They should never have been allowed to leave the city alive," Cesare declared. "We need to take action, Cosimo! Hunt down a couple of Tommaso's distant relatives and throw them on a bonfire in the Piazza della Rosa. Show these cousins *and* Venice who they are dealing with."

Cosimo shook his head. "Forget Alessandro and Galeotto," he said. "Write to the Venetians and inform them that there are enough opportunities for us both to profit. Perhaps we could come to some agreement on pricing and divide the spoils between us. Better that than come to blows. They have only just disentangled themselves from one conflict, why enter into another?"

"More words," Cesare muttered.

"Yes, nephew." Cosimo was struggling to keep his tone even. "More words. Our fame, our reputation, our fortune, are all based upon our words. We are, in fact, a city of words."

To mask his irritation, he picked up a pile of letters and began to leaf through them. Pietro took that as a signal to return to the topic in hand, embarking on a detailed appraisal of the state of relations with Venice while Cesare groped blindly for the wine jug on the floor. Cosimo offered an occasional murmur, only half-listening. At the bottom of the stack, his fingers alighted upon a letter tied with a black ribbon. He hesitated. A quick glance around the chamber was enough to satisfy him that neither of his companions were paying him close attention. Carefully untying the ribbon, he broke open the seal. Inside was a short message crafted in an exquisite hand. The note was neither dated nor signed and consisted of just two sentences.

> *Three days hence I will permit you to accompany me on a walk through the Old Market. You will follow two paces behind me on your knees with your mouth wide open, and anything I choose to place upon your tongue you will swallow.*

A small tremor passed through Cosimo's hands as he refolded the letter and slipped it back inside the envelope. He looked up to find Pietro waiting expectantly.

"Well?" Cosimo said. "Go and deliver our message to the Venetians!"

The Master of the Scrolls spread out his hands. "Look out of the window, my lord—the hour grows late. Though his citizens give thanks that their new Artifex works tirelessly on their behalf, the business of government pauses for the hours of darkness."

Cosimo sat back in his chair. He nodded. "Very well. Tomorrow, then."

Pietro scurried gratefully out of the room, bowing until almost bent double. The Artifex's gaze crept back towards the black-ribboned letter.

"They dye their hair in piss, you know."

Cosimo blinked.

"The Venetians," Cesare explained. "That's why they're all blondes. They dye their hair in their own piss."

"Thank you, nephew," Cosimo said wearily. "We will perhaps omit that particular detail from our correspondence."

He was relieved when Cesare hauled himself up from the divan, jug and goblet in hand, and sloped out of the study. Leaving the letter on his desk, Cosimo rose and went over to the bookcase. He ran a hand down the side panel, thoughtfully rubbing a dark stain in the walnut with his thumb. One stormy evening six months earlier, Tommaso Cellini had stood in this very spot to reach up to the top shelf of his bookcase and, in the act of pulling down a volume, had brought the whole structure down on himself amid a shower of volumes. He was killed instantly. The Artifex's shattered body had to be retrieved from beneath his impromptu wooden coffin, a look of utter astonishment stamped across his face and the book he had been reaching for—a copy of his own *Poetia*—still in his grasp. A fitting death for a tyrant, Cosimo thought, crushed by the weight of his own self-regard. Perhaps this irony might explain why, upon his succession to the Palazzo Nero, Cosimo had reversed Pietro's order to have the bookcase chopped up for kindling and had restored it to its original position and condition, where now it stood, casting its uneasy shadow over him.

The night was in its infancy, and there was a great deal to do. Cosimo settled back behind his desk, carefully placed the black-ribboned letter to one side and picked up his pen.

II. *Black Crepe*

THE HOUR HAD long passed midnight, the candles in the galleries and corridors of the Palazzo Nero shrunk to waxen stubs. Cosimo walked silently through the halls. As a rule, he confined himself to the suite of offices in the northwest tower, retiring at dawn to a bedchamber where he laid his head for two or three itchy, restless hours. But that evening he was distracted, numbers mischievously swapping around on the page before his eyes. He had risen from his desk with the intention of merely stretching his legs, but as he continued through the palace Cosimo realized he was being drawn, as though pulled on a piece of twine, in a specific direction.

He cared little for the Palazzo Nero by daylight, for all the celebrated delights of the blushing camellias in the courtyards and the golden frescoes on the walls of the *salone*. Only with the coming of night did the building's true majesty reveal itself. Its architect, the great Arnolfo, had been commissioned in his declining years by the Artifex Bartolomeo Strozzi, despite the old man's increasing irascibility and failing eyes. By the time the first stone had been laid, Arnolfo had gone completely blind, and in the palace's groined vaults and high arched windows Cosimo sensed his acceptance of the shadows that had enveloped his world, and the ultimate darkness that awaits all men. He ascended a sweeping staircase and made his way along a loggia on the second floor. The domes and roofs of the surrounding palaces were visible through the open outer wall, a sharp wind weaving in and out of the columns. Busts gazed out stonily from nooks that appeared periodically along the opposite wall. Somewhere in the streets, a dog barked.

At the end of the loggia, a statue of Petrarch stood guard over the doors to the east wing. The poet's gaze was turned to the heavens, a laurel crown entwined around his brow. Cosimo took a steadying breath and turned the door handle. A corridor stretched out before him, its walls adorned with mirrored glass. Reflections confronted one another, deepening and multiplying: within their endless reproductions, Cosimo felt the unsettling possibility of other worlds. When he stepped into the corridor, the door shut behind him with a loud click. A complex series of springbolts had been installed throughout the east wing, ensuring that certain doors locked when they fell shut. Tommaso had had the bolts removed and replaced every few months, creating a shifting labyrinth of which he alone knew the exact design.

This knowledge proved particularly useful on the nights he spent, stripped to the waist and whip in hand, hunting screaming girls around the corridors and bedchambers.

Only a handful of people in Cadenza were aware of the brutal and predatory nature of Tommaso Cellini's sexual appetites, the extent of the violence and death that had pockmarked his reign. His gatherings were clandestine affairs, secret invitations issued to carefully selected individuals: waifs and orphans, down-on-their-luck prostitutes and wide-eyed innocents from the countryside and outlying villages. Only once the doors to the east wing had locked shut did the true nature of the evening reveal itself. The Artifex's guests were forced to drink intoxicating concoctions before coupling together at his whim and command, creating groaning friezes of flesh in which the performers doled out pleasure and pain as directed. Tommaso dredged the Stygian depths of his imagination in order to satisfy his appetites, the engorged heir of Elagabalus, spilled seed of Tiberius on Capri. Come the morning, the nightmare reached its climax with the entrance of Tommaso's personal guard into the east wing. The *becchini* scoured the bloodied halls for survivors, butchering everyone they found. Extreme care was taken to ensure that no word of Tommaso's nocturnal activities could escape beyond the springbolts.

Upon entering the wing for the first time, Cosimo had shuddered at the sight of the frantic scratches on the doors, the mirrors' bloody handprints. He had ordered the floor scrubbed and the sheets burned, the manacles pulled from the walls. But these were futile gestures, he knew—too many wrongs had taken place inside the fetid antechambers, the air itself corrupted beyond redemption.

That night, the past felt dangerously close at hand: from the bowels of the building, Cosimo fancied he could hear distant sobs and screams, the crop's sharp retort. His heartbeat quickened as he emerged from the mirrored corridor into an atrium. Double doors were set into each of the four walls, a shallow pool in the centre of the room. He knelt down beside the water and examined his reflection. How must it have felt, he wondered, to crawl about these floors harnessed and tethered, while Tommaso's whip issued its sharp reprimands? He closed his eyes at the thought, allowing himself a moment of delicious, dry-mouthed possibility.

Close by, a door slammed shut, sending a shiver through the pool. Cosimo straightened up and went over to the doors in the north wall. Pressing his ear to the wood, he caught the sound of footsteps, soft as fluttering wings. He frowned. The left of the two doors was unlocked—he slipped through it into a narrow gallery. Rectangles of black crepe hung at regular intervals along the wall. The night was sharper here, more pressing; the footsteps had died away. Halfway along the hall, directly beneath a glass rotunda, one of the crepe covers had fallen to the floor, forming a rustling puddle in the moonlight. Cosimo stared up at the portrait it had revealed.

Tommaso Cellini was a tall, lean figure with a shaven head and sunken eye sockets. There was a burnished cast to his skin, which had given rise to a rumour that Saracen blood ran in his veins—presumably with the Artifex's approval, given that the rumour had been permitted to circulate. He was dressed without fanfare, his sole ornament the swan-beak quill in his left hand. Tommaso carried a pen in all of his portraits, a pointed reminder that he was first and foremost a poet. His *Poetia*—composed, with startling precociousness, at the age of seventeen—was an undisputed masterpiece. In the wake of his ascension to the Palazzo Nero, Tommaso had written only infrequently, each new work greeted with ever-more vaunting praise. His thin mouth toyed with the notion of amusement as he gazed down at his successor.

Unsettled, Cosimo bent down to pick up the crepe, only to step back in alarm. The base of Tommaso's robes had begun to run, dark liquid seeping down the wall. The painting was bleeding. Cosimo tore it from its hanging and hurled it to one side. It wasn't blood, he realized, but ink. Behind the portrait, a word had been scrawled on the wall:

Scio

A single word, dripping with the menace of the inexplicable.

III. *A Man of No Consequence*

COSIMO SCUTTLED THROUGH the east wing, rattling locked doors and cursing Tommaso's name, until finally he stumbled across the mirrored corridor that led back to Petrarch's statue. Empty stairwells echoed to the sound of his hurried tread. By the time he had climbed the northwest tower back to his office, Cosimo's breath was coming in panicked gasps. He closed the door behind him and rested against it, gulping in air.

Inside his chamber, beasts of twilit imaginings were stirring. Chests squatted like gnarled toads and tallow snakes balanced upon candlesticks; a giant moth clung to the wall, stretching out shadowy wings of woven thread. Cosimo hurried over to the bookcase and dropped to his knees, removing a large volume with a metal clasp from the bottom shelf. He fished a key from a chain around his neck and unlocked the clasp. The book was hollow, its insides stuffed with envelopes all tied with black ribbon. Cosimo counted them carefully. Upon reaching the bottom of the pile, he let out a sigh of relief.

There were nearly forty letters in all: five years' worth of correspondence, all composed in Hypatia's elegant hand. Cosimo had first enlisted the ink maid's services when he was still an anonymous Folio clerk, in a brisk and scrupulously polite letter which had outlined his wishes whilst stressing the need for absolute anonymity. They had remained in contact ever since, throughout Cosimo's rise through the backstairs of power. He paid a flat sum for every letter, which he had voluntarily increased with every promotion. In return, the ink maid had subjected him to an unceasing torrent of abuse, taunting him with accusations of impotence and cowardice. She had spelled out detailed plans to confine him in binds and shackles, to blind him and gag him until he could barely breathe, reducing him to a state of complete helplessness, dependent upon—and at the mercy of—her every whim. She had threatened him with violence: to lash him until his skin turned black, to cut him until he ran with blood, to grind him to powder beneath her sharp heel. She promised him humiliation, ordering him to clean her close stool with his tongue, to pleasure himself before an audience of her friends as they laughed and pointed at his paltry manhood. Every word a weapon, judiciously selected; every sentence a slap from a blessed angel.

As Cosimo closed the hollow book, there was a movement over by the divan. The shadows parted to reveal a figure gliding forth from the depths of the office. Cosimo's eyes narrowed.

"What are you doing here?" he hissed. "I didn't summon you."

"And yet you require my help," the man replied calmly. "The mark of the true servant is the anticipation of his master's needs, wouldn't you say?"

He smiled ingratiatingly, revealing a gap between his two front teeth that lent a fluting whistle to his speech. The man was short and pudgy, wispy curls of blonde hair topping a round, childlike face. Dressed in plain robes, hands clasped, he could have passed for a friar at the abbey on the Via Arezzo. He carried himself with the humility of a man of absolutely no consequence.

"A true servant would hesitate to be so presumptuous, Silenzi," Cosimo countered. "I am perfectly fine."

"Then, please, accept my sincerest apologies," replied Silenzi, bowing. "I fancied I spied you returning from the east wing in a state of some distress and feared that you had seen something to trouble you. Evidently I was mistaken."

Cosimo took a seat behind his desk and looked out moodily over the slumbering city. "You saw the message?"

"I am afraid so. My Latin is not that of an educated man, but I believe it means "*I know*". Were I occupying your exalted position, I would wish it removed as soon as possible. It does raise certain... questions."

"Do you think?" Cosimo said witheringly.

"Granted, it is only a single word, but what it lacks in length it makes up for with the drama of its presentation. And as a wise man once remarked, this *is* a city of words."

Over the course of their acquaintance, Cosimo had resigned himself to the fact that he could keep no secrets from his agent. The palace was riddled with secret rooms and passageways installed by Tommaso, a shadowy network through which Silenzi had somehow found a way to navigate to ensure he was perpetually in earshot—no conversation too private, no confidence too personal to overhear. How else to explain how he had first introduced himself? Cosimo had been summoned to the Palazzo Nero to investigate a shortfall in the Artifex's accounts: as he worked late into the night, he had looked up from his papers to find Silenzi standing patiently before his desk. At the sight of this apparition, Cosimo had cried out in fright, and it was some time before he had come to understood that the man meant him no harm—that, on the contrary, Silenzi was offering him his services. Had Cosimo even accepted? He could not remember; but the angelic-faced *putto* had been at his side ever since.

In the three years that had followed, Cosimo had learned no more about his agent than he had during their initial encounter. He thought he detected the traces of a southern accent, but beyond that Silenzi remained an enigma, a man written entirely in italics. He volunteered no details of his life, nor ventured to explain his motives in assisting Cosimo. He asked for nothing in return for his services— neither women nor boys; coin, power nor position. He did everything that Cosimo required, quietly and efficiently, and Cosimo despised him to the very marrow of his bones for it.

"The message could mean anything, or nothing," he told Silenzi irritably. "What do they *know*, exactly?"

"They have chosen not to say. But a cautious man would proceed as though it were the very worst thing imaginable."

A humourless laugh echoed around the study. "And what would that be, Silenzi?"

"Caution prevents me from saying too much. Though it appears that your first thought was to check that your private letters had not fallen into malign hands."

"You would bring this up again?" Cosimo snapped. "I have heard your thoughts upon the matter many times."

"And I am unwavering in my belief that your association with this woman is a risk you should not be taking. It may prove your downfall."

"I have known 'this woman' longer than I have you, and she has given me no reason to doubt her. Her work demands discretion, and I pay her a handsome sum for it. She would not betray my confidence."

"There are ways of making sure."

"No!" Cosimo said sharply. "Leave Hypatia be. Do you not think someone might have noticed Cadenza's most notorious ink maid running around the palace daubing messages on the wall?"

"Perhaps we should look closer to home, then," Silenzi suggested. "Your nephew, for example. He is surrounded by restless young men who would prefer to see a warrior reside in this office. There are whispers that Cesare seeks to increase his standing with the scholars of the city in the hope of improving his reputation."

"Cesare and the *scholars*?" scoffed Cosimo. "He has neither the subtlety nor the patience for intrigue. All he wants to do is drink, fight and whore."

"Pietro, then."

"Hah! His own shadow frightens him. He would not dare."

"He survived the service of Tommaso Cellini for more than a decade," Silenzi reminded him. "I would not underestimate him."

"You see enemies everywhere."

"The better to ensure your safety."

"This is ludicrous!" Cosimo exclaimed. "I am hardly the first man in Cadenza to have correspondences with an ink maid. Tommaso spent his nights knee-deep in dead girls, for pity's sake! What price my letters next to that?"

"The late Artifex's activities remained a secret, my lord," replied Silenzi. "I fear that if the contents of your private letters were to be made public, it would do your reputation great harm."

"How so?"

Silenzi paused delicately. "The people think you are weak, my lord."

"I am aware of that."

"The tone in which you allow the ink maid to address you, the indignities you permit her to threaten you with… they might be thought only to confirm that impression."

"So if it were *me* threatening to whip Hypatia, there would be no problem?"

"She does not lead this city. You do."

Cosimo rubbed his eyes. "Then let us waste no more breath discussing it," he said. "You will remove the message?"

Silenzi bowed his head. "As my lord commands. Though if we do not find its author, I fear it may not be the last such message you receive."

"For all I know, it could have been you who wrote it," Cosimo said darkly.

A ghost of a smile flickered across Silenzi's lips. "*Now* you are thinking, my lord," he said, in a whistling whisper.

IV. *Sunk in Mourning*

AN ICY WIND had greeted the day of Cosimo's coronation, whipping in off the Adige and sending the black ribbons bedecking the stalls of the Old Market into a shivering fit. Merchants were doing a brisk trade selling reprints of Tommaso's *Poetia* and the first hagiographies—composed with startling speed—of the deceased patrician's life and rule. As Cosimo's carriage clipped past the market square, the dangling ribbons provided an uncomfortable reminder of the severed straps he had discovered attached to the bedposts of the Palazzo Nero's east wing.

Since the days of Bartolomeo Strozzi, the Artifex had been elected by the Council of Seven on the basis of applications offered up in the form of poetic, dramatic or scholarly works. In the wake of Tomasso's death, requests for submissions had been hammered into library doors across the city. Amongst the elegantly wrought sentences and sculpted stanzas that came forth in reply, one offering had caused astonishment: sheaves of *ricordanze*, memoranda of the Folio's business dealings; tables of land sales and purchases, records of incomings and outgoings, the delicate weighing of income and expenditure. Dry as wheat, brutally austere in its rejection of cadence or poetry, it was an artistic outrage.

It won Cosimo the city.

News of his appointment had left the citizens—whom, for the most part, had never heard of him—bemused. Why not the great poet Rinaldi? Why not Lorenzo or his rival Borso, let the Duelling Counts settle their feud once and for all! How could a city teeming with scholars and poets, maestri of metre and verse, have fallen under the control of a *bureaucrat*? Yet Cosimo had judged his application shrewdly. Tommaso's reign had come at a cost, the aggressive expansion of business and endless carousing leaving Cadenza's lines of credit running dry in Florence, Antwerp and London. As far as the previous Artifex had been concerned, these were petty concerns. He had continued to spend money up until the moment of his death, planning a series of extravagant feasts to mark the twenty-fifth year of his reign—which Cosimo had promptly cancelled. Now that Tommaso was no more, a scrupulous accountant was precisely what was needed.

The citizens of Cadenza, naturally, had no idea of the parlous state of their city's finances, and Cosimo's carriage swept into the Piazza della Rosa through a thin crowd. Muted applause greeted his descent from the vehicle. In the middle of the square, the Well of Calliope had been staunched, the trio of pools at the Muse's feet smooth black petals. Cosimo unclipped the ermine cloak from his shoulders and handed it to Pietro, who bowed and stepped back. This next journey, he would do alone. It was not without its dangers—the new Artifex had only recently dismissed Tommaso's *becchini*, to great ill-feeling, and as Cosimo's footsteps echoed around the piazza he found himself eying the sky for an arcing arrow, the deadly shiver of a crossbow bolt. But it would not do to be seen hurrying. Upon reaching the Well of Calliope,

Cosimo did not break stride, stepping over the stone lip and wading fully clothed into the ink.

For months afterwards, he would shudder at the recollection of the fountain's wet embrace. Cold fingers teased their way up his thighs; when they touched his groin, he let out a shocked gasp. He pushed on to the heart of the pool and stopped, waist-deep in ink. Previous Artifexes—those fortunate enough to be crowned on hot summer days—had used this moment to make dramatic declarations, but Cosimo feared the shock of the cold had snatched the voice from his throat. Taking a deep breath, he closed his eyes and submerged himself in the ink.

Darkness overwhelmed him. Liquid seeped inside his ears and nostrils, pressing against his lips and seeking entrance to his mouth. Cosimo anchored himself to the bottom of the fountain, fighting back panic. Tommaso had spent more than three minutes inside the well during his coronation, he reminded himself—here was an opportunity to show the crowd waiting on the piazza that Cosimo Petrucci was possessed of a similar mettle. He settled himself to wait, grimly ignoring the burning of his lungs.

It was then he heard it—the noise that he had dreaded might come, the noise that dogged his waking nights: a maddening thudding sound, like an insistent fist against the door. Cosimo pressed his hands over his ears. How could it reach him here, in the well's sable depths? He felt ghosts crowding in around him, the murk thickening with their disdain. The thudding grew louder and louder, reverberating around inside Cosimo's skull until he feared it might shatter. He opened his mouth to scream, and received a sickening tide of ink down his throat. The entire fountain seemed to be trembling. He could take it no longer: clawing his way up through the pool, he broke the surface with a flurry of arms.

Cosimo hauled himself spluttering from the fountain, to find Pietro hastening forward with his cloak. Fitful applause decorated the square. Half-blind and deaf, ink swilling treacherously around in his stomach, Cosimo was ushered across the flagstones to the steps of the Palazzo Nero. There were no more thoughts of arrows and crossbow bolts, every fibre of his being focused on escaping from view of his citizens. The palace doors yawned open as Cosimo stumbled up the steps, and he passed through into a vast entrance hallway. Only then did he fall to his knees.

"Congratulations, my lord," Pietro whispered, as the new Artifex spat black over the chequered floor.

V. *Broken Spines*

Cosimo drummed his fingers on the desk.

"It has been almost a week," he said. "Why have I heard nothing?"

Pietro performed a shuffling dance of abasement before him. "We expect to hear from the Venetians any day now. Rest assured, I stressed our position in the strongest possible terms."

"Evidently," Cosimo said icily. "Did Tommaso also have to wait this long for a reply?"

"He wrote no letters to reply *to*, my lord. The previous Artifex allowed no correspondence with the Venetians."

"If it's news from Venice you require, Uncle, I have something that might be of interest." Cesare's voice was muffled by the arm draped over his face as he stretched out along the divan. "Word coming out of the canals has it that Alessandro and Galeotto Cellini have taken quarters near the Arsenale. They have met with Gritti, the Doge, and are plotting to take back Cadenza."

"Lies," Cosimo said flatly.

Cesare's hand snaked out along the floor, groping for his jug of wine. "I have it on good authority."

"A snatch of tavern gossip while deep in your cups, no doubt."

"Better that than a contemptuous nothing," Cesare replied. "You're wasting your time writing to the Venetians. Mark my words, Gritti and the Cellinis are probably chortling over your letter as we speak."

"*Enough*, Cesare!" Cosimo slammed his fist on the desk. "The matter is closed."

His nephew sank into sullen silence. As Cosimo gazed at his pile of letters—every correspondence he could wish for, save for the one his city needed, and the other that his heart desired—he became aware of Pietro edging closer to his desk. The old man reminded him of a white-tipped gull, circling a morsel of food.

"I trust you will forgive me for saying so, my lord, but you look tired," Pietro said. "Why not take this night to try and rest?"

"Of course I look tired," Cosimo snapped. "I am always tired. Were I able to sleep, I would not be tired."

"You must surely sleep at some point. No man can survive without it."

"I am not like other men."

"Then you must get what little rest you can," Pietro insisted. "This office is a demanding mistress and will drain every drop of vigour you possess. If we can stay a patient course, I am certain you will receive the letter you desire."

Cosimo looked up sharply, but Pietro's expression was one of ingratiating innocence. Pinching the bridge of his nose, he waved the Master of the Scrolls away. Cesare scooped up his jug and slunk out without a word. The riverside taverns would ring with black words and threats against the Artifex that night, Cosimo knew. He had to be careful: he had few enough allies as it was, without alienating what passed for his inner circle.

The hour was approaching midnight when finally Pietro left him. Cosimo shuffled vainly again through his letters. For the first time ever, Hypatia was late—and when he needed her the most! He sprang up from behind his desk, scattering notes across the floor, and marched out of the room. The councillors and attendants who crisscrossed the halls like busy chess pieces had long since retired; the palace was his alone. Cosimo swept up the staircase to the loggia on the second floor, wary of watching eyes beneath the city's distant eaves. At the doors to the east wing, he stopped by the statue of Petrarch and glanced around the hall. Reaching up to the poet's laurel crown, he pushed down on the highest leaf. There came a low rumbling of stone and the wall behind the statue slid to one side, revealing a flight of steps spiralling downwards.

Cosimo walked inside and pressed a lever, slipping into darkness as the wall closed up behind him. Ignoring the tinder and sconce by the wall, he descended through the earth's massy tiers using the faint light at the bottom of the stairwell as a guide. He came out into a vaulted cellar lit by a brazier filled with red-hot coals. The secret rooms beneath the Palazzo Nero had been a gift from Arnolfo to Bartolomeo Strozzi, and every subsequent Artifex had been grateful at one time or another for the privacy they afforded. Tommaso had been no exception: indeed, the great poet had gone about the business of torture with great assiduousness among the filthy straw and gnawing rats, personally administering paper cuts to tender parts of flesh and watching spines break upon the rack.

Piteous moans greeted Cosimo as he entered the cellar. Two men were shackled to the wall, gaunt puppets with their arms suspended high above their heads. Naked save for a cloth around the groin, their filthy flesh was covered in scratches and gouges, their hair unkempt and eyes wild.

I will chain you naked to a stake and beat you with sticks and thorny branches, Hypatia had promised Cosimo.

"Gentlemen," he said, with stiff courtesy. "The talk of the city has you enjoying the delights of a Venetian spring. What would you give for that to be true, I wonder?"

"My lord," said Alessandro Cellini, a weak rasp through cracked lips. "Water, please, I beg you."

Cosimo crouched down by a wooden bucket near the brazier and drew a cup of water. He held it first to Alessandro and then Galeotto's lips. Alessandro let out a spluttering gasp and rested his head against the wall. His brother—who appeared to have taken the worst of the beatings, his nose broken and his left leg twisted awkwardly beneath him—shied away as Cosimo turned his face from side to side, inspecting his bruises.

"You should not be here, my lord."

A low voice, whistling out of a recess behind them.

"This is my palace, Silenzi," Cosimo said coldly, without turning around. "I believe I will come and go as I please."

"Your place lies upstairs, in the halls of government," the *putto* replied. "Leave these unhappy rooms to my care."

At the mention of Silenzi's name, Galeotto began to gibber senselessly, a language shaped by pure terror. Cosimo beckoned his agent through into a soot-stained antechamber.

"It has been several months now," he whispered. "Is it not time to end their suffering?"

"You are a compassionate man, my lord," Silenzi said softly. "But there are occasions when leadership requires a harder heart. We know well that there are plots brewing against you inside the city—can we be certain that Tommaso's cousins have told us everything?"

Cosimo glanced through the archway at the shrivelled prisoners. "What else can be done to them, that has not been done already?"

The fire from the brazier bathed Silenzi's cherubic features crimson. "There is always more," he said. "It can always be longer, or harder, or deeper."

Cosimo bit his lip, and nodded quickly. Gently taking the cup of water from his hands, Silenzi glided back into the cellar and emptied its contents into the brazier, filling the room with steam. Cosimo strode out through the hot clouds towards the steps.

You will wash yourself in the water I pass, Hypatia had written, *and drink the leftovers until no drop remains.*

"Kill us!" Alessandro screamed after him. "I beg of you, my lord, in the name of all that is human and holy, let us die!"

A howl of pain cut him off—Galeotto? Cosimo hurried away up the stairs until the prisoners' cries grew fainter and fainter. By the time he reached the surface and closed the secret door behind him, it was as though they had never existed at all.

VI. *A Strange Humour*

NIGHT HAD TURNED the narrow lanes of the Printing Quarter into murky canals, oozing with innuendo. Jet-black steeds whinnied under the reproach of the coachman's whip. Inside the carriage, Cosimo peered out from behind the curtains at the unfamiliar paths and passages of his city. Never before had he come this way—he had not permitted himself to succumb to the temptation. Yet now, even as he watched, the carriage attacked a steep hill and the outline of a bell tower thrust into the night sky. He banged on the roof.

As the coachman pulled over to the side of the street, Cosimo looked up to the balcony at the top of the tower, and the room he imagined to be Hypatia's bedchamber. He pictured her falling asleep, swooning gracefully onto silken sheets. In her dreams, did she imagine in turn the Artifex paused beneath her window? Perhaps he was dreaming too. Since the arrival of the ink maid's latest letter that morning, Cosimo had been light-headed with delirium. Now, for the first time, he hesitated. He had risked a great deal just coming here. The coachman, a grizzled old man who communicated entirely in grunts, he felt he could trust. But who else had seen him leave the palace?

Cosimo glanced at the seat beside him, where the sight of the black-ribboned letter hardened his resolve. He snatched it up and jumped down from the carriage. The coachman sat silently in his seat, his gaze fixed pointedly at his shoes. Cosimo strode over to the darkened tower and rapped on the door. Footsteps came to meet him—the door flew open, bathing Cosimo in a slanting rectangle of light. He flinched, taking a pace back as a silhouette filled the doorway.

"I would speak with Hypatia the ink maid," Cosimo said, in as commanding a tone as he could summon. "Where is she?"

"This is no hour for visitors," the man replied flatly.

"I am no visitor. My name is Cosimo Petrucci: these streets are mine, and every man and woman who walks them are my subjects. I will speak to them any time of the day or night I choose."

The attendant peered at him through the darkness. His eyes widened.

"Forgive me, my lord," he said quickly, with a low bow. "I had not anticipated such an august guest at this hour. You are most welcome to enter, but I am afraid my mistress is not here to greet you."

"Is that so? And where might she be?"

The attendant gave him an unhappy smile. "I do not know. Would that I did. A strange humour has come over her these past weeks, leaving her at the mercy of whim and reckless impulse."

Cosimo scratched his cheek. "I could say the same for myself," he said.

"I hope my lord would not think me presumptuous to ask whether there was anything that *I* could help him with?"

He thrust a black-ribboned letter in the attendant's hands. The man hesitated before opening it—a welcome sign of discretion. Upon reading the note, he frowned.

"It says simply '*Scio*'," he said. "I do not understand."

"Nor I. I had hoped that Hypatia might furnish me with an explanation."

The attendant held the letter up to the light and inspected it. He shook his head. "It is a fair approximation of her hand, but my mistress did not write this letter."

"Really?" Cosimo said quickly. "Can you be sure?"

"I have served in this house for ten years and more, my lord. Enough letters have passed through my hands for me to know a forgery."

"But if Hypatia did not write it, who did?"

"That I cannot answer. But it was no one who lives here."

Cosimo nodded, accepting the letter's return. *Scio*. Whoever his unknown correspondent was, they knew about Hypatia— and her letters.

"Is there a message you wish me to give to my mistress?" the attendant inquired.

"Only that I am keenly awaiting to hear from her." Turning to leave, Cosimo paused. "Better yet, do not tell her that I was here."

He nodded. "As you wish, my lord."

The man remained in the doorway as Cosimo retreated to his carriage, dogged by the suspicion that his journey had been a terrible mistake. Only when the coachman had geed up the horses and the vehicle was rattling away down the hill did the attendant finally close the door, and the rectangle of light shining across the street abruptly wink out.

VII. *Of Sumptuous Midnight*

RETURNING TO THE palace, Cosimo stared through hot and itchy eyes at pages of *ricordanze* until their numbers blurred into a meaningless blot. Finally, he pushed his papers to one side and headed to his bedchamber, through the watery yellow hallways of the dawn. Inside his room, however, night still reigned. Cosimo had allowed himself a single luxury on becoming Artifex: curtains crafted by the Arab velvet makers of Cairo, transported to Italy via the quays of Venice. The drapes were the colour of sumptuous midnight, capable of repelling the most dazzling of sunrises and submerging the room in a darkness thicker than the Well of Calliope. Cosimo kicked off his shoes and lay down on the bed. Even in the hollow depths of his exhaustion, he knew he would not sleep. The noise would not allow him.

Cosimo had been raised in a townhouse on the Via San Francesco, within sight of the swaying pines of the Garden of Leaves. His family's outward respectability was a façade, behind which lay a brooding, joyless household. Both mother and father routinely beat him, for arbitrary and often imperceptible misdemeanours—his father during the night, cloaked in a stinking fug of wine; his mother during the day, with remorseless, tight-lipped precision. Worse was when they turned upon each other. As he lay in bed, Cosimo had pressed his hands over his ears to try and block out the noise, the shadows on his wall flinching and writhing in time with his mother's screams. His parents' reconciliations were sealed by love-making so brutal that it appeared nothing more than a continuation of their previous scuffles: a lust both violent and shameless, of bruises, scratches and black eyes. Night after night, the young Cosimo huddled beneath his blanket, fists bunched and eyes shut tight, willing with all his soul for the throttled shrieks and rattling headboard to cease and deliver his room into silence: total, glorious silence.

Both parents were now dead. Yet come nightfall, the walls of Cosimo's bedchamber still trembled. No matter where he laid his head, from squalid tavern attics to the resplendent quarters of the Palazzo Nero, there was no escaping the torturous racket. It was a drum that beat through the hours of darkness while other men slumbered; by daylight, Cosimo fancied he could still hear it, a faint echo at the edges of his hearing. Yet now, to his surprise, Cosimo's bedchamber lay quiet. He let out a sigh, his limbs melting slowly into the sheets. He felt himself teetering at the edge of a vast precipice, warm and inviting. To surrender was sweet bliss...

At a rustle by the window, Cosimo's head snapped up from the pillow. He opened his eyes to see a shadow detach itself from the curtains, coalescing into the shape of a man.

"Silenzi?" Cosimo said blearily. "Must you dog my every waking moment?"

"I remain your loyal and faithful hound," his attendant replied, with a gap-toothed smile.

"And what is so important that you would disturb my rest? Have you deemed the few meagre grains of sleep I am granted each night an indulgence?"

Silenzi shook his head sorrowfully. "You are growing careless, my lord," he chided. "To pay a visit to the ink maid's home was a regrettable act of folly; to converse with her manservant, to show him your letter, something else altogether."

Cosimo shrank back in his bed. "You saw us?"

"What kind of servant would I be, if I abandoned my master when he needed me most?"

"I have no more need of you," Cosimo replied hoarsely. "You have served me enough."

"Your actions suggest otherwise. Why not send *me* to the bell tower? I could have sought the information you desired, and made certain that no one could talk about it afterwards."

"Hypatia's attendant told me she is missing."

"So I gather."

"If I have not been sufficiently clear previously, know this, Silenzi: if you have so much as touched a hair upon her head, I will see to it that Alessandro and Galeotto have company in the cellars."

Silenzi spread out his hands. "I have left the ink maid be, as you instructed. Perhaps she has been spirited away by an admirer, or taken by Plagiarists. Perhaps she has thrown herself in the Adige. Regardless, it is a blessing."

"So say you."

"The night is darkening around us, my lord. I fear our work is not yet done."

"What do you mean?"

Crouching at his bedside, Silenzi said, in a fluting whisper: "Your refusal to pursue Tommaso's cousins has aroused the suspicions of the Master of the Scrolls. Pietro knows what kind of man your predecessor was, and is aware of the existence of the rooms beneath the palace. If he learns of the guests we keep, he may become a threat to us."

"You would have me kill Pietro now?" Cosimo said icily.

"I would have you ensure his silence."

"And how long then, before we turn our attention to the next victim? How long before you silence Cesare, my own blood? Tell me, Silenzi, how many people would you have me kill?"

"It would be prudent at this point to lower your voice," Silenzi advised him. "These halls are not without their secret ways. A raised voice can easily find its way from one room to the next."

"Do not lecture me about my own palace, man!"

Spots of colour arose in the attendant's pudgy cheeks. When he spoke again, a note of pique had crept into his voice.

"Tell *me*, my lord: have I ever done anything in your name that you did not desire—truly? Have I not eased your path to the most powerful office in the land? But for me, would not Tommaso Cellini still be Artifex right now?"

Cosimo stared at him.

By unspoken agreement, they had not spoken of the deed since its commission. Cosimo wasn't sure who had suggested it first, or whether either of them even had—or rather, that the necessity of its execution had become so apparent that neither had needed to put voice to it. Silenzi had shown him how, of course. Meticulous diagrams laid out a system of pulleys and counterbalances that could be secretly installed around the bookcase in Tommaso's office, causing it to topple over when a certain volume was pulled from the shelf. It had been Cosimo who had selected the *Poetia*, a ghoulish gamble on the Artifex's self-regard. One chill autumn night, when the springbolts on the east wing doors were locked fast, Silenzi had crept forth from Cosimo's chambers with wire and tools to install their trap. No one saw him, naturally.

"I will not forget what you have done for me, Silenzi," Cosimo said carefully. "Nor will I ever. But we have achieved all we set out to do: I am the Artifex now. This time of murder is done."

"Power does not decrease enemies, my lord. It only serves to multiply them, many times over."

"Be that as it may."

"You have no further need of me?"

"I would have you wait for my summons."

Silenzi sketched out a taut bow. "As you wish."

He withdrew to the adjoining chamber, pausing on the threshold.

"We have more in common than you think, my lord," he murmured. "You are precisely the kind of man this city needs after Tommaso—principled and dedicated; an administrator, not a poet. Yet the people despise you for it. By the same token, I am precisely the kind of man *you* need. And I, too, am despised for it."

Silenzi backed out of the bedroom, softly closing the doors behind him. Cosimo rolled over and closed his eyes, hunting through the black wastes of his mind for the precious threads of sleep that had been so tantalizingly close at hand.

In the next room, a loud banging struck up against the wall.

VIII. *Scio*

RAIN DRUMMED IMPATIENT fingers upon the window of Cosimo's office, the city a smeared outline in the glass. The room was shrinking into darkness, the bookcase's shadow lengthening across the flagstones until it rested on the empty divan by the opposite wall. Pietro huddled in the glow of a candle on the cupboard. He was talking quickly and nervously, each word a butterfly.

"...the response from the Venetians is, alas, not that for which we might have hoped. They have rejected our offer of a deal over contract writing and have summarily closed the channels of communications between our two cities. I have contacted our friends in Florence and Rome and for now they remain steadfast, but I fear that if we do not—"

Cosimo wearily waved him silent. He pointed at the divan. "Where is he?"

The Master of the Scrolls coughed. "Forgive me, my lord. Cesare went out into the city two nights previous and has not been seen since."

"Have the guards sweep the libraries," Cosimo said, with a bitter laugh. "Perhaps my nephew has been studying to impress his new scholar friends, and has fallen asleep over his books."

Pietro looked confused. "My lord?"

Cosimo rubbed his bloodshot eyes. First Hypatia, now Cesare: one by one, his only acquaintances were abandoning him. Three weeks had passed without word from the ink maid—Cosimo itched to roll in the inky squalor of her letters. Had he not earned her chastisement, did he not deserve to have his face ground into the dirt? His only consolation was that Silenzi had stayed true to his word and had absented himself since their dawn confrontation; it was the only way Cosimo could be sure that the *putto* had played no part in the ink maid's disappearance—or Cesare's, for that matter.

Yet, at the same time, it meant sacrificing another of his closest confidants.

Leaving him with Pietro.

Cosimo looked up to find the old man approaching in singularly hesitant fashion, bobbing and bending until he had placed himself almost prostrate across the desk before the Artifex.

"Is there anything you wish to discuss, my lord?" he whispered. "I see you grapple with unspoken dilemmas. I know you pace the palace's loneliest corridors at nights. As Master of the Scrolls, I exist to serve your will—your problems are mine to solve."

"I see," Cosimo said flatly. "Is that what you told yourself when Tommaso's *becchini* were dragging dead whores out of the palace by their ankles?"

Pietro pulled away from the desk. "My duty is to protect the Artifex, my lord," he said reproachfully. "And through him, the city itself. Cadenza is strong when its ruler is strong. I do not choose the man who calls this palace home; I merely work with the tools I am given."

"I am not your tool."

"And I cannot be yours, if you will not let me!"

"What makes you so certain that I have need of your services, Pietro?"

The old man glanced around the study before replying. "I have received troubling news from the Printing Quarter of murder most violent, committed in the quarters of a notorious ink maid."

Cosimo felt a skeletal hand fasten itself around his throat. "The maid is dead?"

Pietro shook his head. "No, my lord, her attendant. His body was discovered in his quarters on the ground floor, head sliced clean from the neck." He hesitated. "There was a message... written on the wall above the body. In blood. A single word."

Cosimo closed his eyes.

"*Scio.*"

He could only nod at the terrible inevitability of it. "And why would you think that I would care about a servant's death?" he murmured.

"Because I know that barely three nights ago you travelled to Hypatia's bell tower and spoke with this man."

"How?"

"You do not own the small hours, my lord," said Pietro. "If you travel in a palace carriage through the Printing Quarter in the dead of night, *someone* will recognize you. It is not the kind of secret easily kept."

"What about you, Master of the Scrolls?" Cosimo leaned forward. "Will you hold your tongue?"

"My lips are sealed. But I know, and whoever killed the attendant does too. Scio, my lord. Scio."

As the rain redoubled its assault upon the Palazzo Nero, Cosimo tapped his fingers on the desk. Pietro dared a knowing smile. There could be no doubt now that there was one man who meant Cosimo ill, who knew everything about him, the smallest and grimiest crevices of his soul, and meant to use it to his advantage. As he stared at the glowing candle on the cupboard, Cosimo realized only one course of action was left open to him.

He was going to have to kill Silenzi.

IX. *A Terrible Necessity*

IT WAS ONLY later, when he crept out into the midnight hallways, that Cosimo began to appreciate the difference between consenting to a murder and its actual commission. He had been party to killing before—had he not ended the monstrous reign of the most powerful man in Cadenza?—but never had he considered taking a life with his own hands. In his belt, a knife pressed uncomfortably against his side. Cosimo wondered whether he would have the courage to use it.

Windowpanes shook in their settings as he passed by, the world beyond the palace obscured by the growing storm. He was glad for the cover of the howling wind—if Cosimo's plan was to have any chance of succeeding, he had to catch Silenzi unawares. Yet was that even possible? He chased a phantom, who came and went seemingly at will. Who knew what obscure lair Silenzi called home, when not stepping forth on his master's business?

"Where are you, faithful hound?" Cosimo whispered, into the darkness. "Where is my true servant?"

The rain assailed him as he stepped out into a courtyard—tangled up in the wind, Cosimo thought he heard a shriek. He pressed on, trailing wet footprints across the floor of the empty *salone*, the scene of so many lavish feasts and balls, where Tommaso Cellini had captivated his guests with his wit and words, his boundless largesse. Hypatia's voice whispered tauntingly in Cosimo's ear: *You are an insect, a worm. A louse. Tommaso was a man. The city needs a man.* How Cosimo longed to hear from the ink maid! But for all he knew, she was dead; perhaps Cesare also.

And therein lay the reason he had to do this thing. Silenzi could not be returned to the dark corner from which he had emerged, there was no restraining him. The killings, the taunting messages, would continue. Cosimo could not fathom the devilish game the cherubic assassin was playing, but he knew that to obstruct Silenzi was to risk becoming his next victim. After all, what was there to stop Silenzi appearing before some other lowly clerk and promising him the city?

Cosimo passed through another courtyard, his path leading back—as somehow he had always known it would—towards the east wing. As he ascended to the loggia, lightning rent the sky above the Palazzo Nero, bathing the gallery in brilliant white and picking out a robed figure moving serenely along the passage. Cosimo drew back into the nearest alcove and pressed himself against the wall, his heart thumping inside his chest. His eyes fell upon the bust of Arnolfo mounted on the plinth before him. He picked up the marble head, felt its reassuring weight in his hands. Better this way, with one irrefutable blow, than to trust a blind blade to pierce the necessary organs.

Further along the hallway, Silenzi stopped in Petrarch's shadow.

Scio. Scio. Who knew now?

The storm was so loud it seemed to be raging inside Cosimo's skull. As he stole forward, darting from alcove to alcove along the loggia, he heard his mother scream, and the hallway rang to the sound of his father's clenched-toothed grunts. And then, above the wind, it began again, the infernal knocking, the frantic bang and rattle of the headboard.

Cosimo bit back a cry of anguish. There came another flash of lightning; another sudden, violent dawn. As Silenzi reached up towards the false leaf on Petrarch's crown, Cosimo darted out from behind a pillar and brought the bust down with a sickening crack upon the man's skull. Bone shattered beneath him, blood spraying into the air. The body crumpled to the ground. A shrill exclamation escaped Cosimo's lips—only to turn into a scream as the secret panel moved to one side.

"My lord?"

Silenzi stood atop the stairs, his hands clasped behind his back.

Looking down in disbelief through the gloom, Cosimo saw that it was Pietro who lay sprawled at his feet, pieces of Pietro's skull scattered like mosaic pieces across the floor. The Artifex staggered back with a screech, his whole body convulsing. Arnolfo's bust was decorated with white hairs matted in blood.

Lost in horror, Cosimo barely registered the protective arm enfolding around his shoulder, pulling him away from Pietro's bloodied corpse.

"Hush my lord," Silenzi said softly. "It will be all right."

Cosimo couldn't breathe. "I killed him!" he gasped.

"A terrible necessity. But Pietro had left you no choice. He was searching for the entrance to the cellars—he wished to know our secrets."

"I did not mean to do it. Not Pietro!"

"I would not be surprised if this whole affair had been his design," Silenzi said solemnly. "The message behind the portrait, the attendant's murder. I did warn you not to underestimate him."

Cosimo searched Silenzi's face for signs of the truth. He was so desperate to believe him, to make sense of the terrible act he had just committed. But how could he trust him? Cosimo had been so *sure* that it had been Silenzi standing in front of Petrarch—could it really have been a mistake, his weary eyes mistaking one man's form for another?

"You did this!" Cosimo hissed. "You knew what I was planning—you know everything! You made sure it was Pietro I killed."

The *putto's* cheeks pinked. "In this act, my lord, you have acted completely alone. Would that you had confided in me, I could have taken this burden from your shoulders. You are no murderer."

Shrill laughter echoed around the loggia. "Am I not, Silenzi? Will Pietro get up in a moment and dance a jig for us?"

Silenzi prised the bust from Cosimo's trembling hands and set it down beside Pietro. "Please, my lord, come with me. Your work here is done this night."

He led the weeping Cosimo along the loggia and through the stormy palace. When they were safely ensconced in the office in the northwest tower, Silenzi guided the Artifex to his seat behind his desk and whispered words of reassurance in his ear. The bloodied loggia would be cleaned, Pietro's body buried in a distant field far from Cosimo's orbit. No one would ever know his role in this deed.

Upon that soft, solemn vow, Silenzi withdrew. Cosimo sat in the darkness, staring down at his upturned palms. In the conspiratorial gloom of the Palazzo Nero, the blood on his hands looked as thick and dark as ink.

Fifth Canto
Aristotle's Library

I. *Of Moisture and Moths*

THEY INSIST IT is lost: *I do not believe that this is so.* My quest has taken me from Ancient Greece to the shores of Asia Minor and Egypt's silted atrium, without my ever once leaving Cadenza. The Library's ultimate fate cannot be discerned by scouring the land and sifting through layers of sand and earth. It is a tale told on the page, rewritten and reinterpreted in indices and appendices, catalogues and *anagraphē*. The depths of winter have found me scrabbling, fingers clumsy with cold, through forgotten scrolls in a cellar on the Via Tribunali; at summer's height, I have sweltered in the sun-drenched galleries of the Accademia. I have been by turns derided and dismissed, my efforts mocked or attributed to some manic distemper of the brain. It means as little to me as the turning of the seasons.

That there was a Library is indisputable: I chase no mirage. According to the geographer Strabo, Aristotle was the "the first man to have collected books and to have taught the kings in Egypt how to arrange a library." His scrolls numbered as many as a thousand—tight cylinders entrusted with the secrets of physics, philosophy and medicine, theories of laughter and the position of the fixed stars in the heavens. The Library was installed in the Athenian temple of the Lyceum, where Aristotle led his disciples upon strolls along the arcades, leisurely circuits marked with detours and digressions on phantasms and the catfish and cuttlefish. But a death in a distant Babylonian palace would bring an end to this age of rumination. Alexander of Macedon had been a boyhood pupil of Aristotle's—upon the conqueror's demise, the Lyceum became a target for those who wished ill on Greece's rivals. Hounded by hierophants and emboldened politicians, Aristotle abandoned Athens for his mother's estate on Chalcis. He would die before a year had passed.

The Library remained at the Lyceum in the care of Aristotle's successor Theophrastus, who in turn bequeathed it to Neleus of Scepsis. Within months, the shelves stood empty— Neleus ordered the scrolls gathered up and transported to his birthplace, a thousand miles from Athens. Was this epic undertaking a dogged attempt to protect Aristotle's collection from the clouds of suspicion still hanging over the temple, or a simple fit of pique, following the election of Neleus's rival Strato to the head of the Lyceum? The histories were unable to decide: I praised Neleus and cursed his name, depending on my mood.

Scepsis proved unhappy lodgings for the Library. The heirs of Neleus were strangers to the houses of learning, unworthy of the priceless treasures they had been given. Upon hearing that agents of King Attalus were combing the region for books with which to fill the library of Pergamum, they panicked and hid the scrolls in an underground tunnel. There the Library remained, for two hundred years, an exquisite feast for moisture and moths. Eventually the mouldering remains were retrieved and sold to Apellicon of Teos, an enterprising collector and book thief. In an effort to salvage the damaged works, Apellicon made his own copies, only to riddle the text with errors: tiny snake eggs laid in the bindings. He died in the aftermath of the siege of Athens, at the hands of soldiers under the command of the Roman general Sulla. The Library was conveyed back to Rome, where Sulla placed it in the care of the grammarian Tyrannion of Amisus. Tyrannion set about making copies of his own, which were in turn drawn on by Andronicus of Rhodes, who arranged them into catalogues known as *pinax*.

A final, fleeting glance of Aristotle's volumes remained, inside the idle house of Sulla's son, Faustus. Cicero, a neighbour, would visit to gorge himself on the contents of his collection. Yet Faustus's spendthrift ways forced him to put his possessions up for auction. At which point, to my anguish, the Library disappeared from view completely.

Here even I—a man who has devoted his life to the pursuit of knowledge—must acknowledge the limits of scholarly inquisition and learning, when they run contrary to the desires of the human heart. My quest was seemingly at an end, yet I could not accept that the Library had been dealt such an unhappy fate. I stood on the benches of the Piazza della Rosa and raged against the histories, my breath hot with zealous fire. At the height of the Carnival of Wit, my impassioned speeches drew a crowd, among their number a man—a scholar by dress, and melancholy of humour—who listened intently. The next day, he returned to hear me again; upon the third, he approached and pressed a piece of vellum into my hand. The fragment contained an unremarkable passage from the gospels for which the scholar offered no explanation, responding to my questions with a sad-eyed stare. I shooed him away, marking him for a madman or a charlatan, a bastard son of Apellicon.

Only on returning to my desk the next morning did the true nature of the man's offering reveal itself. In the generous light of the library window I apprehended a *scriptio inferior*, a faint second layer of text on the vellum. It recounted a series of conversations at an ancient banquet—with growing curiosity, I trawled through the gossip and the gluttony until my eye latched upon the name Neleus of Scepsis. Neleus, the narrator contended, had preserved the libraries of Theophrastus and Aristotle both, before selling them to "our king, Ptolemaios called Philadelphos, who transferred them to Alexandria, the beautiful, along with those which came from Athens and Rome."

Alexandria the beautiful! The suggestion, at once irresistible and sublime, brought tears to my eyes. Surely here was a more fitting home for Aristotle's collection than the dank burrows of Scepsis. May the gods punish me for ever traducing the name of Neleus!

Yet even as I sat back in my chair, clouds gathered in the window, casting my desk in sudden shadow. I did not need to consult the histories to know what sort of fate awaited the Library in Alexandria. The city's decline was famous enough, a tragic tale blotted by *obelos* and *estigmé*; of warehouses engulfed in fire and statues turned to piss-pots; of bookshelves shivering at the thundering fists of the mob at the library doors; of scrolls flung on bathhouse fires, obliterating the wisdoms of the ancient world; of a civilization sinking into ignorance and civil discord.

Little wonder, the scholar's wordless despair. The Library was lost.

II. *An Esoteric Passage*

IN THE DAYS and weeks that followed my discovery of the vellum fragment, I was consumed by listlessness. The written word brought me no ease; I eschewed books for dice and wine, seeking solace in the arms of lost women. Where once I had gazed up at the Niccolo's glorious friezes, now loomed the arches of the Ponte Nuovo. Friends denounced my shameful ways; my patrons disowned me. I roamed the city, loudly haranguing the libraries I had once revered and cursing the bitter place to which they had led me.

Even now, however, I could not abandon my scholarly habits. I embarked on a new course of learning, absorbing the wisdoms of my restless companions of the night. In a forger's workshop overlooking the Old Market, I examined works I knew to have been destroyed for centuries; in the salon of a dying courtesan, a poet recited, to hushed disbelief, a verse accusing Tommaso Cellini of unspeakable crimes. I came to discern a second layer of activity at work within Cadenza, a *scriptio inferior* hidden beneath the everyday correspondences of its citizens. A disgraced clerk whispered to me of a library situated somewhere inside the city that opened its doors to no readers, and whose contents did not appear in the Folio's accounts. In the small hours after midnight I spied a wagon laden with books creaking from reading room to reading room, and began to record its movements on the arches of the Ponte Nuovo. How many hours did I spend, lost in contemplation at the chalk constellations I had created?

Over the weeks and months, the heavens gradually ordered themselves, allowing me to divine a pattern in the wagon's mysterious comings and goings. Late one evening, as a storm vented its fury on the Accademia, I lay in wait as it drew up outside the library. A Folio official appeared in the doorway, vainly trying to protect a ledger from the driving rain as he directed men in the loading of volumes. The operation had a furtive air, yet I knew that these were no thieves. Impatient for answers and impetuous with drink, I crawled inside the back of the wagon while the men were looking the other way. Voices cursed the rain as I hunched down beneath the flaxen covering.

Wine had dulled my wits into near-insensibility, and I lost consciousness almost at once. I awoke with a start to find the wagon rolling through the sodden streets. A wheel shuddered into a hole in the road, tipping the vehicle and flinging me to one side, whereupon I banged my head against the wooden slats. As I lay dazed amid the scattered volumes, I was struck by a vision at once glorious and terrifying in its intensity. Before me came another cart filled with books—this time upon the road from Venice to Cadenza, its driver swaying to the undulation of the pitted countryside tracks. It was Angelo Uccello, the city's founder; behind him, the volumes that would form the collection for Cadenza's first library, the House of Uccello. Volumes that the histories had chosen, for obscure reasons, to leave nameless.

And then, I saw it.

As clear as chiming dawn, I saw it.

Aristotle's books had travelled from the Lyceum to Scepsis, and thence to Alexandria... but what if the trail had not ended there? Many contended that Uccello was a man of Alexandria, whose ancestors had walked the aisles of the Museaum. Did it not follow that the books he had first brought to Cadenza might have come from that very place? And might there not have existed, buried among the shaded alleys, some cool cellar in which Aristotle's scrolls could have sheltered while the others burned? Man had proved himself too ignorant and feckless to care for the Library—what recourse was left to its protectors, other than to spirit it from the clutches of those who would harm it and declare it lost?

And where better to hide it, than a city of libraries?

Gripped by the ecstasy of revelation, my incautious cries alerted the Folio's men to my hiding place. Rough hands dragged me from the cart and delivered a ferocious beating. Every blow served only to confirm my suspicions—I laughed with joy, spurring my attackers into still greater violence. When I came to, the cart was gone. I picked myself up and limped back to the Ponte Nuovo, my head pounding with possibilities. If Angelo Uccello had indeed transported Aristotle's library to Cadenza, it surely followed that *it must still be in existence somewhere in the city*. Why else would the Folio maintain a shadowy house of books beyond the reach of its citizens, and guard its secrecy so fiercely? What if I had been searching the city, not for knowledge of the Library's eventual fate, but the Library itself?

A fever of absolute clarity took hold of me. With the clearing skies of morning I returned to the great houses I had forsaken, only this time I ignored the books on the shelves and began to search the libraries themselves, seeking out private chambers and corridors. Time and again, I was ejected from the Accademia, until it was made clear I was no longer welcome inside the city's reading rooms. I resorted to subterfuge and deceit, taking advantage of unlocked doors and broken windows. Across Cadenza, librarians perched hawk-like on their stools, scouring the aisles for sight of me. The Folio demanded my arrest and imprisonment: I responded by burning my scholar's robes, together with a stolen copy of the third volume of Hecataeus's *Genealogies*.

I discovered birds' nests and subterranean rodent kingdoms, volumes scarred by fire and flood; even, in an attic filled with proscribed texts, a pair of entangled lovers. But of the Library, there was no sign. The Folio's wagon adopted a new course, erratic and unknowable, armed guards deterring further inspection. I reached the conclusion that, if one of Cadenza's libraries *had* once housed Aristotle's own, then it did so no longer. Perhaps it was now hidden inside the workshop of a humble smith or glass-blower. Or perhaps, at the end of some esoteric passage inside the Palazzo Nero, a chamber filled with scrolls awaits the Artifex's pleasure. I think this possibility the most likely, though I must reluctantly accept that I will never be able to test my supposition. The palace gates will not part for a man such as myself. All I am left with is a tantalizing *perhaps*.

Do not think I have lost all reason. It could be that I am a sceptic in the truest sense of the word, destined to search but never to find. The thought has occurred to me that the actual design of Aristotle's library may not be a physical construction but a conspiracy of the imagination, a suggestion to inspire the thirst for knowledge. Have I, in my attempts to discern its whereabouts, already devoured the contents of the philosopher's collection? The thought comforts me on grey days when the pages of the books turn to glass and I am confronted by my wild appearance. And yet, were this to prove the ultimate truth, could I honestly not admit to a flicker of disappointment?

At night, I dream of an underground chamber, a circle as perfect as any by Giotto's hand. A thousand scrolls, perfectly aligned upon the shelves. Each one a world.

Sixth Canto
St Peter in Chains

I. *The Bibliotheca Secreta*

THE MONKS GATHERED before dawn, when the hallways of the abbey were still robed in darkness and the kitchen hearths were dry-mouthed and flecked with ash. Heads bowed, sandals treading lightly on cold flagstones, the men filed into the chapel and arranged themselves along the pews. Coughs punctuated the dutiful hush. The service of *Prime* began with song, the monks' voices coming together in a sonorous swoop through the chapel. At the far end of the back row, one of their number—of middling height but broad-shouldered, his cropped black hair flecked with grey—stayed silent, his eyes closed, and his face tilted slightly to the heavens.

Fra Bernardo dreamed of the sea.

He was standing on the edge of a lagoon, gazing out towards the distant horizon, where the sun reigned so brightly that he could not discern its outline amid the brilliance of its lustre. Water rippled around his ankles. The waves were singing to him with the voice of his brothers, urging Bernardo to submit to their embrace and let them carry him out to sea. He stepped into the water, darkening the hem of his white robes. The light warmed his face. But as he began to wade deeper, the waves abruptly ceased their song, and the lagoon began to shimmer and fade. Delivered abruptly back to the chapel, Bernardo opened his eyes to find them damp with unexpected tears.

He coughed to disguise his embarrassment, drying his eyes on his sleeve. The brothers took their seats and Fra Matteo, the elderly infirmarian, commenced to read from the psalms. As his voice carried about the chapel, cracked and sere, Bernardo felt the hairs prickle along the back of his neck. Twisting around, he spied Abbot Marsilio watching him from the back of the chapel—Marsilio's amanuensis, Thaddeus, a dutiful presence at his shoulder. The abbot was a cadaverous man, lean and pale, his body pared by a lifetime of denial. He waited for the prayers to end, expressionless as the monks filed out of the pews, before motioning to Bernardo to join him.

"You wish to speak with me, Abbot?" Bernardo asked.

"Outside," Thaddeus replied. "There is someone we wish you to meet."

It was not unusual for the amanuensis to speak on Marsilio's behalf, assuming the role of mouthpiece as well as scribe. As a rule, the abbot said as little as possible. He treated every word as though it were a personal gift from God himself, only parting with them with extreme reluctance.

The three men walked in step out of the chapel. Spring had stuttered, the cold dawn fringed with mist. A young man paced up and down the path, gnawing on a fingernail. He returned Bernardo's bow of greeting with a quick nod of the head.

"This is Filippo," said Thaddeus. "He is a librarian at the Bibliotheca Domenico. They have asked for our assistance in a matter of some urgency."

Bernardo spread out his hands. "I would be glad to provide whatever help I can, but I am no scholar. Perhaps another, more learned brother—"

"We know well where your talents lie, Fra Bernardo," Thaddeus said firmly. "The abbot would have you go with Filippo to the library. See what has taken place and report back to us."

"As you wish," said Bernardo, bowing his head.

Apparently satisfied with what he had heard, Abbot Marsilio walked smartly away towards the scriptorium, forcing Thaddeus into obliging pursuit. Filippo bolted in the other direction, in the direction of the abbey gates. The chapel doors swung close behind Bernardo. He sighed and went after Filippo. Shadows were flitting in and out of the trees in the apple orchard: monks, carrying baskets of fruit. From the vegetable garden came the rhythmic chop of spades as they bit into the earth. Pungent scents of marjoram and thyme carried on the breeze. Bernardo had proved no more adept working with the soil than he had the books at the lectern, yet still he could appreciate the gardener's quiet craft: the nurturing of growth, from seed to flower, the bringing of life and colour into the world.

Beyond the abbey gates, Filippo was already halfway down the Via Arezzo. He stopped and turned, peering back up the hill to see Bernardo strolling after him.

"Is everything all right, Fra?" the librarian called out, a touch impatiently.

"I am fine," Bernardo replied. "Indulge an old man by slowing your pace and telling me the cause of this great rush."

Filippo bit his lip. He shook his head. "The Chief Librarian will explain," he said. "He is waiting for us."

They continued in silence to the bottom of the hill. Down in the Old Market, the merchants had already begun to set out their stalls, unveiling quills fashioned from ebony and swan beak, the finest calfskin parchment and small pots of ink worth their weight in gold: objects of veneration, sacraments in the worship of the written word. In private, the Pope was said to rail against Cadenza's obsession with books, declaring it to be tantamount to heresy. It was true that Tommaso had shown the church only cursory respect, and his replacement Cosimo was still an enigma. As for the great writers of Cadenza, they appeared happy enough writing childish poems insulting one another's genitalia, but when it came to proclamations of faith and the great religious questions, all they had to offer was an uncomfortable silence.

Filippo barely glanced at the wares as he hurried through the stalls, flinching at the traders' cries. Bernardo, who had no wish to spend his morning chasing the young man through the city, was relieved that their destination was close at hand. The Bibliotheca Domenico was housed on the Via dei Lucchesi, a pleasant, tree-lined avenue branching off to the southwest from the Via Tribunali. As Bernardo neared the library, through the stone pines he glimpsed a man waiting on the steps outside. Filippo hastened to his side.

"Ludovico, this is Fra Bernardo," the young man said, as Bernardo climbed the steps—more breathless than he cared to admit. "The abbot has instructed him to help us."

"You are most welcome," said Ludovico. "Thank you for coming so quickly."

Beneath the polite surface of his words, Bernardo thought he detected a strain in the Chief Librarian's voice as he ushered him inside: the tone of a capable man faced with a trying situation.

"Have you visited our library before, Fra Bernardo?" Ludovico inquired.

"I have not," he replied. "I have learnt by heart the Psalms and the Gospels. I see little reason to read anything else."

"In this city, that makes you something of a rarity."

Bernardo inclined his head. "So I am led to believe."

"Then, please, allow me to be your guide."

Leaving Filippo in the atrium, Ludovico led Bernardo through into the hall. Rows of bookcases divided up the space on either side of a central nave into narrow aisles. As he walked through the chamber, Bernardo saw that the volumes were attached to the shelves by chains. The aisles were bisected by long benches, allowing readers to sit and study at the slanting lecterns that ran directly below the shelves. The hall was cool and still, cascades of dust glinting in the light coming in through the high Venetian windows.

"This is the *bibliotheca publica*," the Chief Librarian explained. "Here all of the books are on display, and are available for scholars to read at the lecterns."

Bernardo carefully slid one of the books off the shelf and examined the metal clasp affixed to the front cover. It was

connected by a chain to a rod running the length of the
underside of the bookshelf, providing just enough give for
the book to be placed open on the lectern.

"The chains are necessary?" asked Bernardo.

"Absolutely," Ludovico replied. "Some of these volumes
are the only edition of their kind—we cannot conjure
replacements out of the air. The theft of a single book is a
crime of unimaginable loss. At least with the chains, we can
continue to place our collection at the scholars' disposal."

Fra Bernardo stood beneath the window.

"Murano glass," he said approvingly.

"You recognize the work?"

"There were similar windows in the church where my
mother worshipped."

"You are Venetian," Ludovico said. "I wondered if I
detected an accent."

"All that remains," Bernardo replied, gazing up at the
window. "Cadenza has been my home for many years now."

From somewhere within the bookcases came a loud
harrumph. Bernardo glanced at Ludovico.

"The library is open?"

"We saw no reason to close the *bibliotheca publica*," the
librarian replied. "Our problem lies upstairs."

He padded away down the nave. As Bernardo followed
him through shelves of shackled volumes, it felt as though he
were exploring an exotic aviary: caged birds, with delicate
parchment wings. Where books had been left on the lectern,
small windows had been opened on the shelves into the
neighbouring aisles. Through one, Bernardo spied a shock
of white hair, and a brow lined with concentration; through

another, a blinking eye inspected him, only to hurriedly withdraw upon meeting his gaze.

A staircase at the back of the hall led up through an archway between two bookcases. Fra Bernardo peered up the steps.

"Where does this lead?" he asked Ludovico.

"The *bibliotheca secreta*," the librarian replied, as he began to climb. "Here we keep the books and manuscripts that are too rare or too valuable to leave open on the shelves."

"Even in chains?"

"Even so. The books in the *bibliotheca secreta* may still be loaned out to scholars, but only if they can provide a suitable letter of credentials and an item of comparable worth as security."

At the top of the stairs, a corridor came to an end at a locked door. Ludovico opened it with an iron key. The *bibliotheca secreta* was little more than a cell, unfurnished save for a row of wooden chests lining the far wall. Grey light drizzled in through a barred window near the ceiling.

"I take it the books are locked away in these," said Bernardo, gesturing at the chests.

Ludovico nodded. "Exactly so. They are maintained by the armarian, who looks after the catalogues and deals with the scholars' requests for loans."

"Oh?" Bernardo glanced around the room. "And where is he?"

Ludovico went to the chest directly beneath the window and opened the lid. Looking over the Chief Librarian's shoulder, Bernardo glimpsed a patch of naked flesh, smeared with blood.

"Here is the armarian," Ludovico said grimly.

Bernardo let out a long sigh.

"Ah," he said. "Now I understand."

II. *A Small Box of Hell*

LYING FLAT UPON his stomach, his arms resting by his sides, the armarian's body had been arranged with almost tender precision. His back was coated in dried blood, obscuring the flesh all the way from his shoulder blades to his exposed buttocks. There was no sign of the man's clothes. The room was untouched by disorder, without so much as a spot of blood or a grimy fingerprint. It was as though some diabolical force had constructed a small box of Hell and deposited it inside the *bibliotheca secreta*, before withdrawing to the netherworld to watch the bloodied eddies of its handiwork ripple out.

"His name is Silvestro," the Chief Librarian said, looking down at the corpse. "When we entered the library this morning Filippo found the room empty and went to check the chests. This was what he found."

"I see," said Bernardo. "You arrived at the same time as Filippo?"

"As we do every morning. We walk to the library together—he is my nephew."

Bernardo gave his cheek a thoughtful tap. "Have you had chance yet to see whether anything has been stolen?"

"I examined the *bibliotheca secreta's* catalogue whilst Filippo sought help. All the books are here that should be." Ludovico eyed the monk. "You suspect the work of thieves?"

"I do not know enough to suspect anything at all. The library is locked overnight?"

He nodded.

"Who has the keys?"

"Only myself and Silvestro."

"Yet there is no sign that anyone forced the door open. There is no sign of… anything."

There came a knock at the door. Filippo edged inside the room.

"Forgive me, Uncle," he said weakly. "Aquila is downstairs. He demands to know why the *bibliotheca secreta* is closed."

"Tell him we are checking our inventory," Ludovico replied shortly, "and it will be open presently."

Filippo hesitated. "He saw Fra Bernardo enter the library and has deduced that something is wrong. I can try and delay him, but it *is* Aquila…"

Ludovico massaged his temples. "Fine," he said. "Tell him what has occurred here—but you must *swear* him to secrecy. We cannot risk wild rumours spreading beyond these walls."

"And once you have finished with this impatient scholar," Bernardo added, rolling up his sleeves, "I would be grateful if you could bring me warm water and a cloth."

Filippo nodded, bolting the room with visible relief. When Bernardo crouched down beside the chest, he was greeted by a stench rising from within, a noisome curdle of blood and excreta. He forced himself to ignore it, studying the position of Silvestro's body.

"If you do not mind my saying, Fra Bernardo," Ludovico ventured, "you are dealing with this unhappy situation with admirable fortitude."

"This is not the first dead body I have encountered," Bernardo replied.

"I see." The librarian looked thoughtful. "I had wondered why the abbot had sent you in his stead. Now I think perhaps I understand."

Several minutes elapsed before Filippo reappeared in the doorway, struggling with a wooden pail filled to the brim. Bernardo dipped the cloth in the water and wrung it out. He felt the two men's eyes on him as he leant forward and began wiping the caked blood from Silvestro. The water in the pail turned crimson. As he cleaned the armarian's back, Bernardo saw that his flesh had been scored with ugly, jagged cuts. Slowly an image revealed itself: two diagonal lines intersecting one another, each topped with a loop and culminating at the base with three short lines leading off at right angles from the lower section.

Forming the sign of a pair of crossed keys.

"Lord have mercy," Ludovico muttered.

"It would have taken time to do this," said Bernardo. "Were he alive, God forbid, there would have been noise. Screams. A thief would have left the body where it fell; there is hatred in this design. Did Silvestro have enemies?"

"Enemies? No man would be capable of this!" Filippo exclaimed. "This is the work of the Dev—"

"Hush, boy!" Ludovico snapped. He knitted his eyebrows in thought. "I cannot claim to know Silvestro well—he was a Florentine, not long arrived in Cadenza. His position brought him into occasional dispute with some of the scholars, but to the best of my knowledge he was generally respected. Certainly there was no one who would wish *this* fate upon him."

"Do many scholars frequent the library?"

"We are a modest institution," Ludovico admitted. "A small purse in a city filled with treasures. There are but a handful of scholars who visit us regularly, as well as the occasional brother from your order seeking theological references."

Bernardo glanced at Filippo. "And this Aquila? He is still downstairs?"

Filippo nodded. "But he is studying. He will not take kindly to being disturbed."

"Is that so?" murmured Bernardo, drying his hands on his robe. "Then let us run the gauntlet of his disapproval together."

He left Ludovico to lock up the *bibliotheca secreta* and returned to the main hall with Filippo. The librarian led Bernardo through the aisles to a bench beneath the window, where a thin-faced man stood at the lectern. He wore the grey gown of a scholar, adorned with elaborate damask designs around the cuffs and hem. White, shoulder-length hair spilled out from beneath the four corners of a silk biretta. His eyes—small and piercing, and set above a sharp nose—were narrowed in concentration as he read.

"May I present the great Aquila," said Filippo. "One of the foremost scholars of Cadenza."

"God give you good morning," said Bernardo.

Aquila ignored him, his lips twitching with annoyance at Filippo's embarrassed cough. Only when Bernardo walked up and closed the book in front of him did the scholar look up: a cool, hard gaze.

"Forgive my interruption," Bernardo said, "but I would have a moment of your time. A man has been murdered."

"So I have learned," Aquila replied. "But I fail to see what that has to do with me."

"Silvestro was the armarian—you would have had cause to speak with him whenever you wanted a book from the *bibliotheca secreta*, would you not? You told Filippo such, this very morning. So he would have been known to you."

"The Artifex may offer a nod to the groom who saddles his horse," Aquila said archly. "Must it follow that he is acquainted with the man's habits and histories?"

Bernardo smiled. He had met men like this before. "You are a man of some stature here."

"My reputation and my patronage proceed me. Unlike some of my contemporaries, I had no need to seek Silvestro's favour."

"But others were not so blessed."

Aquila sighed. "This city has fostered the mistaken belief that the path to learning is a gentle one. Yet many of the scholars lost among these aisles would be better purposed at the lathe or the loom, or in the fields with their hand upon the till. One can only imagine the frustration that gnaws at such a labourer. The crude measures to which he must resort to further himself."

Bernardo stared at him. "You believe that a man could be so desperate to read a book he would resort to murder?"

"How far would you go to read the word of God?"

"We are not speaking of Bibles here."

"Every book is holy to me."

"That is heresy," Bernardo said quietly.

"Not in this city, it isn't—and I'd wager you know that just as well as I." Aquila reopened his volume. "Now, if you will forgive me, I must return to my work."

Filippo bobbed at Bernardo's shoulder, willing him away. Bernardo held up a finger. "One final question, if I may. The Chief Librarian says his is but a small collection. Would you agree with that assessment?"

"I could hardly disagree."

"And yet you are one of the city's foremost scholars. Why are you not at the Library Niccoló or the Accademia?"

"I have reading desks in those places also, Fra Bernardo," Aquila replied. "I came here today as I thought I would not be disturbed—erroneously, it would seem. Would your time not be better served discussing this matter with Guido? I would have thought he could provide far greater insight than I."

"Guido?" Bernardo turned to Filippo and raised an inquisitive eyebrow. "Who might that be?"

The young man coughed. "Another scholar."

Aquila snorted loudly.

"Truth be told, Guido is something of a problem," Filippo admitted in a whisper, as he led Bernardo away. "He is a choleric man, given to disagreements with the other scholars. Only last week he confronted Aquila over Ptolemy's *Tetrabiblos*, a volume he has been waiting to loan from the *secreta* for many months. When Guido found out that Silvestro had loaned Aquila the book instead, he cursed them both and stormed out of the library."

"Then I am grateful Aquila mentioned him," Bernardo said mildly. "Seeing as you did not. Do you know where I might find him?"

"I have an idea, but really, Fra, you would not be wise to go there."

"A murder has been committed. An insult to God. You would be surprised where I am willing to go."

Filippo shrugged. "Don't say I didn't warn you," he said.

III. *The Serpent's Hiss*

BEYOND THE EASTERN fringes of the Old Market, a tight passageway sloped down from the square towards the Printing Quarter. As Bernardo descended through the city, the calls and caws of the market traders faded behind him. Shabby dwellings leaned in overhead until their foreheads were almost touching, blocking out the sun. The alley's capricious twists and turns reminded him of Venice, of nights spent stealing across lonely bridges and through submerged courtyards, his cloak wrapped tightly around him and the taste of salt in the air and on his lips. Bernardo had served a different master back then: the Council of Ten had been the true rulers of Venice, lords of a shadow city of cells and secret chambers where black-mantled inquisitors went to work on those foolish enough to earn their displeasure.

The *Vigna del Signore* tavern squatted in the dregs of the alley, wreathed in the pungent fumes of a neighbouring tannery. Inside, the shutters were drawn across the windows, keeping the morning at bay. Men hunched around stunted candles, the odour of stale wine and urine draped over the room like a sour shroud. A fair-skinned tavern girl with hair the colour of straw mopped at a stain on the counter. She put down her cloth as Bernardo entered, her eyes widening at his white robes and the cross hanging around his neck.

"God give you welcome, Fra," she said. Not an Italian by

birth, Bernardo judged. "Although I fear you may have taken a wrong turning."

"Then I would be in good company," Bernardo replied, glancing around the room. "I seek a man named Guido."

She nodded over to a table in the corner, where a scholar sat nursing a bottle of wine. Bernardo offered his thanks. The girl reached out and caught the sleeve of his robe.

"Take care when you speak with him," she said, in a low undertone. "Guido has a temper."

"Then I shall endeavour to stay on his good side," Bernardo replied evenly.

He smiled and ventured deeper into the tavern, where the shadows parted reluctantly with their hold over Guido. The scholar's skin was pockmarked and his hair thinning: a young man, succumbing prematurely to the indignities of old age. He grimaced as Bernardo approached.

"What do you want?"

A sour voice, like corked wine. A sour man.

"I wish to talk with you, Guido," Bernardo said politely. "My name is Fra Bernardo. May I sit down?"

"Can I stop you?"

Bernardo took a seat on a rickety stool. Guido picked up the bottle and upended it over his glass, eking out the last drops.

"More wine, Anna!" he called out raggedly to the girl behind the counter.

She acknowledged him with an ironic curtsy and came over with a fresh bottle. Guido pushed a handful of coins across the table, his eyes pursuing Anna's hips as they returned behind the counter.

"So then, Fra," he said, pouring himself a glass. "To what do I owe the honour of your visit?"

"There was an incident at the Bibliotheca Domenico," Bernardo said. "A man is dead."

Guido nodded. "What kind of incident?" He smiled humourlessly. "What kind of man?"

"A librarian called Silvestro. He was murdered."

"Hah! The Lion of San Marco?" Guido lifted his glass and unsteadily toasted Bernardo. "Now *that* I'll drink to. Here's hoping it was a painful end."

"An unworthy sentiment. You would rejoice in another's suffering?"

"I would rejoice in the easing of my own."

"I heard there had been a disagreement with Silvestro."

"A *disagreement?*" echoed Guido incredulously. "You do not understand, Fra Bernardo. He wouldn't let me have the books I needed. How can I make my name as a scholar if he denies me the very tools of my trade? You might as well ask a carpenter to fashion a bookcase with his bare hands."

"Call it an argument, then. Sharp words exchanged. Tempers rising."

"Someone's been chirruping in your ear," Guido said, his lip curling. "Who was it, I wonder? Lorimus, ever delighted by the sound of his empty chatter? That lisping dandy Battista? Or was it Aquila, the Prince of Pomposity himself?"

Bernardo leaned forward, his voice dropping to a hiss.

"Listen to me," he said. "I take no interest in your petty scholarly disputes. This is more than that; more even, than murder. Whoever killed Silvestro took great care to make sure his body was left lying face down. You know what that means."

"His soul was destined for Hell," Guido said darkly.

"For *Hell*, Guido! Why did the killer think that? What had Silvestro done to deserve such savagery, such hatred?"

Guido leaned his head against the tavern wall. "I take it you know the Book of Matthew, Father. 16:19?"

Bernardo frowned. "*I will give you the keys of the kingdom of heaven, and whatever you bind on earth shall be bound in heaven, and whatever you loose on earth shall be loosed in heaven.* The words of Our Lord Jesus to Simon Peter. But how does that concern Silvestro?"

"St Peter would become the gatekeeper of Heaven, would he not? Now, imagine a world where the Devil has his ear."

The curtain over the cellar doorway shivered, a cool draught blowing on the back of Bernardo's neck. In his mind's eye, he saw a chest yawn open inside the *bibliotheca secreta*, revealing the image of a pair of crossed keys sliced into a man's back.

He shook his head. "Are you saying this because Silvestro let Aquila have the *Tetrabiblos*?"

A reedy laugh escaped from Guido's mouth. "You know nothing," he said. "A blind man stumbling around a maze on a moonless night."

"Then why don't you enlighten me," Bernardo said sharply, "instead of talking in riddles? Or must I wait until you are sober?"

"I will not have you judge me!" Guido snapped. Flushed, he grabbed the bottle by the neck and held it up before Bernardo. "This wine was made from grapes grown by *your* beloved abbey; this bottle brought directly from your cellars. How often have I seen Fra Cecco in here, toasting to his health and eyeing up the wenches?" He jabbed a finger towards the door. "The name of the bloody tavern is The Lord's Vine!"

"It is no sin to make wine; it is no sin to drink a glass, either. The sin lies in the over-indulgence."

Guido laughed. "Says the swordsmith to the killer, as he hands him a blade." He slumped back into the shadows. "And I have nothing more to say to you."

Bernardo bowed his head and rose from his stool. Throughout his exchange with Guido, Anna had been watching them with open curiosity. The tavern girl raised an eyebrow as Bernardo returned to the counter.

"Did you find what you were looking for, Fra?" she inquired.

"No answers. Only more questions. How long has he been here?"

"Upon our door opening. He was already in his cups then. The Lord knows how long he's been drinking."

Bernardo nodded. The cutting of the armarian would have required a calm eye and steady hands, neither of which the choleric young scholar possessed—at least at this moment. Had Silvestro been found with his skull caved in and the chests ransacked of their books, then perhaps... unless Guido's drunkenness were an act, of course. Was he capable of such deception?

"You look troubled," Anna said. "A glass of wine to ease your pains?"

Bernardo shook his head. "Alas, I cannot. But I gather there are other members of my order who are happy to partake here."

"Fra Cecco, you mean? He is harmless enough, though his hands are busier than I would prefer." She gave him a look of artful shyness. "I bruise easily, Fra."

Bernardo reddened. "I am grateful for your assistance, child," he coughed. "God be with you."

He made for the tavern door and went out into the alley, careful not to look back.

IV. *A Momentary Twinge*

THE WIND TAUNTED Bernardo as he walked through the grounds of the abbey, ruffling his hair and tugging at his robe. The sun was a fugitive among frowning clouds. There had been a time, he could own, when the morning's discoveries would have given him a certain macabre thrill, but now his stomach was complaining, and he was still searching for his breath from the climb up the Via Arezzo. He had been hoping to return in time for *Terce*, but as Bernardo neared the chapel, he saw that his brothers had already departed the pews. The knowledge that he had missed a service left him feeling strangely unmoored, an empty rowboat drifting upon the tide.

"Fra Bernardo!"

Thaddeus was hastening through the vegetables, struggling to keep pace with Abbot Marsilio's loping stride.

"My lord Abbot," said Bernardo. "Thaddeus."

The abbot gravely inclined his head.

"You have visited the library?" Thaddeus asked.

"I have."

"The boy Filippo was correct?" His voice dropped. "There has been a murder?"

Bernardo nodded. "Of a most brutal and inexplicable nature."

"But this is terrible!" the amanuensis exclaimed. "What possible reason could a man have for killing a librarian?"

"I cannot say," Bernardo replied. "There was a wound on Silvestro's back, purposefully shaped to form a pair of crossed keys. It could refer to the books he kept locked in his chests, or to St Peter himself. One of the scholars implied that Silvestro was somehow abusing his position."

"You were sent to the library to find a killer," Thaddeus said primly, "not to blacken the name of the victim."

"I cannot find *who* committed this crime without knowing *why*."

"Fra Bernardo, we are all aware that you have certain... experiences that may assist you in the investigation of this matter. But please remember that our institutions share their founder and are forever entwined. The reputation of the Bibliotheca Domenico reflects upon the abbey, and vice versa."

"Then let us hope that we are all behaving in a manner befitting God's grace," Bernardo replied. "This morning I was told that Fra Cecco has been making merry in a Printing Quarter tavern."

"Have care, brother," Thaddeus warned. "The Master of the Cellars is one of our most respected brothers. Our burgeoning vineyards stand testament to his craft."

"So long as it only grapes he is plucking, and not tavern girls."

The amanuensis gasped, his cheeks turning pink with

indignation. Marsilio silenced him with a wave of the hand, shooting Bernardo a look of wry disapproval as he walked away through the apple trees. For once, Thaddeus didn't give chase. He waited until his superior had passed out of earshot before rounding on Bernardo.

"This is no matter for jest," he snapped. "The abbot may see fit to indulge you, but do not think that every brother shares his faith in your abilities, or your judgement. Resist the urge to delve into matters of an ungodly nature."

"I can try," Bernardo said evenly. "But if you would have me look for a murderer, I am unlikely to find him if I am only allowed to search the heavens."

"You think that evil cannot tread in holy halls? In my youth, I saw foul devils creep forth at night to sow doubt and temptations amongst my brothers as they prayed—and heard their screams and sizzling flesh, under the reproach of a righteous rain."

"I too have seen the Devil at work. And without a righteous rain to fight it."

"Then you understand the need to conclude your business as swiftly as possible."

Bernardo spread out his palms. "It has been a matter of hours, Thaddeus! I am working as quickly as—Aah!"

He bent double, gasping for breath.

"Fra Bernardo! Whatever is wrong?"

He was aware of Thaddeus's consoling hand on his shoulder. It felt as though someone had driven a sword deep into his belly, white-hot pain slicing through him.

"A momentary twinge," Bernardo said, through gritted teeth. "It is of no concern."

"Forgive me, brother, but it would seem more than a twinge," said Thaddeus. "Should we summon the infirmarian?"

"No, no," he replied quickly.

"It is no trouble, I really think—"

Bernardo forced himself to stand upright.

"You see?" he said, with a strained smile. "I am fine. Thank you for your concern, brother."

He stared at Thaddeus until the other man nodded.

"As you wish," he said gravely.

Bernardo watched, silently cursing himself, as the amanuensis headed off towards the scriptorium. Were tongues not wagging enough as it was, without him collapsing amongst the vegetables? He had told no one, not even Fra Matteo the infirmarian, about the lump lodged in his gut like a small cannonball of pain. Yet still Bernardo caught his brothers' subtle glances at the leftovers piling up in his bowl at mealtimes, heard the sympathy in their voices when they inquired about his health. Now the monks in his eyeline were careful to focus on their digging and picking. Lurid rumours of Bernardo's past had earned him a certain reputation he had done little to quell.

The leaves on the apple trees shivered in the wind. A hailing shout carried across the grounds. Bernardo turned, to see a young novitiate hastening up the path towards him.

"What is it?" he called out irritably.

"Forgive me, Fra Bernardo," the boy replied, breathlessly. "But there is someone who wishes to speak with you."

* * *

246

V. *Pork and Cabbage*

A LITTER WAS waiting for Bernardo outside the abbey gates, taking him south across Ponte Mercato to the Verso, where a small palace perched comfortably on the banks of the Adige. Upon stepping down from the carriage, an attendant directed him through the courtyards to a pergola at the rear of the building. Bernardo walked along the vine-tangled path and emerged on to a sunlit terrace, where he found Aquila seated at a table looking out over the river. A small glass of wine was set on the table before him. At the sight of Bernardo, the scholar smiled.

"Thank you for coming, Fra. Please, join me."

Bernardo sat down stiffly, shaking his head when Aquila offered to pour him a drink. The long journey in the litter had done little for his stomach, the peremptory nature of Aquila's summons even less for his mood.

"You wished to see me."

"A fine view, is it not?" Aquila declared, gesturing out across the river.

"Most pleasant."

"Not the canals of your Venice, perhaps, but not without its own charm."

Bernardo gave the scholar a sideways glance. "Librarians like to talk, it would seem."

"Voices do carry, and libraries are such *quiet* places," Aquila said slyly. "You would be amazed at the things you can hear. The morsels and tidbits."

"No doubt," Bernardo replied coolly. "I can only hope that one of these tidbits concerned Silvestro. It is a long journey from the abbey."

Aquila traced a finger around the rim of his glass.

"I have had chance to think further since our previous conversation," he said. "I wonder whether I could be of more use to you."

"You could hardly be less."

"I sent you to Guido, did I not? Was your conversation a fruitful one?"

"Not how I would describe it."

He nodded. "Alas. Increasingly the case."

"Does he possess scholarly gifts—Guido?"

"Perhaps, beneath the bluster and the fog of drink. But a scholar's life requires utter dedication, a singleness of purpose that excludes all other distractions—be they women or wine, family or friends." Aquila steepled his fingers together. "I suppose a man of holy orders would understand."

"Guido seemed cheered by the news of Silvestro's death," Bernardo said. "He implied that something was amiss at the library."

Aquila took a considered sip of wine. "As a Venetian, you will know the story of the relics of St Mark."

"Naturally."

"During the Abbasids' reign over Alexandria, a pair of merchants travelled to the city and found the saint's remains in a church sarcophagus. In order to remove the relics from the Saracens' clutches, they smuggled them on board a ship bound to Venice, hidden in chests beneath layers of pork and cabbage…"

"…so that the Saracens would be unable to search the chests and find the relics. It is an old story."

Aquila gazed steadily at Fra Bernardo over his glass.

"Are you suggesting that there were other things in the chests of the *bibliotheca secreta*?" he asked the scholar. "Things that might move a man to kill another?"

"Things as precious as a saint's relics."

"Such as what?"

"What do you think, Fra? It *is* a library."

Bernardo frowned. "But Ludovico told me that no books were missing from the catalogue."

"And as far as he knew, none were," Aquila replied. "The Chief Librarian is the very model of probity. Alas, the same could not be said for Silvestro. In Florence, as a young man, he fell under the sway of Friar Savonarola and was cloistered at the convent San Marco—ah, Savonarola was a member of your brotherly order, was he not?"

"He was a Dominican, as I am sure you know," Bernardo said carefully. "He was also denounced and burned at the stake, as you are also well aware."

"True, true. When the city turned on Savonarola and laid siege to San Marco, Silvestro was one of its last defenders. Or so he liked to tell people."

"The Lion of San Marco, Riccardo called him."

"With characteristic wit. Now, I need not tell you that, under Savonarola, gangs of young men had taken to the streets of Florence to purge the city of objects deemed sinful vanities: mirrors and musical instruments, playing cards and dice. But more than just trinkets were thrown on to the fire in Savonarola's name. Your brothers burned statues and priceless works of art; books, even..."

"It was another time, another city. What does any of this

have to do with the Bibliotheca Domenico?"

"You may take the man out of Florence, but a Florentine and a merchant he will always remain," Aquila declared. "Silvestro had been given an early lesson in the value of the forbidden. By the time he arrived at Cadenza, he had amassed a collection of his own books, which were not included in the official catalogue of the *bibliotheca secreta*. These volumes were of such value that just to glimpse them would require additional payment beyond the items presented as security."

"Payment that would go to Silvestro alone."

"Naturally."

"What kind of volumes would these be?"

"Texts that, for one reason or another, the church in its wisdom deems better placed beyond the reach of human eyes—irrespective of the judicious use to which a learned scholar might put such a volume. And if the reading of such forbidden texts required the handing over of valuable items to the armarian..."

"...then those items would also not appear in the catalogue," Bernardo finished. "And might also be missing."

"That would seem a plausible summation."

"And might it be possible that *you* gave Silvestro something in order to read one of these books?"

On the river, a swan took to the air with a powerful beat of its wings. Aquila smiled thinly.

"So you believe this deed to have been the work of a thief, after all," Bernardo said. "Silvestro was killed for the valuables laid down for these forbidden books?"

"The workings of the criminal mind are beyond my fathoming," Aquila replied, with a shrug. "That task appears to have fallen on your shoulders. One can only hope that they prove broad enough. I heard that the grisly contents of the *bibliotheca secreta* left you quite unmoved. What manner of monk are you?"

"I was not always a monk," Bernardo said.

"Evidently. Savonarola maintained that a human's life is a soldier's life: a war of the soul to overcome sin and gain entrance to Heaven. I wonder which battlefields you have seen."

"Are they not all alike, if it comes to that?"

"A Venetian who has fought and is reluctant to speak of it," Aquila mused. "It could only be Agnadello."

Bernardo shifted uncomfortably in his seat. The scholar clapped his hands together with delight.

"I am correct! How satisfying!... Come now, Fra, do not scowl so. You have nothing to fear. Unlike librarians, I know how to keep a secret."

"Comforting to know," Bernardo murmured.

As he went to rise from the table, Aquila stayed his hand.

"Fra Bernardo?" he asked lightly. "Should you come across a silver chalice decorated with angels around its stem in the course of your investigations, do please remember this conversation, and my humble attempts to assist you."

Bernardo nodded abruptly. He walked off the sun-dappled terrace, leaving Aquila to finish his wine alone, a smile of amusement playing across the scholar's lips.

* * *

VI. *Vigil*

FROM THE SHADOWS beneath a listing stone pine on the Via dei Lucchesi, Bernardo kept watch over the Bibliotheca Domenico. The door opened only sporadically—over the course of several hours, he had counted just five scholars and a monk passing in or out of the library. Back when he had served the Ten in Venice, Bernardo would have thought nothing of such a vigil, yet now his calves and lower back ached. The encounter with Aquila had left him brooding with irritation: taunts about Savonarola were one thing, but Bernardo had not been prepared for unwanted memories of Agnadello to be ransacked from the locked chests of his mind.

Nor did he feel closer to achieving the purpose of his mission, to uncover the truth behind the armarian's murder. According to Aquila, Silvestro had been a follower of Savonarola in Florence, yet the Friar had railed against the very profane works he had gone on to collect. How far had Silvestro strayed from the teachings of his former master? Could it truly be that he had incurred the wrath of Hell, and paid for it with not only his life, but his eternal soul?

It was raining by the time Filippo emerged, shooting a nervous look up and down the street as his uncle locked the library door behind him. Bernardo allowed them a few seconds' head-start before following, careful to keep to the lengthening shadows as they headed for the Via Tribunali. Now that his quarry was in sight, a calmness had come over him, as though he were enacting the steps of an old and familiar dance. At the Old Market, the two librarians parted:

Filippo bid Ludovico farewell before scurrying down the Via della Pergola towards the river. Bernardo cut down an alley to head him off. He came out into an empty courtyard and positioned himself behind a colonnade. Presently, footsteps echoed around the arcade. Bernardo waited until the last moment before stepping out in front of Filippo, who threw up his arms with a startled cry.

"Fra Bernardo!" he exclaimed. "What are you doing here? I thought you were a thief!"

"I am no thief, though it is a thief I seek," he replied calmly. "I wished to ask you about Silvestro's books. The ones he kept hidden from the catalogue."

Filippo blinked. "What books? I don't understand."

"Allow me to enlighten you. There were other books in the *bibliotheca secreta* that Silvestro kept hidden from Ludovico, texts forbidden by the church. Silvestro was loaning them out to scholars in exchange for money."

"Forgive me, I have no idea what you are talking about," Filippo said, with a nervous laugh. "If I may pass…"

Bernardo placed a palm in front of his chest. "I am afraid I must insist," he said. "You have been dancing around like a cat with scalded paws since I met you. At first, I thought it was just the shock of Silvestro's murder, but now I suspect it was more than that. You were worried about what I might find out."

"Have you taken leave of your senses? Let me pass, Fra!"

"By all means, carry on your way," Bernardo told him. "But eventually you will have to answer me. A single word from my abbot is all it will take to convene a special council of the Folio, and they have ways of prising words from reluctant lips. Do not be surprised if Ludovico is brought in for questioning alongside you."

"My uncle? But he has done nothing!"

"Then talk to me now, while I can still protect him. Yours would not be the first sins I have heard."

Filippo gnawed on his lip. Whether or not the abbot could in fact convene a special council of the Folio was a matter for debate, but the threat was all that mattered. In windowless rooms below the water's edge in Venice, Bernardo had learned much about a man's character under pressure. He judged the librarian a weak man, a soft fruit needing little squeezing.

"I will tell you what you wish to know," Filippo said finally, "but you must swear to keep it from my uncle. Silvestro had arranged to meet a man in the library the night he was killed, regarding the loan of a book from the *bibliotheca secreta.*"

"Who?" Bernardo demanded.

"I knew better than to ask. Silvestro offered no names, only the title of the volume."

"Which was?"

Filippo went silent. Losing patience, Bernardo seized the startled librarian by the tunic and dragged him beneath the arcade, slamming him up against the wall.

"Tell me, Filippo, or I swear to God, I'll beat it from you."

"You wouldn't dare! You're a monk!"

Bernardo opened his hand and slapped him across the face.

"You have no idea what I am," he said. "What was the book?"

"Fra, no!"

He struck him again. "What was it?"

"*Picatrix*!"

An anguished cry echoed around the courtyard. Filippo slid to the ground, his head in his hands. Bernardo's palm was stinging. He dropped to his haunches beside the librarian.

"I know nothing of this book," he said. "Tell me about it."

"It is a grimoire," Filippo replied miserably. "A compendium of Arab magic. It came to Europe along the caravan trail, promising those who dared open it the secrets of the planets and the arts of reanimating the dead. A book so dangerous that its very printing has been forbidden for over a century."

"And yet, thanks to Silvestro, it found its way to the Bibliotheca Domenico."

"He had spent years collecting volumes on the dark arts, grimoires and their ilk, books no other librarian would touch. When I joined the library, he took me into his confidence and told me all about them. I saw the *Book of Honorius* with my own eyes, and I heard Aquila boasting that he had borrowed a copy of the *Key of Solomon*. Why else do you think he patronizes our library? It is a backwater, ignored even by the Folio: the perfect hiding place."

"Ludovico knew nothing of this?"

Filippo shook his head. "There is a loose stone behind one of the chests in the *secreta*. Silvestro kept his volumes hidden there, along with the valuables he was given as payment and security. My uncle has no idea of its existence. I checked after you left the library—all the books were there, save for *Picatrix*. The valuables, too."

"Including a silver chalice, I believe," Bernardo said. "And have these valuables now passed into your possession?"

Filippo stared at him. "Do you think I am mad?"

"Why else keep quiet?"

"I saw what happened to Silvestro. I have no wish to suffer the same fate."

"Then help me catch his murderer."

Filippo laughed weakly. "Do you really think this murderer can be *caught*, Fra Bernardo? You think him a man of flesh and blood? What kind of man could carve another's back like that, treat flesh like parchment? Open your eyes!" His voice dropped to a whisper. "Silvestro spent his life collecting the Devil's books. Now the Devil has come to take them back."

It had started to rain, grey lines slanting down through the courtyard's lengthening shadows. Filippo gazed defiantly back at Bernardo. He rose and began to pace up and down, his brow knitted in thought.

"Let us assume that the murderer took this *Picatrix*," he mused. "Would one forbidden volume be enough to satisfy him? Or does he also desire the *Key of Solomon*, and the rest?"

"I should have burned them when I had the chance," Filippo said. "But I could not bring myself to do it. Cursed they may be, but they are still books."

"The pride that this city takes in its volumes," Bernardo murmured, shaking his head. "It is a sin."

"You would tell me this, Fra? I have seen men come to blows over a single book, tearing pages from each other's hands; esteemed scholars who think nothing of lies and outrageous slander against their rivals in the hope of moving ahead of them. When Guido found out there was a copy of *Picatrix* in the library, he was so desperate to read it he offered Silvestro his own finger in exchange. Silvestro laughed in his face. He took pleasure in refusing Guido."

"*How can I make my name as a scholar, if he denies me the very tools of my trade?*" Guido had complained, back in the tavern. All he had wanted was access to the *bibliotheca secreta*, but the armarian had stood in his way. Only now, of course, Silvestro was dead...

Bernardo marched over to Filippo and hauled him to his feet.

"What are you doing?" Filippo cried.

"You have a key to the library, do you not? Then let us hurry, and pray we are not too late."

VII. *The Ordinary Compass*

WHEN HAD BERNARDO last had cause to run? As a hot-headed youth, lost in sin, he had made hasty exits from rowdy taverns and ladies' bedchambers; in the service of the Ten, he had swooped along moonlit canals in pursuit of the city's enemies. Then there had been Agnadello—the desperate, slippery flight down from the ridge above the vineyards, Frenchman on all sides, his countrymen lying dead and bleeding and Alviano taken at sword point. No option left but to run, and to pray that the horror he had witnessed on the battlefield would not give chase.

He had been a different man back then, a younger man. Now Bernardo laboured through the rain-lashed streets, his lungs filled with fire and his hand pressed against the painful stitch in his side. Somehow, he had managed to leave Filippo behind him, but as Bernardo turned into the Via dei Lucchesi and the Bibliotheca Domenico loomed through the storm, he saw he did not need him. The entrance was wide open.

He hurried up the steps and along the atrium, leaving glistening footprints upon the marbled floor. At the threshold to the *bibliotheca publica*, Bernardo stopped and leaned against the doorframe, his gasping breaths swallowed up by the darkness. He wiped the rain from his face. Books huddled against one another in the shadows as the wind hurled spiteful handfuls of rain against the windows. Draughts toyed with rustling links of chain. At the far end of the nave, where the night was at its thickest, there was a faint glow.

"Guido?" Bernardo called out.

Lost in the lonely reaches of the reading room, the light had taken on an eerie, unsettling quality. Bernardo had never been superstitious: even as a child, the shadows beneath his bed had held no terrors. Yet, as he ventured towards the illuminated aisle, he was seized by a nameless dread—not normal fear as he knew it, herald of danger or pain, but a warning from some unknowable place beyond the ordinary compass of man. Each step became an effort of will. Where in God's name was Filippo? Creeping to the edge of the shadows, Bernardo pressed himself against a column and peered around the corner.

The aisle was lit by a single candle, a slender, twisting flame on the lectern. Guido's body hung upside-down from the bookshelves, tangled up in chains like a fly caught in an iron web. His head was suspended above the ground, his mouth open in a silent scream and gore running down from the two black pits where his eyes should have been. Bernardo stumbled back, gorge rising in his throat.

At the far end of the aisle, the shadows shifted to reveal a pale face.

"Lord preserve us!" gasped Filippo. "What horror is this?"

He slumped to a reading bench with a wail, crossing himself and stammering a prayer.

"Be quiet, man!" Bernardo snapped. He massaged the bridge of his nose. "I need to think."

The aisle lapsed into wounded silence. Inching around Guido's butchered remains, Bernardo retrieved the candle from the lectern. He bullied Filippo to his feet.

"We must leave this place, Fra," the librarian whispered, clutching at his arm. "Before the Devil turns its wrathful gaze upon us!"

Bernardo shook his head. "Not before we have checked upstairs."

The shadows crowded threateningly around them as Bernardo marched the reluctant Filippo out of the aisle and up the staircase at the back of the hall. The door to the *bibliotheca secreta* stood ajar. Inside, the armarian's chests had been overturned and pulled away from the walls, revealing a small recess in the corner of the cell. Filippo peered nervously into the darkness.

"Well?" said Bernardo.

"All gone," Filippo told him. "Treasures and volumes both. The *Book of Honorius*, the *Key of Solomon*... the Devil has reclaimed its own."

Bernardo brought his fist down on the nearest chest, his knuckles biting painfully into the wood. He turned on his heel and strode out of the room. Trembling with fear and anger and frustration, he felt an overwhelming urge to hurl his candle into the shelves. Let this library of blighted volumes burn, and the Devil find some new home for his murderous games!

Outside, above the growing storm, he heard Filippo call after him from the doorway.

"Where are you going, Fra Bernardo?"

"To Hell!" he shouted back.

The ground churned up at his passing, mud splattering his robe. At the Old Market, instead of turning up the Via Arezzo towards the abbey, Bernardo marched across the empty square and disappeared down the alleyway that led into the Printing Quarter. He almost missed the turning for the *Vigna del Signore*, the tavern sunk deep in darkness. Flat, unfriendly gazes greeted his entrance. Bernardo ignored them. A pair of Frenchmen were playing cards at the table Guido had occupied earlier that day—he took a seat at the next table, as Anna came hurriedly out from behind the counter.

"Why, Fra, you are drenched!" she exclaimed. "It is no night to be walking the streets."

"I will take wine, if I may," Bernardo said, breathing heavily.

"If you are looking for Guido, he left here several hours ago," Anna told him, pouring him a glass. "And in no better humour than when he arrived."

"Did anyone else speak to him, after I left?"

She shook her head, leaving him with the bottle. Bernardo's hand shook as he raised the glass to his lips; he took a deep sip. Blessed relief, delivered from the cellars of his own abbey. He should be there now, he knew, reporting Guido's murder to Abbot Marsilio. Filippo could not be trusted to do the right thing, and with the disappearance of both the forbidden texts and the valuables, no trace remained of Silvestro's illicit dealings. Aquila would have to find his own chalice, Bernardo thought to himself, with a hint of sour amusement.

He poured himself a fresh glass, which vanished as quickly as the first, and after it a third. How else to make sense of the inexplicable? Two men, now, had been murdered. Guido had somehow found his way inside the library, yet both keys now resided with Ludovico, whom all seemed to agree was a good man. There had been no sign of a break-in, which left only two possibilities that Bernardo could think of: that there was a third key somewhere, or that the murderer had no need for one, and could come and go at will...

"Why, Fra Bernardo! I had not thought I would see you here."

The voice, thin and reedy, was instantly recognisable. Bernardo looked up to see Fra Cecco standing by his table. The old man was shrivelled up in a set of voluminous white robes, his eyes turning milky, skin wrinkled as a spoiled grape.

"God give you good evening, Fra Cecco," he said cordially. "I understand that you are no stranger here."

The old man puffed out his chest. "As Master of the Cellars, it is my duty to oversee the journey of our abbey's wine. From grape to bottle to glass."

"An admirable dedication to your craft. Sit, brother. Share my table."

As Fra Cecco settled himself upon the stool, Anna appeared at his shoulder with a fresh glass.

"I am glad you have company," she told Bernardo pointedly. "You appear to have worked up quite a thirst."

"Why, gentle Anna, it is no sin to drink a glass," he replied merrily. "The sin lies in the over-indulgence!"

She shook her head and returned to the counter, taking care to skirt beyond the reach of the Master of the Cellars. He cackled and turned back to Bernardo.

"You are the talk of the abbey, brother," he said. "It is said that Abbot Marsilio has entrusted you with a task of great importance."

Bernardo grunted, and took another swig of wine.

"I heard about the armarian's death. Silvestro came to this tavern also, you know."

"Is that so?"

"We shared a table from time to time. The occasional hand of cards. The Lion of San Marco! What heroic tales he would weave, when deep in his cups! And never the same story each time."

"You did not believe him?"

"What do I care what happened in Florence, a quarter-century ago?"

"Sometimes the truths of the past can shed light upon the mysteries of the present." Bernardo filled his glass. "Go on, brother."

"If Silvestro were to be believed, the monks of San Marco did battle with a darker foe than their fellow citizens," Fra Cecco confided. "Before Florence turned on them, the convent was besieged by demons and monstrous beasts, riotous and foul-mouthed, who disturbed their night-time prayers. Gangs of Ethiopians lay in ambush for them as they walked alone and beat them about the head. The brothers fought them off with psalms and holy water."

"Psalms and holy water," Bernardo repeated thoughtfully. "Did he make mention of spell books?"

The old man shook his head.

"What of the volumes of the Bibliotheca Domenica?"

"If he did, I did not listen. My eyes are failing me, brother. I save them not for the written word but for things of beauty, that a memory may cherish long after the sight has failed."

He sipped his wine and cast a sidelong glance at Anna as she leant over to serve the Frenchmen, snickering with delight.

"Remember yourself, brother," Bernardo told him. "The eye of God is on this place, just as it is any other."

"Why, forgive me!" Fra Cecco exclaimed. "I had not realized that the abbot's mission was to defend a tavern girl's chastity." He grinned slyly. "Unless temptation has waylaid you in the course of duty."

Bernardo's expression darkened. "This day has left me in a strange humour," he said, in a low voice. "It would be wise not to mistake my mood."

"I seek no quarrel with you, Bernardo. I shall leave you. Perhaps, for a coin or two, Mary Magdalene will anoint your toes—or any other tip you might proffer her."

Bernardo lunged across the table and smacked Fra Cecco's glass from his hand, spraying the neighbouring table with wine. The old man squealed as he went sprawling from his chair. With a snarl, the Frenchmen sprang from their seats— Bernardo turned and swung at the nearest, catching him a glancing blow before his companion struck Bernardo in the jaw. The Vigna del Signore danced and spun; he heard a woman's scream and Fra Cecco wail and then he was falling, a dizzying plummet into nothingness.

VIII. *Agnadello*

BERNARDO AWOKE TO find himself lying on a bed in a small chamber beneath the eaves. Anna's concerned face hovered above him. Though still numbed with wine, his jaw throbbed where he had been struck. He would feel worse, he knew, before he felt better.

"Where am I?" Bernardo mumbled.

"In my room above the tavern." Anna pursed her lips. "I offered your surrender to the enemy, and they granted me leave to remove the wounded from the battlefield."

He closed his eyes, running his tongue over dry lips. "I am a foolish old man who does not deserve such consideration. Forgive me, child."

"You frightened me! In the morning you appear to me as a wise man of the cloth; in the evening, a rowdy poet come Carnival time. Whatever possessed you?"

"Guido is dead," Bernardo said hoarsely. "I found his body before I came here. A great violence had been wrought upon it."

Anna paled. "Fra! How terrible! It was only this morning that I saw him... Guido was not a kind man, I know, but he did not deserve this. Who would have done such a thing?"

"I do not know. I think I came here because I was fearful of what the truth might be. To seek refuge at the bottom of a bottle."

"Or at the end of a Frenchman's fist."

"A quicker route to oblivion," he agreed. He gingerly touched his jaw. "Though more painful besides."

Anna shook her head. "Never before have I seen a monk strike a man."

"Not all of my life has been spent in the chapel," Bernardo told her. "I was a very different man before I found God."

"What sort of man?"

"A loyal servant of Venice who took up arms in its name: first as an agent for the Council of Ten, then as a solider. Military orders were my gospels. But then came Agnadello."

She gave him a questioning look.

"Of course," he said ruefully. "You are too young: the name would mean nothing to you. There was a time when Venice's power earned it the enmity of the League of Cambrai, which resolved to break up its empire and seize its lands. An army of Frenchmen under their King Louis crossed the Adda, and Venice sent an army of its own to meet them. It was led by two cousins, Aviano and Pitigliano. I served under Aviano. When our rearguard came under attack from the French, he ordered that we go to their assistance. We took a stand on a ridge overlooking the vineyards of Agnadello. At first our forces beat them back, but then their reinforcements arrived: Swiss pikemen, sharp-tipped grey waves stretching as far as the eye could see. Aviano appealed to his cousin for help, but Pitigliano kept marching south. What followed was a massacre."

"How did you escape?" asked Anna. "Did God save you?"

Bernardo shook his head. "There was no God that day, child," he said. "Only the Devil. Through the smoke and the screams, I saw him—a demon striding across the battlefield, revelling in the anguish of men, and succoured by the blood soaking the earth. I dropped my sword and ran for my life. Through blind chance, I managed to get down from the ridge and sneak through the French lines. Four thousand Venetians were slaughtered that day, their corpses littering the countryside like dead dogs. I kept running, roaming from town to town like a vagabond. When I reached Cadenza, the sound of the bells drew me up the Via Arezzo… and there I saw the abbey. I have remained there ever since. Until today, I fancied that the Devil had forgotten about me. What a fool I am."

"Are you saying you believe that the Devil killed Guido?"

"If it is not the Devil at work in the Bibliotheca Domenico, then it is a soul which has abandoned itself to the purest evil. I am not sure there is a difference."

Anna placed her hand upon his shoulder. "Whatever it is you must face," she said solemnly. "You have the strength and the heart to overcome it."

He eyed her ruefully. "You believe that? Even after this night?"

"Even so."

Bernardo lay his hand upon hers for a moment before rising. His head was starting to ache, and he could feel the wine swilling unhappily around his belly. He rubbed his face.

"I must return to the abbey before morning prayers. The abbot will be expecting me."

"You look pale, Fra," Anna said. "Are you sure you are all right?"

"I am fine," he said firmly. "I must go."

"Will I see you again?"

"I hope so. If you do not, you may know that the Devil has caught up with me."

"Then I shall pray for your safe return."

Bernardo slipped down the stairs and out of the tavern. Although the storm had subsided, the heavy rain had turned the Printing Quarter into a series of treacherous channels. Lost in the pitch-black alleys, Bernardo had to feel his way blindly along the walls, his sandals sticking in the mire. Rounding a corner, he slipped and fell heavily, banging his knee against a stone. He muttered an oath and hauled himself back to his feet.

Just when he was starting to lose hope that he might ever escape the labyrinth, the queasily leaning buildings above his head drew back and Bernardo emerged out on to the Old Market. He stumbled across the square and up the Via Arezzo, where the abbey's forbidding silhouette awaited him.

IX. *The Offices of God*

THE MOON SLID out from behind the bell tower as Bernardo entered the abbey, tracing a pale figure over the puddle-strewn pathways and the glistening apple trees, and up to the dormant windows of the monks' quarters. Bernardo's stomach was churning, a sea beset by violent storms. He fixed his gaze on the chapel doors, seeking a steady point as the world heaved and swam. Stumbling up the steps, he fell to his knees in the aisle. His guts rose up to meet him, and for a terrible moment he thought he was going to be sick. He took a series of slow, deep breaths, his lips moving in a silent invocation.

Gradually, his nausea subsided, allowing Bernardo to take a seat among the pews. His robes were splattered with mud and he was cloaked in a pungent musk of wine and sweat. The first service of the day would soon be upon them—he could not allow his brothers to see him like this. Bernardo had descended as far into the troughs of sin as he could; he would tell Abbot Marsilio that he had failed in his mission and request that he be allowed to resume his normal duties. He would swallow his pride and see if the infirmarian could help ease his stomach pains. And he would pray to God for forgiveness for the grave sins he had committed.

As Bernardo rubbed his face with his hands, moonlight seeped in through the chapel window, catching upon a silver chalice set on the altar.

A flap of wings on the river. A sun-dappled terrace.

Do please remember this conversation, and my humble attempts to assist you.

He stared at the chalice in disbelief. The shadows inside the chapel took on an insidious hue as he rose and slowly approached the altar. Picking up the chalice, he turned it over in his hands, which began to shake at the touch of the winged angels carved in relief around the silver stem. Just as Aquila had described. The sheer brazenness of it was almost unthinkable. And yet... who knew of the cup's significance, beyond Aquila, Bernardo and the killer himself? And with that thought came another, even more unsettling. Could it be that the chalice had been placed here expressly for Bernardo to see? Was the Devil's gaze upon him, even now?

Bernardo's footsteps echoed around the empty pews as he hurried out of the chapel, clutching the chalice tight to his chest. The moon had fled behind the clouds, leaving him to cut across the quadrangle in darkness. He ducked through the archway that led to the scriptorium and climbed a narrow flight of steps. At the third floor, he beat loudly upon a door with his fist. Footsteps hastened within. The door flew open.

"Fra Bernardo?" said Thaddeus. "What is the meaning of this? We were expecting you hours ago!"

"I must speak with the abbot."

"Now? It is the middle of the night! He is asleep."

"Then let us wake him. Look, Thaddeus!" Bernardo held up the chalice. "I thought it was the Devil at work, but it was vanity; blind, stupid vanity. The murderer left this in the chapel so that I might know him, he walks among us, in these very hallways!"

"Calm yourself, brother!" scolded Thaddeus. "You are talking like a man possessed. Why, look at your robe, it is filthy!"

"Forget my damned robe! There was another murder tonight at the library: a scholar, hung upside down and his eyes cut out. He was trying to find illicit volumes that Silvestro had been secretly loaning out. This chalice was one of the treasures used to secure such a book! Who else but the killer could have left it here?"

Thaddeus furrowed his brow. Glancing along the corridor, he ushered Bernardo inside his study. It was a cluttered chamber with piles of books upon the desk and shelves. By the window, a pair of candles burned in sconces either side of a reading lectern. Bernardo laid down the chalice on the desk and rubbed his side.

"This cannot work unless there is another key to the

Bibliotheca Domenico," he told Thaddeus. "Is it possible that there is another, here in the abbey?"

"Our institutions are grapes growing upon the same vine," Thaddeus replied. "Naturally, Abbot Marsilio has a key to the library. But you cannot suspect that he would know anything about this!"

"I do not know what to think. The truth of this matter is so mired in sin that I will consider it no longer. Please, Thaddeus, give the abbot this chalice and tell him what I have found. I cannot walk this path any further."

The amanuensis pursed his lips. "You disappoint me, brother. We may not see eye to eye, but I have never had cause to doubt your courage, your steadfastness in the face of adversity. Do you so readily propose to walk away from the battlefield? Is it not true that a human's life is also—"

"A soldier's life."

The two men stared at one another.

"Why, Bernardo!" Thaddeus exclaimed. "You should spend more time in the library. I had not thought that you were aware of such wisdoms."

"I remain no scholar," Bernardo told him. "But those very same words were spoken to me earlier this day, by a scholar keen to share his great wisdom. They were first uttered by the Friar Savonarola, were they not?"

"Perhaps. Does it matter?"

Bernardo barely heard him. Sunlight brightened the corners of Thaddeus's study, water lapping at his ankles. He had been returned to the blessed lagoon of his morning's vision in the chapel. Light as revelation, glorious and divine.

"I have been searching for the truth in the wrong city," he

said quietly. "I had thought that Silvestro's murder was the result of his deeds in the Bibliotheca Domenica. But the answer lies in Florence, does it not? In the convent San Marco."

"I confess I do not quite follow you, brother. Perhaps we might discuss this in the morning, when you have had chance to rest?"

"Let us speak of it now. You can enlighten me."

Thaddeus laughed. "What would I know about San Marco?"

"You told me yourself, by the apple orchard. How in your youth you had seen brothers battle demons with a righteous rain that made their flesh sizzle. That was holy water. The halls of which you spoke were those of San Marco. You are a Florentine, Thadde—!"

A stab of white-hot pain cut him off; he bent off, clutching at his gut. Thaddeus watched expressionless as Bernardo gasped and sank to the floor. Pain had robbed him of his breath— he could only watch, blinking back tears, as the amanuensis picked up Aquila's chalice and stood over him.

"Another twinge, brother?" he inquired.

He raised the silver cup above his head and brought it down sharply on Bernardo's temple. The world folded in around him.

X. *A Red Hat of Blood*

A TORRENT OF icy water shocked Bernardo back to consciousness; spluttering, he shook his head. He was stretched out across the cellar floor in the centre of a ring of candles, cold stone against his back. His head was pounding and his gut ached. He tried to sit up, only to discover that his hands had been bound tightly around a four-legged wooden stand beneath one of the barrels.

Thaddeus righted his empty pail and placed it carefully beyond the candles.

"God give you welcome, brother," he said. "Be sure that these cellars are far beyond the ears of any of our order, so you may sing to your heart's content. No one will hear you."

"It was you," gasped Bernardo. "You placed the chalice in the chapel. You killed Silvestro and Guido."

"A peddler and a drunk," Thaddeus said dismissively.

"Human lives, all the same."

"You were once a soldier. Tell me, how many men died upon your blade?"

"I did only as I was ordered," Bernardo replied weakly. "Even then, I turned my back on violence in order to praise God's name."

"In whose name do you think I committed these acts? I wield my dagger to further God's glory, not my own."

"You have been led astray. I have seen your handiwork. There is no glory in what you have done. Only evil, grotesque and unholy."

A flicker of annoyance crossed Thaddeus's face.

"Fra Bernardo, I would have thought you of all people would understand," he said reproachfully. "You are not a son of this tainted city; you know as well as I that the churches stand empty and neglected while sin seeps like pus out of every library aisle. Every word is worshipped here, save the Word of God!"

"That gives you no cause to kill!"

"So declares Bernardo the great warrior, who beat a coward's path from the battlefield." Thaddeus's voice dripped with contempt. "I will not retreat, nor will I lay down my sword."

"A human's life is a soldier's life," Bernardo repeated.

"To know those words is one thing. But to have lived them... well, that is something else entirely." Thaddeus's eyes were shining. "I was but a young man when Savonarola took control of Florence, barely more than a child. Together with my brothers we patrolled the city in robes of purest white, cleansing houses of the vanities that the people had collected and hurling them into the flames: dice and jars of scent, mirrors and masks, obscene pictures and books. Where the children had once celebrated Carnival by hurling rocks at one another, we erected altars on the street corners. We took a city mired in sodomy and sin and turned it into a House of God!"

"And what of Silvestro?" Bernardo said sharply. "Where was his place in this House of God?"

Thaddeus's face darkened. "He was no man of God," he said. "Silvestro was a sinner who joined our cause only to further his own, pocketing the vanities we confiscated. When the forces of opposition surrounded San Marco, he was given the keys to the convent doors while the rest of us took up arms to defend it. The great bell tolled above our heads, summoning others to our cause in God's name. If we could only have lasted out the night, I believe the Friar could have been saved."

"What happened?"

"Can you not see it, even now? Silvestro had been entrusted with the keys to the Kingdom of Heaven. Yet he took them and opened the gates, handing them over to the forces of darkness, who crossed his palm with silver and let him flee into the night."

Bernardo closed his eyes and lay his head back on the floor. Matthew 16:19. A pair of crossed keys. It had not been about the *bibliotheca secreta*, nor Silvestro's illicit trade. It had not been about books at all.

"As I watched them march Fra Savonarola out of San Marco through a howling mob, his hands bound behind his back and showered in spit," Thaddeus said bitterly, "I swore that his betrayal would be avenged. And when I saw Silvestro's face among the bookshelves of the Bibliotheca Domenico, I saw that this was more than a gift from Heaven— it was a challenge from God, to prove my devotion to Him. Learning of the vile trade Silvestro was plying under the library's auspices, I arranged to meet him under the pretence of loaning the *Picatrix*. That night, I visited my wrath upon Silvestro, exacting full payment for Savonarola's betrayal. But his other unholy tomes remained festering in their hiding places. I returned to the library earlier this night to search the *bibliotheca secreta*, only to be disturbed by the scholar. Once I set to work on him with my blade, he was only too eager to tell me where to find what I sought."

"The valuables, too," Bernardo said. "You took more than just books, Thaddeus."

"Spoils of war. And every last piece offered up to the Lord. You saw the chalice in the chapel, did you not? I have no desire for baubles and trinkets. In the words of the Friar: *I want no hats, no mitres large or small. A red hat of blood: this I desire.*"

"You have lost your mind."

Thaddeus knelt beside Bernardo.

"What will the abbot say, do you wonder, when they find you down here?" he murmured. "Burned alive on a pyre of forbidden books, the stench of wine still thick in the air. Will he think that the Devil has taken his revenge? Or will he conclude that the Devil walked among them all along?"

"Do what you will," wheezed Bernardo. "I have little but pain to look forward to on this earth. I do not fear death, and I care nothing for the misapprehensions of man. God alone knows the truth: you will not escape His judgement, Thaddeus."

"In that, as in all things, I am His faithful servant. Now come, brother, let me fill your glass."

Pinching Bernardo's cheeks between his fingers, Thaddeus turned on the tap over his head. Wine streamed down over Bernardo's face, stinging his eyes and pouring into his mouth and nostrils. He gagged, thrashing about helplessly as Thaddeus held him down. A sweet, choking tide filled him. Abruptly, the torrent ceased: Bernardo twisted over and vomited wine on to the floor. Through his tears, he saw Thaddeus rise to fetch a hessian sack from outside the ring of candles. The amanuensis shook out a heap of old books on to the flagstones.

Gripped by a sudden desperation, Bernardo tried to pull his hands free from the stand. The wine barrel above his head wobbled. Tensing his muscles, he drew on the last remnants of his strength and yanked on his binds—and was rewarded

with a loud crash as the barrel toppled off the stand. Rolling
in the other direction, Bernardo dived out of the candle ring,
reaching out imploringly towards the wine rack. His fingers
latched around the neck of a bottle. There came a sharp tug as
Thaddeus yanked him back by the feet; in the same motion,
Bernardo twisted around and smashed the bottle over the
amanuensis's head.

Pieces of bloodied glass showered across the floor. Thaddeus
reeled away, clutching his face. Bernardo seized a shard and
began frantically slicing into the ropes around his wrist, numb
to the cuts he dealt his own hands. He freed himself and
scrambled to his feet. Beyond the candles, Thaddeus wiped
the blood from his eyes and drew a dagger from his belt.

"Come, brother," Bernardo panted, beckoning him
forward. "I will give you the red hat you desire."

Thaddeus charged forward with a howl, brandishing the
knife high above his head. Bernardo caught him by the
wrist before he could bring it down, and the two men went
stumbling beyond the candles into a barrel. As they wrestled,
Thaddeus's face contorted into a hate-filled mask: the cellar
melted away, and Bernardo was back among the carnage at
Agnadello, the smoke and the screams and the blood, the
Devil bearing down on him through the vines. He slammed
Thaddeus's hand against the wood, knocking the knife loose.
The amanuensis lowered his head and butted Bernardo in
the nose. He fell backwards against the barrel, stars of pain
exploding before his eyes. A hand latched around his windpipe,
trapping the breath in his throat. Bernardo snatched a candle
from atop the barrel and thrust it in Thaddeus's eye.

Flame sizzled upon soft membrane, a bestial screech

echoing around the cellars. Bernardo dropped the candle and seized Thaddeus by the robes, hurling him to the flagstones in the middle of Silvestro's books. His pain had dissolved in the forge of seething rage. Bernardo sat astride his writhing assailant, pinning him down with his weight. He snatched up the *Picatrix* from the pile of volumes and, with two hands, began beating Thaddeus about the head with it.

"In the name of the Ten!" he roared. "In the name of Venice, in the name of Cadenza, in the name of God!"

He knew not where the words had come from. He was barely aware he was saying them.

"In the name of the Ten, in the name of Venice!" he cried again. "In the name of Cadenza, in the name of God!"

Again and again, Bernardo drove the book into Thaddeus's face.

"In the name of the Ten, in the name of Venice! In the name of Cadenza, *in the name of God*!"

Picatrix fell one final time, harder than before, and the body beneath him shuddered and went still. Thaddeus's features had been reduced to a bloody pulp. Bernardo cast the blood-drenched volume to one side. He rolled away and lay gasping on the floor, the candles shivering in horror at what they had just witnessed.

XI. *The Devil's Library*

AT THE SIGHT of Bernardo at his door, bloodied and slumped against the jamb, Abbot Marsilio's eyes widened in astonishment. Bernardo told his tale there in the doorway, in short, halting sentences, without preamble or embellishment. His offer to escort the abbot to the wine cellar to view the scene for himself was refused with a grave shake of the head—Bernardo headed instead to the bathhouse, where he scrubbed his face and hands until the water in the basin ran black.

The sky was lightening by the time he was done, but there was still time to go to his cell and change into a fresh robe before the abbey bells rang for *Prime*. Bernardo fell in with his brothers, absorbing their alarmed stares at the cuts and bruises on his face. In the chapel pews, he closed his eyes and raised his voice in song, searching in vain for the brilliant lagoon that had appeared before him only hours earlier. At the service's end, he ignored the protest of his aching limbs and headed to the vegetable garden, where he muddied his robe and blackened his fingernails planting cabbages, his spade churning out a crude liturgy as it dug into the earth.

"Fra Bernardo?"

He lay down his spade. The voice, measured and unfamiliar, was Abbot Marsilio's. He had approached without warning, his sandals cushioned by the damp grass. In his hands, he carried Thaddeus's hessian sack.

"Are they Silvestro's books?" Bernardo asked.

The abbot nodded. "All save one, which I burned in the cellars. Your tale had not prepared me for what I saw down there. It is a dark path you have walked in our name."

He handed Bernardo the sack.

"What am I to do with these?"

"That remains to be seen," the abbot replied. "The decision rests with you. You have earned that, at least."

"Then surely they should be destroyed," Bernardo said. "What do they offer the world, except misery and violence?"

"Nothing, perhaps," the abbot conceded. "Yet is the world truly a better place for their destruction? What would that tell us more about: the books, or the men who read them?"

"Abbot or not, you are still a man of Cadenza."

"Are not you also, after all these years?"

Bernardo puffed out his cheeks.

"I will take them to Ludovico," he said eventually. "He deserves to know the truth of what took place inside his library, and who was responsible for Silvestro and Guido's deaths."

"What about the valuables given to the armarian as security?" the abbot asked. "The silver chalice, and the others I found in the abbey's coffers?"

Bernardo considered the question. "They do not belong to the library," he said, "and I feel no hurry to return them to men so keen to explore the arts of devilry. If our imprudent scholars wish to recover their possessions, let them come here and ask for them in person."

The abbot's mouth twitched with amusement. "I imagine some would be reluctant to enter a house of God with such a request."

Bernardo pictured Aquila sitting on his terrace; his small, satisfied sips of wine. "An expensive yet valuable lesson," he replied.

"Come and find me when you return from the library," the abbot replied. "We shall seek God's forgiveness together, you and I."

Brushing the soil from his hands, Bernardo hitched the sack

of books over his back and walked wearily towards the abbey gates. As he passed through the front entrance, he spotted a figure waiting in the doorway opposite the abbey. Anna was dressed in a simple woollen gown, pale and hesitant in the morning sunshine. A smile flickered across her lips as she ventured across the street towards him.

"God give you good morning, Anna," Bernardo said, bowing. "I had not expected to see you again so soon."

"I was worried about you," she replied gravely. "Would you walk with me?"

He hesitated, his eyes darting back towards the abbey.

"I see," she said. "It would seem I am fit only for the midnight hour, and places beyond the Lord's gaze. My apologies, Fra."

Anna turned on her heel and walked away. Bernardo hastened after her, catching her arm.

"Forgive me," he said. "These last hours have been… testing. I have an important undertaking before me, and I would be honoured if you would accompany me."

For a moment, he thought she would refuse him. Then Anna bit her lip and nodded; together, they walked down the Via Arezzo.

"I see you have earned yourself more bruises," she said, eyeing the cuts on his hands. "What happened?"

"There was a devil walking amongst us," Bernardo told her. "He has been unmasked and will have to answer to God for his misdeeds. It is over."

"Is it though, truly? I worry that there is something you are not telling me."

Bernardo smiled wryly. "Perhaps it should be you investigating the city's secrets."

He stopped, shifting the sack of books to another shoulder. Anna's eyes were wide with concern.

"Fra?"

"I am ill," he admitted. "I do not think anything can help me."

"Do you know... how long?"

He shook his head. "There was a fight," he told her. "Earlier this morning, a desperate struggle. When I was younger I fought with the fury borne of the fear of death. But this time, there was a moment when I wondered whether it might be easier, if another hand could strike me down."

"I will not judge you for that," Anna said fiercely. "And neither will God, if there is any grace in his soul."

"Oh, there is grace enough, child," said Bernardo. "Oceans of it."

The Old Market was quiet that morning, the sun warming the flagstones around the fountain at the square's heart. At that moment—more than ever—Bernardo felt attuned to every nuance, every tiny, perfect detail in God's plan.

"And what about now?" Anna asked. "Do you still wish to die?"

"My wishes are irrelevant," Bernardo replied. "It is only God's wish that matters. Someday soon He will come to claim me." Sunlight playing on the fountain's dancing waters. The weight of the Devil's books in his hands. Anna's smile. "But not today, it would seem."

Seventh Canto
Phobos, Muse

I. *Clowns*

IN THE HOT and rowdy confines of a wineshop off the Via Maggio, Maddelina Giodarno found cause—not for the first time in her life—to curse her own cleverness. She had gone to elaborate lengths to present herself in a way that she felt certain would attract the attention of one particular man: Jacopo di Ferrara, a writer of middling repute who was currently celebrating his new translation of Lucilius's *Satires*. To this end, Maddelina had dressed in a white doublet, short black pantaloons and chequered tights. Her hair was tied back, her face hidden behind a grinning mask boasting an upturned nose of a length that bordered on the obscene. The casual observer might easily have mistaken her for a man, but Maddelina was counting that Jacopo could decipher her true figure through her costume. He was, after all, renowned to be a keen student of the opposite sex.

Flawless in its conception, Maddelina's plan had encountered certain practical obstacles in its execution. For one, it required Jacopo to actually *see* her. The wineshop was overflowing with patrons eager to take advantage of the largesse of the writer's father, the Duke di Ferrara, upon whose orders the cellars had been thrown open. To make matters worse, Jacopo was holding court by the counter, where the throng was at its tightest. The hours that Maddelina had spent practising what she considered to be an enigmatic sashay had been wasted. The one time she had battled through the duelling elbows to position herself in the poet's line of sight, a stinging waft of tobacco smoke had found its way through the eyeholes of her mask, momentarily blinding her and bringing on a violent coughing fit.

It would have been easier, she acknowledged ruefully, if she had been Vittoria. But Maddelina was not her sister, with all her celebrated womanly virtues, that suggestion of softness that men seemed to find so beguiling. Maddelina was too tall, too abrupt, her conversation sharp with stinging nettles and needle pricks. Vittoria could part crowds with a single sigh; Maddelina roused amicable tables into argument. From experience, she knew that her boyish aspects did make her more desirable to certain types of men—however, as far as she knew, Jacopo had no inclinations in that direction. More was the pity.

Maddelina sipped glumly on her wine. She only ever compared herself to her sister when she wanted to punish herself. With each passing minute, the din around her intensified. Rousing cheers greeted the sound of smashing glass. A noblewoman with dyed blonde hair and high heels after the Venetian fashion slipped and toppled over, screeching with laughter as she hit the floor. A pair of snarling poets had to be pulled apart, index fingers boring into one another's chests; amid the furore, a castrato scrambled up on to the counter and sang a filthy song in a delicate, heartbreaking quaver. The evening was gaining speed, hurtling towards its climax. Maddelina was running out of time.

"Why, Macchus," an amused voice said behind her. "So glad you could make it."

Maddelina turned around, offering up a silent prayer of thanks. Jacopo di Ferrara had excused himself from his station at the counter and was casting an admiring glance over her costume. He was a full head shorter than her, with tightly curled dark hair and darting eyes set into a fleshy, porcine face. His clothes were notable for their elaborate stitching and silk brocade, his belly nestling inside a fur-trimmed doublet and his stubby limbs swaddled in puffy sleeves and hose of rich mustard. It was a warm night to be dressed in such finery—Jacopo's brow was damp with perspiration, his cheeks flushed with wine and praise.

Maddelina sketched a performer's bow, earning a mime of polite applause from the poet.

"You must forgive us for neglecting you, Macchus," he said solemnly. "The Atellan Farces are plays for simpler times, mere countryside fare. The trickster Macchus could walk through the great libraries of the city without a single nod of recognition, let alone this humble wineshop. Look around you at this cast of knaves and buffoons: I doubt they have read anything of consequence in their lives, let alone the Atellan Farces. Whereas I have written extensively on that very subject." Jacopo took a sip from his wine, his eyes not leaving hers. "But presumably you knew that. Clever girl."

Maddelina made a show of looking shyly down at the ground, even as she fought the urge to poke the condescending poet in the eye.

"And look, you brought friends, Macchus!" Jacopo exclaimed, his face lighting up. "By the doorway I spy Dossenus, the wise hunchback. And there is Bucco! Dear Bucco, with his fat cheeks and flabby mind!"

Near the wineshop's entrance, a stooping figure lingered awkward and alone; along the counter, a portly man with a chortling mask and crimson-stained jerkin took a deep swig from his flask. Opening his mouth, Bucco unleashed a belch of such force he had to reach out to steady himself. Yet Jacopo seemed delighted, laughing as he turned his attention to the divan, where a third masked figure—a leering old man with a single tooth—was squeezed in between a pair of ladies. When the poet raised his glass in greeting, the old man responded by pointing at Maddelina and making a squeezing motion with both hands, as though checking fruit for ripeness.

"It seems lusty Pappus has taken a fancy to you," Jacopo chuckled. "He may be a doddery old fool, but his eyes remain keen for beautiful women."

Maddelina blinked. "You flatter me, sir. How could you know that I am beautiful?"

"It is too late for modesty, my dear, however becoming it sits upon you," he replied, with an airy wave. "Who else but a beauty would hide herself behind Macchus's great nose and a man's garb, and still have the confidence of commanding the attention she desires?"

His reply caught Maddelina off-guard—she had never

considered the possibility that there had been vanity at the heart of her designs. An elbow caught her in the small of her back, propelling her towards Jacopo. He caught her smoothly and raised himself up on tiptoes, his lips hovering by her ear.

"Call it a poet's vanity," he murmured, "but throughout the course of this night, I have fancied your gentle gaze upon me."

Maddelina's pulse quickened. "You have me at a disadvantage, sir," she whispered, with an attempt at breathlessness. "The heat of this room and the eloquence of your words have left me quite faint. Might we take some air?"

Jacopo inclined his head gravely. "Of course."

Offering his arm, he led Maddelina with exaggerated ceremony through the throng. Pappus barked like a dog as they passed the divan, and she had to skirt away from the old man's hands as they grasped for her bottom. The room seemed to be shrinking around them, the jostling crowds pressing her closer to Jacopo. She was relieved when they emerged into the alley behind the wineshop, gratefully gulping in the cool night air. Jacopo's fingers were walking a delicate path down her back—almost before she had realized it, the poet had manoeuvred Maddelina, through subtle insinuation rather than outright force, into the shadows by the wall.

"You have worked *extremely* hard to gain my attention, my dear," Jacopo said. "Now that you have it, whatever will you do with it?"

He threw his arms around her and lunged up towards her

mouth. Instinctively Maddelina shied away, catching Jacopo in the eye with the tip of Macchus's resplendent nose. He bit back an oath, his short arms still clamped around her sides. All of a sudden, her plan appeared to be working a little *too* well.

A polite cough inserted itself into the night air. Releasing Maddelina, Jacopo spun around to find himself face-to-face with the leering Pappus.

"You forget yourself, old man!" the poet said indignantly. "The lady and I were sharing a private confidence."

Pappus placed a hand over his mouth, his shoulders shaking with silent laughter. He thrust his groin merrily back and forth, accompanying it with a pumping motion of the arms.

"How dare you!" Jacopo exclaimed, his eyes bulging. "Off with you, clown!"

Pappus cocked his head to one side. Then, with a shrug, he stepped forward and kneed Jacopo in the privates. Maddelina winced as the poet let out a ghastly groan and folded in on himself.

"Bucco?" Pappus called out. His voice was that of a young man's, clipped with tension. "Where in Hell are you? It's time!"

He produced a sack from the inside of his cloak and whipped it over Jacopo's head. The poet let out a terrified squawk and lashed out with his feet, catching his assailant in the kneecap. As Pappus went hopping away in pain, the door behind Maddelina flew open and Bucco came barrelling out from the wineshop, his breeches falling down from around his waist. He crashed straight into Pappus, ricocheting off the smaller man into Maddelina and knocking the both of them to the ground. She cried out in disgust as a stinking armpit pressed against her mask. Pinned beneath Bucco's vast frame, Maddelina could only watch in dismay as Jacopo went reeling away down the alley. The terrified poet was still struggling to remove the sack from his head, and his bid for freedom came to an abrupt conclusion when he ran headlong into a wall. Jacopo collapsed to the floor, poleaxed; hobbling after him, Pappus gave him a spiteful boot up the backside for good measure.

Maddelina's glorious plan was lying in tatters. Squeezing out from beneath Bucco, she put her fingers in her mouth and whistled. A carriage rolled up to the mouth of the alley. Dossenus the hunchback stared down impassively from the coachman's seat as Pappus and Bucco manhandled Jacopo inside. The commotion had drawn a small crowd outside the wineshop—Maddelina gave them an elaborate salute before turning and running away down the alley, scrambling up beside Dossenus as he lashed the horses with his whip.

The carriage fled into the night, rocketing through the furtive twists and turns of the Printing Quarter. With every muffled thump and curse that emanated up through the vehicle's roof, Maddelina expected to hear an answering shout in the darkness, a challenge or a cry to halt, the alarmed clang of a watchman's bell. But the city had sworn itself to silence. The Adige barely stirred as the carriage hastened across the deserted Ponte Nuovo. Only when they reached the banks of the Verso did Dossenus finally ease off the horses, guiding them down a road leading away from the river before drawing to a halt outside a churchyard gate. The hunchback leapt down from his seat and opened the carriage door, helping Bucco haul the prone Jacopo—still wriggling in his sack—through the gate and along a path between the pitch-black graves. Maddelina pushed up her mask and wiped her forehead on the back of her sleeve, her shoulders sagging with relief. She climbed down to find Pappus waiting for her.

"It is done," he said.

Maddelina grinned. Grasping Pappus by the nose, she lifted up his mask. Behind it Raffaele was breathing heavily, his eyes shining with triumph. Pulling the dark-haired poet towards her, she kissed him on the mouth.

II. *A Merry Galliard*

As with all truly secret societies, the origins of Cadenza's Plagiarists were unknown, its roots a tangle of obscure mythologies. The identity of its first members had been lost to history, their motives unknowable. Over the centuries their number must have topped a hundred, yet none had ever spoken publicly on the matter, or even admitted their involvement. As it was, plagiarism remained a phenomenon entirely peculiar to Cadenza, and the source of much head-scratching in Florence, Venice and Rome.

Its practitioners were young scribes and poets; its victims, well-to-do members of the urban literary elite. They were kidnapped and held captive until their families agreed to pay a small ransom. On receiving their payment, the Plagiarists would release their prisoner and disband, having first selected a new ringleader to form their successors. It was assumed by the wider citizenry—erroneously, as it happened—that all of the great poets and scholars had at one time been Plagiarists. Yet, for many a would-be-kidnapper, the ransom letter would prove the highlight of their career. The notes had become an art form in their own right, each new circle of Plagiarists vying to outdo the last with the elegance of their demands. There were rumours of a secret volume containing copies of every letter written—melancholy sonnets and impish scrawls of graffiti alike—but if such a book did exist, only the kidnappers had ever had chance to read it.

For many Cadenzans, plagiarism was nothing more than an elaborate prank, a charade to which the citizens of the city had tacitly agreed to play along. For others, it existed as a form of patronage or taxation, a way of redistributing a small amount of wealth to those in need. Over time the kidnappings had become a kind of honour, establishing victims at a certain level of literary eminence. Admittedly, this was not an honour bestowed without a certain amount of peril—for all involved. The Plagiarists could be mistaken for common footpads, incurring knife wounds and broken bones in the face of unexpectedly doughty defence. The poet Giuseppe Damian, meanwhile, drowned after leaping into the Adige to escape his pursuers, while a Plagiarist ring under the stewardship of a choleric scribe named Fabrizio caused an outcry by sending their captive's severed ear to his mother. Only a petition from Cadenza's most respected writers had prevented the Artifex from outlawing the practice altogether. Fabrizio was banished from the city; his successor, the irreverent poet Claudio Barberini, redeemed the tradition by faking his own kidnapping in order to extricate several hundred ducats from his notoriously parsimonious uncle—a deception never confirmed but widely publicized, much to the city's amusement.

The shifting and uncertain nature of plagiarism, dependent on the character of those practising it, served to ensure that its victims' families took the ransom seriously and paid it in good order. For their part, the kidnappers took pains to keep their demands reasonable—like the steps in one of Caroso's dance manuals, there was a formal pattern to this merry galliard, and no small consideration of etiquette. After all, if the traditions of plagiarism were not honoured, it was little more than brigandage.

III. *Footnotes*

IN A SECLUDED CORNER of the graveyard di San Felice, a set of steps led down into a disused crypt piled high with the flotsam and jetsam of religious observance. Among the rotting pews and chipped statues, teetering stacks of ruined hymnals, a makeshift table had been fashioned from a tomb lid with a crack running along its length. A nest of candles presided over a modest feast: crusts of bread, hunks of cheese and slices of meat; a bottle or two of wine.

With the curtain having fallen over their first act, the Plagiarists had discarded their masks and costumes. Maddelina and Raffaele had cast aside their roles of Macchus and Pappus, while fat-cheeked Bucco had transformed into fat-cheeked Isidore, a choleric printer and forger who was one of Orsini's latest discoveries. Dossenus had removed both his mask and hunch, while still retaining the serious air he shared with his portrayer Carlo, a countryside poet and recent acquaintance of Raffaele's.

At the far end of the room, behind a locked and barred door, resided the final player in the drama. Jacopo di Ferrara had also been unmasked, the lofty princeling of the wineshop reduced to a pale and miserable puddle in the corner of his cell. He refused Maddelina's offer of food and water with a wounded cry, tears springing to his eyes as he begged to be released. She locked the door with a shake of the head and made her way back through the pews.

"How fares our guest?" Raffaele inquired.

"Like a true Stoic," Maddelina replied. "I assume you heard the sobs."

"Our great prize," Isidore declared sourly, raising his glass. "Have you read his *Satires*? He might as well have daubed Lucilius's grave with excrement."

"Jacopo is no artist, I grant you," Raffaele replied, as Maddelina stretched out her legs and placed her feet in his lap. "Without his father to prop him up, none of his efforts would see the printed page. Which is precisely why we've taken him. As we know, all great writers are penniless."

Carlo chewed on a crust. "Gianni di Bosaro was so poor that he wore the same shirt for ten years, and ate nothing but bean soup and bread."

"Gianni di Bosaro?" Raffaele's mouth twitched. "Was he a goatherd?"

"He wrote the *Mysteries*," Carlo replied. "I'm surprised you haven't heard of it. It is a beautiful work."

"No doubt, no doubt," Raffaele said airily. "Full of rustic vitality, and most diverting on long countryside nights."

He winced as Maddelina jammed her heel in his crotch.

"There are those in the city who have read Gianni too," Carlo said quietly.

Raffaele nodded, smirking. Drink often pushed him to the verge of obnoxiousness, although this time Maddelina was inclined to let him have his moment. They had been lovers for several months: it had been Raffaele who had confided to her, as they lay exhausted and entwined in the small hours, that he had been chosen to form the next circle of plagiarists. It was a boast he had soon come to regret. Maddelina had pressed him incessantly to be included, borrowing some of her sister's letters to back up her assertion that she was learning the ink maid's craft. Privately, she reasoned that such a claim displayed both a resourcefulness and a certain economy with the truth that would make her an admirable co-conspirator. She was also aware that, having betrayed the Plagiarists' strict code of silence, Raffaele was in no real position to deny her.

Isidore had scoffed openly when Maddelina had first been introduced, and Carlo had studied Vittoria's letters with an intensity that made her nervous. Yet both had ceded to Raffaele's say-so, and gradually she had been accepted as one of the group. She wondered what they might have achieved without her. While the targeting of Jacopo had been Raffaele's idea, the plan and the costumes owed their existence to Maddelina. Isidore spent most of his time drinking or bellyaching, while Carlo hardly spoke at all. His sole contribution had been to suggest holing up Jacopo in the churchyard where he worked as a gravedigger. Maddelina would have preferred to have secured some attic or tower top, though she supposed that Jacopo could have called out across the rooftops for help. Down here, no one would hear him. Little wonder Plagiarists tended to seek out Cadenza's lower levels, its sewers and cellars: the dank footnotes of the city.

She looked up to find Macchus's face grinning back at her. "Why so sad, Lady Maddelina?" the trickster asked, in Raffaele's voice.

"I'm not sad," she said. "This all just seems a little..." She puffed out her cheeks. "Ungallant."

"Un*gallant*?"

"I swear Jacopo honestly fears we might kill him."

"Who says we won't?" Macchus said mischievously.

She swiped the mask away from Raffaele, who snickered and helped himself to more wine.

"Best that Jacopo believes us to be serious," Isidore said, his fingers seeking out an itch amid his rolls of belly fat. "If people thought we were in jest, why would anyone pay up?"

"Why, for the honour, of course!" Raffaele cried, leaping dramatically onto his chair. "The Duke di Ferrara is one of the richest men in Cadenza, and his son one of its least inspiring writers. We are paying Jacopo a compliment his talents do not deserve. The duke will be *grateful*." He produced a letter from within his cloak with an unsteady flourish, almost falling from his seat. "Deliver this as we agreed, and let us see the extent of his gratitude."

The ransom note had been the source of stinging debate between Raffaele and Carlo, both of whom clearly considered themselves to be the superior writer. They had crossed swords over every word, each trying to surpass the other with the precision and delicacy of their phrasing. Finally, after a prolonged argument over the most fitting sign-off, Maddelina had snatched the letter from them and declared it finished.

Isidore belched loudly and took the letter from Raffaele, slipping it into the sweaty recesses of his jerkin. As he ambled towards the steps, the burly printer glanced uneasily at the broken headstones.

"Here's hoping the duke pays up in good time," he rasped. "Spend long enough down here and we might as well pen our own epitaph."

"Mark my words," Raffaele said confidently, settling back in his chair and winking at Maddelina. "Jacopo will be home before the day is out."

IV. *An Appropriate Evaluation*

THE FEAST WAS long ended, the wine bottles drained dry, and the jubilant toasts given way to gnawing silence. Raffaele paced impatiently across the flagstones while Carlo stretched out along a pew, flicking through a hymnal. Maddelina shifted uncomfortably in her chair. It felt as though Isidore had been gone an age—she wondered irritably whether he had stopped off at a tavern on the way.

Just as her eyelids were threatening to droop shut, the cellar door flew open and the forger came stomping down the steps, a wineskin swinging carelessly in one hand.

"Finally!" Raffaele exclaimed. "Where have you been?"

"Following your orders," Isidore said hoarsely. "I gave an urchin a *soldi* to deliver the ransom and bring back the duke's reply. The boy didn't return for hours—apparently the duke retired for lunch and his afternoon nap before deigning to put pen to paper. This was his answer."

He tossed the note on to the table. Maddelina reacted quickest, slapping away Raffaele's hand when he tried to grab it from her. She read aloud:

To the Plagiarists of Cadenza,

> *For the sum of money you have requested, I would expect you to be offering the great poet Rinaldi in return, or perhaps the ghost of Tommaso Cellini himself. But given it is my son you have seen fit to carry off, that clumsiest of wordsmiths and most shameful of scions, perhaps you should return with a more appropriate evaluation of the man and his talents.*

Your gracious servant,
Duke Enrico di Ferrara

Raffaele laughed incredulously. "He's *bartering* with us? Incredible! Does he have no respect for the traditions at all?"

"We did kidnap his son," Carlo pointed out. "Traditions or not."

"Of course we kidnapped his son, you ass," Raffaele snapped. "We are Plagiarists! For centuries, writers and poets have been held to ransom in this exact fashion—and every last one of them greater artists than the blubbering milksop locked up back there."

"That's the problem," Maddelina said, re-reading the letter. "The duke has too much contempt for his son to pay up."

"So what do you suggest?" Raffaele retorted. "We sit in the dark and wait for him to have a sentimental moment?"

"Send him a finger."

Three faces turned slowly towards Isidore. The forger shrugged and took a swig from his wineskin. "Watch his Lordship pay up then," he said.

"We are *not* cutting off Jacopo's finger," Maddelina said icily.

Raffaele sat back in his chair. "It need not be his finger, necessarily."

"Then whose finger do you suggest?"

"We are sitting beneath a graveyard, Maddelina. Does not one finger resemble any other, should it come to that?"

Her eyes widened. "Have you lost your mind? You're talking about desecrating the dead!"

"I'm *talking* about getting our money. If the duke doesn't pay up, this has all been for naught."

Isidore tossed his empty wineskin into a font. "By all means, continue this debate," he rasped. "But my head is full of your words and my feet sore from fruitless errands. I'm going for a drink."

"We agreed to stay down here together!" Maddelina protested.

"How many gaolers do you think he needs?" Isidore said,

jerking his head towards Jacopo's cell. "He'll still be here come morning."

Raffaele sprang from his chair, gathering up his cloak and throwing it around his shoulders.

"And where are you going?" said Maddelina.

"To compose another letter to our good friend the duke," Raffaele replied. "It would seem a firmer tone is necessary."

He bounded away up the steps before she could argue, calling after Isidore. Maddelina sank back with a sigh of exasperation, earning herself an amused glance from Carlo. She glared at him.

"Thank you for your contribution."

He held out his hands. "What would you have me say?"

"I don't know! Something that might make those two treat us like fellow Plagiarists rather than members of their *fideli*."

"Go after Raffaele if you want," Carlo shrugged. "I'm happy here."

"I don't want to go after Raffaele. I'm not his dutiful hound."

"Then don't bark at him when he leaves."

"*Bark* at him? Why—!"

"Hello?"

From behind the cell door came Jacopo's voice, thin and insistent as a rusted hinge. Maddelina and Carlo exchanged a wary glance.

"What is it?" Carlo called out.

"Take pity on me, sir, and give me parchment, pen and ink!"

"You can write again when your father pays up," he shot back. "Until then, the great writers of Greece and Rome may rest easy."

"Is it not enough that you torture me with casual talk of cutting off fingers, without also mocking me?" Jacopo quavered. "I beg of you, if you are intent on removing the instruments of my fortune, there is one final thing I would commit to paper."

Carlo rubbed his face. Rising from his pew, he went over to a lattice screen resting against the wall. Maddelina looked on curiously as he delved behind it, pulling out a sheaf of parchment and pen and ink.

"I used to come here to write," he explained.

"Used to?"

"I decided that my instruments of fortune were best put to other uses," Carlo replied, with a rueful smile. "Such as digging graves and kidnapping poets."

He unlocked Jacopo's door and slid the writing implements across the floor. Through the gloom, Maddelina caught a fleeting glimpse of the poet as he scuttled back to the corner of his cell. The night's exertions were catching up with her; selecting a pew to curl up on, she lay down and rested her head on her arm. Within moments, a black curtain fell across the world, sleep spiriting her away.

MADDELINA AWOKE WITH a start, jerking upright to find an angel with a broken wing gazing disapprovingly down at her. Her arm was numb, her sleeve damp with her own saliva. As her surroundings slowly swam into focus, she saw Carlo seated by a candle at the table. There was a small stack of paper before him.

"How long have I been asleep?" groaned Maddelina.

"A few hours," Carlo replied, without looking up. "Jacopo hasn't stopped writing since. At this rate, he will run out of paper."

She sat up. "How long is this masterpiece of his going to be?"

"Who knows? He is so frightened for his life, I wonder whether it may be a ploy to extend it for as long as possible."

"If it keeps him quiet, I say let him write on," Maddelina said. "Although if you ask me, it is a sore waste of good parchment."

Carlo scratched his cheek. "That's the thing."

"What?"

He pushed the pages across the table. "You might want to take a look at this," he said.

V. *Golden Words*

RAFFAELE RAISED AN eyebrow. "It's *good*?"

He had swapped his habitual station at the Accademia for an isolated mezzanine of the Bibliotheca Niccoló, his feet propped up on the desk and his arms folded, his chin resting dejectedly on his chest. A stack of books rose unsteadily into the air by his elbow. The counter was littered with half-finished ransom notes.

"It's better than good!" Maddelina replied excitedly. "It reads as though an angel has taken Jacopo as his vessel and is singing golden words through him."

"But it's Jacopo! He couldn't shit a golden word if you fed him florins for a year."

She thrust the poet's parchment into his hands. "See for yourself."

Raffaele scanned the first lines, a frown worming its way across his forehead. His feet came off the desk. By the end of the first page, Raffaele's thumbnail was between his teeth. When he turned the final page to find there was no more, he looked up at Maddelina.

"This is a mistake," he declared. "There is no way Jacopo could write this."

"A mistake?" laughed Maddelina. "We kidnapped him and locked him in a cell beneath the ground! If he was hiding Rinaldi in there, don't you think we might have noticed?"

Raffaele examined the pages in wonder. "The control here... the writing is so beautifully restrained, so sure of itself. I would never have thought Jacopo capable of it."

"He thinks we are going to kill him," Maddelina said. "Perhaps the threat to his life has unlocked a door within him. By taking him prisoner, we have set him free!"

"Then by all means, lock me up beside him," Raffaele replied gloomily.

Maddelina affectionately ruffled his hair. "He is asking for more paper," she said.

"Mmm?"

"Jacopo. He wants to carry on writing."

Raffaele blinked. "So what are you doing here?"

"I thought you might want to see it first. I wasn't sure if you would want him to continue."

"You weren't sure?" He stared at her in disbelief. "Do you think I would stand in the way of artistry such as this? Get him what he needs."

"But what about the ransom?"

"Go, go!" Raffaele shouted, gesturing frantically towards the door.

Maddelina rolled her eyes and headed down from the mezzanine. Halfway down the stairs, she turned to see Raffaele sit back in his chair and toss his ransom letters into the air, obscuring himself in a disgruntled blizzard of parchment.

VI. *Fugue*

JACOPO WROTE THROUGH the night, gripped by a fever he could only relieve with the furious scratch of quill on parchment. Sporadic exclamations of frustration and inspiration punctured the quiet. As hastily as Maddelina and Carlo serviced the poet with paper, so he slid back fresh, wondrous lines under the door, the ink wet upon the page like dew. At last, the crypt fell still. When no new pages appeared for a time, Maddelina peered inside Jacopo's cell. At the sight of the exhausted writer face-down on the floor, snoring softly, she smiled.

"The maestro succumbs to sleep," she whispered to Carlo. "Who would have thought it possible?"

"Phobos and Deimos are his muses now," he replied, joining her in the doorway. "He hears the gallop of their hooves and feels their hot breath on his neck. He writes quickly in the hope of outrunning them."

Carlo seemed at ease down here in the darkness, among the broken statues and damaged books. It was hard to square this character with the drunken poet whose scandalous actions at the Ridolfi salon had earned him brief notoriety amongst the city's literary circles and had, by association, threatened Raffaele's own position inside Lorenzo Sardi's *fideli*. Why, therefore, Raffaele had subsequently invited Carlo to join the Plagiarists was an intriguing question. Did it stem from sympathy for his fellow poet, or—as Maddelina suspected—a secret desire to spite his master? Expecting a dangerous rabble-rouser, she had initially found Carlo something of a disappointment. Yet she had grown glad for his company. The two of them had been left to watch over Jacopo on their own: Raffaele had made a fleeting return to the crypt, pausing only to read Jacopo's latest pages before heading off to deliver his latest ransom letter to the Duke di Ferrara. Isidore, meanwhile, had disappeared altogether.

Carlo gathered up Jacopo's pages and carefully arranged them. "I wonder if Raffaele has persuaded the duke to reconsider," he said. "Do you think he might lower the ransom?"

"Knowing Raffaele, he probably raised it," Maddelina replied, examining a stain on her crumpled doublet. "Although at this point, I would return Jacopo for a hot bath and a change of clothes. I'm beginning to wonder who the real captives are."

"Yet only one door is locked," Carlo said, nodding towards Jacopo's cell. "What is to stop you from going outside?"

"And leave you down here alone with him?"

He raised up his arms and stretched, stifling a yawn. "We could take a walk around the graveyard," he suggested. "Isidore was right about one thing—Jacopo isn't going anywhere."

Maddelina hesitated. It was all very well for Raffaele and Isidore to come and go as they pleased, but as the sole woman in their ring, she was concerned that leaving her post might be interpreted as an admission of weakness. That said, only Carlo was actually here, and there seemed no point holding herself hostage to her own pride. Leaving the poet to his slumbers, they climbed out of the darkness together.

The graveyard di San Felice was deserted, its tight, intricate paths abandoned to the chirruping crickets. Tiers of crumbling mausolea stretched out before them. For a time neither Maddelina nor Carlo spoke, revelling in the sun's warm glow and the breeze on their faces. By daylight there was no hiding their dirty clothes and dark rings beneath their eyes— each glancing at the other, they laughed, acknowledging the absurdity of their situation. With a courtly flourish, Carlo offered Maddelina his arm. As they walked slowly through the tombs, he began, hesitantly at first, to tell the stories of the dead, weaving tales of murdered lovers and foolish adventurers, gallants and rogues, frustrated artists and tragic innocents. He named it cemetery lore, secrets gleaned from the contents of tombs and whispered graveside confessions. Maddelina was enthralled. At a plinth bearing a carved book and quill, she stopped to peer at the name etched into the stone.

"A minor poet," Carlo told her. "They are all minor poets here. The great writers are buried in the catacombs beneath the Accademia."

Maddelina straightened up, shading the sun from her eyes.

"Do you really think that preferable?"

He shrugged, and for a moment Maddelina thought she

glimpsed in his expression another secret history—one of youthful pride mortally wounded, and grand ambitions dashed to splinters. Carlo moved away, pressing on down a flight of balustraded steps. He turned into a broad gravel path lined with trees, whereupon he stopped so abruptly that Maddelina marched straight into him. Further along the way, a woman sat on a graveside bench. She was dressed in a long-sleeved velvet dress, her hair tied into a simple plait and draped over one shoulder. She rose at the sight of them, smoothing her gown in a manner Maddelina recognized instantly.

"Vittoria!" she called out. "What are you doing here?"

"Looking for you!" her sister replied. "I waited at the bridge this Sunday but there was no sign of you. If I hadn't had the good fortune to run into Isidore, I don't think I would have found you at all."

Maddelina shot Carlo an alarmed glance. "Isidore? What did he say? Where did you see him?"

"At the House of Orsini. The patron has been kind enough to give me a room on the Verso, although I do not know how long I can impose on his hospitality. It doesn't matter, Maddi. Please listen: I came to tell you something. It may be some time before you see me again."

"Wait, why—whatever has happened?"

"I have displeased my correspondents," Vittoria told her. "Andrea also. The last words we shared were not kind ones—things were said that cannot be unspoken. I walked out of the tower and will not return. He was faithful to the last, though I gave him little cause to be. I… I will say no more, my heart is broken."

"Vita, all this mystery makes me nervous! Let me speak

with our aunt and uncle, I can persuade them to let you stay with us."

Vittoria shook her head. "You know that they cannot open their doors to me, Father would never allow it. Do not worry, Maddi, I will be fine. I will not be far away."

Maddelina grasped her hands. "You must write one more letter," she said forcefully. "To me, to let me know you are safe. Else I shall comb the city looking for you."

"Very well," Vittoria laughed. "We will see each other again, I promise. Take care, Maddi."

She enveloped her sister in a rustling embrace. As she hugged Vittoria, Maddelina saw that one of her sister's sleeves had ridden up, revealing a glimpse of inked writing spiralling around her wrist. She pulled back, a question on her lips, but Vittoria pressed a finger against them before Maddelina could speak. With a final squeeze of the hands, the ink maid slipped away through the graves.

Carlo gazed after Vittoria, absentmindedly running a hand through his hair.

"I've seen that look before," Maddelina said drily.

He blushed.

"That one, too," she said. "I had no idea that you even knew my sister, let alone that she meant so much to you."

"She... comes here sometimes," Carlo stammered. "We had cause to speak once, I do not know if she remembers... I merely..."

He trailed off, seemingly aware of the futility of continuing.

"I see," Maddelina said. "Be warned, my fellow Plagiarist— my sister has a habit of collecting men's hearts, and she has no use for any of them. Don't let her kidnap yours."

"A free heart is a lonely heart," he said quietly.

"The cry of a poet, if ever I heard one."

"And I suppose your heart is safer with Raffaele. He will take great care of it, I am sure."

"Do not trouble yourself over my heart," Maddelina retorted. "You have no more claim to it than Raffaele does."

"You do not love him, then?"

She was saved the need of a reply by the sound of a gate rattling angrily on its hinges. Raffaele came stalking through the cemetery, a black look on his face.

"Ah," said Carlo. "This doesn't look like good news."

Raffaele kicked out at a shrub, only to hop away swearing as his foot connected with a gravestone hidden inside it.

"No," Maddelina agreed. "Probably not."

VII. *Exeunt*

A VIOLENT SUMMER squall had descended on the Verso, glowering clouds laying siege to the graveyard di San Felice. Rain poured from the sky, leaving glistening tears on angels' cheeks and running down through the crowded earth. Inside the disused crypt, a single drop gathered on the ceiling, falling through the air and landing with a splat on the stack of parchment in the centre of their makeshift table. The Plagiarists shared a troubled silence.

"So let me see if I have this aright," Maddelina said slowly. She toyed with her Macchus mask, the trickster grinning at some private jest.

"The Duke di Ferrara now refuses to pay a single *soldi* for his son's return. We are running low on food for Jacopo and have no money to pay for more. And Isidore has vanished down the bottom of a wine bottle, leaving the three of us to carry on alone."

Raffaele nodded. He had acquired a hunted look, his eyes sunken and nails bitten to the quick. "Things are not," he conceded, "going to plan."

"Jacopo might disagree," Carlo said. "This kidnapping will be the making of him, mark my words. Once people read what he has written, his reputation and his fortune are assured."

"*If* people read his work," Raffaele corrected.

Maddelina looked up sharply. "And what do you mean by that?"

"We cannot just release him!" he said. "It would be the end of plagiarism! We owe a responsibility to the tradition."

"So we should keep him down here forever?"

"Perhaps." Raffaele tapped his cheek. "Or perhaps ask Jacopo to pay his own ransom."

"With what? All he has, his father has given him."

"Not true." Carlo sat up suddenly. "Not now."

Maddelina followed his gaze to the stack of papers on the table between them. Her eyes widened.

"His manuscript? But what could *we* do with it?"

"Anything we wanted," Raffaele replied. "If people thought we wrote it."

"But we didn't write it, the author is fast asleep on the other side of that door! Forget the traditions and florins and *soldi*—we are writers, first before everything. Authorship is sacred."

"You said it yourself!" Raffaele tried, a little desperately. "If we hadn't kidnapped Jacopo, he never would have written a word of this. Surely there is an argument that we can count ourselves among its authors?"

"Hah!" Maddelina's voice was alive with contempt. "Save your rhetorical pirouettes for the *fideli*. Every word in this manuscript came from Jacopo's pen and Jacopo's pen alone, no matter how you would try to convince yourself otherwise."

"Then you leave me no choice," Raffaele declared. "What I cannot claim rightfully, I will steal."

"And what about Jacopo? How far will you go to ensure his silence?"

"We will give him a choice: he can walk free and leave his manuscript as a token of his gratitude, or he can stay down here and admire his work in solitude."

"You have lost your mind! To kidnap a poet is one thing, but to take his work and claim it for your own... it is unconscionable."

Raffaele sprang out of his chair and grabbed Maddelina by the arm. "You know nothing!" he said, through clenched teeth. "This is not some passing amusement for me—this is my life's dream, my entire world. How long would you have me wait upon Lorenzo like a servant, bowing and scraping and hastening to his every whim?"

The wind rattled the crypt door in its frame, droplets of water peppering the cracked tomb lid. Raffaele pushed Maddelina away and snatched up Jacopo's manuscript, clutching it tightly to his chest.

"Don't look now, Raffaele," she said icily. "But I think your mask has slipped."

Carlo held up his hands. "Maddelina…"

"Do not think your silence excuses you from this, either," she said, rounding on him. "The pair of you can do as you will—a farce is one thing, but I'll play no part in a tragedy."

She tossed her mask to the startled Carlo, who caught it. Turning on her heel, Maddelina strode out of the crypt and into the storm.

VIII. *Homecoming*

At dawn the next day, a shivering poet stepped down from a carriage on the muddy banks of the Adige and began stumbling in the direction of the Old Market. News of Jacopo di Ferrara's release from captivity received a muted reception in the wineshops and reading rooms, pointed comments on the falling standards of plagiarism aside. Maddelina herself only learned of it several days later, when she entered the Piazza della Rosa to find Raffaele performing on the benches. Even from a distance, she recognized Jacopo's words flowing from his mouth. The crowd erupted with applause as Raffaele came to an end; bowing modestly in acknowledgement, he blew a kiss at Maddelina as she swept past.

In her annoyance, she barely registered the path her steps were taking—to the river, and across the Ponte Nuovo. Within the hour, Maddelina found herself standing outside the graveyard di San Felice. She walked through the tombs beneath a cloudless blue sky, damp grass sparkling in the sunshine. The entrance to the disused crypt stood open. After a brief hesitation, Maddelina ducked through the door.

The Plagiarists had taken their leave of the crypt, the last candles long since burned down. Broken statues mourned in darkness. As Maddelina picked a path through the pews, a sudden movement across the floor startled her—upon spying a mouse scurrying behind the lattice screen, she let out a nervous laugh. She entered Jacopo's cell to find it empty, a single sheet of paper lying on the floor. Maddelina knelt down. It was blank.

"If you're looking for Macchus," a voice said behind her, "I'm afraid you're too late. He rests at the bottom of the Adige with his fellow Atellans."

She whirled around. Carlo was lying out across a listing choir stall, a book lying open on his chest.

"I imagine Jacopo was pleased not to join them," Maddelina said. "I just saw Raffaele performing his work at the Piazza della Rosa. He took the manuscript, then?"

"It wasn't my decision," Carlo said evenly, sitting up. "I told him there was more honour in returning Jacopo freely than taking his work, but he wouldn't listen."

Maddelina slumped into a chair, picking at a piece of moss growing on the cracked tomb lid.

"I shouldn't have shouted at you," she said finally. "It was Raffaele I was angry with. And myself. I think I always knew what kind of man he was at heart... how desperate he was for success. I felt stupid for encouraging him. I should never have become a Plagiarist."

"Why did you?"

"Honestly?" Maddelina flicked the moss onto the floor. "I thought it would be fun."

"Wasn't it, in places?"

The cellar lapsed into silence.

"There is something I have to do," Maddelina said finally. "Will you come with me?"

Carlo closed his book and got to his feet. They left the graveyard together, walking side-by-side across the Adige back to the Recto. Maddelina told Carlo nothing about their task and he asked no questions as to their destination. The sky blushed red with the onset of evening, the presses of the Printing Quarter falling quiet. A warm breeze chased laughing children through the streets. On the brow of the Via Liguria, Vittoria's bell tower dramatically announced itself—Maddelina led Carlo up the steep incline. The first time she had made this journey, little more than a year ago, she had been breathless with excitement at the prospect of being reunited with her beloved Vita. Now Maddelina found herself wondering whether she would ever see her sister again.

They stopped outside the entrance, grateful for the chance to catch their breath. Carlo craned his neck up towards the belfry.

"Hypatia's tower," he said. "This place has quite a reputation."

"Among gossips and jealous poets, perhaps," Maddelina retorted. "Which are you?"

"I am not the one hesitating at the threshold."

"My sister told me not to come here."

Carlo gave her a wry look. "So, naturally, you ignored her."

"I'm worried! Something has happened to Vita, but she is trying to protect me from it. Why has she stopped writing?

Who is angry with her? Where is Andrea?"

"What do you think a building will tell you, that she did not?"

"Step aside, and maybe we shall find out!"

Carlo bowed obligingly, making an exaggerated sweeping gesture towards the door. Maddelina took a deep breath and pushed it open. The tower was wrapped in silence and shadow. The door to Andrea's ground-floor quarters was locked shut; Maddelina knocked softly, but the attendant did not appear. She climbed the narrow staircase to find her sister's room in a state of disarray, the writing table overturned and the looking-glass smashed, tangled bedsheets hurled across the floor. Letters were strewn everywhere, trampled and torn and splattered with ink. Behind Maddelina, Carlo let out a low whistle.

"We are too late," he said. "A thief has beaten us to it."

"A singular sort of thief, that would leave precious stones behind," Maddelina replied, pointing at the necklace on Vittoria's dressing table. "I'm not sure anyone else *has* been here."

"You think she did this herself?"

"Perhaps. I honestly do not know."

Carlo hung back in the doorway. He seemed unsure where to look, as though bound by an exaggerated respect for the mysteries of Vittoria's bedchamber. Rolling her eyes, Maddelina got down on her hands and knees and began collecting up her sister's letters.

"What are you doing?" he asked.

"Sooner or later, *someone* will come up here and find these letters," she said. "Do you want them being read out in taverns and salons in the name of amusement? Or people being blackmailed over the contents of their desires?"

Carlo ventured over to the bed and studied a letter lying on Vittoria's pillow.

"Remarkable," he said.

"What?"

He held it up. "You and your sister have identical handwriting."

Maddelina said nothing, crawling around the other side of the bed.

"It was quite a speech you delivered to Raffaele," Carlo mused. "The sacredness of authorship, the shame of passing off another's work as your own. You spoke with such righteous conviction, it was quite stirring."

She raised her head up above the bed. "You knew all along, didn't you?"

"I suspected," he said. "You did not strike me as a woman who wished to spend her days penning fantasies on behalf of lovelorn librarians."

"So why didn't you say anything?"

Carlo shrugged. "Raffaele had a mind to treat me as though I was a member of his household. I had a feeling that your presence might redress the balance a little."

"The liar and the thief," Maddelina said humourlessly. "Perhaps we were a perfect match for one another, after all."

"Perhaps you were."

She glared at him. "If you have finished casting down judgements from your sainted perch, perhaps you might help me?"

Carlo glanced down at the letter, his expression one she

couldn't quite decipher. Then he folded it up and joined her on his hands and knees. They gathered up Vittoria's correspondences, rummaging beneath the bed and behind the wardrobe, fishing sodden letters from the icy bathwater and brushing ash from the charred parchment in the hearth. Pledges of love and fidelity, exquisite threats of pain; every wink, every slap: they collected them together in a chest for Maddelina to hold for safekeeping until the day her sister might reappear. When they were done she closed the lid, sealing a box full of honey-tongued kisses.

IX. *Son of Macchus*

UPON BIDDING FAREWELL to Carlo, Maddelina felt an unexpected twinge of sorrow, the sense of a chapter coming to an end. Yet before the week was out, she found herself hurrying once more along the uneven paths of the graveyard di San Felice. She ignored the crypt this time, making for the opposite corner of the yard, where she spied Carlo sitting on the wall. From a distance, he appeared to be deep in conversation with the ground, but as Maddelina turned into the row she saw that he was talking with a silver-haired gravedigger submerged in a half-dug hole. The old man's face wrinkled with delight at the sight of Maddelina.

"Good morning, sirs," she called out.

The gravedigger gave her a rotten grin. "As we deliver one body to the earth, so another emerges from it," he said. "Mark my words, it does not do for one so young and fair to spend such time beneath the ground, with only the dead for company. A rose must stay loyal to the soil, it is true, but she needs the sun's kiss on her face to flower."

Maddelina laughed with surprise. "A philosopher-gallant!" she declared. "You would turn me into a pretty bloom, sir, but I fear I am of a different nature, less delicate and covered in thorns."

"A garden with but one type of flower would soon grow weary on the eye. Nor, I venture, would it smell so sweet."

"Easy, Pappus," Carlo told him. "This lady is unacquainted with your bold tongue."

"My tongue is bold no longer," the old man replied, unabashed, "nor other parts of me, that I would wish upon them the forthrightness of youth. What I would not give to feel, just one last time, the fiery surge at the maiden's approach."

"I fear you have lost me, sir," Maddelina said. "The fiery surge?"

"Why, love, of course!" he exclaimed. "A love that in its earliest, most innocent form, transforms pale cheeks to brightest red, and ready wits to tongue-tied silence. I envy the pair of you."

Carlo slipped hastily down from the wall and steered Maddelina away by the elbow. She twisted around to look back at the beaming gravedigger.

"What exactly is he suggesting?"

"Pay Ercole no heed," Carlo said quickly. "He is quite, quite mad. What are you doing here?"

"Haven't you heard?"

He scratched his head. "Heard what?"

"You haven't heard?"

"I suppose not."

"I can't believe you haven't heard!"

"Maddelina!"

She wheeled around gleefully. "Raffaele has been expelled from Lorenzo's *fideli* and has fled the city in disgrace. The story he stole from Jacopo was not Jacopo's own, but the work of another!"

Carlo whistled through his teeth. "Embarrassing."

"Embarrassing? It is the end of plagiarism! Kidnapping people is one thing, but kidnapping their *work*? Who would want to be a part of that?"

"So much for Raffaele's grand tradition," he said.

"Is that all you have to say?"

He spread out his hands. "What else is there?"

"It doesn't make any sense!" Maddelina pressed. "We were in the crypt for the entire time Jacopo was writing—no one else so much as spoke to him. There's no way he could have committed an entire volume to memory. So how did he do it?"

"Oh, that's easy," Carlo said carelessly. "I gave him the book."

"You did *what*?"

"It was the only way. Jacopo was never going to see the light of day unless he could offer Raffaele something of equal or greater value to the ransom. So I slipped him the book while you were sleeping, and told him to copy it out and pretend it was his own."

"But he had already asked for pen and ink!"

"In order to compose a ringing denunciation of the Plagiarists who had kidnapped him," Carlo told her. "And his cruel father for abandoning him. Truly, Jacopo is the worst writer I have ever read. Without help, he'd still be down there now."

Maddelina stared at him. "Why didn't you tell me any of this?"

"You were Raffaele's lover! I couldn't risk giving him any reason to suspect what I was doing."

"But you knew he would have to read the manuscript. How could you be sure he wouldn't know it for a copy?"

He reached inside his tunic and handed Maddelina a slim volume. She examined the title in disbelief.

"*Mysteries*, by Gianni di Bosaro."

"It is a minor work," Carlo said, without a trace of a smile. "But full of rustic vitality, and diverting enough on a long countryside night."

At the sound of Maddelina's laughter ringing around the gravestones, his eyes came alive with a twinkle—son of Macchus, blessed with a trickster's glee, and the pure joy of the clown.

Eighth Canto
Lazaretto

I. *Seven Days*

IT BEGAN WITH spilt ink, ugly black blossoms unfurling across parchment. The first sign of infection was a violent trembling of the hands—pens slipped, and sentences slid off the page; ink pots were left bleeding on their sides. It was followed by a sudden exhaustion, which left the afflicted wheezing and breathless upon the stairs. They struggled into bed only to discover that the blotches had passed from page to skin, painful blisters sprouting across their chests.

The second day brought a cough that rattled ribcages. Bedsheets were dappled with red flecks. Those tending to their loved ones fell prey to the same malady, the illness passing from house to house on the hot breeze. Quick-witted traders inside the Old Market made a killing selling nostrums and protective charms; forged certificates of health. They packed up their stalls and returned home to count their earnings, rolling up their sleeves to find the imprint of disease on their own arms.

On the third day, people began to die. The infection feasted on the body of its victims, devouring blackened skin and leaving clots in throats and lungs. Limbs became so inflamed that their agonized owners begged for their removal. With panic setting in, citizens began fleeing for the countryside—word came forth from the Palazzo Nero to close the city gates. Those who had avoided the taint of infection retreated into their houses, locking doors and boarding up windows. By the fourth day, the screams were threatening to drown out the bells. Church aisles clogged with penitents begging for forgiveness. The priests accepted their confessions and promptly took ill hours afterwards. Unrest festered in cellars and taverns: there were rumours that the Artifex had retreated to his quarters, content to let his citizens die. A barber surgeon gave a rousing speech at the Black Lion urging the storming of the Palazzo Nero, only for a shuddering coughing fit to cut him off mid-sentence. At the sight of blood on his handkerchief, his audience hurried for the doors.

On the fifth day, corpses appeared on the piazzas.

Upon the sixth, a great hammering and banging could be heard beyond the city walls. Those watching fearfully from upper floors and tower windows saw a structure rise jerkily into the air, a wooden skeleton with an off-white canvas skin. Men bearing shovels dug a trench around the makeshift building and filled the shallow course with water.

The seventh day saw a ragged company step forth, hauling carts behind them. Wheels creaked and wobbled along deserted streets. Grim-faced men gathered up bodies—the sick and the dying and the dead alike—and ferried them out through the east gate of the city.

To where the lazaretto waited for them.

II. *The Dedication*

A LITTER HASTENED along the Via Tribunali, sketching a nervous path around the dead bodies on the ground. A grey ceiling of smoke hung over the city, the ashes of bandages and bedsheets plunging Cadenza into near-permanent dusk. To the east, beyond the towers and cupolas, the outline of the lazaretto was visible through the gloom, the pesthouse attached to the city like a blighted appendix. From his vantage point inside the litter, Aquila imagined himself travelling through a vast necropolis, the streets abandoned to the dead and the disciples of decay: crawling maggots and clouds of flies, emboldened rats slinking out from their underground nests. With a scholar's eye, Aquila translated the poses of stricken corpses into hieroglyphs, creating a small, complex alphabet of suffering.

The litter came out on to the Piazza Tommaso and cut a hasty diagonal across the flagstones in the direction of the Bibliotheca Niccoló. Aquila waited for it to be set down before stepping out on to the square. The air was warm as dirty bathwater. Flecks of ash spiralled down from the sky: the last, vengeful rain of Sodom. Gathering his scholar's robe, Aquila made his way up the library steps, leaving his attendants huddled by the litter, casting unhappy glances around the piazza.

At this hour, the hallways of the Niccoló would ordinarily be thronged with gossiping scholars, but Aquila had only the echo of his footsteps for company as he made his way towards the reading room. The plague had scattered the writers of Cadenza to the four winds—Battista had fled to his

Umbrian villa with his lover, while Giancampo was in hiding in Venice. It was said that Lorimus had barricaded himself in the top room of his townhouse and was refusing his family's entreaties to unlock the door. Others had taken refuge within the Palazzo Orsini, where the corpulent patron had thrown a party with the promise that the plague would end before his stocks of wine. Aquila had ignored his invitation, which he suspected Orsini had sent only to amuse himself. Let his peers numb their minds with drink: Aquila would not be deterred.

The reading room was suffused with the same grey gloom that covered the rest of the city. Perfumed candles stood guard against the murk and rotting odours. A handful of desks were occupied, the crackle of turning pages audible in the hush. As Aquila passed beneath the rotunda in the centre of the hall, the hairs on the back of his neck prickled. He turned around. A golden-haired young man was watching him from behind the librarian's counter. The boy's features were so delicate, his figure so slender, that he seemed to waver on the boundary between male and female. Aware of Aquila's gaze on him, the librarian blushed; hot sun upon a peach.

Although minded to have words with the boy—who had no business subjecting a scholar to such impertinent scrutiny—Aquila elected to continue on his way, ascending a spiral staircase to the gallery. The upper level of the library was divided into a series of private boxes reserved for certain patrons. Aquila's lay at the end of the row, behind a curtain of crimson velvet. Still musing over the golden-haired boy, it took the scholar several seconds to realize that his box was already occupied.

Cesare Petrucci sat on the desk; his boots planted firmly on Aquila's chair. The Artifex's nephew was setting about an apple with a small knife, feeding slices to himself on the blade. He cut an imposing figure, broad-shouldered and strong, his movements informed by a rugged certainty. Framed by a shaggy mane of brown hair, his features were handsome enough in design, if diluted by a combination of drink and boredom—a lifetime of ease, devoted to vice.

Aquila waited.

"You are a hard man to find," Cesare remarked finally.

"That would depend on where you look," Aquila replied. "In the circles of scholarly erudition, this is known to be my favourite reading desk in the city."

Cesare dissected a sliver of apple skin and flicked it on to the floor. "I do not move in the circles of scholarly erudition."

The box fell into a pointed silence. In his previous dealings with Cesare, Aquila had detected a brutish intelligence at work—a mind muscular yet pedestrian, moving along straight channels like yoked oxen in the fields. The Artifex's nephew was a man entirely ignorant of the limits of his own intelligence. Yet at the same time, Aquila reminded himself, Cesare's blood ties had earned him a place within Cosimo's inner circle at the Palazzo Nero. Such power was not to be taken lightly.

"I am not in the habit of chasing after people," Cesare told him. "Especially with the city in the grip of plague. Right-minded citizens are taking cover behind closed doors, leaving only criminals and madmen abroad." He looked Aquila up and down. "And rats."

Aquila absorbed the sting calmly. He could handle the

rhetorical thrusts of Cesare Petrucci. "Unbeloved he may be, but no one can deny that the rat is a creature of great industry," he countered. "He will descend into the deepest, darkest sewer, shrinking not from the vile conditions as he goes about his business. A city of rats would be one of fortitude and endeavour."

"A city of rats," repeated Cesare. "The notion seems to please you."

"I am merely confident that our current unhappy situation will soon be at an end. Your uncle is taking steps to combat the plague: the lazaretto—"

"My uncle is losing his mind," Cesare said flatly. "He spends all day in his study gibbering about phantoms. The lazaretto was built at *my* command."

"Then the city owes you its thanks," Aquila said generously.

"Cadenza needs a leader. If Cosimo cannot be that man, then I will."

"I can see that your time is in great demand, my lord. I feel unworthy to have taken up so much of it already; please, do not let me detain you any longer." Aquila gestured at his books. "As you can see, I also have work to do."

Cesare held up his hand. "This will not take long," he said. "Several months ago, at your request, I entrusted into your care a silver chalice. You told me that this item would allow you to read a volume of great importance, and swore that it would be returned to me in a matter of days. As your patron, I saw fit to grant you this request. Yet weeks have elapsed without a single word from you. I sent message to your house on the Verso, only to be informed that you had taken new quarters in the city—where, your man would not say. I had no option but to travel forth into the plague-ridden streets to search the libraries for you, tracking your spoor through the bookshelves. Now that we are finally face-to-face, I would have you answer one question for me: where is my chalice?"

Aquila feigned a look of surprise. "My lord, I was sure that you would have heard of the terrible events at the Bibliotheca Domenico. The armarian was brutally murdered, along with a brilliant young scholar whom I had taken under my wing. Your silver chalice was among several valuables stolen from the armarian's safe-keeping. Despite strenuous efforts, I have been unable to recover it."

Cesare cut another sliver of apple, nodding to himself. "Murder, you say."

"Of a most horrifying and unnatural aspect."

"Yet I gave *you* the chalice. Did you not think to replace it?"

Aquila laughed. "Had I those kind of riches at my disposal, I would hardly have need for a patron in the first place," he said. "I am a humble scholar, condemned to penury. But, gracious Cesare, please remember what this offering has bought you."

Cesare waved his knife vaguely. "Remind me."

"A dedication!" Aquila announced grandly. "A most humble offering of thanks to the great Cesare Petrucci, patron of the arts, from Cadenza's foremost scholar. Every mind of consequence in the city will read this book and see your name sitting proudly beneath the title. They will appreciate not only your generosity, but the judiciousness with which you saw fit to bestow it. Surely this is worth the price of a mere chalice."

"A dedication," Cesare repeated.

"Indeed."

"I am to just… accept my loss."

"With my humble apologies, and sincerest regret."

Cesare had sliced his apple down to the core. Glancing around the desk, he dropped the browning remains into Aquila's ink pot and wiped his hands on his breeches. He put away his knife.

"Very well," he said.

Aquila stepped back, respectfully lowering his gaze as Cesare strode past him and pushed his way through the curtain. Only when the rippling velvet had fallen still did the scholar peer out into the corridor, allowing himself a small smile of satisfaction at the sight of the empty passage. A movement in one of the alcoves gave him pause. It was the golden-haired boy from the counter downstairs. As their eyes met, the librarian darted nervously back into the shadows.

Aquila drew the curtain shut. The quieter the city, the greater the distractions seemed to become. But at least the querulous ox had been placated, and at no cost to his purse. Using the hem of his robe to brush away the dirt Cesare's boots had left on his chair, Aquila settled down in front of his books. He dipped his quill in the inkwell and began to write, humming softly to himself as he did so.

III. *Two Men of Honour and Distinction*

THAT NIGHT, A thunderous banging jarred Aquila from sleep. He gasped as his eyes sprang open, nearly falling out of bed in his haste to grab a candle. Lighting the wick with a shaking hand, he went stumbling down the stairs in his nightshirt. The hammering grew louder as he went along the corridor, the door wincing on its hinges. Aquila flung it open, an imperious dismissal on his lips. But at the sight of the two figures before him, he drew back, aghast.

The shorter of the men was horribly disfigured, his features buried beneath swollen lumps of pink flesh that had pushed his eyes, nose and mouth from their natural stations. It was a mockery of a face, a clown's mask viewed through the bottom of an alchemist's flask. His companion was tall and gaunt, with a sickly pallor and a vacant, sullen gaze. His hairline began at the top of his crown, lank strands extending down to his shoulders. The pair were dressed in ragged uniforms, their cloaks stained with mud.

"Pray, do not be alarmed, gentle sir," said the first man, holding up his hands. "Ciro and Benozzo at your service. I humbly apologize for the lateness of the hour. The only consolation I can offer is that my features are best viewed under the cover of darkness."

There was an unexpectedly courteous tone to his speech, emerging as it did through scabbed and spittle-wet lips.

"I would rather not have to view your features at all," Aquila said icily. "What do you want?"

"If we might be permitted entrance," suggested Ciro, "I will happily furnish you with an explanation."

"Absolutely not!"

Ciro shot a glance at his companion, who remained expressionless. There was something about Benozzo's gaze—the complete absence of light in his eyes—that Aquila found profoundly unsettling. In the pages of an Arabian grimoire he had read of the ghūl, a malign spirit that haunted graveyards, feeding on corpses. Aquila had dismissed the notion as the product of savage fancy, but now, confronted by these men on his doorstep in the dead of night, the certainties of the reading desk had evaporated.

"It would be in your own benefit to talk indoors," Ciro tried. "If your neighbours should be drawn to their window by the sound of our voices, your reputation may suffer as a consequence."

"So I should invite a pair of brigands into my home instead?" Aquila laughed. "Perhaps I can help you select my finest silver whilst I am at it?"

"Brigands?" Ciro shook his head. "I am wounded by the accusation, gentle scholar, sorely wounded. Ciro and Benozzo are men of honour and distinction. We served in the employ of the late Artifex Tommaso Cellini, proud members of his most faithful guard."

Aquila paused. "The *becchini*?"

"We preferred to think of ourselves as soldiers rather than gravediggers, but it turned out that the city knew more than we did," Ciro replied. "When our master died we were no longer welcome in the Palazzo Nero, and people do not open their doors for men with our unfortunate physiognomies. The cemeteries were the only home we could find. Now we dig by profession as well as reputation. What else could we expect—should we have taken to the stage instead, to set maidens' hearts a-fluttering? Can you imagine the screams?"

The candle's flame shuddered at Ciro's grotesque smile. Aquila could only wonder whether he had woken up at all, or if he was lost in some kind of feverish dream. He went to shut the door, only to find Benozzo's boot wedged firmly in the jamb. At the same time, Ciro managed to insert himself inside Aquila's house, ducking beneath his arm and moving purposefully along the corridor. Aquila went after him, protesting indignantly. The gravedigger sauntered into the study, letting out a low whistle at the sight of its vast bookcase.

"We are in the wrong trade, Benozzo," he called out. "If only you could work a pen as you do a shovel!"

A grunt answered him from the corridor. Benozzo walked stiffly into the study, his dead gaze passing over the rows of volumes.

"Even by Cadenzan standards," Ciro said admiringly, "this is an admirable collection of books. It must have taken years to acquire."

"My library is no concern of yours," Aquila replied stiffly. "I demand that you leave this house at once."

The gravedigger sucked in through his teeth. "Not possible, I'm afraid. You see, this building is to be put to the torch."

"What?"

"On account of the plague."

Aquila stared at him incredulously. "What nonsense is this? There is no plague here! I am in perfect health!"

Ciro produced a crumpled piece of parchment from inside his shirt. "That's not what it says here," he said, flicking the paper decisively. "This is an order directing us to come to this address and take steps to halt the spread of the plague. Signed by Cesare Petrucci himself."

He pointed to the bottom of the order. At the sharp,

forceful lines of Cesare's signature, a cold sweat broke out across Aquila's flesh.

"I can give you money," he said hoarsely.

"It is not our debt you need to pay," Ciro replied meaningfully.

"This is about the chalice? But I told Cesare, I do not have it!"

Ciro held out his hands. "Then you will understand our position," he said. "You can't expect a pair of lowly gravediggers to disobey a direct order from the Artifex's nephew."

Aquila marched over to his writing desk and took a seat. "What I would have you do," he said, scribbling furiously, "is take this letter to Cesare Petrucci. While I find his actions deplorable, I will see that his debt is paid in full. If he will just grant me two or three days—"

"Benozzo, if you will?"

A hand grabbed Aquila by the hair and wrenched his head backwards. The pen fell from his grasp. A second hand latched itself around his throat, pinning him to the chair. Helpless, Aquila could only watch, upside down, as Ciro calmly walked over to his writing desk and picked up the ink pot. Dirty fingers jammed themselves between Aquila's lips and prised them open. Ciro tipped the pot's contents down his throat.

Sickly liquid filled Aquila's insides. He spluttered and gagged—the hands at his hair and throat relented and he fell out of his chair, retching ink over the floor. Through his tears, he saw a boot rushing towards his face. It landed somewhere near his eye, snapping Aquila's neck back with the force of the impact. Benozzo had come alive, unleashing a brutal flurry of kicks at his ribs. Curling up into a ball, Aquila allowed his mind to flee from his study, leaving the blows and buffets to land in some distant, other place.

He had no idea how long Benozzo beat him. At some point, he was dimly aware of Ciro shooing his partner away. Aquila forced open his right eye and saw the disfigured gravedigger crouch down beside him.

"There will be no more letters," Ciro said, almost apologetically. "It's too late for that. Really, you should have made amends with Cesare when you had the chance."

"What will you do with me?" Aquila mumbled, through a mouthful of blood and ink.

"As I said, this house has been condemned. We must take you away."

"Away? To where?"

"Do not trouble yourself, scholar. There are suitable quarters awaiting you just beyond the city walls."

A dark shadow on the eastern skyline. Aquila's stomach lurched.

"The lazaretto? But you cannot... please, I beg of you! I am a healthy man!"

A thick gurgling sound escaped from Benozzo's mouth. It was laughter, Aquila realized numbly.

"Forgive me, it does not quite look that way at this present moment," Ciro said. "But we have talked enough. It is time to leave."

"Wait! In the name of all that is holy, please wait!"

Ciro and Benozzo did not wait. Taking an arm each, they dragged Aquila out of the study and along the corridor, smearing trails of red and black across the tiles. As he was manhandled into the street, Aquila saw for the first time the cart waiting for him in the shadows. An arm, purple with festering buboes, hung limply down through the wooden slats. Aquila fought and screamed but what strength he possessed had been beaten out of him, and he was powerless to stop the gravediggers from tossing him into the back of the cart, on top of a mound of rotting corpses.

IV. *A Spectacle of Misery*

THE RATS CAME out to greet the cart as it rumbled along the Via Maggio, darting in and out of the wheels and chittering with irritation as Ciro swiped at them with his staff. In the back of the wagon, mouths hung open vacantly, eyes staring into nothing. Fat flies perched on sores and the craters of exploded buboes. Aquila kicked out at the corpses, shuddering at the touch of their cold flesh upon his feet. He tried to cry for help, but the city had turned his back on him, its doors and windows closed in silent rebuke. His chest was full of snapped twigs. Somewhere beyond the city walls, a fire was burning, suffusing the East Gate in a reddish glow. In desperation, Aquila scrabbled to the rear of the cart, his one good eye fixed on the empty road behind him; Ciro tutted and beat him back down with his stick.

As they passed under the shadow of the city walls, Benozzo raised his hand up to the guard and the East Gate juddered open for them. Aquila had passed this way many times, on pilgrimages to libraries and private collections in Venice and

Ferrara. Never before had the sight of the fields struck him with such dread. The earth was pockmarked with yawning pits, bodies piled high beside the idle carts. Those already consigned to the ground had been buried in haste, stray limbs trailing carelessly around the edges of open graves. Against the backdrop of a writhing bonfire, it seemed to Aquila that the arms and legs were still moving: a chthonic horde, rising from the restive realms of undeath.

Ciro passed Benozzo a wineskin and the gaunt gravedigger took a swig, wine dribbling down his chin. The cart splashed through the stream surrounding the lazaretto. From the city, the pesthouse had been an unsettling presence on the skyline. Up close, its canvas skin shivering in the wind, the makeshift building seemed to ooze with an unnatural life of its own. A knot of armed men stood guard by the entrance—Germans, Aquila judged, by their guttural tongue. He called out to them for help in their own language, but the guards only laughed as Benozzo dragged him down from the cart and ripped the nightshirt from his body. The splattered rags were tossed on the bonfire, and Aquila was hauled naked inside the lazaretto.

He went stumbling through a series of rotten alcoves, cowed and beaten and clutching at his privates, sallow-faced patients drawing back in their beds at his shameful procession. Through a doorway lay another chamber, somehow darker than the rest, where a row of dirty straw mattresses had been laid out across the floor. Here the inmates presented a spectacle of misery such as Aquila had never seen: sunk in bedsheets stained green and brown, decay festering in their groins and armpits. The smell was indescribable. As Aquila staggered along the aisle, a hand shot out, fingernails digging into his arm. He recoiled in horror as a woman lunged forward from her bed. She was dressed in a nun's habit; her torn veil revealed a youthful face, unblemished by plague sores. But her eyes were abandoned to madness, her throat muscles straining with a silent scream. When Benozzo strode forward menacingly, the nun let go of Aquila, fumbling inside her habit for a wooden crucifix. The gravedigger swiped the cross from her hands with a snarl, hammering it against the wall support until it splintered into pieces. She fled back to her mattress with a terrified squeak.

The *becchini* bundled Aquila over to an empty berth in the corner where Ciro proceeded, tumours wrinkling with concentration, to shackle him by the wrists and ankles to a metal spar driven into the ground.

"That should do it, scholar," he said. "You may rest easy now."

They withdrew, leaving Aquila whimpering on his back. His stomach was sick with ink and his brow was burning up. Alone, consumed utterly by fear, Aquila felt even time abandon him, the minutes and hours losing meaning until the only thing left to tether him to the world were the shackles clamped around his limbs. He closed his eyes and abandoned himself to the darkness.

V. *Dead Scholars*

AQUILA DREAMED THAT his study was in flames. The fire burned with an animal ferocity, a stalking thing of vengeance devouring his works, the doorway ringed red as it belched out the sulphurous breath of Hell. Seized with panic, Aquila reached out to rescue a volume, only for the bookshelf to give way with a groan, spraying him with hot sparks. He was driven back to the corner of his study, where he discovered an unexpected staircase leading down through the floor. With a wail of despair, he surrendered his books to the inferno.

As he went reeling down the steps, Aquila discovered to his astonishment that his library now extended down deep into the earth: floor after floor of burning bookshelves, the walls hewn from brimstone and the ground coated in tar—a ziggurat of dizzying dimensions, alive with fire. He descended through the levels, fighting his way through passages clogged with smoke. At the seventh tier, a molten river raged along the central aisle, breaking in golden-tipped waves against the massed banks of volumes. Aquila ducked through the gap between two toppled bookcases, only to shrink back in alarm.

In the next aisle stood Cesare Petrucci, leafing through the pages of a smoking book. Gleaming shackles encircled his wrists and ankles, binding him to the shelf. The Artifex's nephew was so enraptured by the contents of his volume that he seemed not to notice the flames spreading to his doublet—Aquila tried to call out a warning, but the words came out in a shapeless wheeze. Cesare looked up and smiled. Reaching inside his book, he produced an apple of pure fire from its innards and took a bite. He screamed: a high-pitched, unnatural sound. Aquila wanted to run but his feet refused to obey him. Looking down, he saw that he had begun to sink into the tar. Cesare writhed in his bonds, his flesh charring and the features melting from his face. The tormented library burned hotter than ever, books turning to ash and showering over Aquila as he was sucked into a sea of tar.

AQUILA AWOKE WITH a gasp to find himself lying fettered and naked in the darkness. His vision of the burning aisles had been so vivid that it took him some time to recall his true surroundings. At the realization that he was back in the lazaretto, Aquila's relief gave way to creeping dread. He had been delivered from one nightmare to another, and this was a horror from which there would be no easy awakening.

As he lay back in the straw, trying to quiet his thundering heart, Aquila's ears pricked up at the shuffle of footsteps in the next room. An old man in a scholar's robe and sandals limped through the doorway. He was bald headed, with a flowing white moustache and beard. Aquila could not name him, yet there was something familiar about the scholar's features, the suggestion of a face once glimpsed across a reading desk or passed by in the library hallway. Fear giving way to curiosity, he propped himself up on his elbows and whispered a greeting. But the old man seemed not to hear. Aquila could only watch, frustrated, as the scholar hobbled away.

A fine mist was drifting through the shadows from the other side of the ward, where a bathtub had been positioned in one of the berths. Its inhabitant was cloaked in a shroud of steam, water sloshing over the sides on to the floor. With growing unease, Aquila saw the scholar re-emerge through the mist, talking rapidly under his breath as he paced up and down. This time, he looked over towards Aquila as he passed by his berth—eyes widening, the old man scurried away in fright.

The steam grew thicker, enveloping the lazaretto in its clammy grip. Following the scholar's gaze, Aquila looked down at the foot of his mattress. There, beyond his exposed genitals, a man's severed head had been set in the straw by his toes. Its eyelids were closed, dried blood caked around its lips. With a shriek, Aquila tried to climb from his bed, but his chains held him fast. The bathtub began to rock on its legs—a despairing arm reached out through the steam, parting the clouds to reveal a man's face, racked with agony. Gripping the sides of the bath, he threw back his head and screamed.

The severed head's eyes flicked open.

Aquila gazed in horror as it opened its mouth, revealing a black tongue pierced with a pin that mangled its words when it tried to speak. The head cackled as Aquila lashed out at it with his feet. Blood sprayed the straw. The scholar came back into the room and Aquila screamed for help, only for the old man's legs to give way beneath him. He collapsed to the floor with a groan, which was answered in kind from the depths of the bathtub, whose gushing waters had turned crimson with blood.

As Aquila begged and pleaded for mercy, beseeching in tongues that he himself did not recognize, his tormentors melted into the steam. When it lifted, they were gone—in their place stood a lugubrious-looking man with a high forehead, dressed in a plain brown robe with a cross hanging around his neck. His heavy-lidded eyes were filled with sadness. Aquila implored the monk to deliver him from his pain, but the man dolefully shook his head. Behind him, Ciro and Benozzo came creeping out from the shadows, their blighted, leering faces shifting and warping. As Aquila wrestled against his shackles, he felt a darkness rising up from beneath his mattress—or was it that the mattress was sinking into the ground? He was grateful when the abyss claimed him, and he could hear and see no more.

VI. *Angel*

IN THE MIDST of the darkness, a single beam of light reached down like a golden ladder. Aquila stirred, summoning what remained of his strength to claw his way towards it. Upon reaching the light, he began to float slowly out of the abyss, drawn by a single bright pinprick far above his head. Tiny bubbles of noise popped around him. Aquila forged upwards, suddenly desperate to feel the sun's bright kiss on his face just one more time, a few seconds' reprieve from the all-encompassing night. The noise grew. The light brightened.

Aquila blinked. His left eye would only open a fraction; through his right, the world slowly swam into focus. Sunlight stained the canvas roof. His ribs ached with every breath, dried blood on his wrists and ankles where he had thrashed about in his shackles. The straw was damp beneath his naked body. Aquila groaned and a shadow fell over him, framed by sunlight—a soft, girlish face, topped with golden hair. The boy lifted a cup to Aquila's lips. Water, sweet as strawberries inside his parched mouth. Aquila nodded and lay back on the straw, closing his eyes.

"I am alive." he said faintly.

The boy nodded.

"What is your name?"

"I am Bartolomeo."

Aquila ran his tongue over his cracked lips. "I know you. The other morning, in the Bibliotheca Niccoló. Downstairs, and in the corridor as Cesare left."

Bartolomeo blushed. "Forgive me for spying on you," he said, in a lilting, musical voice. "I had meant to warn you that Cesare was waiting at your desk, but when I saw you all the words in my head took flight in fear. You did not return to the library the next day, and I began to worry that some harm had befallen you. I went to your house and knocked at your door—your neighbours shouted down that you had been taken away in a plague cart. I came to the lazaretto at once."

"To search for me?" There was wonder in Aquila's voice.

"The health officers are so desperate for assistance, they let me in without question. I have been tending to you these past hours. You have been suffering from a fever, but I believe the worst is over."

"Fever? I thought it was the plague. I have seen such things you would not believe. Piles of rotting corpses come to life, a library aflame, the great scholars of the ancient world on the verge of death. And then..." Aquila faltered. "Then I had a vision that St Peter himself came to my bedside. He was dressed in a monk's robes, and there was such sadness in his eyes..." He swallowed a sob. "I begged him entrance to Heaven, but he refused me."

"Do not despair, gentle Aquila," said Bartolomeo. "The man you saw was not St Peter, but the confessor. He tends to the lazaretto's sick—his eyes are sorrowful on account of the deaths he has witnessed. The gates of Heaven would never close for a man such as you."

Aquila sought out the boy's slender wrist with his hand.

"Why?" he murmured. "We are but strangers, who have not exchanged a word. Why would you travel into Hell for me?"

Tears glistened in Bartolomeo's eyes. "We may never have spoken, but I have read every word you have written," he said. "You are the great Aquila, the finest scholar in all Cadenza. It is nothing for me to come to this place to aid you. I would kiss your sores, if it came to that."

Aquila squeezed his hand, too choked with gratitude to speak. Bartolomeo smiled shyly. O, golden angel!

A ragged cry went up from the other side of the room. Bartolomeo flinched, and slipped his hand free.

"I must go," he whispered. "Be warned—your fever may have passed but your life remains in grave danger. I hear the *becchini* talk in the small hours, their voices loud and loose with drink. Ciro and Benozzo are in Cesare's pay and have instructions to kill you if the plague does not. We must free you as soon as possible."

Flashing a shy smile of farewell, Bartolomeo rose from his bedside. Aquila had to fight the urge to call out his name and beg him to stay—he could not bear to be left alone again. Yet even as the golden-haired boy disappeared into one of the lazaretto's putrid cubbyholes, Aquila felt something small and precious fluttering inside his chest: the first stirrings of hope.

VII. *Quarentena Brutta*

FROM HIS MATTRESS in the corner of the lazaretto, Aquila began cautiously mapping out his surroundings. From fragments of conversations, he learned that the pesthouse was divided into two sections: the *purga di sospetta*, a quarantine for those suspected of having the plague; and the *quarentena brutta*, the isolation ward for confirmed cases. Aquila was quartered in the furthest recesses of the latter, where the lazaretto abutted against the eastern wall of Cadenza. The only way out of the building was through the front entrance, which meant passing through the *purga di sospetta* and then under the watchful eye of the German guards—provided, of course, Aquila could escape from his shackles first.

Here in the *quarentena brutta*, even the light seemed infected, painting the room a watery brown. The floor was splattered with blood and pus. A great stink rose up from the mattresses. The afflicted jabbered and howled, trapped in their own worlds of suffering. When the surgeons came to lance their buboes, their ministrations were greeted with hideous shrieks of agony that verged on the ecstatic.

With the lengthening shadows of evening came forth the confessor, who emerged from his private room at the other end of the ward. He was a grave-looking man with a high domed forehead, his robes brushing against the floor in a sorrowful susurrus as he moved from bed to bed. So solicitously did the confessor tend to his patients, clasping their diseased hands as he soothed them to silence, that Aquila might have mistaken him for St Peter anew, were it not for the presence of Ciro and Benozzo bobbing along behind him.

Aquila began to thrash and scream every time the *becchini* passed by, summoning the frenzy of a Turkish dervish and taking private satisfaction from their cruel smiles. For now, at least, they appeared to be enjoying Aquila's suffering too much to finish the job that Cesare had given them.

He lived for glimpses of Bartolomeo, flitting in and out of the wards like a heavenly will-o'-the-wisp. One early morning the boy appeared, framed by the dawn, smiling and carrying a ring of keys that Ciro had drunkenly left by a bedside. While the *becchini* slept off their wine, Bartolomeo unshackled Aquila and led him around the *quarantena brutta*. A vicious beating and days of confinement had left the scholar weak as a lamb, barely able to walk. He leaned on his golden-haired attendant as they picked a path through the sick, imagining themselves strolling through the Garden of Leaves like an uncle and his dutiful nephew. As they talked softly, Aquila came to understand the breadth and depth of the ardent feelings that had driven Bartolomeo to descend, like Dante, through the agonized tiers of the condemned— and, at the same time, even as he was led back to his bed and its iron restraints, Aquila felt his own gratitude blossoming into something more tender and unexpected.

HE HAD NOT thought he would see Bartolomeo again that day, but as the pesthouse paused at evening's edge the boy reappeared. He set down a pail of water and began scrubbing at the floor around Aquila's bed, careful not to look up.

"We are undone," he whispered. "I fear Ciro left his keys for me to find by design—now the *becchini* fall silent when

I pass, and the patients turn their backs against me in fear. I can feel Benozzo's gaze on my shoulder blades as I go about my work. There are rumours about him, the terrible things that he has done. His eyes… he frightens me!"

"Courage, sweet Bartolomeo," Aquila told him softly. "Free me and we shall battle the ghūl together, like Ta'abbata Sharran."

The boy looked up at him then, his eyes wide and radiant. Reaching inside his robe, he pulled out a small blade and slipped it beneath Aquila's mattress.

"Together we shall," he said fiercely. "We escape tonight."

A scream pierced the murk of the *quarantena brutta*— startled, Bartolomeo knocked over his pail, sending water sloshing over the ground. He hurriedly righted it and moved away from Aquila's bedside, making a brief pretence of cleaning before bolting for the *purga di sospetta*. Aquila settled back on his mattress, feeling the reassuring press of the boy's blade against his back. Only a few more hours, he told himself, and he would be gone from this hellhole forever.

VIII. *Darkest Hour*

AQUILA AWOKE WITH a start. The night was at its deepest, the darkness almost total. A sweltering breeze rolled through the aisles of the lazaretto, heavy with the stench of sickness and rancid flesh. Canvas rustled and floorboards creaked, giving Aquila the queasy sensation that he was at sea, aboard a plague ship rotted free from its moorings.

Where was Bartolomeo? As he lay upon his mattress, sweat beading on his chest and brow, the *quarentena brutta* felt unnaturally subdued, as though a rag had been shoved in its mouth. Twisting his neck slowly to the right, Aquila saw that a stool had been drawn up beside his bedside. A hunched figure was watching him intently. He shrank back in dismay as Ciro's ruined face emerged from the shadows.

"Having trouble sleeping, scholar?" he said quietly. "Pray, allow me to tell you a story. As a man of learning, you are probably aware that a man's private behaviour may be quite at odds with his public reputation. Our beloved former Artifex was just such a man. Tommaso Cellini had very particular tastes and passions that he could afford to satisfy only occasionally. When the urges became too much, he would send out invitations for a private gathering at the Palazzo Nero: to pretty girls and boys from distant villages, exotic foreign courtesans, Printing Quarter whores. With nightfall, his guests would come tiptoeing into the east wing, dressed in their fine clothes and giggling with excitement at whatever grand ball or feast they had been promised. Instead, they found only Tommaso. At some point—when their fine clothes had been discarded, and they had learned the true nature of the evening in store for them—they would try to flee. But the doors would be locked behind them. The Artifex was free to demand the most vile and depraved acts from his guests, to visit the very darkest corners of his imagination. And do you know why? Because he knew that, come the morning, his faithful *becchini* would come to clear up after him.

"Now, this might sound like fun, but it was hard work,

let me tell you: chasing screaming *puttane* around a maze of locked doors, slipping in blood and sweat and vomit. We saw things unfit for human eyes, things that are hard to forget. But the Artifex was not a generous or a grateful man. He just wanted his mess cleaned up as quickly as possible. So, from time to time, we would make a little sport of our own. Our captain would select a live one and, once we'd finished killing the others, we'd play with them for a while. All of us would take a turn dipping our quills before we'd put them out of their misery.

"Such was our work, in the service of the Artifex and the city of Cadenza. For years we bloodied our blades in Tommaso's name, and not one of us ever breathed a word about it to anyone. And what was our reward? Upon Tommaso's death, Cosimo had us tossed out of the palace like so many dead whores. They called us the *becchini* and left us fit for nothing else—so now me and Benozzo have none but corpses for company, still toiling away for a city that despises us."

A tide of groans swelled around Ciro as he talked, the plague ship sailing on through churning, infernal waters. Aquila stared at him in horror.

"Why are you telling me this?"

"Because you think we're all so *stupid*," he hissed, wiping a string of saliva from his chin. "Even here, shackled to your sickbed, you look at me and Benozzo as though we're nothing more than livestock. Running around with that catamite of yours when our backs were turned—did you think that we wouldn't notice? Cesare wants you dead, scholar, and we will happily oblige him. But we'll have our fun first."

Aquila's chest tightened. "What do you mean?" he whispered.

Ciro settled back in his chair with a smile. "Our captain left the *becchini* a year or so before Tommaso died, but he still knows the value of a loyal soldier. From time to time, when he gets the itch for a little sport, he finds me and Benozzo. This plague has been a gift from above—when we go out into streets to round up the sick, we keep a lookout for a juicy morsel here and there, a ripe fruit to bring back to the lazaretto. Who would dare question us? Out in the city our word is the law, and within these walls we follow the will of God's agent. If you follow my meaning."

At his words, a series of images flashed before Aquila's eyes: a fair nun, her skin untouched by sores, holding up a trembling crucifix; a lugubrious face, heavy-lidded eyes filled with sorrow; the doorway in the corner of the *quarentena brutta*, leading off to a chamber set aside for the confessor's personal use.

A man's private behaviour may be quite at odds with his public reputation.

"Monsters!" Aquila gasped.

"We are loyal servants of this city, moulded by its needs and desires. If we are monsters, what does that make Cadenza?"

"No one asks this of you. The only master you serve resides in Hell."

"Then upon his summons, we will drag everyone here to the depths of infernal agony—starting with you and your little friend."

Aquila tried to rise, but his shackles hauled him back. "Bartolomeo is innocent!" he cried. "Your quarrel is with me!"

"And we will get to you in good time," Ciro replied firmly. "Once Benozzo has finished with the boy."

Letting out a ghastly moan, Aquila reached under his mattress and scrabbled for the knife Bartolomeo had left him. A frown rippled across the bulging lumps on Ciro's face. He rose from his stool and limped around the mattress, just as Aquila's fingers closed over the slim blade. There was a gleam of silver in the darkness. Ciro hissed with alarm and lunged to grab the dagger—Aquila threw out his hand, slashing the gravedigger across the throat. Hot blood sprayed over him. Ciro staggered backwards with a gurgle, clutching at his neck as his tumours throbbed and the front of his tunic turned crimson. He collapsed to the ground, legs twitching in distress before falling still.

Aquila stared at the knife. Blood was dripping from his face and palms on to the straw. His breaths were coming in shallow gasps, his hands shaking uncontrollably. The mattresses of the *quarentena brutta* were alive with hoots and howls. If a guard should come through this way and see the body, both he *and* Bartolomeo were dead. Blocking out the bedlam, Aquila imposed the studious calm of the library upon his mind, arranging his thoughts like volumes on the shelf. He took a series of slow, deep breaths. Sliding down as far as his shackles would allow, he used his feet to drag Ciro's body across the floor towards him. Aquila manoeuvred the corpse around so the pockets were within reach and dug out a set of keys. With trembling fingers, he set to working himself free from his shackles, willing the room quiet as he fumbled with the keys in turn. At last the final lock sprang open, and Aquila was able to stand.

Looking down at Ciro, it occurred to him that he might don the gravedigger's clothes and escape the pesthouse before the alarm was raised. But then a vision of Bartolomeo came before him, the young man's eyes shining as he knelt at his bedside, framed by sunlight. Aquila forced his aching limbs into action, dragging Ciro's body on top of the mattress and throwing a blanket over it. There was not time for more—gripping hold of his knife, Aquila hobbled naked through the *quarentena brutta*. The lazaretto fell into a watchful hush. Fear washed over Aquila as he approached the confessor's chambers, its entrance cloaked in swirling darkness.

I would kiss your sores, if it came to that.

He pushed open the door.

Before him was a small, candlelit room, steeped in sulphur. No crosses hung on the walls, nor were there holy books or altarpieces—it was a chamber hidden from the gaze of God. The confessor stood at a cabinet with his back to the room, sleeves rolled up as he carefully washed his hands in a basin of water. There was blood in the bowl. Aquila's heart hammered against his damaged ribs; a black veil descended over the room. He fell on the confessor with a yell and buried his knife in the man's back, driving the blade up to the hilt. The monk let out a hideous gasp, staggering forward into the cabinet and overturning the basin. Aquila clung on grimly, his feet slipping in the spilt water, digging and gouging to widen the dagger's bite. He felt, with satisfaction, the strength ebbing from the confessor. Let him die this death a thousand times over.

The monk stopped struggling and slid to the ground. Aquila let go of the knife. He rubbed the back of his arm across his eyes, which were stinging with sweat and blood. His head was dizzy; he felt certain he would be sick. With every second that he tarried, the danger of discovery increased, but he could not countenance leaving this place yet. Where was Bartolomeo?

As he stood, swaying with exhaustion, Aquila became aware of the sound of trickling water. He stared down at the upended basin by the cabinet. A cool draught played around his ankles. Throwing his weight behind the cabinet, Aquila pushed it to one side. Behind it, a hole had been punched in the lazaretto's canvas skin, a black maw rustling in the breeze. He got down on his hands and knees and peered inside. Between the pesthouse and the imposing stonework of the city walls ran a patch of rough earth, enshrouded in gloom. Water was spilling out from the confessor's chambers and down into a shallow pit lined with corpses, their pale skin lambent and ethereal in the darkness. Resting uppermost upon them lay the broken body of Bartolomeo. His robe was torn and his delicate features bruised and bloodied—a golden angel fallen from the heavens. Choking back a sob, Aquila grasped the boy's hand and held it to his cheek.

Inside the pit, something stirred.

Aquila screamed as Benozzo erupted from the scattered limbs—the ghūl of lore, naked and inhuman, his nails blackened and lips bloodied. He reached out with a guttural roar and grabbed Aquila's arm, dragging him down on to a bier of cold flesh. Pain exploded inside his chest. Benozzo's jaws snapped at the air, his fetid breath engulfing Aquila in the stench of the dead. Their bodies were locked together in a violent embrace, skin slippery with blood and sweat. There was barely room to move, let alone to fight, and Aquila had so little strength left. Ta'abbata Sharran had fought and killed a ghül but he was a brigand poet, with an outlaw's boldness and strength. What hope had Aquila—oh, brave scholar warrior, vicious wielder of the pen!—against this being of Hell?

He cried out as Benozzo raked his nails across the face. Grabbing him by the hair, the ghül pushed him deeper into the pit, burying him amongst the corpses. Lifeless faces pressed up against Aquila's own. In desperation, his hands searched blindly for something, anything, he could use as a weapon. Benozzo grinned and ran a white tongue across his lips. As the ghül descended upon him, Aquila felt his fingers close around a solid object: with a cry of defiance, he thrust it upwards.

There was a grunt of surprise in his ear. Benozzo pulled away, his grip loosening as he stared down in incomprehension at the piece of wood jutting from his belly, Aquila's hands still fastened around the bloodied end. It was, he realized belatedly, a fragment of a broken crucifix. Benozzo curled up into a ball, whimpering like a dog in pain as he tried to pull the jagged shaft from his stomach. Aquila scrambled away, gasping for air as he clawed his way through the dead to the edge of the pit and dragged himself free. He crawled back through the canvas opening and collapsed on his back inside the confessor's chambers, utterly spent, listening to Benozzo's softening whimpers until the ghül let out one long, final exhalation, and the grave claimed him for eternity.

* * *

IX. *To Falter at the Last*

AQUILA HAD NO idea how long he lay there, so still that there was no distinguishing him from the dead strewn around him. The silence pounded in his ears. Finally, he found the strength to pick himself up. Retrieving the basin from the floor, he refilled it with water and washed the blood from his face. His thoughts were precisely ordered now, his hands no longer trembling as he removed the confessor's robe and slipped it over his own body. He would have to trust the darkness to mask the hole his knife had carved in the garment's back. Aquila drew up his hood and walked out of the room.

No hands reached out for him as he passed by the mattresses of the *quarentena brutta*—whether from veneration of the confessor's holy station, or terror at his true activities, Aquila would never know. Too late, he remembered the knife he had left on the floor of the confessor's chamber. There would be no going back now. He passed through the doorway into the *purga di sospetta*, whose denizens huddled in their beds, gripped by quaking silence. The entrance offered a tantalizing glimpse of fields and sky. As he approached, Aquila saw the German guards had abandoned their watch to warm themselves around the bonfire's embers. Two of their number were arguing, to the amusement of the others. They barely looked up at the cowled Aquila as he swept past them.

The heavens were lightening with the coming dawn. Aquila had escaped the lazaretto, yet he dared not celebrate, with the city gates still closed before him and a trail of corpses in his wake. As he waded across the water course, a shout went up from the bonfire—Aquila forced himself not to look back. To falter, to run, would be to give himself away at the last. A swift exchange of Germanic insults was greeted with laughter. Aquila fixed his gaze on the gates, the distance to Cadenza seeming only to grow with every step. He bunched his fists inside his sleeves. If the guards came for him, they would have to run him through where he stood. He would not allow himself to be taken back to that place.

The city walls drew nearer. Aquila quickened his step, stumbling over wheel ruts in the ground. He hailed the guard atop the East Gate and raised his hand in greeting. The man nodded sleepily and stepped down to the winch. As the gate creaked open, Cadenza revealed itself, inch by inch. Even now, Aquila expected the cry of alarm to go up, for the Germans to come running after him. Yet somehow the gate had opened wide enough for him to step through, and he passed across the threshold a free man—oh, truly, he was free!—a sob escaping from his throat, and he had to fight the urge to fall to his knees and kiss the ground beneath his feet.

Before the gate clanged shut behind him, Aquila glanced back for the first and final time, and saw the lazaretto slink back into what remained of the night.

X. *Venus Weeps*

DAWN BROUGHT THE rain, recasting Cadenza in shades of slate and ash. Puddles flinched upon the piazzas. As Aquila limped barefoot through the city, its once-familiar ways now glorious avenues of fresh wonder, each raindrop fell on him like a blessing: he turned his face to the heavens to accept them. His spirits had fled to some giddy place of grief where tears and laughter came hand in hand. He had killed three times that night. Bartolomeo was dead. *Venus weeps, and Cupid, sunk in mourning…*

On the Via Maggio, Aquila drew back warily behind a stone pine as a carriage clipped down the thoroughfare. Though the streets remained deserted, the corpses that had littered the ground had gone—a sign, perhaps, that the worst of the plague was over. He willed the rain to fall harder and faster, to wash away the stench. Let the Adige rise up over its banks and pour forth through the streets. Let the cohorts of pestilence flee back to their rotting underground palaces or be drowned in the churning tide!

Lost in his fervid vision, Aquila's steps slowed of their own accord. He had returned to his townhouse. In the grip of fever, he had seen it engulfed in flames, yet here its proud columns stood undaunted. On the steps, Aquila's strength failed him at the last, and he had to reach out to steady himself. The wind whistled a warning—feeling a shadow either side of him, he whirled around. No one was there. There was no need to be frightened now, he told himself sternly. The *becchini* were ghosts now. What was left to fear, that had not already been done to him?

His house was shrouded in gloom, the floor dirty with ink and bloody scuff marks and the odour of soured meat seeping up from the cellars. Yet the gilded halls of the Palazzo Nero could not have looked so welcome to Aquila's eyes. He wandered into his study as though in a dream, tears springing to his eyes at the eager nuzzle of his volumes against his fingertips. The chair by his reading desk remained where it had fallen the night that Ciro and Benozzo had come for him. When Aquila went to right it, he caught sight of himself in the looking-glass on the wall, and let out a gasp. His face was gaunt, the flesh around his left eye still swollen and purple. Aquila had tried to clean himself in the confessor's room, but in the half-light of the study he saw that his hair was matted with blood and there were gouges across his cheek and neck. But it was the eyes—his own eyes!— that stilled the breath in his throat. Wide ovals, rendered wild and unsteady by the horrors that they had witnessed. *Things unfit for human eyes*, Ciro had said, *things that are hard to forget.*

As Aquila examined his reflection, he paused. Beneath the raindrops' heavy tap against the shutters, the quiet of the empty townhouse, he detected another noise lurking at the very edge of his hearing. Without turning from the looking-glass, his eyes moved beyond his shoulder to a murky corner of the room, where the bookshelves ran off into the shadows beyond his reading desk.

"Who's there?" he called out. "Show yourself!"

He recoiled as a man shuffled awkwardly out from the shadows, noting with mounting revulsion the red rashes and blackened fingertips, the cloak of pestilent perfume hanging about him. Oozing sores obscured the man's face, yet Aquila knew him instantly by his unkempt brown hair and the gold rings on his fingers.

"My lord Cesare!" he exclaimed. "What are you doing here?"

"Avoiding the eyes of any that would look upon me."

Cesare spoke slowly, with great effort. "This house is *supposed* to be unoccupied."

"I am sorry to disappoint you," Aquila replied stiffly. "I was taken away in error. For, as you can see, I am not ill."

"So I see." The breath crackled in Cesare's chest. "How resilient of you."

"Alas, it would appear you have not been so fortunate."

"It was the damned ink!" he growled. "The Venetians must have found a way to infect our supplies with their disease. They turned our books into weapons against us; every word, every accursed letter we wrote, was a violence against ourselves."

"Is that so? Truly, a most terrible turn of events," Aquila said, his voice hollow. "Shall I summon your attendants to take you back to the palace?"

"I am going nowhere," Cesare replied. "There remains an account to be settled between us."

Aquila calmly returned his gaze. "I have suffered enough for a thousand silver chalices. My debt to you is repaid."

"I do not care about the chalice. What matters gold and silver, jewellery and coins, compared to *this*?" He swept his hand across his destroyed face. "If I had stayed inside the Palazzo Nero, the Venetians would never have been able to touch me. I could have wrested power from my uncle while the rest of the Seven cowered in the Star Chamber. The damned city would have sung my name with joy! But instead, I had to leave my rooms. To search for *you*."

At his words, Aquila was struck by the clearest vision: Cesare in his private box at the Bibliotheca Niccoló, lowering a browning apple core into a pot of ink and wiping his hands on his breeches.

"You cannot blame me for this," Aquila said quickly. "The only ink you used on my account was the warrant you signed condemning me to Hell. But I escaped."

A thick chuckle echoed around the bookshelves. "You cannot escape Hell, scholar!" Cesare told him. "It is not a cage or a prison cell. The Devil cares not for locked doors, he does not forget—he will always claim what is rightfully his. And in this, I am his faithful agent."

"I escaped," Aquila repeated defiantly. "I will not let you lay a finger upon me. Not now."

Cesare coughed, spitting up a red wad onto the study floor. "If you listen, you can hear the hooves," he rasped. "A black carriage, travelling through the dead of night."

Aquila grabbed a heavy volume from the shelf and raised it in warning but Cesare came at him anyway, a smile on his scabbed lips. He swatted the book dismissively away as Aquila tried to swing it at him. Even ravaged by disease, Cesare was still so *strong*—an ox, seeking to grind him beneath his hooves. A back-handed blow sent Aquila crashing backwards into the looking-glass. He fell to his knees, blood gushing from his nose and mouth. The strength was leaching from his body, as though he had been enfeebled by the sheer unfairness of it all. Cesare's shadow fell across him.

"No!" shrieked Aquila, holding up his hands. "This cannot be! I escaped!"

"And yet the city will still shudder at the word of your death," Cesare vowed. "Consider this *my* dedication to you."

He descended upon Aquila and sank his teeth into his neck, biting through the skin and ripping flesh and tendons. A single, horrified scream rang out, a discordant note startling the rain, and then the house of the great scholar Aquila fell silent.

Ninth Canto
A Crack in the Glass

A sharp, glittering rain comes from the east, stinging the flagstones of the Piazza della Rosa. The veiled lady guides my hand to the start of her tale and begins to read aloud. In a street of silent presses, a falling scrap of paper disturbs the night.

Tommaso Cellini raises a glass to his lips and smiles.

ORSINI'S PLAGUE BALL has turned rotten, a putrid stink reigning in the patron's halls. Windows lie shuttered and barred; corridors echo with hoots and screams, hoarse cries for more wine. As I stumble through the palace's bewildering turns, a pair of disheveled nymphs run giggling past me, hands entwined and their hair spilling carelessly down around their shoulders. Amid the dying candles, an alcove is alive with limbs, fingers busy with stays and drawstrings, the urgent search for bare flesh. Time has lost all meaning; the entire world shrunk to these frantic halls of revelry.

There was a time when I walked these corridors as though they were my own, but now every room is a fresh mystery.

The perpetual night encourages abandon—the noble citizens who first paraded through Orsini's doors now squat in corners to relieve themselves and pass out on the stairs. They came to escape a dying city, only to succeed in creating a horror of a different kind, slipping free from their civil binds to sink into the embrace of the unrecognizable and obscene.

From somewhere within the palace, a spinet plays a wild spiralling melody, my antic companion as I climb a flight of stairs and arrive at a narrow balcony. Soft moans float up from the black depths of the *salone* beyond the balustrade. I take up the candle burning low on the cupboard and venture along the balcony. Portraits line the wall. Their subjects' names are lost to me, but some dim impression of their reputation remains: poets and writers all, the stable upon which Orsini established his fortune. At the end of the row hangs a painting larger than the rest, set in a mahogany frame. A cry goes from the *salone* as I near it—whether in pleasure or pain, I cannot say. Raising my candle with a palsied hand, I gasp. Someone has taken a flame to the portrait, burning away its face completely. Where once there was a mouth, nose and eyes, only a jagged hole remains.

As I gaze up at the poet's absent face, the spinet plays faster and faster, unseen fingers dancing across its keys.

Situated in the lagoon to the north of Venice, the foundries of Murano are blazing cloisters devoted to the worship of glass. Furnaces burn through the day and night, stoked by black-knuckled stizzadors. To preserve the mysteries of cristallo, lattimo and rosechiero, Murano's glassmakers are forbidden from ever leaving: exalted prisoners, trapped on small islands of fire.

I FLEE THE *salone* balcony and follow the steps down to a dingy passageway, rattling door handles until one gives way. Sunlight comes as a violent surprise. Blinking, I raise a hand to shield my eyes. The spinet falls abruptly silent.

I have come out into a walled courtyard wreathed in pungent clouds of lavender and mint. Exhausted fauns slumber on the benches, lulled by a trickling fountain of red wine. The walls are manned by armed guards, who gaze down impassively as a curly-haired young man directs a stream of urine against a tree. He lets out a sigh of relief as I skirt around him, making for a door set into the palace's outer wall. My hand closes around the iron ring.

"I would not, if I were you."

Whirling round, I see the corpulent figure of Orsini waddling towards me. Though he wears an ornate golden mask, I would recognize the patron at any time. My hand snatches guiltily away from the handle.

"The Dalmatians are under strict instructions," he tells me mildly. "Beyond these walls, the rats feast on corpses as they fester in the streets. Death carries on the very air itself. I cannot let you out any more than I can allow anyone else in. The Dalmatians will kill anyone who tries."

"I meant no insult. I was only..."

He waves a chubby hand. "You need not explain. Though it pains me to think that you are so weary of our company that you would choose the plague pit over it."

"I was unworthy of your invitation, my lord," I reply quickly. "I would not have come, but your men were most insistent."

"I learnt long ago that you could not be trusted to see the sense of things, Rinaldi," Orsini says firmly. "You were once the first and foremost poet in Cadenza, your verses as beautiful to behold as the grandest palace or the fairest maiden. And yet, were it not for my men's insistence, you would now be rotting in a pit with the farrier and the fisherman."

"And I am grateful, but—"

"What use have I for your gratitude? Look around you, man! Do you not see what I have created? This is no mere *ball*. I have offered my guests refuge from a dying city, fed and fattened them. They owe their very existence to my whim and sufferance. And how do they treat this greatest of gifts?" He made a sweeping gesture around the courtyard. "They drink themselves into a stupor and soil my hallways with their shit and seed. Freedom has turned them into petty emperors, debased gods. Or perhaps... is it not freedom, but fear that makes a man act so? Fear of the spectre of death that stalks the alleys outside?"

"I cannot say."

A tsk escapes Orsini's golden mouth.

"Is the artist within you truly so cowed, so reduced, that he cannot appreciate the spectacle that I have created for him?" he presses. "Is he not *inspired*?"

I shake my head. "I am no artist, my lord."

He presses a piece of paper into my hand so subtly that I am only aware of the act in its aftermath.

"A line," Orsini murmurs. "A single word. *Anything.*"

A warm breeze blows across the courtyard, dappling the paving stones around the fountain with flecks of claret. The paper trembles in my hand. Apologies and objections spring to my lips, but by the time I look up, Orsini has gone.

Cristallo, lattimo and rosechiero.

A table of wine glasses, raised in celebration.

"A SONG! A SONG!"

Voices flood the courtyard. From the door erupts a sudden crowd, an ashen-faced poet struggling at their head. Catching sight of me, his eyes widen in recognition—he calls out my name as I duck down behind a statue of a winged *putto*, but it is lost among the cackles and cries. A snoring reveller is dragged from a bench, and the reluctant poet goaded into climbing onto the impromptu stage. He runs a hand through his hair, nervously licking his burgundy-stained lips.

"A song, Alberto! A song!"

Alberto clears his throat. "I propose a verse… in honour of Cosimo Petrucci."

The announcement is met with cool silence. In the days of Tommaso Cellini, an offering to the Artifex would be a safe choice. But Tommaso is the Artifex no longer. Alberto falters, aware of the dangerous mood of his audience. Yet to change his mind would only invite further derision. He clears his throat and begins his recital, in a thin voice that struggles to reach the corners of the courtyard. The poem is fawning and clumsy and will satisfy no one. Peeping out from behind the statue, I cast a glance up to the walls, wondering whether the Dalmatians will have to intervene.

And spy, against the sun, a black speck.

Alberto breaks off, ducking as a glass flies through the space his head had occupied a second earlier. He holds up his hands in protest. Far above him, the black speck takes on the shape of a falcon. My hand tightens around the *putto's* stone wing. Alberto tries to climb down from the bench, and is shoved unceremoniously back.

"A song, damned poet!"

Belatedly, Alberto decides on a change of tack, launching into a popular poem of Tommaso's. But he has long since lost his audience. The falcon is streaking through the sky along a perfect diagonal, set on a course straight for the heart of the courtyard. A murmur passes through the crowd as it notes the bird's uneasy trajectory. On the wall, one of the Dalmatians reaches for his bow. Alberto turns and looks up into the sky.

The falcon dives down into the courtyard, straight and true as an arrow, crashing headfirst into the ground directly in front of the horrified poet. There is a horrible sound of small bones snapping. Jeers and catcalls turn to screams as the crowd scatters: Alberto is dragged from his bench, sinking beneath a trampling tide of boots. The bird is a crumpled mess of broken bones and bloodstained feathers. I slump behind the *putto* and jam my fingers in my ears, my chest heaving with sobs.

After that, there are no songs.

There are eighteen glassworks on the island of Murano, each known by a sign hanging above the door: the White Lion and the Mermaid, the Phoenix and the Rooster. A bestiary, its pages singed with brimstone.

I TAKE SHELTER in the midnight aisles of Orsini's private library, which nestles in the upper reaches of the palace and alone in the building appears to have been spared the Plague Ball's violent excesses. Walls of volumes stand guard around me. There was a time when I too boasted a collection of fine books—carriages and liveried attendants besides, gems and fur-lined cloaks. In the months following Donato Pitti's feast, I paced my library from sunset to sundown, searching fruitlessly for words that would not come. I started a hundred poems, each stroke of my pen an ungainly scratch on the paper. Seized by a creeping fear of the blank parchment I could not fill, I locked the doors to my library and rebuffed all suggestions that I return. In time, my books went the way of my carriages and fur-lined cloaks. I have given them no thought since.

My ears prick up at the careful click of the library door. Lying flat on my belly, I crawl over to the shelf and press my eye to a gap between two books. Candles dance in the darkness, casting their fickle glow over a trio of faces: golden-masked Orsini, accompanied by a man I recognize as Lazzaro Negri, esteemed member of the Council of Seven; behind them comes a veiled lady dressed in black. She heads to the cupboard to pour wine while Negri stands at a lectern. My patron waddles over to the shelves, holding up his candle to examine his volumes.

"Well?" he says, without turning around.

Negri hesitates. "I would prefer to speak alone."

"Speak now, and with freedom," Orsini replies. "Vittoria is the most discreet woman in Cadenza. She is also a true artist, and as such can come and go as she pleases within my house."

He accepts a glass from Vittoria and bestows a kiss on her hand. Negri refuses her offering with a brusque shake of the head. Unruffled, she takes his glass for her own and settles into a chair. Negri seems unhappy, but has little option other than to continue.

"I have received grave news from the Palazzo Nero," he announces. "The Artifex has barricaded himself inside his rooms and will not leave."

"A wise precaution, in the circumstances," says Orsini.

"It is a move not of self-preservation, but madness. Cosimo claims he poses too great a danger to be allowed his freedom."

"More dangerous than the plague?"

"He has lost his mind. His inner circle has disintegrated and he refuses to meet with the Seven. No one is ruling this city."

The patron staunches a yawn. "You confuse my rooms for the Star Chamber, Signor Negri," he says. "Knowing well what I have risked to grant you entrance, you repay me with dry talk of palace intrigue."

"I came here to save a city," counters Ridolfi. "Do you think that Venice will hesitate to march on Cadenza once it learns that we are helpless and adrift? How many of your beloved poets will flourish, with the Doge's yoke across their shoulders?"

"What would you have me do—man the city walls?"

"I would have you do *something* to help defend them. You have long mocked the Seven and the business of government, but the number of men with standing and influence shrinks with each passing day. In the Star Chamber, I can set wheels in motion, but your reach extends to places that mine does not—you have the city's ear. Let us decide upon a new Artifex together, here in this room, this very night. Present the people with a saviour in whom they can entrust their hope. The plague has pushed them to the edge of rebellion; it will take the merest spark to ignite them."

"You seem to forget that the Palazzo Nero is already occupied. The Artifex is crowned for life. You cannot simply ask Cosimo to step aside."

"I am not talking about offering him a choice," Negri said bluntly. "Cesare Petrucci has let it be known that he is willing to do what is necessary."

"The *nephew?*" Orsini said scornfully. "I would rather Cosimo remain in power, his wits addled and drool dripping from his chin."

"If not Cesare, then another. Choose your horse, Orsini. But mark it well: this Artifex's reign ends here."

At this, my patron finally turns and looks at Negri, his expression unreadable behind his mask. The night thickens and complicates around them. As I wait for Orsini's reply, a rustle draws my attention to the third member of their party. Vittoria takes a sip of wine, her gaze fixed directly on my hiding place. I break away from my spyhole and press myself, trembling, against the shelf. Sweat beads on my brow. A second passes. Another. Vittoria says nothing.

Whatever else passes between Orsini and Negri is lost to me. I close my eyes and hold my breath until they finish their wine and take their leave of the library, wishing myself a man without a face, with neither ears nor eyes, and no notion of the conversation that has just taken place.

Coiled around Murano's easterly tip, the foundry at the sign of the Viper lies at a slight remove from the others. Fire spits from its crimson mouth.

ALONG AN EVER-DARKENING corridor, I run for my life, a group of angry men at my heels. Why they pursue me, I do not know—perhaps in search of redress for some imperceptible slight I have given them, or simply for the sport of it. At their thunderous tread, I cast a fearful glance over my shoulder, and spy a door lying ajar. I duck through it and close it behind me, willing my shuddering breaths to silence.

Oaths and footfalls, shrill laughter.

The corridor falls quiet.

Slumping against the door jamb, I let out a sigh of relief. Only then, do I realize I am not alone. In the shadows beneath a shuttered window, the veiled lady from the library stretches out on the divan.

I sketch a startled bow. "My lady. Forgive me for interrupting you."

"Be welcome, sir," Vittoria murmurs. "It seems you had little choice in the matter."

"They must have mistaken me for someone else," I tell her.

"Too much wine has been drunk, too many nights spent in darkness. If we do not leave this place soon, I fear that more blood will be spilt."

"You may be safer out in the city," she says. "There is word that the plague is easing."

"Then why does Orsini not tell his guards to open the gates?"

"Who can say? Perhaps he is enjoying himself too much." She moves her legs, clearing space on the divan. "Come, sit beside me and catch your breath."

I hesitate.

"You have nothing to fear," she tells me. "Unlike those fools outside, I know exactly who you are."

"But how?"

"Why, your reputation proceeds you, sir!" Vittoria exclaims, roused. "The name Rinaldi is spoken with reverence in salons across the city, your verses recited by its foremost poets. Our greatest hope is that you will one day offer us a new work. How long has it been, since you last wrote?"

"I do not know," I confess. "A long while. I am not the man I once was. Something... shattered."

"Can it be put back together?"

"Orsini believes so."

"And you?"

"..."

Vittoria nods. "I was once somebody else too, until my name became too heavy to carry and I could bear it no longer. It is hard for others to understand."

Reaching down beneath the divan, she pulls out a wine jug

and pours herself a glass, filling it to the brim with a black liquid.

"What is that?" I ask.

"A gift from friends in Venice," she replies. "It comes from Constantinople, where the natives drink it. It brings joy and courage and insight. And… ease."

Vittoria raises her glass up behind her veil, offering me a glimpse of a small, perfect mouth.

"You are welcome to join me, if you like," she says.

I take a seat beside her and accept the proffered glass. The drink is bitter on my tongue; she gives me an encouraging smile. It is a long time before either of us speaks. Gradually, I become aware of the pandemonium of Orsini's halls fading, my agitation easing into a delicious nothing. A joy fills me, so vast and so profound that it takes a solemn, almost grave aspect. Within my mind, long-forgotten doors swing open, offering new perspectives and original thoughts: a palace of possibilities. I look down in disbelief at the swirling black water, unable to comprehend what alchemical magic could so transform my humour. The foolishness of man, to spend centuries channelling his endeavours into the pursuit of gold, when this glorious elixir—gateway to ecstasy!—was so close at hand.

Later, after we have drained the jug dry, Vittoria offers to tell me a story. She moves aside the folds of her gown to reveal lines of writing inked across her flesh. Guiding my hand to a point upon her upper thigh, she begins to read.

"In my youth, I liked to ride…"

*   *   *

Everything comes from the east. The black water, Tommaso's wine glass, the sharp rain that fell on the Piazza della Rosa—all fashioned in Venice, one way or another, our lives and deaths decided in the twists and turns of its calli and canals.

I awaken in the backroom of a printing shop, its presses pounding their wooden fists against the wall. Vittoria is gone, the grotesque decadences of the Plague Ball now but a memory. How I arrived here from the House of Orsini is a mystery. Under the influence of the black water, time has lost all certainty: I feel I have spent the full measure of a hundred lifetimes inside this rude inn, tormented by the maddening march of words through the next chamber. By candlelight, I toss and turn on a bed of straw, my hands clamped over my ears. A stack of parchment lies untouched on a writing desk.

At length, a door bangs open and a man enters. He is brutish and unshaven, his armpits damp with sweat. I shrink back into the corner of the room.

"I beg of you, sir!" I plead. "Whatever wrong I have done you, take pity on me and free me from this place!"

He spits on the floor. "Do you see a lock upon the door? Leave as you wish. I agreed to house you only as a favour to Orsini. He is resolved that you should write again."

"Write?"

Impatiently, he mimes a scribbling gesture.

"But I told Orsini, I cannot!"

"Then do not tarry on your way out. The presses of Isidore hunger for words, they care nothing for empty reputations and mewling excuses. I saw the hovel they dragged you from when the plague struck—you don't have a *soldi* to your name. Where will you go? The great palaces of Cadenza will not open their doors to poets who do not write."

"Their doors can stay closed. I am happier in a hovel."

Isidore picks at a patch of red flesh on his neck. "You are a myth," he says. "No matter what Orsini says, you are no poet."

"I do not know who I am," I tell him.

His face darkens, and for a moment I fear he means to strike me. Instead Isidore stomps back into the other room. He returns clutching a jug of black liquid, which he slams down on the writing desk.

"Orsini said you would want this," Isidore says.

Cristallo, lattimo and rosechiero.

A table of wine glasses, raised in celebration.

The printing shop has fallen quiet. Isidore's presses stand seething and mute; inside the airless backroom, parchment stuffs the ratholes. An empty jug lies spent on its side. I turn restlessly in the straw, my stomach cramping and my skin crawling with invisible insects. Gradually, through the pain, I become aware of shouting. Struggling to my feet, I creep to the door and push it open.

Isidore stands by the window, a wineskin in his hand. As I look beyond his hulking silhouette out on to the street, I cannot help but wonder whether my mind is still under the sway of the black water—for somehow, on a sultry summer's afternoon, it is snowing. Questions die on my lips; I know better than to interrupt Isidore when he is in his cups. At the creak of the floorboards beneath my foot, he turns.

"Finally," he says. "I thought you'd died back there."

I edge past him and step hesitantly out onto the street. It is not snowflakes spiralling down through the air, I see now, but scraps of paper, tossed out from the upper stories and settling on the ground. On every one, an insult scrawled in an unsigned hand. *Bastard offspring of a miser! Piss-stained coward! Catamite of Venice!* The target of their wrath is clear: Cosimo Petrucci must be arrested and imprisoned, strung up and beaten, tossed headlong out through the city gates! A foul-mouthed chorus, warning of a coming war.

"What say you now, poet?" barks Isidore. "I swear you are the only man in the city who cannot put pen to paper."

The streets are alive with discord. As a coarse ash of invective rains down, Isidore circles around, staring up at the anonymous windows.

"But what does this mean?" I ask him.

He scratches a grizzled cheek. "The beginning of the end," he replies.

Through the swirling parchment, two guardsmen come marching towards us, the blades of their long pikes glinting in the sunlight. As I scramble to my feet one of them grabs me and snatches the paper from my hand. His eyes narrow.

"Did you write this, old man?"

I burst out laughing, the noise sounding wheezing and strange to my ears. Isidore shakes his head. The pikeman bunches up my smock in his fist.

"You think I jest?"

He deals me a shuddering blow to the jaw. The world spins and swims. As I reel away, I am aware of dissenting cries from the buildings around us. A stone flies down and cracks against the guardsman's helm. Isidore backs away into his shop. It is no longer paper falling from the windows but slate and stones, wood and glass. The guardsman raises the butt of his pike to strike me again, only for his companion to drag him back by the arm.

Cosimo's men retreat, to a growing roar.

Outside the sleepless furnaces of Murano, pebbles are reduced to dust in the crushing machines. Tongs and scissors set to work on glass softened by the merciless heat.

The crowd gathers outside Isidore's printing shop, ankle-deep in mud and spiteful verse, wielding sticks and tools—the merry, makeshift instruments of rebellion. I am hoisted into the air, bruised and bloody-lipped and begging to be set down. But the crowd is a raging torrent, surging through the alleys towards the Piazza della Rosa. Chants against Cosimo find willing voices; at one point, a banner bearing a falcon takes flight behind us. Back in Orsini's library, I heard Lazzaro Negri speak of rebellion, but they were mere words. I am caught in the eye of a people's fury, innocent author of a revolution.

On the Piazza della Rosa, ashen faces look on from the windows of Accademia as the crowd storms the square, demanding that the Artifex come before them. The thin line of pikemen behind the gates of the Palazzo Nero takes one look at the approaching masses and backs away up the steps. Calliope's inky pools shiver. As the rioters break ranks and charge forward, the wave carrying me finally breaks, throwing me to the flagstones. I cover my head with my arms as men run over and around me. The crowd swarms around the palace gates, rattling them and hitting them with their sticks.

As I struggle to my feet, high above us comes the sound of breaking glass. Heads turn and necks crane. From a window in the northwest tower, a body comes plummeting down: a ruler faithfully answering his people's summons. There is nothing of the falcon's grace and speed about Cosimo Petrucci's descent, his arms and legs flailing as he falls. His body shudders as it impacts on the flagstones. He does not move again.

The gates buckle and give way, allowing the crowd to swarm around the bloodied remains of their former lord. They kick and stamp on the body and strip it of all clothing. To growing cheers, word goes around the square: the Artifex is dead. Cosimo's corpse is hauled up into the air and paraded around the square, to mocking shouts and whistles of derision—for the March of the Poets, for Tommaso, for the city Cadenza had been before his presumptuous accession. The procession heads out into the streets, stoking the fires of outrage until, on the Ponte Nuovo, Cosimo's limbs are torn from their sockets and his head severed from his torso. What remains of his body, once the people have finished, is tipped into the Adige, where it slips away on the current to find some dank, distant resting place: unwanted master of a city that was never his.

I take refuge by the Well of Calliope, huddling up against the fountain's trefoils. Come dusk, a large shadow falls over me. Isidore marches me back to his shop, unwilling to cede Orsini's reward for my housing. I do not have the strength to resist, bent double with stomach cramps as I am and desperate for peace and anonymity, for a rathole or a crack so small to slip through that the world cannot find me. As I lie in the straw, words multiplying at a thunderous rate in the next room, the image of the falling Cosimo runs through my mind. Could it be that I have played a role in his demise, unwitting and unwilling a participant as I was? I was not the author of the scurrilous note the guardsman found in my hand; I have not written for twenty years.

Inexorably, the past comes to claim me. Memories of a feast I have tried so hard to forget.

Though Murano's craftsmen were forced to remain on the islands, tales of their arts rippled out far beyond the Venetian lagoon. Rumour and fable laid on top of one another, like precious bands in glass.

"To the poet!" a voice goes up, to a murmur of approval around the table.

The name-day feast of Donato Pitti has drawn a host of illustrious guests from Cadenzan society, none more so than the man seated beside me. Tommaso Cellini circles the rim of his wine glass with his finger. The Artifex has sipped his wine with conspicuous care, only now—after courses of boar and sausages, oysters, and twice-roasted goose on baked onions—reaching the bottom of his first serving. A blue serpent winds around the stem of his glass, which has been fashioned from Murano *cristallo* and is inlaid with brilliant bands of gold and quartz. There were murmurs of admiration when Tommaso's attendant first produced it from its wooden case, the snake seeming to dart and dance in the candlelight. Yet the Artifex is in a cool humour this night. The news that Donato's daughter Lucia—a noted beauty—is too ill to attend the feast appears to have irked him, even as he waves away the host's profuse apologies. Tommaso pays little attention to the conversation, which is at once overly timid and too obviously tailored for his approval. I have noticed that he does not laugh, permitting himself nothing weaker than a smile of condescension. I am not frightened of him. But I am very *aware* of him.

Now we wait to see if Tommaso will permit the toast. He is a poet himself, of course; one of the finest in Cadenza, as I believe myself able to judge. Will he take offence at the tribute being offered to another? Across the table from us, Donato Pitti gestures urgently at a servant to fill up Tommaso's glass. Name day or not, every meal the Artifex attends is in his own honour, in one form or another.

"My lord?" Pitti ventures.

The Artifex taps his nail against the glass serpent. "It is a fitting suggestion," he declares. "What do we celebrate here, if not the passage of time, and our noble efforts to leave an imprint upon it—even if it is but the faintest breath on a mirror of interminable dimensions? That faint breath is immortality. Only in Cadenza does the poet sit proudly beside the ruler."

"Only in Cadenza is the ruler himself a poet," I say.

This seems to please Tommaso, who nods.

"This is the City of Words, is it not?" he says casually. "We celebrate our great poets and scholars for they are the authors of our greatness. On the page, for all to see, now and a thousand years hence."

Eager applause greets his declaration. As the rest of the table joins the toast, the Artifex leans in towards me and whispers: "Are you not honoured, Rinaldi?"

"I have no words, my lord," I reply.

Tommaso raises his serpent stem, and smiles.

His glass explodes.

The table is in uproar, shouts and screams puncturing the dull fog that has descended over my senses. Wiping a hand across my cheek, I gaze down at the glittering fragments of glass on my palm. Tommaso clutches at his bloodied face. Yet in the dreadful, interminable seconds that follow, somehow it is not the Artifex who holds my gaze, but Donato Pitti. He sits absolutely still, his expression that of a man who has seen his fate foretold: a proud house reduced in an instant to dust and rubble and ash.

Only then, do I understand what has just taken place.

Of all Murano's secrets, the most closely guarded was kept behind the sign of the Viper, glimpsed only fleetingly within the island's endless reflections: a glass,

*decorated with a blue serpent, which had been fashioned
to shatter on contact with poison.*

In the depths of my despair, Vittoria comes to my rescue.
Isidore's presses stamp their feet in approval at her passage:
she appears in the doorway as a veiled shadow, a jug in her
hands. Rising from my stinking bed of straw, I stammer an
apology. She graciously waves me away.

"I am glad to see you, sir," she says. "I heard you were at
the head of the crowds when the Palazzo Nero fell."

"You did? But how?"

Vittoria smiles. "Orsini's eyes are everywhere. Who else
can make the streets rain with parchment?"

"The poems against Cosimo were his doing? He moves
against the Artifex?"

"He moves to save the city."

"With whom as its leader?"

"Someone befitting the City of Words. Cosimo was an
honourable man, but he did not understand Cadenza's soul.
Our leader should be a poet. A great poet." She steps forward
and clasps my hands, whispering in my ear so quietly that
each word is a breath of fresh air. "Why do you think Orsini
had you housed here, in the very heart of the uprising? He
does nothing by chance."

"I do not understand!"

"It is you, Rinaldi. You shall be the new Artifex!"

"Madness!" I gasp, pushing her away. "I cannot... I will
not... I cannot...!"

"Courage, brave poet," says Vittoria. She brushes her

thumb across my bloodied lip. "You have nothing to fear. It will all be taken care of. Come, sit with me, and let us seek out a happier place together."

Numbly, I let her guide me down into the straw. We drink the black water, filling our veins with ink. The burning across my skin mellows into a delicious warmth; all questions vanish, my pain melting away. Vittoria sighs, a veiled angel of dark alcoves. The presses fall silent.

Later, as the water's pull begins to ebb, I ask her whether I can hear the end of the tale she began in Orsini's. She hesitates briefly before nodding, slipping free from her gown to lie naked before me in the darkness. With a trembling hand, I trace the flawless path of the story that covers Vittoria: down her thigh and encircling her foot, continuing up the length of her calf to the generous curves of her behind; up her arching back and along her shoulder blades to her neck and cheek, down breast and belly. Only when my finger reaches the bottom of her veil does Vittoria tense, but she makes no move to stop me. I lift up her veil and follow the story to its end. Both of us are crying.

As I lean in to kiss the tears from Vittoria's cheeks, the door bangs open and a young couple burst inside the room. Their faces blanch at the sight of us. I try to rise but the man shoves me back, sending me sprawling into the straw and upending the jug of black water. Vittoria screams as the girl hauls her from the straw, grabbing her wrist and dragging her towards the door. With her companion's help, they wrestle Vittoria from the room.

I lie stunned on the floor, a thunderous banging inside my skull. At a stroke, all that I have left has been taken from me.

Vittoria is gone and I am alone in the cacophonous gloom of this house of words, black water seeping away through the cracks.

Cosimo hurtles down to the piazza, his body shattering into a thousand sharp pieces as he smashes against the ground. Fire rages through the Printing Quarter, engulfing Cadenza's palaces and libraries; a paper city, burning away to nothing. The veiled lady slips her arms around Isidore's neck and whispers in his ear. Orsini raises his golden mask, revealing a face obscured by a swollen purple bubo. Debased gods squat.

Tommaso raises his glass to his lips, and smiles.

Tenth Canto
The Siege of Caterina

I. *The Folly*

KNOW THEN THAT at that moment a man appeared at Cadenza's East Gate having been away from the city for a great many years. He had travelled thousands of leagues from one end of the civilized world to the other, from England's cloudy isle to the parched lands of the Levant, observing armies in the field of battle. Upon his return to Italy, he had written a scholarly work about the pursuit of warfare, lecturing on the subject at the universities of Padua and Bologna; the renowned general, Andrea Gritti, had received him in Venice. Only now was this man, who went by the name of Stefano Pellegri, returning to the city of his birth.

The road to Cadenza was thronged with travellers, two hosts following opposite paths of the compass and differing greatly in countenance and disposition. From the west came the citizens fleeing the city, possessions bundled on their backs, bedraggled flotsam on a tide of misery; from the east marched the soldiers of fortune, bellicose pilgrims invigorated by the prospect of plunder and bloodshed. Stefano fell in step with a band of Swiss pikemen, trading his wineskin for rumours from the road. Cadenza's plight seemed to worsen by the hour: its great houses ravaged by plague, streets simmering with unrest; and now the Artifex leapt to his death, torn limb from limb by his own citizens and his body parts displayed about the city. It was common knowledge that Venice was considering a march on its impudent rival. In Stefano's estimation, Cadenza would almost certainly fall before the year was out.

And yet, for all the gathering clouds, he could not deny the skip of his heart at the sight of the light glittering on the languid stretches of the Adige, the libraries' steepling towers soaring up beyond the city walls. Memories that Stefano had fended off during long nights on cold stone floors and pitted fields, tense campfires on the eve of battle, now came back to him in a flood. Quickening his step, he bid farewell to the pikemen and pushed through the crowds gathered around the East Gate.

He entered a watchful and uneasy city. Men carried their arms openly; flat, suspicious gazes marked his passage. Stefano made his way through the deserted squares of the former Pitti neighbourhood towards the Ponte Mercato, following directions in a letter he carried inside his jerkin. The streets were at once unknown and strangely familiar— yet by the same token, Stefano reflected, was he not altered greatly from the headstrong youth who had left Cadenza? A stray cannonball at the Battle of Pamplona had robbed him of his left eye and arm, leaving him with a patch over his socket and a sleeve pinned to his shoulder. His skin had been weathered by sandstorms and foreign suns; his frame boiled down to hardened sinew. He smiled rarely. Even the closest companions of his youth would struggle to recognize him now, the merry tavern wit now battle-scarred and sober.

Stefano crossed over the Ponte Mercato to the Verso, where he headed east along a pleasant riverside avenue. A set of gateposts topped by stone galleys marked the residence he sought: he walked up the approach to an imposing palace and knocked at the door. Upon presenting the steward with his letter, Stefano was led wordlessly through to a great hall adorned with tapestries depicting scenes of crowded battle, the clash of the spear and the lance rendered in vivid threads of red and gold. In the middle of the hall, Duke Agostino stood poring over a set of maps. The banker was a large man with fierce eyebrows and a florid complexion. His bald head shone brightly as a copper coin. In contrast to his fine surroundings, the duke was dressed plainly, in a brown doublet without embroidery or ornament. He looked up eagerly as the steward announced Stefano.

"Welcome, sir!" he exclaimed, in a booming voice. "I had wondered if I would see you. These are unhappy times for our city."

Stefano bowed stiffly. "I have seen unhappier cities," he replied.

"You are a son of Cadenza, I believe."

"Born in the shadow of the Library Niccoló. Although it has been many years since I last called it home."

"I was glad my message found you in Venice. Word has it you spoke with Gritti."

"I did."

"You should have slipped a knife through his ribs."

"Small reward for his hospitality."

"The people of Cadenza can only hope that the general shows similar decorum when his army comes knocking at the gates."

"The people of Cadenza are running for the hills," Stefano said bluntly. "Anyone who stays is a fool."

Agostino raised an eyebrow. "Your manners, sir, are more soldier than scholar."

"Forgive me, my lord. I have spent these last ten years in the company of fighting men, whose courtesies lack the polish of the salon. Your letter spoke of a matter of great urgency."

"Yes, yes," said the duke, with an irritable wave of the hand. "I remember well what I wrote to you. First, there is something I would have you see."

Turning upon his heel, Agostino marched out of the hall and embarked upon a complicated journey through his palace to a room at the top of a tower. He unlocked the door with a key from a chain around his neck and gestured impatiently at Stefano to enter. Inside the chamber was a lectern, a book resting on its slanted surface. At Agostino's urging, Stefano went over and examined the cover.

"*De re militari*. Roberto Valturio."

"Lorenzo de' Medici's own copy," the banker told him proudly. "I will not tell you what it cost me to leave Florence with this under my arm, but cities have been sacked for less. The woodcuts are especially fine, I think."

Stefano turned the page. "It is a masterpiece."

"The finest book on warfare ever written," Agostino

agreed. "And I have read all of them of worth, including your own. Through my studies, I have come as close to the battlefield as a man can without strapping on armour and bloodying his blade." He let out a deep sigh. "Yet, little was I to know, that the opening of this volume would unleash a misery to rival that contained within Pandora's jar."

"My lord?"

"The truth is, sir, that I find myself entrenched in a bitter conflict within the walls of my own household—a battle joined without trumpet or fanfare and unmarked by valorous deeds. No swords ring out, not a drop of blood has been shed. Yet with each passing day, my honour receives a further crippling blow."

"You may have to speak more plainly, my lord," Stefano said. "There is little appetite for riddles amongst men of war."

Agostino reached across him and closed the book on the lectern.

"It would be easier if I showed you," he said crisply.

The duke locked the door behind him and descended the tower, striding through a hall lined with his own portraits. An archway led out into the central courtyard, where a squat bastion reared up before them, pugnacious as a clenched fist. It seemed to have sprung directly from the pages of the Valturio, a defiant outpost on the frayed and lawless edges of Christendom.

Stefano scratched his cheek. "What is this?"

"The act of sheerest folly," Agostino replied.

As he cast his lone eye over the building, noting with admiration the carved corbels beneath the parapets, Stefano caught sight of a movement at the top of the tower. There was a flash of bright silk, a shock of long, golden hair.

"And this would be…?"

"The fair Caterina," said Agostino. "My lady wife."

II. *The Night of Sorrows*

STEFANO HAD SEEN too much in the way of battle and bloodshed to be given to idle romances. Yet as he gazed up at Lady Caterina, it felt as though the natural world had conspired to announce her in the most glorious fashion possible, the aroma of blushing roses filling the courtyard and the late-summer sun providing a generous golden frame. She stepped gracefully along the parapet, a single stalk of corn swaying in the breeze, her smiling face upturned towards the sun. Did Stefano imagine it, or had the birds—mute on his passage through the city—now burst into song?

Agostino cleared his throat.

"Forgive me," Stefano said hurriedly. "I am not sure I understand."

"Then perhaps I have enlisted the services of the wrong man," the banker said curtly. "You have seen a defensive tower before, have you not?"

"Of course. But manned by soldiers and bowmen, not ladies in silk gowns. Your wife resides within the tower?"

"And will not step foot outside it, nor even open the door," Agostino told him. "She remains completely beyond reach, deaf to all my entreaties."

"Incredible. How has this come to pass?"

"Know this, sir: I am a man of business. I deal in accounts and contracts, not pretty words and poetry. Fair as Caterina is, there are other brides in this city of equal beauty, and with fewer years chalked up among their debts. But her father, Guiliano, possesses something the others do not—contacts in Antwerp, who have hitherto remained deaf to my overtures. The alignment of our houses promised great financial opportunities. I had been warned to expect some resistance from Caterina, whose boldness and headstrong nature have caused her father no end of unhappiness. In her youth, Guiliano had been forced to end her childish dalliance with a musician, and Caterina had fiercely resisted all subsequent attempts to match her. Yet I was surprised to find her most agreeable in nature; she even requested to see the Valturio, complimenting it in a manner that gave me great heart. She confessed that she lived in fear of the growing threat of Venice and was sorely troubled by my resolution never to abandon Cadenza. So artfully did Caterina sow the seeds of the notion, it seemed to spring forth from my own imagining: to ease her fears, I would build a bastion in my own courtyard as proof of my devotion. When I told her of my plan, she showered me with affection and agreed to take my hand.

"An army of men laboured ceaselessly to complete the tower before our wedding day. It was stocked as though for a true siege, with weapons and provisions and access to a well. All seemed set fair, yet I had been played for a fool—upon our wedding night, Caterina excused herself from my bedchamber and fled to the tower with her duenna, locking the door behind them."

"When was this?"

Agostino chewed on his lip. "A year ago," he said finally.

A coughing fit assailed Stefano with such ferocity that the banker was moved to strike him on the back. Stefano shied away, holding up his hand.

"Truly, I am fine," he said weakly. "A most vexing situation, my lord. But if what you say is true, then the marriage has not been sealed in God's eyes. Surely the church would make no objection if you annulled this union and took another bride?"

Agostino drew himself up. "And concede defeat? Have I not been humiliated enough? The only way I can hope to reclaim my reputation is to walk into Ridolfi's salon with Caterina on my arm, offering me all the doting affections that one would expect from a wife. But if I am to have any hope of achieving this, I need to get her down from that damned tower!"

"To which end, you would seek my assistance."

"If the Doge of Venice would have you speak with him on military matters, surely you can steer this minor domestic stand-off to a happy conclusion?"

"I have seen wars and bloody sieges; whole armies slaughtered, cities razed to the ground," Stefano told him frankly. "But nothing like this."

"You told me you were a man of Cadenza, sir. Believe me when I say: I am its last hope. You have walked its streets—do they not teeter on the brink of anarchy? Any day now, the Venetians will march against us, yet the Palazzo Nero lies empty and the Council of Seven squabble amongst themselves. My fortune can win me the city, but I cannot hold it without respect. I have tried soft words and flattery; I have hammered on the door until my knuckles bled. I have paid poets to stand beneath the tower windows and offer tender verses. But still Caterina ignores me."

"She cannot stay up there forever."

"She has lasted a year," Agostino reminded him. "And with your friend Gritti eyeing our city, I cannot rely on her growing weary any time soon. All that now remains to me is the machinery of war."

Stefano hesitated. "I do not deny the city is imperilled," he said. "But I will not drag a woman to the marriage bed against her will."

"Do not mistake me for a barbarian, sir," Agostino said stiffly. "This is my wife we are discussing; I will not have her looted and pillaged. I wish merely the chance to speak with Caterina, face-to-face, to win her round with reason. What chance have I now, with these battlements between us? In return for your efforts, I can offer you the hand of Pagolo Monti's daughter, Beatrice. She is a great beauty, noted for her grace and charm, and sought after by the most eligible young men of Cadenza."

"And what does Beatrice think of this proposal?" Stefano enquired. "I doubt that I am any woman's dream, let alone one noted for her grace and charm."

"Beatrice has sufficient of both for the pair of you," Agostino said abruptly. "And she will do as her father commands, who in turn will do as I command. It will be a match greatly to your advantage. Will you help me, sir?"

As Caterina stepped down from the parapet, Stefano saw her glance down into the courtyard for the first time. If she registered her husband talking with a one-armed stranger, she gave no outward sign as she disappeared inside the tower. The sun withdrew with her, the birds falling silent.

Stefano nodded. "I will help you," he said.

III. *Escalade*

STEFANO SPENT THE remainder of the afternoon examining the tower, making sketches and measurements of its dimensions. The fortress was octagonal in shape, similar in design to the *bergfrieds* of the German forest crags, and topped with a tiled conical roof. He could only admire the quality of the rusticated masonry—Agostino had evidently spared no cost to fulfil his pledge to his wife-to-be, unaware that he was sealing his own humiliation with every stone. Its only door was a forbidding barrier hewn from thick oak, dotted with pyramid studs and reinforced with iron bands. The windows began at the third storey, set into the stone beneath a fighting platform encircled by a parapet. As Stefano paced the courtyard, he had the sense of eyes following him from inside the tower.

He was joined on his reconnaissance by Agostino's captain of the guards, Leonardo. A bluff-spoken veteran who had been wounded during Cadenza's defeat at the battle of Rovigo, Leonardo was guided by a cynical pessimism that informed almost every sentiment he expressed, and seemed to give him a strange, cheering comfort. Stefano, who had met countless men of his type around the world's campfires, quickly judged him a competent soldier.

"It is good that you are here," Leonardo confided, in a low voice. "It is high time the duke came to his senses. I would have torn down that accursed tower months ago, but he will not hear of it. He cannot bear the thought of Lady Caterina sustaining an injury—or the damage that might do to his reputation."

"It is a most unusual situation," Stefano remarked. "Though if anyone has lost their senses, it would seem to me to be Agostino's wife."

The captain glanced up at the tower before replying, the words sidling out of the corner of his mouth. "You are closer to the truth than you imagine," he muttered. "But the blame for this lies at the Spaniard's door, not Lady Caterina."

Stefano frowned. "What Spaniard?"

"The duenna. Sence. I had her marked as a witch the first time I laid eyes on her."

"You believe she has enchanted Caterina?"

"How else can you explain what has taken place here? The duke may be a serious man, with little time for frivolity or romance, but Lady Caterina was set for a life of ease. Now she lives like a prisoner inside that tower. You think that a choice she would make freely, were she not under the influence of some malign spell?"

"I am here for my knowledge of swords and siege towers," Stefano replied. "The battle for a woman's heart is another thing entirely."

He returned to the great hall to seek out Duke Agostino, who had immersed himself in strategic plans for the defence of Cadenza. At Stefano's proposal, he glanced up from his maps, frowning.

"Ladders?"

"To these exact dimensions," Stefano told him, laying his sketch out across the table. "I have gauged the tower's height by measuring its shadow against a ten-foot pole. Using these ladders, your men can climb up to the parapet and gain entrance to the building. The door will open easily enough from the inside."

"And if my lady wife should try to prevent them?"

"Rest assured that your men know full well the consequences should any harm befall Lady Caterina. She will be treated with the utmost respect."

"As plans go, this sounds a little..." Agostino waved his hand. "Rustic."

"Sometimes the simplest plans are the most effective. In the heat of battle, it is easy to forget a cunning stratagem."

Agostino inspected Stefano's diagram intently before summoning the steward. By mid-morning the next day, two ladders of the exact length stipulated were being carried through the palace halls. Stefano followed them through to the courtyard, where he found Agostino pacing impatiently beneath the arcade. Sweat was glistening on the duke's domed head.

"Let us tarry no longer, sir!" he said. "Lest you wish a trumpeter to blow you a fanfare?"

"A final suggestion, my lord: give your wife one last chance to leave of her own undertaking," Stefano advised. "If she sees that you are resolved, she may be cowed into submission."

"Cowed into submission?" The duke gave him a sidelong glance. "You have obviously never met Caterina."

"No doubt she is as formidable as she is fair. But there are but two women inside that tower, surrounded by a guard of trained soldiers. I do not expect us to be long detained."

Agostino gestured at Leonardo to step forward. The captain saluted crisply and marched over to the tower. He banged his fist on the door.

"Lady Caterina!" he called out. "Your husband, Duke Agostino, bids you to come out from this place and assume your rightful position at his side. He has shown great patience, but this display of resistance must end. Open the door, or we will be forced to gain entrance through force."

From one of the arrow-slit windows, came forth a salvo of Spanish invective. Stefano winced.

"You speak the language?" said Agostino.

"I picked up a few words at Pamplona. A soldier's vocabulary."

"What did the duenna say?"

"Nothing I would care to repeat. It would appear Sence has also spent some time around military men."

Agostino irritably signalled for Leonardo to return to the arcade. The captain was passed in the courtyard by four of his men—Baccio, Tozzo, Agnolo and Cadere—who were split into two teams, each carrying a ladder between them. Passing under the tower's shadow, the men stood the ladders up against the walls, Agnolo and Cadere holding the legs steady while Baccio and Tozzo began to climb. At the commencement of battle—even this bizarre, almost farcical engagement—Stefano could not deny a small thrill, a volley of tiny arrows shivering down his back.

Baccio and Tozzo made swift progress up the ladders and

were almost at the windows when a figure appeared on the parapet. It was a short, olive-skinned woman, carrying a large black pot. Leonardo's face darkened.

"Sence," he growled.

Moving briskly, without ceremony, the duenna carried the steaming pot over to the box machicolation above Baccio's head and tipped its contents down through the stone bracket. The guard let out an ear-splitting howl, almost slipping from the ladder as he tried to claw scalding liquid from his eyes. Tozzo looked across at his companion, and then down at the ground. He elected to continue climbing. As he scrambled up the rungs towards the parapet, Sence promptly upended the pot's remains over him. Tozzo's screams joined Baccio's echoing around the courtyard.

Down on the ground, Agostino's face turned purple as he watched his men clamber back to solid ground. Shaking off the exhortations of their cohorts, Tozzo and Baccio stomped away from the tower, red-faced and dripping. Stefano beckoned Baccio over and dipped his fingertip in the burning concoction. He dabbed a little on his tongue.

"Iberian stew," he reported.

"She fights us off with *stew*?" Agostino roared. "Get back up those ladders now, you dogs!"

A large shadow fell across them. Whirling around, Stefano saw that Tozzo's ladder had come away from the tower. For the briefest moment, it remained perfectly upright, standing straight-backed upon its legs. Then, with a wobble, it began to fall.

"Take cover!" Stefano barked.

He ushered the duke under the arches as Tozzo's ladder

came down on the arcade with a resounding crash, sending tiles raining down on the gravel and guards diving for cover. It was quickly followed by Baccio's ladder, which fell even swifter and scraped across the roof before joining its companion on the ground. Through a rising cloud of dust, Stefano saw Sence brush her hands and disappear back inside the tower.

The courtyard plunged into an astonished silence. A solitary tile slipped and smashed on the flagstones. Duke Agostino glared at Stefano.

"Still expect us to be not long detained?"

"This may take a little longer than I thought," Stefano conceded.

IV. *Pool of Siloam*

AGOSTINO'S PALACE RANG with the sound of workmen's hammers. In the great hall, the counters on the map of Cadenza jumped in fright; inside the tower reading room, the Valturio trembled on the lectern. The cacophony carried through the hallways all the way down a cellar stairwell, to where a party of men picked their way through the gloom. Leonardo led the way, a burning torch in hand, followed by Agnolo and Cadere; Stefano escorted Duke Agostino. Tozzo and Baccio brought up the rear, their flesh still pink where it had been doused in boiling stew. As they went deeper into the earth, the hammering gradually began to fade.

"How far will you have me descend, sir?" Agostino enquired stiffly of Stefano. "I do not see why this subterranean expedition requires my attendance. Back at the surface, there is an entire city in need of my attention."

"Consider it a fillip for your men," Stefano advised. "At the siege of Mirandola, Pope Julius rallied his troops by ordering that he be carried in his litter through the snow to stand by their side."

"Pope Julius?" Agostino's eyes narrowed. "He was in league with the Venetians, was he not?"

"The warrior pope, they called him."

"And what, pray, would the warrior pope have made of the fiasco I witnessed in the courtyard this morning?"

"It is a fortunate commander who has never overseen a reverse of some kind. The trick is to regroup undaunted and strike a decisive rebuttal."

"I say we try the ladders again," Cadere called out, over his shoulder. "How much stew can they have in there?"

"By all means, let us find out," Baccio replied acidly. "I will hold the ladder while you climb, and Tozzo can pick the boiling carrot from your eye."

Agostino ordered him quiet, and it was with a slightly surly air that the party came out into the cellars. Leonardo's torch wavered in the draughts as he guided them, stooping, through the archways.

"I will wait no longer for an explanation, sir," the duke declared. "What is our purpose here?"

"You said that Lady Caterina had access to a well," replied Stefano. "If we cannot take the tower from above, let us see if we can breach it from below."

"Mining, you mean?" Leonardo growled. "That's a dirty and dangerous business, and just as likely to bury us alive as lead us to our goal. I'd sooner take my chances on the ladders."

"Many a long siege has been ended this way."

"Aye, and there's the rub. Do you know how long it will take us to dig a tunnel through to the well? Short of blasting a hole through the—"

He broke off. In the next chamber, a section of the wall had crumbled in, masonry spilling out across the floor. An icy wind blew into the cellar through a narrow fissure. The captain crouched down beside the hole and thrust his torch inside. He let out a low whistle.

"Looks like someone's done our work for us," he rasped.

Stefano glanced at Agostino. "Is it possible that this is Lady Caterina's handiwork?"

"There are the makings for explosive devices within the tower," the duke admitted. "A hearth and bellows, supplies of pitch, sulphur and powdered lime. But concocting a pot of stew is one thing, munitions quite another. I cannot believe Caterina would be capable of this."

"She does not need to be, my lord," Leonardo said, examining the scarred brickwork. "This is Sence's doing."

"Do you not think we would have noticed, if she had started blowing up walls?"

"This far below ground?" said Stefano. "I would not be so sure."

Agostino stared at him incredulously. "Do you mean to tell me that Caterina and Sence have had the run of my palace this whole time?"

"No wonder we couldn't starve them out!" Agnolo laughed. "They could stroll to the kitchens any time their bellies rumbled. They've probably eaten better than we have."

Yet, with this revelation, came the realization of an unexpected opportunity. Agostino insisted on taking the lead, though he cut an undignified figure as he struggled through the hole, cursing as he caught his bare head on the wall and pushing away Cadere's attempts to help him. One-by-one, they ducked under the brickwork into a natural passage running through the earth. In the distance, came the sound of trickling water. Rocks glistened beneath their feet.

"The well lies ahead!" Agostino called out. "Onwards, men!"

He strode off down the tunnel, his men hastening after him—all save Leonardo. The captain lingered by the hole, chewing on his lip.

"I would not tarry here long," Stefano said wryly. "Pope Julius has the scent of victory in his nose."

"Not once in battle have I seen fortune such as this," Leonardo muttered. "I do not like it one bit."

"You think Sence anticipated our expedition to the cellars? You credit this woman with divine perception."

"Not that. But the Devil's eyes see clearly in darkness."

An echoing shout of triumph sent them hurrying along the passage. By Stefano's estimation, they were passing directly beneath the tower—did he imagine it, or could he hear swift footsteps overhead? The tunnel brightened and they emerged into a cavern. A small pool lay motionless in the hollow, a wooden pail suspended on a rope above the water. Agostino and his guards were milling about the rocks at the pool's edge, examining the walls for handholds.

"Glad you could join us, sirs!" the duke said, craning his neck upwards. "We stand upon victory's threshold."

"And yet, still possible for us to trip at the last," Leonardo called back. "I would not hand the garlands out just yet, my lord."

Agostino gave him a sideways look. "With a fighting spirit like that, little wonder we lost at Rovigo."

"In my experience, fighting spirit tends to be stronger in those directing warfare than those actually taking to the field."

"Do I not stand beside you now?"

Stefano sniffed the air. "Do you smell that?"

"Smoke," said Leonardo. He held up his torch. The upper reaches of the well had been obscured by a shifting grey haze that was drifting slowly down towards them.

"Perhaps Sence burns her stew," Cadere suggested, with a smirk.

"An amusing notion," Stefano said coolly. "But, in my experience, smoke usually travels up, not down."

Leonardo swore. "The hearth has bellows, remember? It is as I told you: the Spanish witch knows that we are here."

"So now you baulk at a puff of vapour?" Agostino scoffed. "Pull down that rope and *I* shall ascend it into the tower."

Baccio and Cadere waded into the pool, bickering over who would hoist up the other into the air. The smoke continued to inch its way down the well. Stefano slowly circled around. Leonardo was right: something was amiss here. Through the hiss of Sence's bellows and the splashing of the guards, Stefano's ears caught a low hum. Baccio squatted down and laced his fingers together, preparing to receive Cadere's foot. Above their heads, the bucket shivered.

Stefano turned to Agostino. "Run," he said.

The duke stared at him. "Run? Have you lost your mind?"

As the first tendrils of smoke brushed against the pail it began to shake, the hum growing to a whine. Baccio and Cadere froze. Grabbing Agostino, Stefano wrestled the indignant duke into the passageway. The smoke thickened.

A black cloud erupted from the bucket.

Suddenly the tunnel was alive with furious insects—Stefano wrapped a protective arm around Agostino, who cried out as a hornet delivered a stinging rebuke to his cheek. The guards came galloping after them, Leonardo cutting fiery swathes through the smoke with wild swings of his torch. Together they stumbled for the safety of the cellars, cursing at the sharp stings on their hands and neck, an incensed swarm hot on their heels.

V. *The Fields of Brescia*

Having been repelled twice in quick succession, the besieging forces withdrew to the great hall. Agostino's guards nervously lined the wall as the duke hunched over his map of Cadenza, toying with a counter. He had changed into a fresh doublet and hose, salve lathered across the angry stings on his cheek and nose. His eyebrows bristled angrily; his complexion, naturally florid, had turned deep crimson.

"Explain to me, please," he said finally, "how one woman can keep an entire guard of fighting men at bay."

Stefano rubbed behind his eyepatch. "Sieges can make heroes of unlikely men, my lord," he replied. "The mathematician Archimedes kept Rome's quinqueremes from the gates of Syracuse with machines of war of his own devising. He built catapults and bolt throwers, burned sails using mirrors that channelled the sun's heat, and fashioned an iron claw that could lift whole ships out of the water and dash them on the rocks."

"Then let us be thankful we only have a Spanish governess to overcome," Agostino replied sourly. "As even that appears to be beyond us at present."

"Sence is no mere woman," Leonardo declared. "She fights like a Turk, so let us respond appropriately. Wait until she next appears in the window and stick an arrow in her eye."

"And how fondly will the lady Caterina view me then, do you think, with her bosom companion bleeding out on the floor before her?" snapped Agostino.

"Perhaps the shock might bring her to her senses," Tozzo suggested.

He ducked as a counter flew through the air towards his head, ricocheting off the tapestry behind him. Scowling, the duke rounded on Stefano. "You, sir, are supposed to be the expert in these matters, yet twice you have led us into disaster. What wise words have you for me now?"

"Leonardo is right," Stefano replied calmly. "Sence is a most unexpected and determined obstacle. If we cannot overpower her, let us see if we can win her over to our cause."

"Win her over?" barked the duke. "How? From the moment Sence entered Caterina's service, the two have been inseparable. Why would she betray her now?"

Stefano shrugged. "Everyone has their price. Offer her five hundred florins to open the tower door in the middle of the night. If done discreetly, Lady Caterina need never even find out."

"And how do you propose I open negotiations? Shall I cup my hand and call up to the battlements?"

"A letter. Delivered in secret and written in Spanish, to disguise its contents lest your wife should stumble across it."

Agostino tapped a counter on the table. "Very well," he said. "You can write it. I told you that Beatrice Monti is a great beauty, did I not?"

"You did, my lord."

"Ordinarily, she would be a prize well beyond your reach. So I would make your proposal a pretty one."

He dismissed the guards and rose from his chair, his steward hastening forward to wrap a cloak around his shoulders. "The Seven gather in the Star Chamber to discuss Cosimo's successor," Agostino announced. "I must try once again to break the deadlock."

"Hard to defend a city, without a leader," agreed Stefano.

"Would that Tommaso Cellini were still alive—he would never have permitted this decline." Agostino gave him a sidelong glance. "I heard talk that Tommaso's nephews were in Venice."

"Alessandro and Galeotto? That rumour had reached Venice as well, although nobody there believed it. Gritti seemed to think they hadn't left Cadenza."

"Impossible! Someone would have seen them."

"If they had the luxury of liberty, perhaps. But every city has its secret rooms, its cells and dungeons..."

"Come now, sir!" Agostino scoffed. "Cosimo Petrucci did not have the stomach for that kind of thing."

"As you wish. But wherever they may be, Alessandro and Galeotto Cellini are not in Venice."

Agostino scratched at a sting on his neck, coating his fingers in salve. Shaking his head, he wiped his hand on his cloak and swept from the hall. Stefano took a seat at the writing desk and composed a brief letter to Sence in her own tongue, outlining the duke's offer. What little Spanish he knew had been gleaned during his convalescence following the Battle of Pamplona and was barely adequate for the task in hand. As he battled with the language, the knights of Agostino's tapestries continued their valiant struggle in the field—less warfare than glorious sport, orderly and bloodless.

On finishing his letter, Stefano returned to the courtyard to find it bathed in bright sunshine. It seemed that good fortune—conspicuous by its absence since his arrival at the palace—now favoured him, for the duenna was out on the battlements, hanging out laundry. He tied his note around a stone and tossed it carefully up towards the parapet. At the fourth attempt, the message disappeared over the side. Sence stooped to pick it up and scuttled inside.

Stefano retreated to a bench beneath the arcades to wait. From here he could look along the arbour through into the garden, where Tozzo sat picking idly at a lute. Stefano's missing arm began to throb. He settled back and closed his eye as the sun warmed the bench under him. Ten years of warfare had left him well-versed at taking rest whenever the opportunity arose—the unexpected lulls of siege time, when the cannon fell silent and the trebuchet slumbered. He fell asleep almost at once.

At a dull thud, his eye flicked open. A small round object

had appeared on the gravel not far from the tower. Rising from his bench, Stefano crossed the courtyard and crouched warily beside it. To find an onion, wrapped in a scrap of parchment.

Stefano smiled.

WITH NIGHTFALL CAME rain, the moon taking obliging cover behind a cloud. Stefano stood beneath the arcades with Leonardo as Tozzo and Cadere unlaced their boots. "This is a mistake," the captain declared. "You do not make deals with the Devil. Who knows what it will ask of you in return?"

"It is a matter of business, nothing more," Stefano replied firmly. "Once we get the signal, the guards can go forth and open the door."

"So you have told us," Cadere interjected, lifting up his leg to show the grimy sole of his foot. "But I still don't understand why we have to take off our boots."

Stefano bit back an oath. "As I have already explained to you," he said patiently, "this is a mission requiring the utmost delicacy and discretion. Sence is most keen that Lady Caterina does not learn of our agreement. She also says the sound of your boots crunching on the gravel is enough to rouse the dead."

"But it's raining!"

"Are you a soldier or not, man? During the sack of Brescia, the fields were so sodden that Gaston de Foix ordered his men to fight barefoot, the better to find their footing."

"If I wanted to fight for a Frenchman, I'd go to Paris," Agnolo retorted.

A light appeared in the tower's highest window.

"The signal!" Stefano hissed. "Lady Caterina retires for the night. Away with you!"

Grumbling, the guards stole out from beneath the arches, their bare feet soundless across the gravel. Yet no sooner had their shadows melting into the night than a figure appeared in the window. Almost as though in a dream, Stefano watched as Lady Caterina leaned out and unfurled a blanket, shaking its contents into the air. A cascade of tiny silver stars fell glittering to earth, settling on the gravel.

"What fresh mischief is this?" said Leonardo.

"I do not know," Stefano said uneasily. "But Caterina is most assuredly awake. We should call your men back."

"Too late."

The moon emerged from behind a cloud, illuminating the two guards as they crouched by the entrance to the tower. Cadere pressed his ear to the wood and tried the handle. There came a great whoosh of air, and both men were engulfed in a thick white cloud that billowed out from beneath the door. They reeled away, coughing and wiping tears from their eyes.

Stefano scratched his cheek.

"Lime powder?" he said.

The captain nodded. "By the looks of it. Poor bastards."

As his men fled blindly from the poisonous fog, Tozzo screamed and clutched at his foot—only then, did Stefano understand why Sence had insisted they remove their shoes. The glinting objects Lady Caterina had sprinkled over the ground were caltrops, metal spikes designed to slow the advance of infantry. Another trap. The light in the tower window winked out as the yowling guards danced tenderfooted back towards the arcades. Leonardo patted Stefano on the back.

"So much for Gaston de Foix," he said. "What will you tell the duke?"

"That as pretty a proposal as I made," Stefano replied, as the guards hopped and swore. "Sence had a prettier reply."

VI. *Iskoroten*

As DAWN STIRRED, Lady Caterina appeared on the tower battlements. Stefano watched from a balcony as she sprinkled grain about the parapet, laughing with delight as birds descended from the sky and flocked around her. Was she aware that she was being watched? Her joy seemed entirely natural and, despite everything, private: a small moment of freedom.

Absorbed, Stefano did not hear Leonardo's footsteps until the soldier was almost upon him. The grizzled captain nodded a greeting as he leaned against the balustrade and spat over the edge.

"Quite a picture, isn't she?"

Stefano grunted.

"Sleep at all?"

"As much as I needed. How are your men?"

"Bloodied feet and wounded pride," Leonardo reported. "They'll live. Although I had to talk Cadere out of setting fire to the tower by way of retribution."

"This will likely end badly, one way or another."

"It is a farce, plain and simple. We look like idiots."

"Then we are fortunate the city has more pressing matters on its mind," said Stefano. "The only thing it will remember is the moment Lady Caterina leaves the tower and rejoins her husband's side."

On the parapet, birds were battling one another in their eagerness to get close to Caterina. A swift settled on her shoulder—she smiled and stroked its head. Leonardo cleared his throat.

"The duke thinks you are in Gritti's pay," he said.

"The duke is obsessed with Gritti," Stefano replied evenly. "What does the Doge of Venice care what happens in this courtyard?"

"So why *are* you here?"

"I was looking for an excuse to come home. Fate served me a reminder that it had been some time."

Leonardo nodded at his missing arm. "Pamplona, wasn't it?"

"At the invitation of Íñigo de Loyola himself. I strayed too close to the lines and received a cannonball by way of chastisement."

"You are lucky to be alive."

Stefano smiled humourlessly. "When I awoke in the hospital bed, half-blinded and with a stump for an arm, I cannot say I felt overly blessed."

"Does it still hurt?"

"On occasion. Worse are the times when it feels as though it is still there, so strongly that I swear I could reach out and pluck a grape from the bunch." He gazed over toward the tower. "It is hard enough to lose something so precious the once."

"War is an ugly wench," Leonardo declared. "I have no desire to look on her misshapen features again, nor hear her banshee scream in my ears. Whether the Venetians come or not, this is my final battle. And a pretty way to end, too—outwitted by a woman and a Spanish she-devil."

Her supply of grain exhausted, Caterina brushed her hands and stepped down from the platform. The birds took to the air in a fluttering cloud of disappointment.

"Do not sue for peace just yet," Stefano said thoughtfully. "Our luck may change."

AGOSTINO LAUGHED INCREDULOUSLY. "You have lost your mind!"

"Admittedly, it is a bold plan, my lord," Stefano replied. "But time is not our ally, and traditional methods have won us naught thus far."

He had to raise his voice to be heard above the indignant squawks echoing around the hall. They stood before a wall of birdcages, filled with pigeons that the guards had spent the morning chasing, red-faced and swearing, around the Old Market.

"Explain to me again how this foolishness would work," said the duke.

"You are aware that the lady Caterina feeds the birds every morning," Stefano responded. "Come tomorrow, these feathered conscripts will serve as our infantry and march on the parapet, carrying pieces of lit tinder in their talons. The threat of fire inside the tower will serve to urge your lady wife to vacate the building forthwith."

"Impossible, sir!" scoffed Agostino.

"It is how Princess Olga of Kiev took the town of Iskoroten."

The duke leaned in towards Stefano. "I am beginning to suspect," he said, in a low, menacing tone, "that you think me a bird also. A gull, brainless and greedy in equal measure, happy to gobble up every morsel of fable and foolishness you feed me."

"I am only trying to share with you the lessons of war."

"And yet what feeble answers you offer me. Ladders, bribes and fickle birds! Where are your organs of destruction, your mighty catapults and battering rams?"

"I thought that we were to avoid placing Lady Caterina in danger."

Agostino jabbed a finger at the cages. "You're proposing to set the damned tower on fire!"

"At most, a trifling flame or two," Stefano said, holding up his hand. "The chances of any harm befalling her are slim indeed."

"The wellbeing of my wife grows less important to me with each passing hour," the duke said darkly. "Smoke her out, and I will brush the sparks from her hair."

After a thorough examination of the palace's upper floors, Stefano settled on the library for his base, whose windows he judged offered the best view of the tower. He helped the guards carry the cages up the stairs and through the bookshelves. Leonardo pointedly refused to lift a finger, making clear his disdain for Stefano's scheme. Nor did the captain join them the next morning, leaving Stefano to watch over Baccio and Agnolo as they wrapped pieces of lit tinder in cloth and bound them to the birds' talons.

"Let us hope their hands are steady," rumbled Agostino, beside Stefano. Whether owing to the early hour, or the continued thwarting of his designs, the duke appeared in a particularly ill humour. "The Valturio is not the only volume dear to me."

"And as a keen student of the business of war, you will know that the element of surprise is crucial to a successful sortie," Stefano replied. "Should we release the birds in plain sight, Caterina and Sence will gain wind of our designs."

"The business of war," snorted Agostino. He nodded at the pigeons. "Is that what this is?"

At that moment, Caterina stepped out onto the parapet. Stefano made a hurried signal and the guards held up each cage in turn to the open window, shaking the birds free from their pens. They soared into the cloudless sky, bearing tiny parcels of fire. As he watched them flock towards the tower, Stefano was assailed by sudden doubts. Could it be that Leonardo and the duke were right—was this plan the work of madness? What was he risking, arming these mindless creatures with fire and sending them forth to do his bidding?

A loud crash startled him from his reverie. Running to the window, Stefano saw that Caterina had vanished. In her place stood Sence. The duenna was brandishing a pair of metal pans, which she proceeded to clang together while marching along the battlements, screaming at the top of her lungs. Alarmed by the hideous din, the pigeons veered away from the tower.

"Damn her!" Baccio swore. "We should have listened to the captain and put an arrow in her eye when we had the chance!"

Stefano ignored him. He watched, a sinking feeling in the pit of his stomach, as the birds banked as one, a grey blade slicing through the sky. Spurred on by the fires burning under them, they settled upon a new course, hurtling back towards the palace... straight towards the library.

"Look out!" yelled Agnolo.

The guards dived to the floor as the birds came streaming through the windows, scattering smouldering fragments of tinder across the floorboards. A pigeon swooped past Stefano, leaving a burning kiss upon his ear before coming to rest with a flurry of wings on top of a bookcase. Smoke rose from the shelves. Agostino ran up and down the aisles, waving his arms and yelling at the birds as they flapped around his head.

"Behold, the fruits of your ingenuity!" the duke shouted at Stefano. "You've set my palace alight!"

He snatched a book down from the shelf and began swatting at the pigeons while his guards tried to stamp out the fires. Sence's pans rang out like church bells. Through the chaos, Stefano caught sight of Leonardo in the doorway. The captain turned away with a shake of his head, ignoring his master's cries for help and abandoning his men to the smoke and the flames.

VII. *The Price of Peace*

A FROSTY SILENCE had descended over the duke's palace, its corridors wreathed in the accusatory odour of singed parchment. Inside the great hall, the map of Cadenza had been abandoned, its city walls left unguarded; Agostino had withdrawn to the lectern in his reading room, seeking solace in the pages of his Valturio. His captain of the guards had left the palace altogether, never to return. With Leonardo gone, the guards milled idly in the courtyard, taking turns to hurl stones at the tower windows. They sloped off, grumbling, when Stefano ordered them away.

He stood alone in the courtyard for a time, staring up thoughtfully at the battlements. When he turned to leave, there came a piercing whistle, and an object came flying down from the third-storey window. Stefano sprang back, throwing up a protective hand before his face, only for an onion to roll to a stop in the gravel by his feet. With a rueful glance about him, he picked up the vegetable and unwrapped the message tied around it. He sat down on a bench to read the message. Having considered its contents, Stefano went up to the duke's reading room and knocked on the door. There was a long pause before Agostino bade him enter. The duke was hunched over the lectern, a wistful expression on his face as he leafed through his beloved volume.

"I bring news," Stefano told him. "Lady Caterina has written me a letter, requesting that I serve as an emissary in a parley between the pair of you."

His eyes widened eagerly. "She is suing for peace?"

"Not in so many words."

"Then what does she want? Spit it out, man!"

"She has made you an offer, my lord. The lady Caterina says that, if you relieve her of her marital obligation, she will vacate the tower at once. Furthermore, she will leave the city, in secret and never to return, offering you the chance to declare her dead in whichsoever fashion you desire."

The duke frowned. "So, after all this, I still lose my wife? What manner of victory is that?"

"Think about it, my lord!" Stefano urged. "For a year, now, the city has believed that the Lady Caterina has rejected you. But if it should emerge that she has been subject to some terrible illness or malady of the mind, say, then your humiliation would be reversed at a stroke. What fidelity and discretion you would have shown, to have entertained the fantasies of your sick wife, without thought for your reputation or standing!"

Agostino knitted his brows in thought. "When put like that, perhaps there may be wisdom in such a move," he conceded. "And Caterina will offer me this, merely in return for my releasing her of her obligation?"

Stefano hesitated. "Not quite, my lord. She has requested one other thing."

"Which is?"

"She wants... my lord, there is no easy way of saying this... she wants the book."

The duke squinted at him. "What book?"

"The Valturio."

"Hah! Never!"

"It is the only—"

Agostino held up his hand. "No more, it is wasted breath. Do you know what I had to go through to obtain this volume? Three days, I negotiated with Lorenzo de' Medici over its purchase, a battle as bitter and exhausting as any taken to the field. I ate not, I slept not. This single book, sir, cost me more than a season's worth of trading profits. It is the most precious thing I have ever owned, Lady Caterina included, and I will not be parted from it. What interest has she, anyway, in the affairs of war?"

"None, she makes that quite plain. But she knows that you value it beyond all other possessions."

"This is no peace offer!" the duke thundered. "It is a declaration of war!"

"The terms may not be ideal," conceded Stefano, "but it would put an end to this affair this very day, allowing you to take control of the Council of Seven and save Cadenza. Would that not be worth it, my lord, in the final reckoning?"

Agostino took the letter from Stefano and tore it into tiny pieces. When next he spoke, his voice was hollow with disdain.

"You have proved a great disappointment to me, sir. I asked for a man of war, not a diplomat with weasel words. Our contract is at an end. Do not think for a second that I will hand Beatrice Monti over to you."

"As my lord commands," Stefano replied, bowing. "I should imagine she will be most relieved."

"It was a mistake to entrust my business to the hands of another. From now on *I* shall take command. Like Pope Julius in the snow."

"What do you propose to do?"

"Caterina has pressed me to my limits. I will not bend any further." Agostino slammed the Valturio shut on the lectern. "If it is war she desires, then war I shall give her, bitter and bloody."

*　　*　　*

VIII. *Warwolf*

FOR TWO DAYS and two nights, the palace had been alive with activity, guards and messengers colliding in the hallways as they hastened to Duke Agostino's bidding. Now, with evening fallen black and swift upon the courtyard, the corridors were still. Rows of crackling torches lined the arcade walls. On the third-floor balcony, Stefano waited. His missing arm was taunting him, a tingling itch that could not be scratched. He had elected to stay on at the palace, at once curious and uneasy as to Agostino's next move, feeling a weight of responsibility for the ominous atmosphere gathering around the tower and its inhabitants.

A jarring trumpet blast announced the duke's entrance, flanked by members of his guard. Regally surveying his surrounding, he caught sight of Stefano at the balustrade.

"Still here, sir?" he called up, with a bark of laughter. "I presumed you had scurried back to Venice with your tail between your legs. By all means, tell your master Gritti what befalls those who would defy me!"

The duke had been drinking, his doublet hanging carelessly open and his eyes gleaming with feverish triumph. His scalp glowed in the flickering torchlight.

"Lady Caterina!" he cried. "You asked for the Valturio, so I shall give it to you. From within its pages I have taken a design and brought it to life with mine own hands. Let me deliver it to your care at once, as proof of my fidelity."

The tower offered no reply.

"Unleash the Warwolf!" Agostino roared.

From beneath Stefano's feet, there came a low rumbling

of wheels, and a battle ram emerged from the arcades. A network of chains supported a thick beam of wood carved into the shape of a perfect cylinder, its point capped with an iron wolf's head, complete with snapping jaws. The carriage's slanted side-screens were covered with animal hides, protecting Agostino's guards as they propelled the siege engine forward. Prowling ominously past the duke, the Warwolf gathered pace as it crossed the courtyard, its wheels flying across the gravel. It collided with the tower door with a resounding bang, bouncing off the wood. The door shuddered.

"Again!" Agostino bellowed.

Beneath the side-screens, the guards reversed their direction, pushing the ram back to its starting position. Stefano anxiously scanned the tower. Where was Sence, indomitable spirit of defiance? The Warwolf lunged forward again, hungrily eating up the ground between the arcade and its target. This time, a crack reverberated around the courtyard when the iron-tipped ram connected with the door—it wheeled back to reveal a jagged fissure running like a lightning bolt through the wood.

Finally, there was a movement at the top of the tower. Sence stepped out on to the battlements, dragging behind her a heavy grappling hook on a chain. Agostino roared encouragement at his men as they reversed the Warwolf. Alone in the courtyard, Stefano watched as the duenna lifted up the hook and balanced it on the parapet. The ram charged forth from the arcades, gravel churning beneath its wheels. Sence waited. Stefano's grip tightened on the balustrade.

"Now," he muttered.

Sence pushed the hook over the edge of the parapet. It landed directly in the path of the onrushing ram, claws biting into the carriage as the Warwolf trampled over it. The ram flew on and the chain snapped taut: Sence hurriedly backed away. At this sudden restraint, the Warwolf bucked and reared up on its back wheels, shaking loose Agostino's guards from its fur like fleas. Slowly, awkwardly, it rose into the air—a wolf no longer but a fish, dangling helplessly on the line.

"The Claw of Archimedes," murmured Stefano, awe in his voice.

Agostino was a vision of rage, haranguing his guards as they picked themselves up from the ground. High up in the tower, Sence took careful aim with a small clay pot and threw. The missile struck the Warwolf flush upon the nose—with a whoosh, the battering ram went up in flames. The duenna disappeared inside the tower. Moments later, the chain began to pay out, sending the battering ram plunging back to earth, where it splintered into burning planks of wood and scraps of hide. Agostino slumped to the ground, staring in disbelief as fire devoured his proud machine; Stefano retired from the balcony, a smile playing on his lips.

And still the tower stayed silent.

IX. *Porta Salaria*

THE NEXT MORNING, a lone figure crossed the courtyard, his footsteps crunching across the gravel. He carried a book beneath his arm—somewhat awkwardly, the book being of considerable size, and the arm being the only such limb in his possession. Skirting around the blackened carcass of the Warwolf, Stefano walked up to the entrance of the tower and banged on the door. A crossbar scraped against its setting, and the door swung open with an oaken groan. In the gloomy interior stood a woman, small and unsmiling. Her sleeves were rolled up, and there was a smudge of ash on her cheek.

Stefano bowed stiffly. "My lady," he said. "You received my note."

"I did, though deciphering it was no easy matter," Sence replied, in Italian. "Your Spanish is terrible."

"My apologies. I learnt the language in haste, under trying circumstances."

"The duke has agreed to my lady's terms?"

"He has come to see the sense of it—with reluctance," Stefano said, holding up the Valturio. "Another reverse like the Warwolf and it will be Agostino who has to leave the city. And I think it is fair to say that his love for Lady Caterina has dimmed."

Sence snorted. "Love. The man does not know the meaning of the word. He cares only for numbers on the page and the jingle of coins in his pocket. To love is to lie at death's door and have thoughts only for another, to give testament to their beauty and grace in the depths of agony, and to feel sorrow only for their absence from your side. That is what I saw in the hospital in Pamplona. That is love, Stefano."

At that, finally, he smiled. "I wish you could have seen my face when I received the duke's letter in Venice. Never in my life had I imagined you would reach Cadenza."

"I gave you my word in Pamplona," Sence said. "I said that I would bring you before Caterina once more."

"You did. I told you then, it was not necessary."

She snorted. "You stood in the path of a cannonball for me, a stranger, saving my life at the cost of an eye and an arm and almost your life as well. What measure a long journey, against that?"

"A long journey, and a year confined within these walls."

"How long did you spend at the hospital? Tally your own accounts as you will, but I remain in your debt." Sence stood aside. "She is expecting you."

Stefano stepped inside the tower. In its cool, musty confines, he saw the other half of the siege's tale, hidden from him until now. The bowls of water laid out across the floor, their surfaces sensitive to the passage of men through the ground beneath them. The hearth where Sence had concocted her scalding stew and filled the bellows with steam. The iron chain running across the ceiling to a storeroom filled with great casks, linking them together to provide the counterweight that had outmuscled the Warwolf. Stefano shook his head in admiration.

He went over to the wooden ladder leading up into the tower and began to climb, pulling himself up with one hand. In the windowless chamber above, he saw the rude cots where the two women had slept; on the third floor, the stockpiled arms and barrels of pitch that Sence had turned against the duke and his men. Through the narrow windows, there were glimpses of the palace's blackened and missing tiles.

A third and final ladder led up to a doorway. Stefano stepped out on the battlements, to be met by a fresh, playful wind. His legs felt weak, the breath short in his chest. Had the ladders taken their toll on him or was this—here, now, for the first time—fear? At his back, the Adige sparkled in the morning sunshine. Birds wheeled above the domes and towers.

"Stefano?"

He turned around. There was hesitancy in Caterina's voice: she stepped towards him and faltered, clasping her hands together. Her face was drawn, a ghostly pallor to her skin and dark rings around her eyes. Yet this Caterina was no less lovely than the golden-framed vision Stefano had glimpsed from the arcade on his arrival at the palace. On the contrary, here was beauty in all truth, dazzling in its honesty and perfect in its flaws. He did not need the birds to sing or the sun to shine to appreciate the woman stood before him.

Stefano dropped to his knee. "My lady."

Caterina looked him up and down. She pursed her lips.

"I suppose this means I will not hear you play the lute again."

He bowed his head. "Nor watch me juggle oranges, if it comes to that."

"You were a better lute player than a juggler."

"I am the equal at both, now."

"You have learnt other things in the meantime."

"As have you, it would seem." His mouth twitched. "I had no idea you were so enamoured with the works of Roberto Valturio. You have caused the duke great sadness by forcing him to part with this."

"He is rich beyond imagination," she said lightly. "There will be other books. Other women."

"I fear I am as poor as I was when I played the lute."

Caterina laughed. "Did you not read the terms of my surrender? I am a dead woman, a ghost. What need have I for money? I do not even want the Valturio. It is a gift, for you, in gratitude for your coming to my rescue."

Stefano looked out ruefully across the wreckage of the courtyard. "I am not sure that you are the one who needed rescuing," he said. "Ten years of warfare, and I have never seen a siege like it. What on earth possessed you?"

"I had to do *something* to bring you home," Caterina replied. "I had resigned myself to a life of unhappiness when Sence arrived at my doorstep with word that you were still alive. It was her idea to turn Agostino's love for the Valturio against him, to have him build this tower and hide behind its doors until you heard word of it. When I saw you talking in the courtyard with the duke, when I realized that he had sent for you, I was scared to believe the truth of my own eyes. I had spent so long praying for your return." A note of reproach crept into her voice. "Ten years, Stefano. You might have written to me."

He laid his hand over his heart. "Truly, I am sorry," he said. "I should never have left Cadenza. When your father refused to give me his blessing for our marriage, he told me he would have you wed before the year was out. I could not bear to see you with another."

"I did not want another. I would have told you that, had you waited."

"I was too angry," he sighed. "Too young, too foolish. I travelled to the edge of the world in the hope of forgetting you. Time and again, I sought out death, wishing for an arrow or a blade to put an end to my misery. At Pamplona, I nearly got my wish. But as I lay in the hospital, delirious with pain, on the threshold of life and death, all I could see was your face. I realized that I could not die without seeing you again. Without telling you that I loved you."

Caterina smiled. Stefano felt a drawbridge open inside his chest, the castle walls around his heart crumbling.

"Oh, Stefano, my love!" Laughing with delight, Caterina ran up and threw her arms around him. "What took you so long?"

Eleventh Canto
Palestrina

I. *The Silent Sisters*

THEY NUMBERED NINE in total, all of them women, sequestered at their desks at intervals across the hall. Clad in grey hessian robes, they worked in silence: a studious hush, punctuated by cleared throats and creaking stools. By day, light poured in through the windows lining the east wall; now, with evening descending, the candles had dyed the pages burnished orange.

The women were known as the Sisters of San Benedetta. Their life's work—or, to view it another way, their sentence—was to examine the books of Cadenza's libraries, making judicial amendments to certain volumes and excising references to individuals or events that might prove troublesome to the Artifex. Thus, while the Pitti family still existed in the memories of many in the city, like their toppled houses south of the Via Maggio, almost no trace of them now remained in the histories of the era. Likewise, all record of the battle at Rovigo, in which Cadenza had been routed on the field by Venice, had been removed; the name of Orazio

Colleoni, a poet who had dared to compose a scathing verse blaming Tommaso Cellini in its aftermath, had been buried alongside it.

It was work requiring great precision and concentration. In some books, only a single word required changing or crossing out; in others, entire chapters needed rewriting. The most offensive volumes, such as a four-volume history commissioned by the Pittis to celebrate their achievements, were simply tossed into a cellar beneath the convent. By fiat issued by the Artifex, every fresh publication had to pass under the sisters' scrupulous gaze. The citizenry may have come to fear the *becchini* and the brutal ring of steel they formed around the Palazzo Nero, but few knew that Tommaso's most implacable defenders were in fact the nine women of the convent San Benedetta—a secret guard, absorbed in the construction of an oubliette that consigned the Artifex's enemies beyond the reach of memory itself.

Even now, with Tommaso dead ten months, the Sisters continued to work. The plague that had ravaged the rest of the city had stalked by the convent—as she worked at her desk, Lucrezia had smelled its hot, sickly breath through the scriptorium windows, her ears alive to the pitiful scratching at the building's entrance. Sister Ginevra had argued in favour of unbolting the doors to give shelter to those afflicted, but Lucrezia had managed to persuade Sister Eleanora otherwise. When all was said and done, they were not, in fact, nuns: they owed the city nothing. In the absence of their warders, Eleanora was in nominal charge of the convent, although the elderly sister increasingly deferred to Lucrezia on the major decisions. This fact did not please everyone, she knew.

She had been sequestered within San Benedetta for the best part of a quarter-century, her skin long deadened to the hessian's dull itch, her figure whittled down to the sparest frame beneath her robes. Sharp cheekbones lent her face drama and shadow. Lucrezia remained strikingly beautiful, although it was a beauty complicated by its lack of softness— thin lips, unused to smiling; a cool, challenging gaze. The years spent scanning pages for Tommaso's enemies had taken their toll on her eyes, leaving her prone to headaches. Even now, as she finished her corrections, Lucrezia felt a twinge of pain somewhere behind her forehead: a distant rumble of thunder on the horizon.

She returned her quill to its inkpot and stepped down from her stool, rubbing the stiffness from her back. Gathering up the book, she walked along the row of desks to the wooden cart at the far end of the hall. No one looked up as she passed, eight heads bowed in concentration. At the sight of the cart, already overladen with volumes, Lucrezia sucked in through her teeth. Carefully balancing her book on top of the others, she wheeled it out into the corridor.

The convent was situated in the corner of a quiet square at the summit of the Vicolo Scarpuccia, in the northwest corner of the Verso. The entrance led directly into the scriptorium; on the other side of the hall, there began a series of three long corridors that folded back upon themselves, like a serpent chasing its tail, around a rectangular cloister. Lucrezia pushed the cart past the refectory and along the West Corridor, a back wheel creaking as she went. The high ceilings and empty rooms only served to amplify noises inside the convent, lending even the simplest sounds—a closing door, an embarrassed squeak of flatulence—a certain lonely grandeur. In the alcoves, the black shoots of evening were beginning to flower. Previously the warders had kept the corridors lit at night, the better to assist their grudging watch over their charges. But now, having been left to their own devices, the sisters had elected to save their candles for the scriptorium, condemning the rest of the building to darkness.

Lucrezia pressed on to the South Corridor, wheeling the cart by the row of cells where the sisters slept at night and the entrance to the orange orchard in the corner of the grounds. She turned left for a third and final time. The light faded. No windows graced the walls of the East Corridor; even at the height of summer, the passageway remained grudging and cold. The sole concession to the outside world was a series of grilles built into the wall overlooking the square, which allowed the sisters a view of the parades at carnival time. Opposite the grilles, a sturdy door barred the way to the cellar.

Shadows enveloped Lucrezia as she headed along the passage, making for the chapel at the far end of the corridor, beside an archway leading up to the tower. Outside the cellar door, the cart stuttered violently on an uneven flagstone— she fought to keep it upright, jarring her wrist as books spilled out over to the floor. Tutting with irritation, Lucrezia gathered up the fallen volumes and continued on her way, clamping her hand down on the stack. The cart should have been emptied before now; her sisters had been neglecting their duties. She should have sent one of the younger girls, Bianca or Maria. They might pout and roll their eyes, stick out their tongue when Lucrezia's back was turned, but they obeyed her all the same.

It was with a certain amount of relief that Lucrezia brought the cart to a stop outside the chapel and unlocked the door. She had completed a circuit that had brought her within the thickness of a partition wall between herself and the other sisters in the scriptorium, yet at that moment she felt far from anybody. The chapel windows glowed in the dying afternoon light. God had taken His leave of San Benedetta many years earlier: the altar had been removed, the crosses and relics packed up and transported to a church on the other side of Cadenza. In their place stood rows of bookshelves, where the Sisters offered up their amended works in the name of Tommaso Cellini. Once a month, an agent of the Folio would come to collect them and return them to the city's libraries. But now, amid the chaos engulfing the city, the volumes were mounting.

Lucrezia steered her cart carefully through the aisles, trying to ignore her aching wrist. Spying an empty shelf in the corner of the room, she began transferring volumes from the cart, standing on tiptoes to slide them into position. She worked quickly and methodically. As she stretched up to place the final book, her hand froze at a dull thud from the next aisle. Stepping away from the shelf, Lucrezia arched backwards and peered around the corner. Halfway along the aisle, a book was lying open on the flagstones, a pointed gap on the shelf marking the place where it had fallen. She walked over and knelt down beside it, tracing a finger across the fine Latin print.

Outside in the square, a sudden bark of laughter made her

start; glancing around the empty chapel, Lucrezia picked up the book and returned it to the shelf. The banks of tightly packed spines seemed to crowd in around her, the aisle narrowing and tightening. Shaking her head, she hurried back to the empty cart and wheeled it out of the chapel back towards the scriptorium, the creaking wheel protesting at every revolution.

II. *Chalk Marks*

THE SISTERS TOOK their supper together in the refectory. Spoons scraped against bowls, pursed lips admonishing the steaming broth with their breath. A solitary chair sat empty—Sister Tullia was still working in the hall and would take her meal later. In the wake of Tommaso's death, the sisters had agreed on a system that required at least one of them to remain in the scriptorium at all times. Like the monks of the *acoemeti*, who arranged themselves in continuous choirs to ensure that their songs in praise of the Lord never ceased, the Sisters of San Benedetta would not rest.

For all that they spent their days in nuns' habits and bowed their heads in prayer before sipping their broth, little else about the convent's inhabitants spoke of the holy. They were sinners to a woman—thieves and murderers, prostitutes and confidence tricksters. The former ink maid now known as Sister Maria had blackmailed her correspondents with compromising letters forged in a scrupulous imitation of their own hand; Tullia, a street walker, had purloined a small fortune from a besotted nobleman. Paola had stabbed her father thirty-nine times while he lay unconscious in her bedroom doorway, his breeches around his ankles, while Eletta had clawed out the eyes of a love rival in a shocking attack on the Piazza della Rosa. Twins Bianca and Francesca had connived to steal heirlooms from an elderly countess; pious Ginevra had set alight a printer's shop on the Via Tribunali, torching books and workers alike. Even aged Eleanora, softly spoken and half-blind, was no innocent. Thirty years earlier, she had arranged the killing of her husband at the hands of two cutthroats, who had lain in wait for him beneath their marriage bed.

The women had paid for their crimes with imprisonment and maiming, their tongues removed to ensure their silence before they were sent to the convent. They communicated with one another through chalk marks on a slate, which they wore on a string around their neck. All contact with the outside world was forbidden and attempts at escape were punishable by death. Yet, despite the city's tantalizing proximity, the glimpses through the grilles in the East Corridor, there had been few such incidents of disobedience. Many of the Sisters had left behind lives of drudgery and misfortune; others were merely glad to have been left with their lives, if not their freedom or their tongue.

Lucrezia's crime was at once the most grievous and the most obscure, shackling her to a name that was not her own and assuring her lasting infamy. The commission of this crime had occurred at a place and time unknown to her: a stroll in the Garden of Leaves upon her mother's arm, perhaps, or her first appearance at the Ridolfi salon with her father; crossing the Ponte Nuovo with her sisters or watching the river boats race along the Adige. All that she knew for certain was that at some point the young Lucrezia—who had then been known by the name Lucia Pitti—had caught the eye of Tommaso Cellini, at a stroke condemning herself to a lifetime's imprisonment and ensuring the death of almost everyone she loved.

She finished her meal quickly, nodding at Sister Eleanora when her bowl was clean and rising from the table. A restless mood had come over Lucrezia that evening and she was glad to be relieving Tullia in the scriptorium. Upon leaving the refectory, she was struck by the sharp drop in temperature, her thin frame offering her little protection from the cold. In previous years, the sisters had gathered in the calefactory to warm themselves on the fire, but now the hearth was barren. Lucrezia went quickly through the corridor to the scriptorium, slipping through the door and closing it behind her.

Inside the hall, eight desks crouched in darkness. Upon the ninth, a candle burned low, the pages of an open book rustling in the breeze from the nearby window. Over the course of the summer Tullia had browbeaten Sister Paola into swapping desks, claiming that she was struggling to breathe in the middle of the hall. Lucrezia had been minded to move her back, but she knew that Tullia would only find some other way to take out her frustration on Paola, and besides, she could not involve herself in every petty dispute that took place between the women. Now, however, Tullia's stool sat empty. Always a reluctant worker, it was entirely possible that she had simply left the convent—there were no guards now, nothing to stop her climbing out of the window. Lucrezia's candle wavered as she picked a path through the desks towards the end of the row.

A hand shot out from the darkness, grabbing her by the ankle.

Lucrezia let out a shapeless scream, reeling backwards into a stool as she shook herself free. Tullia hunched in the darkness beneath Paola's desk, her knees pulled up to her chest and her face a ghastly mask. She shrank back as Lucrezia stared at her. Lucrezia took her slate from around her neck and wrote a question on it, turning the tablet around to show it to Tullia.

What is it?

Tullia shook her head quickly, her eyes flicking up towards the scriptorium's gallery. Lucrezia straightened up. The upper recesses of the hall were lost in shadow; she could see nothing beyond the balustrades. Tullia's slate was lying on the floor halfway across the hall, its string snapped. Lucrezia's footsteps echoed in the silence as she went to retrieve it. She pressed it into her sister's hand and held up her own tablet once more, tapping the question insistently with her nail.

With a palsied hand, Tullia drew a picture on her slate and handed it back to Lucrezia. Two crude figures—one much shorter than the other—their stick arms reaching out to one another as they clasped hands. A worm of unease crawled down Lucrezia's spine.

Who is this? she wrote.

Tullia snatched the slate from her hands and hurled it across the flagstones. Burying her face in her sleeve, she broke down into heaving sobs. Lucrezia drew the young woman towards her and held her stiffly. Tullia's gaunt frame trembled in her arms.

Up in the gallery, a spiteful wind slammed a door shut.

III. *The Toils of Sisyphus*

THE NEXT DAY Borso came to visit, as was his custom every other Sunday. Sitting on a bench among the orange trees, sunlight dappling the leaves above her head, Lucrezia could hear the count's laboured breaths as he toiled up the slope. Finally he appeared above the brow of the hill, ducking his head through the archway into the cloister. As a youth, Lucrezia had thought Borso the largest man in the city, his friends mere children beside him, his booming voice carrying from one end of the Ponte Nuovo to the other. Age had not reduced Borso, though his hair was now grey, and his shoulders hunched. He was out of breath, and trying not to show it. It occurred to Lucrezia that she had condemned him to the life of Sisyphus, to toil up a steep hill only to find himself back at its base come morning. Yet she had never once requested his company—indeed, when Borso had first appeared, keeping a respectful vigil outside the door to the orchard, Lucrezia had fled in horror. To this day, she had no idea how he had found her.

Borso sat beside her and dabbed at his glistening forehead with a handkerchief. Taking up her slate, Lucrezia asked him for news of the city. His expression turned grim. Cadenza was rife with rumours and ominous tidings: a monstrous baby with hooves and tentacles had escaped from the lazaretto during the plague and now haunted the arches beneath the

Ponte Mercato; a blood-red comet had been spied by a scholar from the Mezzanino of the Accademia; in the heart of the Printing Quarter, an ancient stone pine had spontaneously burst into flame. The armies of Venice were reportedly only days from the walls, yet still the Council of Seven bickered and vacillated. Cesare Petrucci—whom Borso had heard had been positioning himself to replace his uncle inside the Palazzo Nero—had disappeared without trace, presumably fleeing the city in anticipation of an unwinnable battle.

Borso talked at length, well used to decorating the orchard with his words. How many hours had he spent here, waiting patiently as Lucrezia chalked her thoughts across the slate? He had never openly declared his love for her, though she fancied he would have done so as a youth, had his best friend not barged in front of him. More than twenty years had passed, yet still Borso came to her, receiving neither encouragement nor thanks for his troubles, nor any hope of reward. It must have cost him a pretty penny to persuade the warders to turn a blind eye to his visits. She hoped that he kept a woman or two in the city—the notion that Borso might have foresworn his needs on her account irritated Lucrezia; she had not asked for such a sacrifice. Would he have remained faithful, had her freedom and her tongue not been taken from her? The last thing she desired was pity, wrapped up as it might be in a flag of chivalry.

She received his tidings without reaction, allowing herself to be lulled by his deep voice, the words her mouth could no longer form. A shaft of sunlight arrowed down through the trees, striking her directly in the eyes. Lucrezia raised a hand before her face: as its shadow fell over her, she spotted something moving in the window of the bell tower directly above the chapel. In the blink of an eye, it was gone.

Borso broke off and inquired if there was something wrong. She shook her head quickly. Seeking to change the subject, she asked him if he was writing, at which Borso coughed and shifted uncomfortably in his seat. Lucrezia's mouth tightened. She despised his petty feud with Lorenzo Sardi and had told him so on countless occasions. Had she not endured enough, without being squabbled over so? Her name; her memory— little more than a carcass to be pawed at and picked over by the wounded beasts of male pride. Even worse than the embarrassment at being the cause of such bad blood, was the thought that the afternoons they shared together represented some kind of secret victory for Borso. During the worst of his exchanges with Lorenzo, she had refused outright to see him. Yet still he returned, every other Sunday, whether the door to the orchard stood locked or not.

Now Borso only shrugged his shoulders, as though the matter was beyond his control—a reminder to Lucrezia that there was more than one kind of vanity. She had never asked for his company. But on certain occasions, as the orchard slipped into evening, she had permitted him to take her hand in his great paw, and together they had sat and watched the stars emerge in silence.

IV. *Vague Things of Air*

LUCREZIA WAS VISITED by a headache that stayed with her for the rest of the day, lodged painfully in the cramped attics of her skull. Sensing her disquiet, Borso took his leave of her—she waited until he had departed through the outer gate before heading back inside the convent. Her eyes struggled to adjust to the gloom after the orchard's bright sunshine, the East Corridor shifting and blurring in time to the throbbing of her head. She went carefully past the entrance to the cellar, wary of the treacherous flagstones, and passed through the archway by the chapel. Climbing the steps up into the tower, Lucrezia unbarred a heavy oaken door and pushed it open.

The room beyond had previously served as a punishment cell for disobedient sisters: there were empty hooks on the walls where scourges once had hung; holes in the stonework where the fetters had been anchored. Stripped of its purpose, an idle, brooding atmosphere remained. The flagstones were coated in a thick layer of dust—there was no sign that anyone had passed this way recently. Perhaps the movement Lucrezia had seen in the window had been nothing more than a caprice, an after-effect of the sun's glare. Her eyes were, after all, increasingly unreliable witnesses.

The Sisters would be gathering around the refectory table, but Lucrezia's headache had sapped her appetite and she was in no hurry to join them. She stood by the window, watching the reddening sun sink over the orchard. The succession of strange occurrences in recent days was troubling her. First a falling book in an empty aisle, then Tullia cowering beneath her desk; now this half-glimpsed presence in the window. Could it be that her sisters were playing games with her?

Tullia had offered no further explanation for their encounter in the scriptorium, glaring at Lucrezia across the dining table the next day as though holding *her* responsible for whatever had taken place. Lucrezia ignored her baleful stares. They had all, at one time or another, succumbed to the convent's mournful atmosphere and spied unwelcome guests in the shadows. There were nights when it felt to Lucrezia as though she walked to her room along hallways lined with ghosts, the men and women she had crossed out from existence forming a solemn, reproachful guard. She paid them no heed—what harm could such spirits, vague things of air spun from breath and mist, visit upon her?

More troubling had been the days when Lucrezia had sensed the eyes of the living following her as she went about the convent. She became watchful for subtle changes in her surroundings: a door lying unexpectedly ajar, a movement in the gallery; half-glimpsed reflections in windows; an unfamiliar carriage on the piazza outside. On days such as these, the warders seemed to busy themselves with chores, their eyes fixed on the floor, and Lucrezia fancied she detected an unspoken tension among her sisters. She had never once confronted them about this, not even Eleanora. Even to her own ears, the notion that she had been subject to some secret observation sounded wild and improbable, and she would not have anyone thinking her vain enough to suspect herself worthy of especial attention. If someone *had* been watching Lucrezia, she felt sure that they were no longer doing so. Not now.

V. *The Reach of Elagabalus*

LUCIA PITTI HAD spent her last night of freedom weaving through the crowds of the Carnival of Wit, her face hidden behind a mask of brilliant white feathers. To her relief, her father had suggested that she forgo his name-day feast to enjoy the celebrations in the streets, sparing her the prospect of Tommaso Cellini's intense gaze across the dining table. The Artifex would be told that she had a fever, Donato told her solemnly. Lucia had thrown her arms around her father, peppering his cheek with kisses of gratitude. She knew well the honour Tommaso was bestowing on their family by attending the dinner, and the consequent risks Donato incurred by allowing her to miss it. For all his courteousness, his urbanity, something about the Artifex unsettled Lucia, her cheeks blushing hot whenever she was subjected to his frank appraisal.

She walked west from the Pitti neighbourhood along the river. Outside the tavern at the sign of the Boar, a pack of young men in hound masks gave chase to squealing maidens, barking and baying at their skirts—Lucia carefully sidestepped around them. At the Ponte Mercato, a crowd had gathered to watch boats festooned with lights and garlands parade along the Adige. A juggler stood on the balustrade, tossing flaming brands into the night sky. Lucia gasped with amazement as he hurled the torches higher and higher, snatching their handles as they descended with unerring precision before returning them to the air.

Through the circle of fire, she caught sight of a large figure striding along the riverfront, broad-shouldered and ungainly, long black hair spilling out from behind his mask. The breath caught in her throat. Borso only ever wore a bear mask at carnival, aware of the futility of attempting to disguise himself. As Lucia watched, he raised a hand in greeting to the hounds as they hailed him, barking his name, but did not stop to share their wineskins. Alone in the city, Borso did not care for the Carnival of Wit, and spent it shut away in a private room in the rafters of the Black Lion. He would be surprised to see Lucia out alone in the streets—she wondered whether she could persuade him away from the tavern to watch the boats with her instead. A smile tugged at her lips as she weaved through the throng after Borso.

The din intensified as Lucia moved away from the bridge, heading towards the intersection of the Via Fiume with the Via Guilia. At the heat of the jostling press, the colour rose in her cheeks. She kept her eyes fixed on Borso's huge frame, thinking up a teasing line to make him laugh. A great cheer went up behind her as the juggler gathered in his final torch with a flourish. Lucia reached out to pinch Borso's arm, only for an antlered reveller to knock into her, sending her stumbling backwards. The Bear strode on. She became aware of a growing urgency to the noise around her, shrieks of alarm. A horse screamed amid the furious lashing of a crop. Looking along the Via Guilia, Lucia saw a carriage ploughing through the crowds, scattering people from its path. Finally, Borso turned. His eyes fell on her. She felt sure he saw her at that moment, through the brilliant feathers of her mask.

The carriage skidded to a halt between them, obscuring him from view. Lucia cried out as the door flew open and a man reached out to grab her by the wrist. She was bundled, screaming, inside the vehicle. Lucia pummelled her assailant with her fists, yet as the vehicle jolted forward, she realized that she knew him. Her uncle Matteo wore no mask, his face bright red and his brow glistening with sweat.

"In God's name, be silent, girl!" he urged. "We must leave the city at once."

Lucia stared at him. "Leave? Why, whatever has happened?"

"Donato, damn him to eternal torment for his foolishness, just tried to poison Tommaso Cellini at his own feast."

"Poison the Artifex? Father? Is this a jest?"

"Do you see me smile?" Matteo snapped. "I told Donato this was a grievous mistake, but he would not listen, and now he has signed a death warrant for us all. There will be nothing left of our house but dust and salt. Tommaso cannot allow it otherwise."

"Uncle, I do not understand!" Lucia said, almost pleading. "Why would Father do such a thing?"

He laughed bitterly. "Why, because of you, child! We have all seen the way the Artifex favours you with his gaze, and Donato knows well the manner of assemblies that take place inside Tommaso's east wing. He would not countenance his daughter disappearing behind its doors."

"I know nothing of east wings and assemblies," Lucia said stubbornly, folding her arms. "But I know my father. He is no poisoner."

"You speak with such certainty, when you know so little!" scoffed her uncle. "Answer me this, Lucia: if Donato had not been planning such a deed, why else do you think you were allowed to leave tonight?"

He cursed and hammered on the carriage roof. The coachman replied with a lash of his whip, a chorus of angry shouts greeting the carriage as it rattled violently through the streets. Booming explosions ruptured the night sky as they galloped along the Via Maggio towards the city gates. Matteo let out an oath. Following his gaze, Lucia saw a line of guards standing abreast in the road, their swords and spears dyed red in the fireworks. The coachman tried to slow the carriage, but it was too late, the black cloaks of the *becchini* were swarming around them. Firm hands reached out to take hold of the horses' bridles. There was a shriek as the coachman collapsed to the dirt, a crossbow quarrel in his chest.

Lucia was torn from her uncle, who was marched away by the grim-faced guards, and taken to a waiting carriage. Struck dumb with shock, she sat motionless as the city slipped past in a blur. They travelled north, to the Piazza della Rosa, and on through the yawning gates of the Palazzo Nero. Expecting to be hurled into a dungeon cell, Lucia was bewildered to find herself instead escorted to a set of rooms in the northwest tower. She stood on the balcony, taking deep breaths in the cool night air in an effort to calm herself. A crowd was gathering in the square below her. It occurred to Lucia that the best thing to do might be to throw herself from the balcony to join them. If what her uncle said had been true—and still, even now, Lucia could not believe him—better a swift death than the agonizing reprisals that were sure to follow.

Yet she did not kill herself that night, even when the truth of her father's actions became impossible to gainsay, nor did she upon the next night, nor the one that followed. Lucia was young and did not want to die. She paced her chambers, neither eating nor sleeping, pleading in vain with the guards on the other side of the door for news of her family. The next evening, she received a summons. Lucia walked hesitantly through the palace to the great *salone*, where two places had been made up at either end of the long dining table. Through a forest of candelabras, she saw the Artifex sat waiting for her. Tommaso was dressed simply, his hair cropped short, studying Lucia with his considered, troubling gaze. She hesitated in the doorway, and he gestured at her to approach.

"I missed you at your father's feast."

"I was unwell, my lord," she replied hesitantly.

Tommaso nodded. "You are aware what occurred in your absence?"

"I... I am not sure. My uncle said... but I still cannot believe, my father..."

"It took me rather by surprise also." A jest? He was not smiling.

Lucia went to the Artifex's chair and dropped to her knees beside him. "Whatever wrongs have been done to you, my lord," she said, her eyes filling with tears, "I beg of you, please spare my family."

He raised her chin with a finger. "It is too late for that, child," he told her. "Donato knew the consequences of his actions. He made his choice, leaving me with none."

"Then you must kill me also," Lucia said fiercely.

"It may very well come to that. My *becchini* are most eager to have you entrusted to their care. But I am inclined to show mercy in that regard, at least."

"Without my family, what do I care for my life?"

"A question you would do well to think over," he replied sharply. "Return to your quarters and reflect on the gift that I am offering you."

So ended Lucia's first dinner with Tommaso Cellini. A second invitation arrived the next evening: she sat stiffly in her chair, refusing to utter a single word as Tommaso picked over a pheasant carcass. He seemed amused by her display, toying with his knife as she ignored his efforts to draw her into conversation. Over the course of their third and fourth dinners—when she arrived late and unwashed, stifling yawns behind her hand—his smile faded. Minutes into their fifth dinner, Tommaso casually announced that Lucia's father had been burned alive on the Piazza di Pietra. Lucia said nothing, digging a fork deep into the palm of her hand beneath the table to stop herself from screaming. For the first time, a flicker of irritation crossed Tommaso's face. He rose from the table and walked out, leaving Lucia to stumble to her room, where she spent the rest of the night in inconsolable tears.

In preparation for their sixth dinner, she dried her eyes and found a comb for her hair, pinching the colour back into her cheeks. She made every effort to look as beautiful as she could, intent on finishing what her father had started and sticking a knife through Tommaso's heart. But she arrived at the *salone* to find the Artifex's chair empty. Lucia, who had not eaten since the news of her father's death, sat down and stared listlessly at her plate.

Finally the *salone* doors flew open and Tommaso appeared. His doublet was unbuttoned to the waist, a cloud of wine around him. He strode over to Lucia and pulled her from her seat by the hair. She was dragged screaming through the palace, a violent blur of chequered tiles and stone steps. They passed nobody in the halls. Pink-cheeked cherubs nestling in the friezes gasped and looked away. Upon a loggia on the second floor, Tommaso stopped before a set of double doors. He slammed Lucia up against a statue, his breath hot on her neck.

"You think yourself untouchable," he said hoarsely. "But even the Vestal Virgins were not beyond the reach of Elagabalus. By rights you should have burned with the rest of your family; it is my largesse to which you owe your breath and the beating of your heart. And yet all you offer in return is this disdainful silence, this monument to selfishness and ingratitude."

Keeping one hand around her throat, he fumbled around his neck and pulled out a key on a chain.

"There are things on the other side of this door..." he whispered. "Acts that I would have you witness. Let us see if we can move you to comment after all."

He turned the key in the lock and the door swung open. A shaft of pale light fell across them; Lucia heard sobbing, a distant groan. The mirrors on the corridor walls were flecked with blood. The Artifex grabbed hold of her face, his eyes seeking out her own. She sensed an inner beast within him straining to be unleashed, its hoarse breaths in his chest. Lucia had been preparing herself for this moment. She forced her body to go limp, like a discarded puppet, and stared blankly at Tommaso—offering him nothing, neither fear nor desire, not even an acknowledgement of his existence. An empty page. The Artifex raised his hand as though to strike her, only to slam the door shut with a furious growl and stride away down the corridor, leaving Lucia alone in the darkness, his finger marks upon her throat.

She never saw Tommaso Cellini again. Around dawn, she was awoken by three men barging into her chambers. They dragged her from her bed and bundled her down a flight of steps leading below the Palazzo Nero into a dark cellar. There, with pincers and burning tongs, they removed Lucia's tongue at the root, roughly cauterizing the wound before abandoning her in the rat-infested straw of a dungeon cell. As the great palaces of the Pitti family toppled amid cheers and choking clouds of dust, their sole surviving member was left to rot underground, Lucia's sun rising and setting with the brief rectangle of light that appeared when her jailors pushed stale bread and water through the door. A rat bit her; she killed it by hitting it with the water jug. She had no idea how long she was to be imprisoned, nor why she fought to stay alive. When finally a man came to visit her, the sound of his tread on the steps sent her into a panic, and she scuttled into the corner as the door opened. It was Pietro, Tommaso's Master of the Scrolls, bearing the news that she was to be allowed to live.

Lucia had to be helped up the dungeon steps, her eyes so accustomed to the darkness that daylight assailed her like beating fists on her skull. Two unsmiling women scrubbed the filth from her skin and brushed the tangles from her matted hair, ushering her into a set of grey hessian robes. Come nightfall, Lucia was bundled into a cart and ferried out through the palace gates and across the Ponte Nuovo to the Verso, making for a convent on the edge of a small square, where she was given a new name under which she was to live for the rest of her days.

All of which Lucia bore in complete silence.

VI. *A Slow Spiral*

THE FOLIO CAME, as was their custom, in the middle of the night, announcing themselves at the doors of San Benedetta with a solemn rap on the convent door. Lucrezia awoke with a start to find Eleanora's hand on her shoulder, her room blinking in the glow of the old woman's candle. She rose at once. Guildsmen went watchfully through the black corridors, holding torches high above their head. Lucrezia was careful to keep her gaze lowered as they passed by.

The clerk was waiting for them in the scriptorium. A studious character with a tonsure and a boil upon his cheek, he looked up from his ledger as they entered and gave Eleanora a nod of recognition. If he had noted the absence of warders from the convent, the fact did not seem to trouble him. He drew a scrupulous line through an entry in the ledger and turned the page. Paola, who had been working in the hall when the Folio arrived, watched the clerk from her desk, gnawing on her fingernail. Lucrezia would have preferred to have seen more of their sisters with her. Should one of them succumb to a failure of nerve—or a slip of the tongue, she thought humourlessly—their designs could be ended that very night.

Touching Eleanora's arm, Lucrezia withdrew from the scriptorium. The convent had stirred into life with the guild's arrival, torches thrust through rusted sconces and draughts nosing into long-neglected corners. Men laden with books walked in an antlike procession from the chapel back towards the front entrance. In the South Corridor, Eletta watched them through a crack in her cell door, drawing back at the sight of Lucrezia. The door to the next room stood wide open: Ginevra knelt by her bedside, her head bowed and her hands clasped in prayer. The other cells were empty. Lucrezia frowned. Where were her sisters?

She continued to the East Corridor, which had grudgingly submitted to illumination. The guildsmen had completed the first wave of clearances from the chapel; already, an aisle stood empty. As Lucrezia stood in the doorway, her ears pricked up at the sound of a voice floating down through the tower archway. Glancing quickly around the empty corridor, she went soundlessly up the spiral steps. The punishment cell was wreathed in shadow; beyond it, a growing light filled the stairwell. A further turn of the steps revealed two figures gathered at a window recess. Sister Maria huddled by a candle on the ledge, partially obscured by the silhouette of one of the Folio's men. He was leaning against the wall, a casual pose that nonetheless blocked off her route back down the tower. Lucrezia's jaw tightened as he whispered something in Maria's ear; she shook her head, her face expressing neither encouragement nor disapproval. She looked down at her hands as the man stroked her cheek with his thumb.

Lucrezia cleared her throat.

Maria started violently, her face turning bright red. Wriggling out from the recess, she ran past Lucrezia down the stairs. Her companion turned. He was younger than she had first assumed, smooth-shaven and wide-eyed, little more than a boy. But handsome.

The clerk will be looking for you, she wrote on her slate.

He gave her an appraising look—brazenly, almost lazily, weighing her up. The merits and demerits of her appearance. Lucrezia held his gaze. How old she must seem to him, as lined and worn as the volumes he had been brought to move. Had he tried to woo Maria on previous visits, she wondered, or had he seized his opportunity this night, with the warders absent from the halls? There seemed little of the wolf behind his puppyish exterior, yet he showed no trace of embarrassment at having been disturbed. Indeed, his lips twitched with amusement as he stared at Lucrezia—a gambler, willing to chance his hand at a second romance. A diversion on a slow night.

Beyond the window, the orange orchard was blanketed in darkness. Footsteps echoed faintly through the corridor beneath them. Tullia and the twins were still unaccounted for. At any moment, the clerk in the scriptorium could spot something amiss and demand to see the warders. There were so many books left to amend, still so much at stake.

The boy stepped closer, warily, half-expecting to be rebuffed. He reached out and cupped Lucrezia's cheek in his palm. She did not move. Emboldened, he leaned in to kiss her on the mouth, only to be pushed away. He hesitated, uncertain. Lucrezia laid her slate on the window ledge and smoothed down her hair. Turning to the boy, she raised up her robe around her waist. His eyes widened as she revealed herself to him, and he began fumbling with the drawstring on his breeches. They came together without preamble, and when he entered Lucrezia the immediate sensation was one of pain—more abrasive than she had expected, an unwelcome intrusion. Yet she could feel him stirring eagerly within her, as though spurred on by her indifference. She wrapped her legs around him as he gripped her waist and lifted her up on to the ledge. A cold gust of wind blew in through the window: she fixed her gaze on the candle as it winced and flinched. The boy muttered something unintelligibly, grabbing hold of her buttocks. Shifting her hips, Lucrezia felt her discomfort ease—she bit his shoulder and he responded by driving harder and deeper inside her, pushing her back against the wall by the window. Here, now, was the first hint of pleasure, of syrup and sap. Lucrezia closed her eyes and felt their breaths align, urgent gasps that had no need for words. The boy bit back a cry as she raked her nails down the back of his neck. He collapsed, shuddering, at his climax.

When it was done, Lucrezia pushed him off her and slipped gingerly down from the ledge. She pulled down her robe and looped her slate back around her neck. There was a smile on his face as he tied up his breeches, some charming or clever line playing in his head. Lucrezia pressed her finger firmly to his lips. The boy left without a word, ruffling his hair as he stepped lightly down the steps, his satisfied expression complicated by a slight bewilderment, and perhaps even a hint of admiration.

Lucrezia blew out the candle and sat in darkness by the window. She would not hurry down after him, red-faced and out of breath—she had no wish for anyone to learn what had transpired on these steps. The act itself did not shame her: it was the ill-discipline, the sheer foolhardiness of it, that left Lucrezia astounded. How could she expect the others to adhere to her plan, to see it through to fruition, when she herself had abandoned them at such a critical juncture—and for such selfish, frivolous reasons!

And yet, to have lived the full measure of a life, without once knowing.

She came down from the tower to find that the East Corridor had been returned to darkness, the chapel shelves stripped bare, and the torches slid free from the sconces. Lucrezia pushed open the grilles in the wall and pressed her face to the eyeholes. The Folio's wagon had gone. Tiny circles of moonlight danced across the wall behind her.

At a giggle echoing through the darkness, Lucrezia straightened up. She slammed the grille shut, the bright dots winking out. The laughter left a mocking trail along the length of the passage as it faded away. She looked back towards the chapel, her eyes delving fruitlessly into the gloom around it. No sign of anyone. Tutting, she turned and walked away.

A cloaked devil sprang shrieking from the alcove, a wicked grin slashed across its face. Lucrezia stumbled backwards, letting out a scream as a second imp barged into her. They hooted and capered around her, pulling at her robes and hair. She grabbed at one of them blindly, tearing off a mask to reveal the flushed face of Bianca. The young thief hissed and bared her teeth. Her sister, Francesca, pushed up her own devil mask and ran to her side.

Fool girls! Lucrezia scribbled angrily on her slate.

Do you like our masks? It was Francesca who replied.

Where did you get them?

The warders' room, wrote Bianca. *From Carnival.*

Did the Folio see you?

We aren't stupid.

Did they see you? Francesca added, with a sly smile. The twins giggled.

That, Lucrezia chose to ignore.

Where is Tullia? she asked.

Francesca shrugged. *How should we know?*

It is late. Go to your rooms.

You are not our warder, Bianca wrote pointedly. *We go where we want.*

Snatching back her mask, she pulled it over her face and curtsied mockingly. Francesca took her hand, and the two girls ran away laughing towards the South Corridor, their cloaks fluttering about them. Lucrezia shook her head. It had been a long night, and the dawn could not be far off. But her mind was racing too quickly for sleep, and one of her sisters remained unaccounted for. She went to Tullia's room and found the cell empty, the bed still freshly made from the previous morning. At the sight of the courtesan's slate poking out from the beneath the bed, a prickle of unease ran down

Lucrezia's spine. She walked back out into the corridor. A sliver of moonlight was playing on the flagstones at the end of the passageway—the door to the orchard had been left ajar. It butted against the jamb as Lucrezia approached.

She stepped outside. The night was hot and airless, stifling the crickets into silence. Shadowy hands reached out towards Lucrezia as she went slowly through the orange trees, stepping over roots and ducking beneath gnarled branches. The chapel tower pierced the black sky. She arrived at the outer gate to find it closed, and tried the handle. Locked. If Tullia had fled the convent, she had not come this way.

There was no need for undue concern, Lucrezia reasoned with herself. The convent was replete with nooks and cubbyholes, countless places where Tullia might be. Yet the orchard's hush had taken on an oppressive air; as Lucrezia made her way back to the convent, she felt branches bend to block her path. Her step quickened. Glancing behind her, she tripped over a root and stumbled into a tree. There came a fibrous creak above her. She looked up. Her legs went weak; she reached out to a trunk to steady herself.

Above the bench where she had sat with Borso, Tullia's body hung by a rope around the neck: a soiled angel, turning slow spirals in the air.

VII. *Holy Words*

THEY BURIED TULLIA in the cloister, carrying her body through the trees wrapped in a sheet. Ginevra had led the arguments that a priest should be summoned to oversee the funeral, but

Lucrezia had flatly rejected the suggestion. This was no time to be inviting strangers into the convent—what manner of questions would a man of God have, to be confronted with the body of a young woman with the mark of a noose around her neck? How long before word reached the Folio, or even the Seven? Sensing she was about to be outvoted, Ginevra stormed out of the scriptorium, her sisters exchanging unhappy glances as the door slammed behind her.

By way of a peace offering, Lucrezia offered to dig Tullia's grave herself; to her surprise, Eletta volunteered to assist her. They carried shovels out to the cloister and set to work in the shade of a cypress tree. Lucrezia dug vigorously, relishing the dirt working its way beneath her nails, the hessian's reproach against her sweaty skin. Beside her, Eletta wielded her shovel in silence. Of all the women of San Benedetta, she was the hardest to fathom, so unremarkable in nature and appearance, yet at the same time responsible for a crime of appalling savagery. Eletta had attacked her love-rival in broad daylight on the Piazza della Rosa, clawing the girl's eyes out with her nails and leaving her screaming and clutching at her bloodied face. It begged the question: had Eletta suffered a momentary explosion of uncontrollable rage, or did her assault offer instead a glimpse of some devil hidden within her? Lucrezia had never been able to decide, and remained cautious in her dealings with Eletta who, for her part, offered no clue as to the truth of the matter. She used her slate only when absolutely necessary, steering clear of her sisters' games and arguments alike, seemingly happiest when cut off completely from the world.

Lucrezia climbed out of the grave and rested her shovel

against the tree, gesturing wearily at Eletta to stop digging. Tucking a stray lock of hair behind her ear, she looked around the cloister. Her mouth was dry—she wished she had brought water. Eletta sat down on the grass and wrote something on her tablet. She held it up for Lucrezia to read.

She did not want to stay here.

Lucrezia sighed and reached for her slate.

There was a vote. We agreed.

Some agreed more than others, Eletta replied.

You blame me for this.

She wanted to leave.

She chose to stay.

Something is wrong here. I will not dig another grave.

Looping her slate around her neck, Eletta rose and walked away towards the West Corridor, leaving Lucrezia alone with the shovels and the shivering trees.

SHE WAS KEEN to wash the sweat and soil from her skin, but upon leaving the cloister Lucrezia did not go to the lavatorium. Instead, she headed for the sisters' rooms in the

South Corridor. Tullia's body had been laid out on her bed, her expression frozen and her neck bruised where she had tied the rope around it. Glancing around to check that she was alone, Lucrezia crouched by the bed and slid Tullia's slate towards her. Upon it was the same drawing the girl had made in the scriptorium. Two figures holding hands, rendered in frantic lines. A single line was written beneath them. Outside, footsteps were approaching—Lucrezia hurriedly rubbed the slate with her sleeve as Eleanora came bustling into the room, and slipped it back beneath the bed. She avoided the elder woman's gaze as she got to her feet, brushing her hands on her robe. Maria appeared seconds later, carefully carrying a basin of water. Together they set to washing and wrapping Tullia's body for burial.

The afternoon light was fading by the time they were done. As they carried Tullia through the cloister, Lucrezia saw that the trees had been decorated with fragments of parchment, pinned to the bark and suspended from the branches—pages from the Bible, sliced carefully from their bindings. Ginevra was kneeling by the graveside. She rose as the procession drew near, offering Lucrezia a look of defiance. They lowered Tullia's body into the ground and stood over it. Bianca bit her lip, trying to stop a giggle, and received an elbow in her ribs from her smirking sister. The wind picked up as Eleanora began shovelling soil over the white sheet. There seemed no need for any more words, with holy pages whispering in the trees around them. Someone was crying: Sister Paola. Ginevra's lips moved with rapid, mute invocations.

When the grave had been filled, the women bid their

farewells to their sister and filed back inside the convent. Lucrezia walked through lengthening shadows to the lavatorium. She filled the octagonal basin with cold water and began to scrub her hands. As a young girl, she had wallowed for hours in deep baths filled with steaming hot water, until her skin had wrinkled like old fruit and she was too weak to lift herself from the tub. What she would have given now, for such luxury?

She dried her hands, noting with distaste the chapped skin around her knuckles. Taking up Sister Maria's looking-glass from the side, Lucrezia examined her face.

And saw a shadow in the doorway behind her.

The mirror clattered to the floor as Lucrezia whirled around. At the sight of Sister Eleanora, her shoulders sagged with relief.

Sorry, the old woman wrote on her slate. *I frightened you.*

Lucrezia stooped to pick up the looking-glass, annoyed and a little embarrassed at having been startled.

What is it? she wrote.

I saw you cleaning Tullia's slate. What had she written?

There was a long pause before Lucrezia replied.

"I am not a thief", she wrote.

Eleanora frowned.

Then why was she sent here?

Muddy water swirled inside the basin. A damp smear obscured Maria's looking-glass. A simple drawing on a slate, rendered in a shaking hand: two figures, one tall and one small. A mother and a child.

I do not know, Lucrezia lied.

VIII. *A Serpent Tongue*

BIANCA AND FRANCESCA fled the convent that night, creeping out through the orchard as the moon hid behind the clouds. They took with them Maria's looking-glass and a bestiary adorned with gold-leaf illustrations, leaving Lucrezia to reflect on the limits of maiming and imprisonment in correcting the essence of people's nature. She could not hide a twinge of annoyance at the manner of the sisters' leaving—without a word of farewell, after all these years, their pockets heavy with the belongings of others: a thief's parting.

With only six women left inside San Benedetta, the sisters had to extend their shifts inside the scriptorium. Lucrezia did not mind the longer hours, volunteering for the lonely stretches after nightfall when the candle's light shrank around her. Better that than lying in bed awake for hours, her ears filled with the sound of creaking rope fibres. She was not the only one finding sleep elusive: two nights in a row, Eleanora had sat huddled beneath a blanket before the empty hearth in the calefactory.

Summer took its leave of the city, pursued by a stiffening wind from the east and the smell of bonfires from the surrounding countryside. In the cloister, Ginevra's Bible pages slipped from the trees like browning leaves. Oranges glistened in the rain. Little of what remained of the sun's heat penetrated the convent walls, its corridors tingling with ghostly breaths and the basins of the lavatorium filling with freezing water. The Sisters lingered over their broth at dinner and went quickly to their rooms at night. Ginevra kept her door open, so the others could see her at prayer. Lucrezia suspected that, behind her back, the pious little viper was putting the fear of God into the others. After so many years in each other's company, the women were finely attuned to each other's moods, and Lucrezia was well aware of the deep misgivings Tullia's death had wrought.

So long as they did not leave her. So long as they could finish their work.

That afternoon, Lucrezia took her lunch alone. The refectory had retained at least a little of its warmth—the lingering aroma of food, some lost echo of pans rattling over the hearth. Rain pattered and dripped from the eaves as she ate. Lost in thought, Lucrezia realized only belatedly that someone was watching her. She sighed and reached for her slate.

What? she wrote.

We pray for Tullia, Ginevra replied, from the doorway. *Join us.*

Lucrezia shook her head.

You pray. I work.

Our sisters need comfort.

Is that what you offer them?

I am God's vessel.

Lucrezia sat back in her chair, her expression one of sour amusement.

As you were when you burned down the printer's shop.

A den of profane works, Ginevra replied implacably. *To destroy it was God's work.*

You killed five men.

Five sinners, beyond redemption.

Then why did God have you locked up here? Lucrezia inquired icily.

Ginevra held her head up proudly. *To do as I did before. To stop evil.*
What evil?

Ginevra wrote a single word on her slate.

You.

Rain drummed against the windowpanes. Lucrezia nodded and pushed away her bowl. Ginevra withdrew without another word, a smile on her lips. *How simple life must be for you,* Lucrezia thought, *clad in an armour of pious pride, untouched by uncertainty and remorse.* It was hard not to envy her, hate her as she might.

While her sisters gathered to pray, Lucrezia returned to work in the scriptorium. She had no appetite for dinner and retired early to her room. As she took off her slate and laid it by her bed, she felt an overwhelming tiredness come over her. She curled up under the sheet and fell asleep almost at once. Her dreams were turbulent and filled with nightmarish images: her uncle Matteo, begging for mercy as the *becchini* set to work on him; her father Donato, strapped face-down under a plank and dragged around the piazzas before a howling mob; her mother and her sisters, screaming as the bonfires devoured them. An entire bloodline, drained away into the gutters; a house lost in choking dust.

Lucrezia's eyes snapped open. She was lying flat on her back, a film of cold sweat on her skin. Her room was a black well. As she tried to disentangle herself from her dreams, she became aware of a noise from the floor by her bed: a scraping sound, mismatched surfaces grating against one another. Lucrezia peered over the edge of her bed. Through the shadows, she could discern the outline of her slate lying on the flagstones in the middle of her cell. She frowned. Had it not been by her side when she had fallen asleep? Lucrezia reached out to retrieve it—and cried out with alarm, as the tablet came alive and slid beyond her fingertips. She snatched her hand back. It skidded to a halt.

Lucrezia's eyes narrowed. She sprang out of bed and dived after the slate as it shot away across the floor, trapping it just before it could slip underneath the door. Her momentary satisfaction vanished at its touch against her skin, so cold it burned in her hand. She had expected to find a piece of string attached to it, leading to some mischievous hand out in the corridor. But there was nothing of the kind. Lucrezia went to her bedside table and struck the flint by her candle. Light filled the room. She gasped, the slate clattering to the floor.

Upon it, drawn in a jagged and violent hand, a pair of narrowed eyes stared up at Lucrezia.

IX. *Dark Altar*

THE NEXT MORNING, Lucrezia took pen and parchment with her to the old punishment cell above the chapel. There, sitting at the window overlooking the orchard, she set about composing a letter. Accustomed to presenting her thoughts on the slate, concisely and uncluttered by emotion, she found to her annoyance that she struggled to express herself on the page. She broke off repeatedly, making small noises of exasperation. Rising from her seat, Lucrezia paced the room, gazing out over the trees for inspiration.

She had spent the rest of the night awake, staring at her slate as it lay innocently beside her candle. Only with the morning light, did she come to regret having wiped it clean, and with it all proof of what she had seen. Would anyone have believed her, regardless? Lucrezia could find no easy explanation either for the moving slate or the unsettling image that had appeared on it. If it had been some kind of ugly joke by one of her sisters, it had been accomplished in a way she could not fathom. Had her dreams spilled over into the waking world, leaving her unable to discern one from the other?

Shaking her head, Lucrezia resolved to compose one final draft of her letter, refusing to linger on the gentility of her phrasing. When it was finished, she folded it up and slipped it inside her sleeve. She was no ink maid—what she had would have to suffice. Gathering up the discarded parchment, Lucrezia picked a path down the stairs and headed back through the convent. At the junction of the East and South Corridors, the light hesitantly reintroduced itself, in shades of cream and straw. Dust played on its pale tendrils. As Lucrezia neared the West Corridor, a distant thud reverberated through the brightening halls. It was coming from within the scriptorium, the doors rattling in their frames. At a scream, Lucrezia broke into a run, the banging growing louder with every step.

The scriptorium was in disarray, books scattered across the flagstones, their pages stained with ink. Chairs lay dazed upon their back. Sunlight was pouring in through the windows, but the rows of desks were encased in a sour and stinging cold. In the middle of the hall Sister Paola lay on top of her desk as it stuttered and shook with a life of its own. She wailed as the desk began to buck violently, its front and back legs lifting clear of the floor in turn, like a furious steed trying to dismount its rider.

Appalled by the scene before her, Lucretia froze, her breath forming white clouds in the air. When finally she forced herself to take a step towards the desk, it went abruptly still. Lucrezia paused, her breath forming white clouds in the air. Paola raised her head and stared at her. Beneath her, the desk stirred. Lucrezia could only watch, with mounting horror, as it lifted slowly off the ground and rose into the air. She ran forward and grabbed her sister's despairing hand, at once encountering a force in opposition, almost strong enough to lift her from her feet. Paola's eyes bulged with a pleading horror.

Gasps and footsteps filled the ice-bound hall. Suddenly there were Sisters around them, Eleanora and Ginevra, Maria and Eletta, flocking around the rising desk. Together, they strained to drag it back to earth. The desk wobbled and lurched violently to one side, knocking the women away and wrenching Paola from Lucrezia's grip. It began to spin, faster and faster—Lucrezia caught a flailing foot to the temple and fell backwards, her head exploding with pain.

Paola's screams built to a peak before breaking off. Rolling on to her stomach, Lucrezia saw her sister had been thrown clear from the desk and was lying face-down on the flagstones. The others stood ashen-faced and frozen. It was then, through the black stars raining down before her eyes, that Lucrezia saw it—a vague figure on the scriptorium gallery, little more than a suggestion of a presence in the air. Its restless outline pulsed with fury.

As Lucrezia stared up towards the gallery, the air blurred. She heard Eleanora shout a mangled warning, and felt the shadow of the desk fell over her. It shivered and dropped like a stone. Lucrezia rolled to one side, feeling the rush of air as the desk slammed down on the spot where she had fallen, its wooden legs snapping with the force of the impact and its compartments crumpling and splintering.

She lay on her back, panting, as the reverberations echoed around the hall.

X. *Farewell*

BORSO CLIMBED THE hill to find Lucrezia waiting for him at the orchard's outer gate. Noting the bruise on her temple, he raised a bushy eyebrow—she thrust her letter into his hand before he could say anything, leaving him standing awkwardly in the gateway. Borso asked whether he could take a seat on the bench to read, and she reluctantly gave way. In firm, composed handwriting, she had informed the count that she would no longer receive him. The orchard would be empty, and the door locked, every Sunday hence. Lucrezia had added that she would prefer it if he left the city altogether, as in the past he had not always shown sufficient regard for her wishes, most notably in his continuing feud with Lorenzo.

Borso had been summarily dismissed before, but something in his manner upon finishing Lucrezia's message told her that he understood the significance of this one. She had expected him—still that last trace of vanity, like a smudge of kohl she could not wipe clean—to try and argue with her, to plead his case. But he folded up the letter and nodded. Lucrezia wondered whether there was a release of some sort, a day of reckoning for which Borso had been both dreading and dreaming of all this time. For all the world, she would have wished another woman for him, a kind-hearted and gentle soul to draw him into her embrace in bed at night.

She wrote him one final question on her slate, a question to which she had been waiting fifteen years for the answer.

How did you find me?

Borso rose from the bench.

"I searched the city," he said simply. "Every street, every building. Why do you think it took me so long to find you?"

He bowed stiffly and took his leave of the orchard, closing the door on the latch behind him. At that moment, Lucrezia loved him as much as she ever had—and would continue to love him for whatever remained of her life, and whatever might follow in the next.

XI. *The Devil's Tread*

THE FIVE REMAINING sisters were waiting for Lucrezia in the scriptorium. One glance at Eleanora's face, pensive and downcast, told her all she needed to know. She swept past them and sat down at her desk, reaching for a pen. A tap on a slate stayed her hand. It was Sister Ginevra.

We want to stop.

Lucrezia looked at each of them in turn.

Why? she wrote back.

We have done all we can.

There are still more books.

It is enough.

Lucrezia closed her book.

You are frightened.

This house is cursed, Ginevra replied insistently. *The Lord frowns upon our work.*

He did not frown when we worked for Tommaso.

Tommaso was our ruler. To her surprise it was Paola, the bruises fresh upon her, who answered. *You are not.*

A challenge, a confrontation of some sort, had been inevitable even before desks had started flying around the hall. The important thing, Lucrezia told herself, was not to lose her temper. She took heart from the fact that they were here at all. The doors stood unlocked and the warders were long gone—why stay to debate the matter? The truth was that the Sisters of San Benedetta were lost without a guiding hand: no one in Cadenza, neither the straw statesmen bickering inside the Star Chamber nor the idle *becchini*, the fawning poets nor their fatted patrons, missed Tommaso Cellini as much as the women he had had maimed and imprisoned.

Adopting a show of contrition, Lucrezia managed to persuade the others to agree to a compromise: they would finish what they had started, but all works save those requiring the simplest of changes would be thrown into the cellar for the damp and the darkness to devour. With the threat of outright rebellion averted—for now, at least—the sisters set to categorizing the remaining volumes. As Lucrezia watched them pile the cart with books, a headache began to build behind her eyes. She left them to their labours.

The corridors blurred as she wandered their shifting lengths, unsure where to go. What places of refuge were left to her inside the convent—her room, where her slate had taken on a life of its own; the orchard, where Tullia had hanged herself; or the cloister, where the courtesan's body mouldered in the earth? Outside the cellar, Lucrezia heard the rusty creak of a wheel behind her and drew back into an alcove. She watched from the shadows as Ginevra guided the book cart along the flagstones, humming lightly to herself. The young woman stopped at the chapel and unlocked the door, golden light spilling out into the corridor and settling about her shoulders in a glittering mist. She manoeuvred the cart through the doorway and disappeared inside.

Lucrezia followed her into the chapel. Shielding her eyes from the glare of the low autumn sun through the windows, she made out Ginevra's silhouette at the bottom of one of the aisles. The girl was stacking books on the shelves—at Lucrezia's entrance, the hummed refrain died on her lips.

I thought you were resting, she wrote on her slate.

No easy matter, now.
No. These halls are busy with evil.
You still think at my command?

Ginevra looked thoughtful. *I cannot tell where the evil ends and you begin.*

Lucrezia's fingers tightened around her chalk. She wrote rapidly on the slate, her handwriting rushed and insistent.

A lifetime of imprisonment. My family slaughtered. Has not evil been done to me?

I did not say I did not pity you.

I do not want your pity!

Pride. Always your downfall.

I do this for all of us, wrote Lucrezia, with a noise of frustration. *Can you not see that?*

Yet when we ask you to stop, you do not listen, Ginevra countered.

Lucrezia took a threatening pace towards her.

I have come too far to be denied.

Am I not trying to help you?

With that, Ginevra turned her back on Lucrezia and calmly resumed the unloading of her book cart. Lucrezia did not have the strength to continue the argument; shaking her head wearily, she turned to leave the chapel. Behind her, Ginevra made a small grunt of surprise. In the act of placing a book on the shelf, her left hand had become wedged between two volumes. She tugged on it, a bewildered expression on her face. Lucrezia rolled her eyes. Yet Ginevra seemed to have forgotten about her completely, straining to free herself. Losing patience, Lucrezia strode over and grabbed her arm— to her shock, she found that Ginevra's left hand was stuck fast, the books pressing in so tightly around it that her skin was reddening at the wrist. She and Ginevra exchanged a troubled glance.

The chapel door slammed shut.

Ginevra was frantically trying to remove her hand, the panic now plain in her eyes. Lucrezia adopted a new tactic, scrabbling at the other volumes on the shelf in the hope of prising them out of their row. But it was as though they had been nailed down. Her fingernail snapped painfully on a spine. Beside Lucrezia, Ginevra stopped struggling. She twisted around, her eyes darting up and down the aisle. The colour drained from her face. Clutching Lucrezia's arm, she silently mouthed the words:

It is here.

Lucrezia froze. The chapel was perfectly still, the window at the end of the aisle glowing so brightly it almost seemed to be burning. Yet she, too, had the sense that they were not alone, the aisles seething with an unspoken anger and the temperature rising unnaturally. A book fell from a high shelf, startling them both as its spine slapped against the flagstones. Ginevra huddled against Lucrezia. One by one, volumes began to tumble, slowly and deliberately, moving along the aisle towards the pair of them. There was a blur in front of the window.

Ginevra's body lifted off the ground and slammed into the bookcase, knocking Lucrezia to the ground. She heard the girl's head connect with the shelf with a sickening crack; looking up, she saw to her horror that the shelves had swallowed up Ginevra's right hand to leave the girl pinned against the bookcase, her feet suspended off the floor and her arms extended either side of her. The string around Ginevra's neck snapped, her slate flying against the wall and shattering. She lifted her head groggily.

The light from the window was driving hot pins into Lucrezia's temple, sweat streaming down her back. A golden ray arrowed in through the glass along the aisle, landing on a patch of Ginevra's robes above the knee. The hessian began to smoulder and smoke. Lucrezia tried to struggle to her feet but already a small flame had danced to life on Ginevra's robe. The girl stirred as the smoke began to billow off her. Looking down, she burst out laughing: a grim, deathly sound.

Ginevra's robes went up in flames, enveloping her in a roaring cocoon of fire. She threw her head back and screamed, her limbs convulsing as she mindlessly kicked and writhed. The heat drove Lucrezia to her knees, weeping helplessly as the room filled with the stench of charred flesh and hair. Fists pounded on the chapel door.

It was over almost as quickly as it had begun. The flames shrivelled and died, leaving what remained of Ginevra to topple to the floor as the books finally released their grip on her. Lucrezia let out a piercing shriek, sobbing and clawing at her robe as her sisters looked on open-mouthed from the doorway, and the blackened carcass steamed and crackled on the flagstones.

XII. *Salt and the Plough*

TEN MONTHS EARLIER, a scream had knifed through the open windows of the scriptorium, startling the Sisters of San Benedetta from their labours. They abandoned their desks, trailing sleeves leaving smudges of ink on the page, and hurried through the convent. There were eight of them, all the Sisters save Sister Eleanora, who had been summoned to talk with the warders. In the East Corridor, they slid open the grilles in the wall and huddled around them. A lone woman ran sobbing across the square, wailing and tearing at her clothes. She slowed and collapsed to her knees, folding up into a small bundle of dismay.

Across the river, a bell began to toll. Its call was taken up in the neighbouring churches and towers, a slow, dolorous procession through the parks and the piazzas, along the aisles of the Accademia and beneath the arches of the Ponte Nuovo, over the river to the Verso, where it wound its way up the Vicolo Scarpuccia. The sisters shot one another questioning looks. Stepping away from the grille, Lucrezia turned in time to see Eleanora hastening around the corner.

There were tears in the old woman's eyes.

Tommaso Cellini, Artifex of Cadenza, was dead.

Lucrezia felt every bell toll physically slam into her, crushing her ribs and lungs, threatening to knock her to the ground. Behind her, she could hear Paola sniffling; Lucrezia clenched her fists, fighting the urge to wheel around and slap her. She thought she might faint. As the sisters slowly filed back to the scriptorium, Lucrezia was dimly aware of Eleanora by her side, offering her an arm to lean on.

Inside the hall, inkwells hiccupped nervously at the thundering bells. In the confusion, it was several minutes before any of the sisters realized that they were alone. Bianca and Francesca crept out into the corridors to check for their warders, only to return shaking their heads. Chalks scurried across slates; hands waved in the air, mouths making strained noises for emphasis.

Can we leave? Maria asked.

Perhaps, Eleanora replied.

Let us go now, together!

Tullia's hand. Eleanora shook her head.

Who will take us in?

Bianca thrust her slate in front of Eleanora.

What does it matter? At least we'd be free.

475

What is freedom, without money or food or a roof over our head? Eleanora shot back.

So we sit here and wait?

Lucrezia tapped her slate.

I have an idea.

In truth, she had held little hope of winning them to her cause. Yet she had no option but to try. This thing could not be done alone, much as she might have preferred it. The younger sisters—most attuned to the possibilities of freedom, and the most reluctant to do anything that might endanger it—were the hardest to convince. Bianca and Francesca refused flat-out, while Tullia laughed contemptuously at her notion. Lucrezia kept tight rein of her temper and calmly countered their objections. She had spent years refining her argument, to shape its nuances in a way designed to win her sisters around, to anticipate and overcome their reluctance by answering their need for one thing above all else: vengeance.

She would have seen Tommaso set on by a pack of ravenous hounds or led bowed and weeping to the stake. She would have seen him die the death of the apostles, upside-down on a crucifix, or buried beneath a storm of rocks. She would have seen the city that lauded him burned to the ground. Yet that had been denied to her. His death had been a distant thing, bloodless and impersonal, felt only through the eddies of panic rippling out across the city. And yet, although he lived no longer, Tommaso was not completely beyond Lucrezia's grasp. She proposed to turn the Sisters' censorious pens upon him, to remove all mention of his name from the volumes of Cadenza. His poems, his reign as Artifex, every accolade and achievement would be removed.

The sisters argued the matter late into the night, as soldiers brawled in the streets and the *becchini* went from house to house, kicking down doors and settling old scores. Even at the last, Lucrezia could not be sure she had won the day. The bells had fallen silent by the time they put it to the vote, eight hands rising into the air in agreement—slowly followed, with reluctance, by Tullia's. And so the Sisters of San Benedetta declared war on Tommaso Cellini.

They set to work at once, hunting the Artifex through the pages of the very books he had ordered them to change: dogged hounds of Diana, striking him down with brisk strokes of their pen. The forger Maria set to work on letters to the Folio, requesting fresh volumes from the Accademia and the Niccoló in a disguised hand. Three nights later, a cart appeared on the Vicolo Scarpuccia. Even with the Palazzo Nero empty, the business of the libraries could not stop. Lucrezia watched the men unload the books with a thin smile of satisfaction. Tommaso's death was not enough. She wanted him obliterated; his legacy, his reputation, erased. She would bury his memory in salt.

Under Lucrezia's supervision, the sisters attacked laudatory odes and works of history alike, erasing flattering dedications to Cadenza's former ruler. In their haste, it became an attack on the city itself. Entire streets were scratched out, bridges toppling into black water; neighbourhoods were razed to the ground. The Sisters laid waste to the very earth in which

Cadenza stood—this city, that had gloried in tyranny and mourned a monster. Its ghosts would line the hallways.

XIII. *A Spoilt and Spiteful Child*

NIGHT HAD FALLEN by the time Lucrezia had buried Ginevra's charred remains in the cloister. This time, no one had volunteered to help her dig. Upon stepping back inside the convent, she heard the beckoning crackle of a fire from the calefactory, and entered the room to find Eleanora perched before a blazing hearth. Her eyes were closed and her feet propped up on a stool. Books were strewn about the floor around her, pages ripped from their bindings. Kneeling down beside the fire, Lucrezia saw sheets of parchment curling and blackening in the flames.

She turned back to Eleanora, who had opened her eyes, and shot her a questioning look. The old woman held up her slate.

Can you forgive me?

Lucrezia wearily rubbed her neck.

That depends. Which books did you burn?

It does not matter. They were already destroyed.

A reproach of sorts, its delivery mild and matter-of-fact. Lucrezia looked around the calefactory.

Where are the others?

Eleanora shrugged.

Gone.

I should have let them go. They asked to stop.

You did not chain them to the walls.

They died because of me.

Perhaps.

I wanted to finish what we started, Lucrezia told her. *Cadenza is doomed. You shall have your victory.*

A smouldering book slipped down the hearth. Eleanora gazed sadly into the flames.

I will not mourn for this city, Lucrezia wrote.

I know. But I am a foolish old woman. I cannot take satisfaction.

You are not foolish. It is a sign of strength to be capable of compassion. Of love.

It is all that has kept me alive.

I envy you, Lucrezia wrote. *I feel nothing but rage.*

Is it any wonder?

I hate, and am hated in turn.

Do not judge the others. They were common women who knew your true name. A nobleman courted you!

I did not ask for that.

All the more reason to hate you.

I thought they would kill me. A knife through the ribs while I slept.

Eleanora pursed her lips.

I would never have allowed it.

I know. I would not be alive otherwise.

They were both, the two of them, skirting around a truth they had found easier never to acknowledge, regarding the true course of Eleanora's affections and desires. In return for her protection, Lucrezia had offered Eleanora all the warmth of which she was capable—the bitter embers left to her after Tommaso Cellini had scraped the inside of her heart raw. It was scant reward, she knew; a debt she could not hope to repay.

I have been so cold here I feared I would not awaken, Eleanora wrote finally.

Why do you avoid your room?

A scratch of chalk on slate.

The ghost of my husband lies in wait for me beneath my bed.

Lucrezia reached out and took Eleanora's hand in her own. She squeezed it gently.
Fear not. It is not your husband.

Eleanora looked up at her.

Then who?

A spoilt and spiteful child, Lucrezia wrote. *Who is far more frightened than you or I.*

Do not be so sure.

Lucrezia smiled gravely and handed Eleanora her slate. As she rose, the old woman scribbled hurriedly on it.

Stay with me. Enjoy the fire.

She leant over and kissed Eleanora's forehead. The old woman closed her eyes with a small sigh. Lucrezia walked out of the room and closed the door behind her, leaving Eleanora resting before the fire as it feasted on the books she had served it.

After the warmth of the calefactory, the corridor was shockingly cold. Lucrezia walked through into the scriptorium, where a final candle burned down on her desk. The shelves on the book cart were bare. She gathered up the candle and went out into the West Corridor. Her headache had returned with increased insistence, sharp needles pressing and probing the soft recesses inside her skull. The candlelight blurred before her eyes, leaving a muddy yellow stain on her vision that remained no matter where she looked. In the cloister, trees bent in supplication before the wind.

Lucrezia pressed on into the South Corridor. Outside Eleanora's cell, she flung open the door. The room ignored her. She placed the candle on the floor and got down on her hands and knees, heedless of the landslide of pain this caused inside her head. Peering into the shadowy nooks, she inspected the space beneath the bed until she was satisfied the chamber was empty. Her own room, she disregarded. Only at the junction of the South and East corridors, beside the entrance to the orchard, did Lucrezia pause. She was tempted to allow herself one final glimpse of the moon above the orange trees, a few moments with the grass beneath her feet. It would have been so simple to slip out like Bianca and Francesca and leave this turbulent house behind her. The Pitti neighbourhood was no more, but at least one door in the city would always remain open for her. What evil spirits need she fear, in Borso's gruff company?

Lucrezia shook her head. The malign spirit that haunted

these walls remained—she would settle her accounts as scrupulously as a Folio clerk. She knew, now, where to find it. Upon stepping into the East Corridor, her candle spluttered and died. The night gathered in around her. As she walked along the passage, Lucrezia could feel the ghosts pressing in around her, the victims of her brisk pen, silent and seething. She carried her head proudly, as her own father had walked to his own end, through a hate-filled crowd. The grilles rattled in the wall like chattering teeth. At the cellar, where they had tossed the laudatory works and poems of the late Artifex, Lucrezia stopped. The handle was cool against her palm.

Taking a deep breath, she opened the door.

The cellar screamed, an ear-splitting screech carrying on a blast of wind. It hit Lucrezia like a fist, driving her to her knees. Shrieks echoed and multiplied inside her skull. She clamped her hands over her ears, her own cries swallowed up in the shrill tumult. Gritting her teeth, she hauled herself back to her feet and stood defiantly in the face of the maelstrom.

The corridor fell silent. Lucrezia did not move for a long time, her heartbeat thundering in her ears. Before her, a handful of steps disappeared down into darkness. They were strewn with loose pages and the empty shells of volumes. In the cellar's restless, inky depths, she could sense something moving—the gnawing presence she had glimpsed in the chapel and the scriptorium gallery, waves of loathing and scorn pouring forth from it. Was it truly scared, as she had told Eleanora? It had been an easy thing to say, in the warmth of the calefactory fire. Yet here, at the cellar's icy threshold, it was Lucrezia's legs going weak beneath her.

As the shadows writhed, Lucrezia was visited by a vision from long ago: another corridor, another doorway, in the shadow of a poet's statue; a mirror sprayed with blood, a hand around her neck. They had taken everything from her. But she had survived. And now it was Cadenza which lay bleeding, ravaged by plague, rotting away at the core. The Venetians would come and put it to the sword, this presumptuous and self-regarding fabrication of a city. The men and women who had gathered on the piazzas to watch Lucrezia's family burn would learn for themselves the cost of such an act.

She stepped back, running her fingers through her hair and guiding it behind her ears. Even now, at the last, that trace of vanity. A thin smile crossed her lips. As she stepped across the threshold, the cellar door slammed shut behind her, leaving Lucrezia to descend alone into the riled darkness, where the ghost of Tommaso Cellini awaited her.

Twelfth Canto
The Carnival of Ash

I. *The Ass*

THE STATUE OF Pietro Zoppo had held court over the Piazza della Signora for more than a century, his head tilted skyward, pen paused upon the page. It was said that the poet had remained alone his entire life, his work unknown until the discovery of his corpse, lying on a bed of crumpled verse, in an attic near the Parco Durazzo. In death, Zoppo had become a patron saint of yearning: it had become the custom for lovestruck Cadenzans to come to this quiet square and slip notes of their hearts' designs into the statue's hand. He would hold on to them for as long as their passions remained, parchment rustling in his steadfast fingers.

Three weeks after the death of Cosimo Petrucci, a bloodshot dawn brought with it the revelation that Zoppo had looked over his final letter. The poet's head had been severed from his body, and was nowhere to be found.

Presently, a pair of librarians could be seen hastening across the piazza. The younger of the two, Giovanni d'Allegri, gazed up fearfully at the decapitated statue but elected to say nothing. His companion, Fabrizio Groto, a choleric man whose humour had only soured with the city's declining fortunes, preferred to walk in silence. Usually Giovanni avoided his company, but with neighbourhoods abandoned and gangs of footpads prowling the alleys, it was no longer prudent to travel alone. He mouthed a small prayer of thanks as the Bibliotheca Marciano came into view, tucked away down a side-street running off from the square. Giovanni was not, by nature, a man of deeply held religious convictions, but it was hard not to feel that God had turned His back on Cadenza, abandoning it to disease and discord and war, headless poets under a sanguineous sky.

At the entrance to the library, Giovanni paused. The door stood ajar, its hinges groaning as Fabrizio pushed it open and peered inside. Muddy footprints crisscrossed the atrium floor.

"Should we go in, do you think?" Giovanni asked, nervously eyeing the damaged doorframe.

Fabrizio shrugged. "Stay out here if you wish."

He stepped over the threshold and ducked inside. Giovanni hesitated. Across the city, once-tranquil houses had been disturbed, murderers and thieves taking up lodgings in their halls. Even the libraries were not safe. Yet what was the alternative—to make the journey back to his rooms alone, and invite the risk of ambush? As Giovanni glanced back at the abbreviated outline of Pietro Zoppo, he fancied he heard a cry of alarm from the next street. With a gulp, he darted after Fabrizio.

The two men's footsteps echoed around the empty atrium.

That summer, plague had swung its tarnished scythe through the aisles of the Bibliotheca Marciano, striking down librarians and scholars at will. One of its first victims had been Girolamo, the Chief Librarian, followed soon afterwards by his golden-haired daughter Alessia, whose name had passed regularly through Pietro Zoppo's fingers. Giovanni, who had himself been hopelessly in love with Alessia, had wept for days on hearing of her death. He had bought a phial of poison from the druggist with the intention of pursuing her into the afterlife, only for his courage to fail him at the last. Alone in the library, Fabrizio had appeared unaffected by the horrors of the plague, accepting the position of Chief Librarian in the wake of Girolamo's demise without comment. He appeared to live only for the volumes on the shelves—less a man than a catalogue index, admitting neither humour nor joy nor love.

Fabrizio had stopped at the entrance to the reading room, his silhouette almost indistinguishable from the darkness. Joining him in the doorway, Giovanni let out a gasp. The windows had been ignited by the sunrise, bathing the chamber in a fiery glow that played and caught on a forest of sharp metal. Nails had been hammered up through the desks, driven through splintering wood, violating every possible surface where a book might rest. Giovanni wandered through the reading room as though in a dream, brushing his fingertips against the cool spikes. At the sight of a volume impaled on the desk, a shudder ran down his spine. He looked over at Fabrizio in disbelief.

"This is obscene! Who would do such a thing?"

"I have no earthly idea," the Chief Librarian replied.

Giovanni sniffed the air. "And the smell! Like... stables."

Fabrizio ignored him. Striding through the nailed desks, he headed down an aisle strewn with torn pages. Giovanni could have wept at the senselessness of it all. He picked up a battered volume and placed it carefully back on the shelf.

"We should go," he said. "Whoever did this might be lying in wait for us."

Fabrizio snorted. "Then let them spring forth from their hiding places and nail me to a desk," he said. "I will not take flight from my own library."

Giovanni had not imagined the Chief Librarian capable of such resolve in the face of danger. Yet he took no comfort from Groto's demeanour; on the contrary, it only made Giovanni more uneasy. It seemed to him that Fabrizio's actions were not brave, as such, but rather a sign of an absence of any feeling at all—a reckless disregard for the consequences of whatever might lurk in the shadows. Giovanni reluctantly trailed after him, the noisome odour thickening around them with every step.

At this very spot, on the eve of the Carnival of Wit, Giovanni had stumbled across Alessia stepping lightly through the deserted aisles in a fox's mask. She danced for her own amusement, accepting the arm of invisible partners with exaggerated ceremony. Pressing himself against the shelves, Giovanni had crept after her, dry-mouthed and breathless with desire. He followed her on an intricate path through the library, before turning a corner to find her waiting for him at the foot of the gallery steps, a smile playing on her lips. Giovanni had fled, red-faced at her laughter and the knowledge that Alessia had been aware of him all along. He would not see her again. Now, for all that he might fear the growing violence and disorder, Giovanni could not bring himself to leave the Bibliotheca Marciano. He was haunted by the thought that Alessia might one day return, upon a wintry dusk, to flit through the aisles where she had once twirled and pirouetted.

Yet why would her spirit visit this place, with its torn books and impaled desks, the sickening reek of spilt bowels? As they pressed deeper into the darkness, it seemed to Giovanni that the Bibliotheca Marciano had been transformed into some blighted and infernal labyrinth. He no longer felt sure of his way through the shelves. Ahead of him, Fabrizo did not slow his pace, irritably swatting away a fly as it buzzed around his head. They were coming to the oldest part of the archives, where volumes gathered dust in perpetual twilight. Rounding a bookcase, Giovanni almost collided with Fabrizio, who had stopped dead in his tracks.

In the centre of the aisle, the carcass of an ass had been mounted on a lectern, its forelegs draped over the top of the slanted desk. Nails extruded from the wretched beast's flanks and withers, pinning it into place. It hung its head as though in shame, a grotesque parody of the scholar at work. His stomach churning, Giovanni saw that the ass had been slit open along the belly, its entrails heaped in a stinking pile on the flagstones. Flies swarmed around the daubs of excrement smeared along the shelves. The smell was indescribable.

Giovanni felt dizzy. Unthinkingly, he reached out and gripped Fabrizio's arm. The Chief Librarian said nothing, his expression unreadable. The ass fixed its dead, dolorous gaze on them. Struck mute by the macabre scene before them, it was all the two men could do to stand and stare.

II. *Chickpeas*

AT THE FRINGES of the old Pitti neighbourhood, the wind had stirred the Adige into open rebellion, sails billowing in distress as boatmen battled with their craft on the water. Ercole hummed a light melody as he picked a path along a riverside alley, heading towards the eastern limits of the city. Here, far from the reading rooms and the piazza benches, the city moved to a different rhythm: the ring of the smith's hammer and the dart of the glover's needle; the slap and slither of live fish upon the jetties. Beneath the industrious clamour, Ercole could sense a growing restiveness. A couple engaged in a furious shouting match across the balconies, while below them children battled invisible Venetian soldiers with wooden sticks. Handbills mocking the Council of Seven were trodden into the muddy path. Within a dingy barber surgeon's, men broke off from their conversation and glared at Ercole as he passed by. A single word had been daubed in black paint on the wall outside—*Scio.*

He descended a set of steps to arrive at a workshop beneath the sign of the Red Stag. Within its hot and grimy recesses, Ercole glimpsed a glass-blower withdrawing an iron from the fire, upon its tip an orb glowing molten red: a small sun, bursting angrily into life. Flames danced in the windows of the furnace. As Ercole went to enter the workshop, a shadow filled the archway. A firm hand blocked his chest.

"No beggars," a voice growled.

"Why, I want for nothing, sir, except entrance," Ercole replied, with a courteous bow. "There are people within these walls with whom I would speak."

The man stared at him suspiciously. His face was scarred and his left ear sliced off at the lobe. He wore a black jerkin and hose, a bright red sash tied about his waist.

"Password," he said finally.

"To enter here?" Ercole replied, a study in surprise. "A most singular workshop this is, with such a forbidding custodian at the door, and a shibboleth required to enter! I find myself thoroughly at a loss, sir—like a Frenchman in Sicily, trying to say chickpeas."

"Are you drunk, old man?"

"Merely providing an illustration from history to underline my befuddlement."

"Who told you of this place?"

Ercole grinned. "A dead man whispered it into my ear."

There was a sharp prick against his chest. He looked down to see a dagger addressing its point against the flesh over his heart.

"Take your jests elsewhere," the guard warned. "They will find a cool reception here."

"I offer no jest, nor insult either," Ercole said evenly. "The dead have much to tell the living, so long as we know how to listen. The unfortunate youth of whom I speak was, I believe, a brother of yours. His body was pulled from the ruins of an apothecary's shop on the Via Maggio two days past."

The pressure on his chest eased fractionally. The guard frowned. "Lucio?"

"He did not offer me his name, nor could I readily identify his features. His life had been ended by a violent explosion that had burned the flesh clean away from his bones. But among his possessions to have survived the inferno, I found a red sash and a scrap of parchment, upon which had been written directions to this place."

"Which you just happened across, whilst rooting through a dead man's things. Are you a thief, old man?"

Ercole drew himself up indignantly. "A most unfortunate supposition, sir! I am a gravedigger."

"And what made you think you could come in Lucio's place, gravedigger?"

"I sensed I would find men of a similar temperament here. And even now, waylaid at the threshold, I sense I was not mistaken. By your attire, I would mark you as a member of Tommaso Cellini's *becchini*—and I believe I have seen you in the company of Ciro and Benozzo, who have served the city as guardsmen and gravedigger both."

"My associations are no concern of yours," came the brusque reply. "By your riddles and roundabout words, I would mark *you* a Venetian."

"I am a wayfarer," Ercole declared. "A happy wanderer, who calls no one particular city home. Canals and lagoons leave me unmoved. The element that calls strongest to me is fire, like the blaze that rages in the furnaces beyond your shoulder. I am a creature of the flames—a salamander, if you will."

The guard's eyes narrowed. "You do know the password, after all," he said. "What else did Lucio write on this note?"

"Enough for me to travel the breadth of the city in search of the sign of the Red Stag, and to submit to the pointed enquiry of your blade at my chest. I would name it a conspiracy, but what is there to conspire against? There is no Artifex, now that Cosimo Petrucci has vacated the Palazzo Nero—much to your satisfaction, I would presume."

"Satisfaction?" The guard spat on the floor. "I would have found a higher window from which to throw him."

"A testament to the thoroughness of your art."

"Mark my words, a thorough job would have seen the rest of the Seven flying down after him," he declared. "The city has become overrun by straw gallants and coward poets, cowering inside their libraries. Do you think Gritti would dare to take up arms against us if Tommaso still ruled? We have no hope of repelling Venice until the *becchini* are back inside the Palazzo Nero and Cosimo's mercenaries have their pikes rammed up their Swiss arses. Cadenza's defence needs Cadenzan men."

"With its regiments of straw gallants and coward poets."

The dagger dug into his chest. "Time to move on, old man. I grow tired of your flapping mouth."

Ercole held up his hands. "I shall trouble you no more. Though it is a select defence you plan to mount, that you would dismiss all volunteers at the door."

"You think that the Venetians will turn tail at the sight of you on the battlements, waving your shovel in the air?"

"I think that Lucio had never worked with saltpetre before and was unaware of its temperamental ways," Ercole replied meaningfully. "A harsh lesson, learned but the once."

"You claim to be learned in explosives now?"

"By profession I work the earth; but as I told you, I am a creature of the flames. I have spent years exploring the mysteries of gunpowder and Greek fire, working with saltpetre, sulphur and resin. No man knows more about the science of transformation. I have overseen the turning of stone walls to rubble and wood and parchment to fire and ash. Tell me, my fellow gravedigger, have you replaced Lucio, or will your plans have to proceed without him? Did you even know he was dead?"

Ercole gazed up inquisitively at the guard, who scratched his cheek. He sheathed his blade.

"If at any point I mark you for a charlatan or a spy," he warned, "you'll not live to tell the tale of what you hear inside this place."

"And I would go to my grave without a word of complaint," Ercole replied, "having been so comprehensively forewarned."

With a shake of the head, the guard stepped to one side. Ercole offered him a bow of thanks and ducked through the archway.

III. *An Unfamiliar Room*

IN THE DEPTHS OF torment, she kicked and thrashed against her binds, staked out on a bed of burning pins. A demon sat upon her chest, heavy and grim, enveloping her in the stink of brimstone and crushing her insides. Her flesh blistered at its touch. The demon gazed down at her with dead eyes, addressing her in a voice of grinding slate in a language she did not understand. She was utterly helpless, even her own name a mystery to her: a brute beast, lost in pain.

Time became meaningless, seconds and years interchanging. The demon's dread weight pressed down on her. In its eyes, she saw visions of hell: a rotting stable filled with naked corpses; a tower encased in darkness, its steps slippery with blood; a well piled with glistening bones. Walls groaned and bedposts streamed with rancid sap. She found herself screaming one name, over and over again—yet Andrea made no reply. Where was he, when she needed him most?

As she writhed, helpless with agony, she felt the sensation of a cold cloth against her brow. Soothing words, whispered softly in her ear. She awoke to find herself lying alone in a bed. The demon had vanished. Her stomach felt as though she had been sliced open with a jagged blade. She had no idea where, or even who, she was. Through the darkness, she saw that she was covered in words, set out across her flesh in black ink. She stared at them in incomprehension.

A letter twitched.

At first, she ignored it, assuming her eyes were playing tricks on her. The letter twitched again, slowly peeling itself from her skin to stand on end. She watched in astonishment as others stirred around it. An alphabet awakened. Suddenly the letters began to move up her body, swarming along her legs and arms and across her stomach to her chest—she let out a scream, trying to brush them away. Still they came, like tiny spiders, scuttling up her throat and over her face. She clenched her jaw shut, but could not prevent them inserting themselves between her lips. Letters wriggled and writhed inside her mouth. She jammed her fingers between her teeth, clawing out the spindly creatures and hurled them to the floor, but there were too many to fend off, an army of insects burrowing inside her ears and beneath her eyelids, crowding into her mouth until she gagged on them, a final scream dying in her throat.

And then Vittoria opened her eyes.

Bedposts stretched up towards the ceiling. In the window, the slender tips of cypresses brushed across a grey sky. An unfamiliar room. Her bedsheets were soaked through, her shift plastered to her body. There were red marks on her wrists where she had been restrained. Somewhere outside, she could hear roosting birds. A light rain tiptoed along the window ledge.

Vittoria sat up and placed her feet on the floor. She rose unsteadily, on newborn legs. A pitcher of water had been left on the side for her—she poured some into a glass and drank it in one gulp, setting off a coughing fit so violent she almost brought the water back up. She wiped her mouth with the back of her hand. The window looked out across a tangled garden to a cemetery beyond the wall; with a jolt, she realized that she knew where she was. At the sight of the pathways of the graveyard di San Felice, the world started to come back to her: Zanni's letters and the Round Room, the arches beneath the Ponte Nuovo, the black water and the words spreading across her skin, the final argument with Andrea, the plague ball at the House of Orsini and Rinaldi, sitting hesitantly beside her... and then Maddelina, erupting into the squalid room behind Isidore's printing shop and dragging Vittoria from the straw. A carriage had been waiting for them outside—Vittoria had tried to fight them off, but Maddelina's companion had been too strong for her. Carlo, the young poet, she remembered now. He had looked shocked, horrified even. As though he had a claim to know her, to measure her fall from grace. She wondered what had become of Rinaldi, and whether he too had been torn from the black water's numbing embrace.

Vittoria shivered. There was no silk robe to slip on here, nor steaming bath in which to sink. She was dirty, her hair tangled and matted. Her relief on waking had been replaced by a gnawing unease—her stomach was cramping, and her heart twitched like a frightened animal in her ribcage. She went to the door and tried the handle. It was locked. Vittoria banged her fists against the wood, calling out her sister's name, but the only reply was the coo and scrabble of birds above her head. She leaned her head back against the door and sighed.

In the corner of the room, she noticed a chest stowed neatly against the wall, partially obscured by the bed. Vittoria knelt beside it and opened the lid. Inside were letters—her letters, or, as she now thought of them, the correspondences of Hypatia. This would have to be Maddelina's doing. Sifting through her ink maid's work, Vittoria was unsure what she was supposed to feel. Relief? Joy? Gratitude? Had she not left them behind for a reason; would she ever be allowed to close a door on the past?

Alone among the fading letters, she came across a sealed note addressed in fresh ink. The name on the front was her own: Vittoria, not Hypatia. At the sight of Zanni's handwriting, her skin prickled, a crackling current running through the words on her flesh. She turned the note over in her hands.

At the door, a key turned in the lock. Vittoria froze.

IV. *Maps and Charts*

THE STAR CHAMBER was located at the top of a narrow flight of steps in the Mezzanino of the Accademia, the entrance to which was guarded at all hours. A modest-sized room, its windows were dominated by the towers and turrets of the Palazzo Nero across the piazza. It was rumoured that the chamber could be reached from the palace via a complex series of secret passageways and stairwells, although no document of such a journey existed. Singularly for the Accademia, there was not a single book to be found inside the Star Chamber. Instead, an array of maps and charts were laid out on the lecterns and framed on the walls. There were sea charts adorned with compass roses and Portuguese maps of obscure coastlines, the fever dreams of sailors as they sweltered below decks. Here, in the midst of a tentatively flowering world, the Council of Seven gathered to discuss the business of the city.

A trio of empty chairs faced Borso Cardano as he sat at the table, drumming his fingers on the wood. The Seven numbered but four at that moment, his only companions being Pagolo Monti, Salvatore Ridolfi and Lazzaro Negri—Tommaso's men all, none of them a day under sixty. Cosimo Petrucci was dead, of course, along with his Master of Scrolls, Pietro. The seventh member, Duke Agostino, was also absent, leading Lazzaro to inquire archly whether he had taken his wife's place inside her tower. Even with her mysterious disappearance, Agostino remained a target for even the feeblest of wits: an archery butt marooned in the field, barbs and sharp missiles protruding from its soft belly.

Aware of a sudden silence, Borso looked up to find three lined faces turned inquiringly in his direction—the aftermath of a question he had not heard posed. He stroked his beard.

"Naturally," he said.

The response appeared to satisfy them, greeted as it was

with vigorous nods. Borso had been elected to the Seven in the wake of Cosimo Petrucci's headlong plunge from the Palazzo Nero. Hardly the most auspicious time for such an elevation—Fiametta, Borso's niece, had told him flatly that accepting the position was an act of madness. Yet he had agreed anyway. Too many citizens had turned their backs on Cadenza, leaving the city listing like a ship caught in a storm. Pagolo Monti had assumed nominal control of the council's affairs, through seniority rather than any abilities of leadership. Under Tommaso, the Seven had occupied little more than a ceremonial role, and upon his death Pietro was said to have guided the council through much of its deliberations. Borso had heard a rumour that the Master of Scrolls had died at Cosimo's hands, which he had scornfully dismissed. He had met the Artifex once and judged him a sober and thoughtful man—too guarded, perhaps, to win the hearts of those around him, too cautious to inspire admiration, but certainly no murderer. Yet lurid tales now circulated the taverns of a crazed ruler who had stalked the moonlit halls of his palace, kept awake by a bloodlust he could not slake.

Cosimo's death had presented the Seven with a pressing dilemma. Tradition demanded that they invite submissions to become the new Artifex and wait for poems to decorate the statues on the bridges and piazzas. Yet they hesitated, haunted by the spectre of their previous mistake. And who was there, truly, to turn around the city's fortunes? So many of Cadenza's great men had been lost in recent months, either to plague or to the promise of safety and ease elsewhere. With every fresh rumour of Venice's approach, or the growth of unrest inside Cadenza itself, so the old men's vacillations increased. The enormity of the situation had overwhelmed them; the one thing that was necessary—decisive action— seemingly beyond their grasp.

Following his first visit to the Star Chamber, Borso had returned home and ordered Fiametta to pack at once for the countryside. But she had refused point-blank to leave the city without him, revealing a stubborn streak that Borso found at once exasperating and privately to her credit. Fiametta was unhappy in Cadenza, he knew, and had been so even before Lorenzo's poisonous verse had been nailed to doors across the city. What was there to stop him from taking her away? Venice was out of the question, naturally, but there was always Florence, Rome or even Naples. And what of other countries—of Antwerp, London or Lisbon? Had Borso not spent enough years here, a prisoner of his own forlorn hopes, devoted to a heart that could never be his?

As he gazed at the maps on the wall, losing himself in foreign streets and unfamiliar pathways, Borso became aware of a growing tumult inside the Accademia. Shouts and hurried footsteps floated up from the reading rooms, voices raised in argument. Pagolo appeared deaf to the growing maelstrom, lost in a droning soliloquy on credit lines. Frowning, Borso heard the guards at the foot of the stairs bark out a challenge, only to be drowned out by the roar of a great host. At the thunder of feet on the staircase, Ridolfi raised his hand sharply. Pagolo broke off and gazed at him inquiringly.

The doors to the Star Chamber exploded open, admitting a crowd of men clutching sticks and clubs. Their faces were contorted with fury, the air busy with cries and oaths. Borso stayed in his seat and gazed calmly back at them. At a shout, the throng parted, allowing the triumphant figure of Duke Agostino to stride to their head.

Pagolo rose from his chair. "What is the meaning of this intrusion?" he spluttered. "Explain yourself, Agostino!"

"I will hear no admonitions from you, sir!" the duke roared back, jabbing a finger at the old man. "Your petty etiquettes mean nothing to me. While this council has sat idly by, slumbering on thrones of ease, this city has fallen into gravest peril. Midnight draws closer and still the Palazzo Nero stands empty. Cadenza needs a true ruler, not this league of treasonous inaction."

"And do you, sir, claim to be that man?" Ridolfi inquired acidly.

"Hah!" Agostino barked contemptuously. "You mistake me for one of your own venal kind. I make no claim to be Artifex. But I bring before you a man of irrefutable character and bloodline, who has suffered unending torment due to this council's grievous error of judgement."

Only now, did Borso see the hooded figure standing behind Agostino. As the duke stepped aside, he came forward with slow, careful steps, and pulled back his cowl. Gasps echoed around the Star Chamber. The man's cheeks were sunken, his skin a patchwork of gouges, weals and bruises: a youth starved and beaten into old age and infirmity. He bowed his head.

"My face, I know, is no longer an easy thing to look upon," he said, in halting bursts. "Yet I trust my name will still mean something to the loyal citizens of this city. I am Alessandro Cellini, brother to Galeotto and nephew of Tommaso Cellini."

There were approving murmurs, scattered cheers. Borso blinked with surprise. He had seen Tommaso's nephews in the salons on several occasions; if memory served, he had even been complimented by Galeotto for his verse. In truth, there had been little to mark them out from the other young bucks of the *fideli*. Yet there was nothing of the boisterous young man in the skeletal presence now stood before the council.

"Following the death of our uncle," Alessandro rasped, "we were apprehended by foreign mercenaries and ferried in secret to the dungeons beneath the Palazzo Nero, where the monstrous madman Cosimo Petrucci had us tortured. We were beaten and cut, impaled with red-hot pins. I watched my brother beg for mercy, even as the tongue was ripped from his mouth. For days after the tyrant's end, I was left in darkness beside Galeotto's corpse, with barely a cup of water to sustain me. Had Duke Agostino not found me, I would not have lived to see this hour. He took me back to his palace and nursed me back from the brink of death, until I was strong enough to walk. Even now, I wonder how much was truly taken from me."

A coughing fit overtook Alessandro, forcing him to break off. Cries of "shame" echoed around the room. The mob's anger was palpable, and threatening to rebound on the council itself. The thought occurred to Borso that he might not escape this place alive. Judging by Pagolo's ashen features, the possibility had occurred to him also.

Agostino held up a frail hand for silence.

"But I survived," he said, his voice low and hard. "The Cellinis do not bend, nor do we retreat. This city has taken a great deal from me. It has cost me an uncle and a brother, the teeth from my mouth and blood from my veins. Yet I will not turn my back upon it. Take me as your Artifex, and I will lead Cadenza out of this trough of discord and return it to the exalted plinth where it rested when a Cellini last called the Palazzo Nero home!"

So loud were the roars that greeted this declaration, the fierce stamp of boots, that the charts on the wall began to shake. As Borso stared around the chamber, lost in tumult, he saw a map of Cadenza shiver as though struck by an earthquake, its walls buckling and crumbling before his eyes.

V. *Brothers*

THE FIRES BEGAN shortly before noon. From his vantage point atop the rooftop terrace at the sign of the Ship, Francesco stood and watched the trails of smoke climb through the sky: slender black pillars, marking intermittent points around the compass. Their acrid tang carried on the breeze. He had expected an accompaniment of screams and ringing steel, but Cadenza was eerily still, the courtyard at Francesco's back a silent well of shadows. Since the Carnival of Wit, the bellicose din of the Arsenale had been quietened, the ranks of Lorenzo Sardi's *fideli* thinned almost to nothing. Raffaele had fled the city in disgrace, while three more had been lost to the plague; dim-witted Paolo had vanished without a word in the turmoil following Cosimo Petrucci's death.

Verses sat half-finished on the courtyard tables—war cries to Mars, strangled in the throat.

Their master was quietest of all. Lorenzo had not written a line since the publication of the *Ode to Fiametta* and showed no inclination to sit at his desk. In the days following the Carnival, his *fideli* had been prepared for a literary onslaught from Borso, yet no poem had appeared—there were rumours that the Bear had expressly forbidden his men to compose any written reply, so set was he on answering in force. Wooden staffs and cudgels had been stockpiled in the corner of the Arsenale; Francesco had been careful not to walk the streets alone. But then the plague had struck, rendering the ongoing antics of Cadenza's Duelling Counts an irrelevance. What matter a young woman's honour, while rats gnawed on corpses in the streets?

Lorenzo had continued to drift back and forth from his palace to the sign of the Ship, apparently as unconcerned by the threat of illness as he was the prospect of Borso's men lying in wait. A wineskin was rarely far from his hand. Upon the night of Cosimo's death, Lorenzo had drunk himself into an insensible rage on the terrace and Francesco had been forced to wrestle his master away from the roof's edge before he fell—whether by design, or blinded by wine and anger, it was impossible to say. Lorenzo's last poem had been a blistering attack on Cosimo that he had composed during the Carnival of Wit, only to have seen it switched for the *Ode to Fiametta* by the secret contrivance of his *fideli*. What had happened to the original *Denunciation* remained a mystery.

Now Francesco was all that remained of Lorenzo's entourage, and even he could not explain why he had stayed. When he had first been admitted to the *fideli* he had venerated his master, believing Lorenzo to be among the greatest artists of his day. Yet he had learnt little of poetry and the craft of writing. His lessons had been conducted not at the desk or in the library, but in the taverns and alleys, scuffling with Borso's followers in defence of his master's name. Yet Lorenzo's behaviour during the Carnival had shown him to be the hollowest of gentlemen. Since the loss of his *Denunciation* the poet had diminished with each passing day: a wrung cloth or an empty amphora, cracked with age. Francesco had begun work on a poem of his own, an account of the city under plague, and the rotting away of one of its favourite sons. A denunciation of his own, of sorts.

"It begins."

Francesco turned to find Lorenzo standing at his shoulder. There was wine on the old man's breath, and he had not changed his robe from the previous day. His eyes, however, were bright.

"The fires have been burning for hours," Francesco reported. "But I see no other sign of intruders in the city. If this is war, it is like none I have ever seen."

"It is war of a kind," Lorenzo replied, scanning the skyline. "But you will see no armies take to the field, and Cadenza stands to lose far more than mere bodies."

"I do not understand."

"Do you truly not see?"

Grabbing Francesco by the shoulders, Lorenzo turned him towards the most northerly trail of smoke.

"The Bibliotheca Ambrosiana," he said.

He pointed to the next plume, to the east.

"The Bibliotheca Marciano."

And then the next.

"The Bibliotheca Niccoló."

"The Venetians are burning the libraries?" Francesco frowned. "But why?"

"Hah!" A single, contemptuous syllable. "Must I spell it out for you, in short and simple words? *It is not the Venetians.*"

"Then who—?"

From the courtyard below, a scream.

Running to the edge of the terrace Francesco looked down to see a serving girl sprawled on her back in the courtyard, a group of men marching brusquely past her. A stray boot kicked over a table, scattering papers to the floor.

"Soldiers come this way, my lord!" Francesco cried. "We must go!"

Lorenzo eyed him with cold amusement. "And how will we make our escape, Francesco?" he enquired. "Shall we spread wings like birds and take to the skies? Or leap like fishes into the river?"

The intruders appeared on the terrace steps. Francesco had thought them soldiers, but they wore no armour, dressed instead in the simple uniform of the labourer and artisan, their smocks adorned with a bright red sash. At their head was a dark-haired youth carrying a wooden stave.

"Paolo!" cried Francesco.

He stepped forward to embrace his old friend, only to falter upon apprehending Paolo's expression. Paolo's lips were set in a cold, thin line, neither warmth nor recognition in his gaze. His companions were smirking. Francesco did not know them by name, but he had encountered their kind before—at horse races and dice games, the wineshops on the river; wherever aggressive gangs of young men gathered.

Paolo gazed slowly around the terrace. "I had expected more people," he said. "Where is everyone?"

"They have all left, one way or another," Francesco explained. "Through the city gates or delivered to the ground. We thought you had died, Paolo!"

"You were right, in a way," he replied. "The old Paolo died when he left this place to march against the imposter Cosimo Petrucci. I was reborn beneath the banners, amongst a brotherhood of citizens, honest and true. The Palazzo Nero trembled at our approach: an earthquake as powerful as any to have struck this land since the House of Uccello was toppled. My hands were wrapped around the gates when Cosimo fell, and I swear it was as though we had shaken him from his tower. How could I return here, after that? To be mocked and derided by those who claimed to be my brothers, and abused and ill-treated by he who claimed to be my master."

"Why, come now, Paolo!" Francesco tried. "Nothing was said to wound, we all took our turn at the sharp end of the joke."

Paolo shifted the stave in his hands. "Then come, brother," he said. "Offer me one of your clever jests now."

The terrace slipped into silence. Only now, did Paolo smile.

"You see? What weight do words carry, against the stick's stout reply? My brothers and I have found a new banner, that of the Salamander. There are no masters, no *fideli*. Nor poetry, either."

"It was you." Lorenzo said flatly. "The burning libraries. This is your handiwork."

"This city has grown weak," Paolo replied. "But is it not the plague of the flesh that has driven it to its knees. The libraries have grown rotten, their shelves weighed down by pretty verses and the haughty speculations of scholars, our citizens rendered idle and unmanly. We Salamanders have doused their poison cabinets with fire. From the cleansing flames will come forth a new civic spirit, vigorous and virtuous, to raise us up together and protect us from those who would threaten Cadenza."

"You would defeat Venice by destroying our books?" Francesco exclaimed. "You have lost your mind!"

Paolo shook his head.

"True revolution stops at no boundaries," he said. "And you would be wise to choose your words carefully when addressing me. I have toppled an Artifex from his palace—do you think I would blink before throwing you from a tavern roof?"

"But that is not why you have come here," Lorenzo said. "Why did you?"

"To extend an invitation," Paolo replied. "We are building bonfires on the Piazza della Rosa in preparation for a celebration this night, a Carnival of Ash. Come, master, see the spectacle we have created. Present yourself once more to those crowds to whom you airily turn your wrist during the March of the Poets."

His companions fanned out behind him, blocking off the path to the steps. This was not, Francesco realized with a sinking heart, a request. He glanced behind him, gauging the drop to the street below. Too far to fall, with any guarantee of survival. Lorenzo sketched a theatrical bow.

"Here's to you, Paolo!" he declared, raising an imaginary wine glass. "I had thought you stupid beyond measure. But I wonder if you will not outlive us all."

Paolo stepped forward and struck Lorenzo across the face with his stave, spraying teeth across the terrace. Seizing the bloodied poet by the robe, he dragged him towards the stairs. Francesco sprang to his master's aid but there were too many men in his way: a blow caught him on the side of the head, and he fell to the ground. He heard Lorenzo eject one final curse—foul-mouthed and majestic—and then a violent storm of punches and kicks broke over him.

VI. *Worcester, Zurich and Ulm*

FOR DAYS NOW, the talk inside the *Vigna del Signore* had been of war, its patrons roused by the threat of invasion. Chafing with indignation at the lack of response from the Palazzo Nero, they banded together to form impromptu militias, sealing solemn pacts with ringing tankards and toasting to the rout of Venice. Anna ignored them, accustomed as she was to the gusts of hot and hollow words that blew around the tavern. When Gasparo arrived, she had paid him little heed at first, even as the youth sought her attention, announcing himself as he sauntered to the counter with a sash tied around his waist, bright red as a cockerel's comb. He drank alone, affecting the knowing air of a man twice his age. When word reached the tavern that houses across the city were burning, Gasparo smirked into his wine.

"It is an unusual humour, that finds amusement in burning

buildings," Anna remarked, as she briskly wiped the counter around him.

"Worry not." He patted his sash. "No harm will come to this place, nor any other honest house of business. It is only the libraries that should fear the Salamanders."

"Salamanders? A grand name, to accompany your fine sash."

"We have lit a fire below the Seven's feet," Gasparo declared, in a voice designed to be heard along the counter. "Our leaders hide away inside their palaces, leaving the city's walls unguarded. From the flames will pour forth more of our red brothers—an army of Salamanders, rising up to smash the Venetians!"

"Why, the Venetians need not trouble themselves, if you burn the city down for them," Anna replied sweetly.

His smile tightened. "I would not expect a tavern wench to understand the truth of such things," he said. "Cadenza has grown soft on balcony songs; what is needed now are war cries, virtuous and strong."

Salvatore, one of the tavern regulars and a scribe by profession, declared the boy to be a fool, and was promptly shouted down by his own companions. As a rule, the patrons of the *Vigna del Signore* showed little interest in the business of the city's reading rooms, but suspicion and ill-feeling towards the libraries had grown in the chaos since Tommaso Cellini's death. There would be fights here, before the night was out.

Gasparo leaned across the counter towards Anna.

"If you doubt me, come to the Piazza della Rosa tonight," he whispered. "See the transformation we will wreak upon this city: dead parchment turned into glorious fire, defeat into victory. A Carnival of Ash!"

He grinned as she looked up sharply at him, and settled back upon his stool. Eventually he grew bored of trying to charm her and turned to bait Salvatore. Putting down her apron, Anna hurried for the door, smartly refusing the offers of escort from the sozzled gallants on the other side of the counter.

Outside, the bells were ringing—a fearful clamour reverberating around the tight steps and passages of the Printing Quarter. Mothers chased children inside from the balconies as shutters closed over windows. Everyone knew the significance of smoke on the breeze: war was coming to Cadenza. Yet Anna had no intention of leaving. There had been travelling enough in her life, and she had no desire to return to the road. She knew full well the consequences her choice might invite, and that the Vigna del Signore was no sort of safe haven. But what choice did she have? Anna had resolved to give Fra Bernardo no further thought, cloistered away as he was with his holy brethren, and no doubt occupied by loftier concerns than the safety of a tavern girl. There was one other man she knew well in the city, but his natural hold on her affections had been compromised by past disappointments and estrangement. Anna had resolved never again to seek him out—yet here she was, hurrying west towards the Ponte Nuovo. Bands of young men were parading along the piazzas, swathed in the same red sashes Gasparo had sported in the tavern. Anna was careful to keep her gaze lowered.

It had been a while since she had last crossed the Adige,

and on reaching the Verso she had to seek directions from a washerwoman for the graveyard di San Felice. The pealing bells quietened as Anna passed through the church gate and made her way through the deserted tombs. Passing through a gate in the wall, she followed a path through the tangled grass towards a ravaged church, its stonework blackened by fire and its tower threatening to topple over.

At the entrance to the nave, Anna pulled back at the sound of voices. Inside the church, a man was standing at the foot of a spiral staircase leading to the lectern, where a woman stared back him, incredulity written across her face.

"You *command* me, Carlo?" she said.

He laughed ruefully. "Would that I had the power! It is your father who commands you to return home, Maddelina, while your aunt and uncle beseech you likewise, even as they ready to leave the city. I merely said that you could not stay here, if you refused to see the sense of the thing."

"There being room for only one Giodarno sister in these halls," Maddelina replied tartly.

"Take Vittoria with you, if you can—her mind is free of the black water now, and she is no safer here than you. If she will not be persuaded, I will look to her safety as best I can."

"No doubt. How gallant of you."

Carlo looked to the heavens and let out a strangled cry of frustration. Bounding up the steps, hands gripping the railings, he addressed her: "Might it not be possible that I would take care of your sister in your name, rather than the furtherance of some other base and selfish designs of my own?"

"Hah! You would have me think you a priest, saintly and

chaste in your work. But I have seen your longing gazes and heard the echo of your lovelorn sighs." Maddelina threw a hand across her forehead in mock despair, guiding an invisible pen across the lectern with the other. "Your heart is still a poet's, puffed up with drama and desire, pumping to the throb of engorged veins."

"My heart beats to the same rhythm as every other man's," he retorted, "and does not belong to your sister, no matter how you would fit it for a trinket for her to wear around her neck!"

They gazed at one another defiantly.

"Where do I take her, Carlo?" Maddelina exclaimed finally. "Who will open their doors to us, now she has covered herself in those words? Father would die before seeing her. What if she goes back to the Printing Quarter instead? The way Vittoria talks to me—it is as though nothing really matters, as though her mind is already resolved."

"Resolved to what?"

"I fear I am about to lose her forever."

"How can you stop her, if that is her design? You cannot keep her under lock and key."

At Anna's cough, the pair turned as one.

"I am sorry to disturb you," Anna said. "I seek my father. He works here, among the graves."

"You must be mistaken," Carlo told her, absentmindedly. "There is no one who works here beyond myself and Ercole."

"And since you are not my father..." she said brightly.

He stared at Anna. "*Ercole*?"

"You would not be the first to find the notion a surprise."

Carlo climbed down from the lectern. "He left several days

ago, without a word," he said. "I have been waiting for him to return. I did not know that he had family in the city."

"Among other things, I would wager. Does he still study the arts of alchemy?"

"In the cellar, yes."

"Would you show me?"

He led her to a set of steps at the back of the nave, and together the three of them descended into the cellar. The furnace in the corner of the cellar had gone out, jars gleaming dully on the workbench. Broken glass crunched beneath their feet. At the chamber's metallic tang, Anna was at once transported back to the rooms of her childhood, dotted around countless cities and countries. It was as though her father carried the stale air stoppered inside a jar, to release upon finding new quarters.

"I am sure he will soon be back," Carlo offered.

"I would not be so certain. Have you not seen the fires across the city?"

Carlo and Maddelina exchanged a glance.

"The whole city is gripped by the fever of war," Anna told them. "A group calling themselves the Salamanders are setting the libraries alight in the hope of bringing others to their banner."

Maddelina's eyes widened. "Have they lost their minds? What good will come of burning libraries?"

"They talk of defending the city from Venice, but they look less like an army than a mob intent on disorder. One of their number spoke to me of transforming parchment into fire and I knew I must come here, for it was as though my father was speaking through him."

"Come, now!" Carlo laughed. "You cannot think that Ercole would involve himself with men such as these!"

"I do think that, exactly that, as one who has known his ways far longer than you," she shot back. "My father is drawn to fire like a moth to the flame, and though he means no ill will his experiments have left a trail of destruction in his wake: a church in Worcester, a guildhall in Zurich, an entire district of Ulm. He worships the elements for his gods, their balancing and harmony his life's work, and he will not have the process of transformation profaned. If he had learned that the Salamanders intended to burn down Cadenza's libraries, he would feel compelled to intervene."

"So is it the city Ercole seeks to protect, or the flames?" said Maddelina, with a disbelieving laugh.

Anna shrugged. "What does it matter, in the end? He is in danger, either way."

"Then I will look for him," Carlo declared, striking his palm with his fist. "Ercole took me in when I had nothing. If he is in danger, I cannot stand by."

"What about Vittoria?"

It was Maddelina.

"She will only leave this city with you at her side," Carlo told her. "Go to her, convince her to accompany you."

"Another command, my lord?"

"I would never command you," he said. "But I will not apologize for wishing you safe."

A smile flickered across Maddelina's lips. "You cannot save everyone, Carlo." She pushed him away gently. "Go, find Ercole. See if you can stop the world from ending."

Anna drew back as Carlo and Maddelina shared a

hesitant, uncertain farewell amongst the pungent phials. Then Carlo accompanied Anna out of the church. They shared a preoccupied silence as they walked through the headstones. At the church gate, Anna suddenly stopped. A man stood waiting for them, straight-backed and alert, his hands clasped patiently behind his back. He was dressed in the white robes of the Dominican order.

"Our holy brother is a long way from home," Carlo said thoughtfully. "What is he doing here?"

Anna smiled.

VII. *A Man of Cadenza*

HE SHOULD HAVE left the city hours ago. He should have left it *days* ago, when the rumours of the Venetian invasion had grown too loud to ignore and the Council of Seven had seized with terror like a rusted stable bolt. He was a pragmatist at heart—there were disgruntled poets who would have found other, harsher words to describe him, but his was a business that nurtured grudges and sore feelings. Yet Orsini had hesitated until the final moment before ordering his servants to pack up his belongings. And even now, with his carts plodding out of the city under the watchful eye of his Dalmatian guards, Orsini was heading in the opposite direction—back towards his palace.

It had been the blazing windows of the Bibliotheca Marciano that had alerted him to his error, smoke pouring from the upper galleries as panicked librarians and Folio officials threw books out into the street. Orsini was about to order his men to help them when he realized, with a start, that he had left a volume of his own behind. He had jumped down from the cart at once, irritably refusing offers from his retinue to accompany him.

Orsini had been in a foul temper all morning. He was as much a creation of Cadenza as any of the volumes fashioned on its presses; the very thought of stepping foot beyond the city walls filled him with consternation. Yet how far he had travelled!—born under the arches of the Ponte Nuovo and raised in the lawless alleys behind the Via Maggio, now he proceeded through a world of salons and palace hallways, the great men of the city vying for his ear. As a child, Orsini had joined the crowds watching the poets perform on the Piazza di Pietra, clambering on barrels and shinning up pillars for a view of the stage; in later years, he would be escorted to a cushioned seat on a balcony overlooking the square. Orsini had seized all the city would give him, engorging himself on rich food and wine, furs and silks, warm young bodies in his bed at night. Several years earlier, on an extravagant whim, he had purchased a sprawling countryside retreat outside Padua. The time had finally come to visit it.

Provided, of course, he ever left the city.

The gates to the House of Orsini stood open—he waddled across the courtyard and hauled himself up the stairs, his breath coming in great gusts through his nostrils. The Plague Ball had scarred the palace: exquisite mosaics left gap-toothed, and tapestries torn. For all their scrubbing, the servants had been unable to eradicate the lingering smell of the ordure that had been deposited in careless mounds on the floor. There had been bodies to dispose of, afterwards. Orsini had opened his doors to the gods of vice and discord and invited the people to frolic before them for their amusement. But the wild chorus of abandon had grown tiresome, a sour jest fallen flat. At the height of the grim bacchanal, he had retired, sunk in melancholy, to a suite of rooms via a secret passage. Retracing his steps now, he headed along the balcony above the *salone*, white rectangles marking the spot where the portraits of his most famous writers had once hung. A single painting had been left behind, the face of its subject burned away completely. Orsini shook his head. Still, Rinaldi eluded him.

Orsini could neither name nor understand the malady that had taken hold of the great poet, and in his frustration he had resorted, he acknowledged, to increasingly desperate measures. He had hoped that, under the numbing intoxication of the black water, Rinaldi could be persuaded to take up residence inside the Palazzo Nero, where he would serve as a glorious figurehead while the real business of the city was conducted by the men around him. But Rinaldi was lost to him now, vanished without trace from Isidore's printing shop. It was entirely possible that the forger had murdered him. Isidore had had the effrontery to demand payment anyway—Orsini had summarily dismissed him, declaring him to be a German hostelier and calling on his Dalmatians to march him from the building. Few of Orsini's peers could understand why he had persisted in trying to coax Rinaldi out of his self-imposed exile, long after it had become clear that the poet had lost his mind. They did not know the ennui that came hand-in-hand with success; nor that, while men and women copulating in his hallways could leave him unmoved, and he could step over dead bodies in the darkness without remark, Orsini's eyes still brimmed with tears at Rinaldi's verse.

Which explained why he was now walking through the empty rooms of his palace, rather than heading out through the city gates. There had not been time to gather up all his possessions: furniture stood abandoned; volumes scattered across the floor of his library. Orsini reached behind a shelf and pulled on a hidden lever. The bookcase rumbled to one side to reveal a set of steps. He found the *Song of Summer* lying where he had left it during the Plague Ball, on a chair by the window in his private chambers. It was Rinaldi's first work, and his greatest—the foundation on which Orsini had constructed his empire. Clutching it to his chest, he turned back and hurried down through the library. Upon reaching the top of the main staircase, however, Orsini realized that he was no longer alone.

Below him, in the empty expanse of the hall, two young women stood facing one another. Curtseying, they reached out to clasp hands and began a stately promenade across the flagstones, moving in time to a music Orsini could not hear. As they passed beneath the windows, diaphanous white gowns on pale skin, they threatened to disappear into the light completely: ghosts of past revels, flitting and twirling through the empty palace. At the *salone* doorway, they spun on their heels and paraded back towards their original position.

Orsini cleared his throat.

"And what, pray, is this?"

The girls paused mid-step and looked up, their expressions

registering neither guilt nor surprise. As Orsini slowly descended the staircase, he saw that their gowns were of fine quality but a poor fit, hanging off their shoulders and trailing hems across the floor. One of the girls went to the cupboard and brought back a pair of slates, passing one to her companion. She scribbled on her tablet in chalk and held it up for him to read.

Alms for the poor.

Orsini gestured towards the cupboard, where a wine bottle stood uncorked beside a pair of goblets. "It would seem that you are taking sufficient advantage of my hospitality as it is," he said mildly. "I do not recall inviting you inside my house."

The two girls exchanged glances. The second one wrote:

We thought it was abandoned. Houses are empty across the city.

It was not, Orsini noted, an apology.

"And you figured mine ripe for a ball," he said. "At least you have dressed the part. You are wearing such fine gowns that I am surprised you need seek charity from anyone."

The complement earned him twin curtseys.

Do you like them?

"They are most becoming. And, as you say, houses are empty across the city."

The girls giggled knowingly. It had not been so long since

Orsini had visited the Printing Quarter, nor did his business preclude dealing with the occasional vagabond—he knew a thief when he saw one. He could almost be charmed by the girls' boldness. Not everything in life could be won honestly, especially for those who had to start with nothing.

"You have wine and a ballroom in which to dance," he told them. "Alms enough, I should think. Do not think me a gull who will dab my eye with a handkerchief merely because you carry a slate. You would truly have me believe you cannot speak?"

Grinning, the first girl opened her mouth wide, revealing a stunted root where her tongue should have been. Orsini repressed a shudder.

"Forgive me," he murmured. "Pray, stay here awhile, if you wish. My house is your house."

She dropped into a low curtsey, her companion theatrically clasping both hands to her breast. Orsini reddened.

"It is a peculiar sort of ingratitude," he said, "to beg for charity, only to scorn those who would offer it to you."

Such charity! Empty rooms and rotting food.

"What else would you have from me? I have already taken everything of value; the Venetians will no doubt help themselves to the rest."

In the hush of the *salone*, a chalk scratched across a slate.

The book.

Orsini glanced down in surprise at the *Song of Summer*.

"Why, this volume would mean nothing to you, child! It is of sentimental value to me, nothing more."

We want it anyway.

The other girl: an immediate reply. Orsini's grip tightened around his book. The nerve of these insolent wenches, to think that they could enter his house and demand his prized possessions from him! Did they not know who he was?

"My men are waiting for me outside," he told them sharply. "Neither my charity nor my patience are inexhaustible. You would do well to leave before they run dry."

Yet, even as he threatened them, Orsini was aware that it was he who was edging backwards towards the courtyard. The girls exchanged a glance. Retreating to the cupboard, they lay down their slates and slipped masks over their heads. When they turned back to face Orsini, he blanched. Their faces were now those of sneering she-devils, with protruding horns and mottled crimson flesh. And in their left hands both, each carried a knife.

Orsini turned and ran, his sandals slapping against the tiles. He heard no footsteps behind him, only felt an agonizing slash across the back of his calf; crying out, he collapsed to the floor, the *Song of Summer* slipping from his grasp. The girls swarmed around him, hissing and spitting, their knives slicing through the air—Orsini held up his hands to protect himself, and received sharp stings across his palms. His cries for help spiralled forlornly up into the vaults. In desperation, he lashed out, catching one of his attackers and sending them stumbling backwards. The other lunged forward, burying a blade deep in Orsini's side. He let out a shuddering gasp.

The girls drew back, their diaphanous gowns splattered with blood. Only now could Orsini see them for what they truly were—fiendish servants of the gods of vice and discord, sent to punish him for his temerity. For had he not turned his back on them, at the sordid height of his bacchanal? Rinaldi's volume was lying in the courtyard archway: Orsini began to drag himself across the floor towards it, the strength leaking from his limbs with every inch. It seemed he would not leave Cadenza after all. A bark of laughter escaped him, spraying the flagstones with blood. He reached out towards the *Song of Summer* and felt his fingers brush against the pages. The sun was shining in the courtyard. A slice of clear blue sky. And then nothing.

VIII. *A Position of Consequence*

As NIGHT DREW the Palazzo Nero into its velvet embrace, at the conclusion of a second-floor loggia the entrance to the east wing stood open. The shallow pool in the atrium quivered in silence; spring-bolted doors held their breath. A corridor of mirrors stared back at itself. Inside the gallery, the paintings had shed their covers of black crepe; a lone torch burned in a sconce on the wall, illuminating the figure of Duke Agostino as he looked up at a portrait of Tommaso Cellini. During the poet's reign, there had been rumours of things that had taken place in these rooms, crimes too dangerous to be voiced outright. Agostino had given them little credence. A man—even one with Tommaso's formidable gifts—could not rise to a position of consequence without earning the enmity and bitter insinuations of those he had surpassed. And yet on a night such as this, alone in the crepuscular gallery with the Artifex smiling enigmatically down at him, his expression speaking of a confidence that he would not share, Agostino had cause to wonder.

He had barely left the Palazzo Nero since Alessandro Cellini's installation as Artifex, a hurried coronation that had taken place without audience or fanfare. Agostino had little desire to return to his own palace on the Verso, where the lectern stood empty in the reading room and rubble was strewn across the courtyard. He had ordered the destruction of Caterina's tower the day after she had fled the city, arm-in-arm with Agostino's erstwhile guest Stefano. Upon learning the true extent of his betrayal, the duke had flown into a rage that had left his guards cowering, counters scattering across his great map of Cadenza as he set about it with a chair. When he had calmed sufficiently to gather himself, he had toyed with the notion of arranging an accident to befall the lovers on the road. Yet this, he had decided, would be the act of a weaker man, mortally wounded by a single prick to his pride. Agostino was a businessman who lived by the sober truth of the balance sheet. He had lost, it was true, a woman he had once desired, and a volume that he deemed irreplaceable. Yet had he not gained a more valuable prize? For more than a year, Agostino had been the subject of crude tavern jests and whispers in the salon, lampooning verses during the Carnival of Wit. Yet now he was Master of the Scrolls, the second-most powerful position in Cadenza. Let them laugh: he would have them choke on their merriment.

For his newfound position to mean anything, however, Agostino needed to guide Cadenza through its current crisis. He had hoped that a new Artifex might calm the flames of sedition and focus the city's mind on the protection of its walls from the armies of Venice. Yet Alessandro Cellini had barely been glimpsed since taking residence inside the Palazzo Nero, leaving the running of the city entirely to Agostino. So many hours had he devoted to the planning of the city's defence, poring over maps and weighing up troop deployments, that at night his dreams trembled to the rumble of siege engines. Yet now, faced with the actuality of command, Agostino had to admit there were problems beyond those he had previously considered. The pikemen upon whom Cosimo had relied to maintain order were deserting their posts in droves, while an unruly mob marched beneath the banner of the Salamander. What remained of the Seven sat cowering in the Star Chamber and there was no sign of the Artifex anywhere in the Palazzo Nero. Was it possible that he, too, had fled the city?

Lifting the torch from the sconce, Agostino abandoned Tommaso to the darkness and made his way out of the east wing. Back upon the loggia, by the statue of Petrarch, a thought occurred to him. He reached up and pressed the highest leaf upon the poet's crown. The secret panel in the wall slid sideways. Ironically, it had been Stefano who had alerted Agostino to the possibility that Tommaso's nephews might be found somewhere in Cadenza—a single truth shuffled inside his pack of lies. With Cosimo's death, Agostino had been able to begin the search for Alessandro and Galeotto Cellini in earnest. A tip-off had led him to a wineshop upon the Via Tribunali and a former member of Tommaso's *becchini* who, his tongue loosened by wine and the lusty blows of the duke's guards, had acknowledged the rumours of a secret passageway behind Petrarch's statue. Agostino himself had led the way down to the palace dungeons, stepping through the piss-riddled straw to find the two prisoners shackled to the wall. He had thought them both dead, only for one of the corpses to come alive with a hideous shriek when Agostino's torch fell over him.

This time, when the duke carefully descended the steps, he saw a light glowing at the bottom. The rats had retreated behind the cellar's idle instruments of inquiry, nesting beneath the rack and scurrying up and down the *strappado* ropes that dangled from the ceiling. Ducking his head beneath the low archway, Agostino moved through into the next chamber, where he found Alessandro Cellini sat before a burning brazier.

"My lord," Agostino said, with a stiff bow. "I have been searching the palace. This is the last place I expected to find you."

"I am well used to these quarters, am I not?" Alessandro replied.

"Used enough for this life, and the next. Would you not be more comfortable in the Artifex's offices?"

"I am in pain wherever I sit. These are my offices now."

"As you wish, my lord. But there are matters we must discuss, urgent affairs of the city—"

The Artifex waved him silent. "Do you know," he said, "when you came before me, for a moment I could have sworn you were Cosimo? He would come down here, to speak with Galeotto and myself. To ask us questions to which we had no answers. He spoke as though there was another with him, always out of view. I had thought Cosimo mad, but now, as I sit here, I do not fancy myself alone. I wonder if I should be surprised, should a figure come gliding out of the darkness to whisper in my ear." He looked up from the fire. "Is that what power is?"

"True leaders heed the wise counsel of their advisors, not voices inside their own head," Agostino replied. "Cosimo should never have been appointed Artifex; his reign will go down as the most foolish and ill-starred in the city's history."

"And what will history say of me, do you wonder?"

"It will remember your bold words at the Star Chamber. How the people cried out for you to follow in your uncle's stead and save their beloved city."

"The people are fools," Alessandro said softly. "They stand beneath banners woven from hollow promises. My uncle had no love for them—how many died at his hands? Yet still they wept upon his death."

"You are not your uncle, just as you are not Cosimo Petrucci. Be a leader to your people. There is a new banner upon the streets, as dangerous as any that have preceded it. They call themselves the Order of the Salamanders and have declared war upon Cadenza's libraries. Even as we speak, they are building bonfires upon the piazzas. My lord, the pikemen must be ordered on to the streets before this disorder spreads too wide to be quelled. I presume these malcontents to be a fifth column, working at the Venetians' behest…"

Alessandro snorted. "They are nothing of the sort."

"But, my lord—"

"Venice has no interest in our affairs, Agostino," he said abruptly. "There is no army marching west. Gritti remains in the Doge's Palace."

The duke blinked. "You have been in contact with Venice?"

"I wrote to him as soon as I had the strength. Galeotto and I met Gritti in Venice years ago, when our cities were on a happier footing. Given the rumours making us comrades-in-arms, I thought it best the Doge knew the truth of the matter." He held up a letter. "This is his reply."

"You cannot trust a Venetian's word! For all we know, they are massing at the gates as we speak!"

"A ghost army, marching upon the breeze," Alessandro said contemptuously. "Go to the city walls, Agostino, and tell me of the fearsome horde you spy. The Venetians have raised no army: *they do not need to*. Cadenza is destroying itself from within. Why trouble to take up a sword, when your enemy will slit his own throat for you?"

The brazier flickered, shadows thrusting and parrying across the dungeon walls.

"If Venice truly does not march upon us," Agostino said, his mind moving quickly, "there is an opportunity here, my lord. We can end the city's pain this very night. Come with me to the Star Chamber and take the Seven in hand. Have the pikemen paid in full and command them to restore order. The Salamanders are no more than a mob. In the face of an organized military force, they will flee like dogs!"

"Do not talk to me of a city's pain. Where are its tender nerves, its soft flesh? It feels nothing."

Agostino reddened. "I did not comb the city's dungeons

to be regaled with sonnets of self-pity. I was looking for a ruler—a Cellini, who would neither bend nor retreat. Your words, Alessandro."

"You would have me fall at your feet and weep with gratitude for my life. I was already dead when you found me. Neither power nor acclaim can revive me."

"Then what use are you to Cadenza, its people?" Agostino was struggling to control his temper. "I might as well have propped up Galeotto on a throne and balanced a crown upon his cold brow."

"My brother was fortunate. His pain has ended."

"But if we do nothing, the Salamanders will burn Cadenza down to the ground!"

Alessandro dipped Gritti's letter into the brazier, holding it up as the end caught, flames hastening across the parchment. He dropped it into the fire.

"Let it burn," he said.

IX. *A Spray of Ash*

AS THE FIRST sparks began to dance above the pyres on the Piazza della Rosa, to roars from the gathering crowds, across the river the great houses on the Verso huddled in darkness. Many stood empty, their insides scraped clean as an oyster shell; here and there, the faint glimmer of a candle could be detected behind a shuttered bedchamber window, where families knelt together, lips moving in prayer.

In the northern reaches of the Verso, no lights burned around the square at the steep conclusion of the Vicolo

Scarpuccia. Inside the convent San Benedetta, an icy draught harassed the deserted corridors. It gained speed as it swept through the rooms, leaving a trail of damage in its wake—pages ripped from their bindings, bowls hurled to the floor and stones flung against the windowpane. In the calefactory, ash sprayed from the hearth upon the floor; inside the scriptorium, ink dripped from a pot tipped upon its side.

Arriving at the West Corridor, the wind seemed to turn upon itself in its frustration, creating a whirling tempest of dust and parchment. It erupted out into the cloister, shaking tree branches and tearing down the scraps of browning parchment pinned to the bark. Converging upon a patch of freshly dug earth beneath a cypress, the wind began clawing at the soil: a mad dog, vomiting up gobs of ink and fragments of shattered slate.

X. *To the West*

THEY HAD TRIED to leave as quickly and quietly as possible, taking with them only what they could not bear to leave behind, and plotting an unobtrusive route out of the city. As the carriage headed west along the side-alleys towards the river, the towers and cupolas around the Piazza della Rosa acquired a lacquer of tarnished gold. Noise grew on the breeze. The streets became clogged with people—at the junction of the Via Fiume and Ponte Nuovo, the carriage slowed to a walking pace. That they were headed away from the bonfires was taken by some among the crowds to be a show of disloyalty: there were jeers and hisses; hands reaching out to rock the vehicle upon its axles. Spit glistened upon the Cardano family crest.

Inside the carriage, Fiametta jumped as a stone smashed against the window. For all the talk of Venetian armies, it seemed to her as though the city had already been invaded— she saw nothing she recognized in the angry faces pressed against the glass. Her escort of guards had deserted her at the last minute, and Fiametta had not had time to wait. Yet, strangely, she was not afraid. She knew little of these Salamanders who had come scuttling out of the smoking timbers of Cadenza's libraries, and cared even less for their destructive crusade. What would be left of the city, once its bookshelves were bare? It mattered not to her. So long as she and her uncle had left it behind.

Borso had agreed to meet her at the West Gate. He would not say where he was headed in the meantime, but Fiametta presumed that his path would take him past a convent on a secluded square upon the Verso, where the woman he loved resided. It would have astonished Borso to learn that his niece knew full well where he went, every other Sunday, dressed in his finest doublet and hose—even more so, to discover that she had engaged the services of a former soldier to tail him and inform her of his movements. Fiametta had spent a lifetime being underestimated, even by those who loved her. She had learnt to use it to her advantage.

Fiametta had never found her place in Cadenza, defined as she had become by a quarrel that had nothing to do with her. She thought the city dizzy in love with its reflection, breathless at the laudatory odes penned in its name. At one time she had tried to write herself—bashful verses, left unsigned at the bottom of her chest. But since the Carnival of Wit, she had given no thought to putting pen to paper. Bad enough, that she had been known as Feasting Fiametta—a name that haunted her at the dining table, whispered behind hands even as she declined dishes and retired hungry to bed—only then to be skewered upon the tip of Lorenzo Sardi's sharp pen, her name pinned to every tavern and library door for the city to mock... she recalled, with a shudder, her uncle that morning, the Bear roaring and swatting at the air as his *fideli* tried to restrain him. Her friends' attempts at commiseration only served to remind her of the brutal verse, even as she tried to push it from her mind. Great misfortune had befallen Cadenza since then: death and horror and unrest. The *Ode to Fiametta* had been largely forgotten—save by Fiametta herself, who remembered every word.

Amid much swearing, the coachman managed to extricate the carriage from the crowd and took to the Ponte Nuovo. The bridge was quiet, the Verso a rising rampart of shadows before them. The West Gate would have closed hours ago, but for Count Borso Cardano—still a member of the Seven—it would reopen. Fiametta willed the coachman to lash his whip, for the horses to strain upon their reins. She wanted them to fly from this city.

As the carriage hastened along the bridge, Fiametta looked out of the window and saw a woman dressed in black standing beneath the statue of Fredino di Rossi. At Fiametta's command, the coachman hauled upon the reins, guiding the horses towards the balustrade. The woman stepped forward from the shadows to greet them, only to fall silent at the sight of Fiametta. Her expression softened. In the soft glow of the carriage lanterns, Fiametta could see the lines of writing marked upon the woman's face and hands. She would have recognized her even without them.

"God grant you good evening, Lady Hypatia."

"And to you, child," came the soft reply. "I see the night is not yet dark enough to mask me. But Hypatia is no more, and she was never a lady. Call me Vittoria."

"I stopped when I saw you standing here alone," Fiametta said hesitantly. "The city is in uproar. I fear there will be violence before the night is out."

Vittoria looked back towards the Recto, its skyline bathed in a growing light. "The violence is already upon us," she said. "But I am not alone."

Fiametta faltered. "Forgive me... I do not see anyone..."

"Zanni is never far away," she replied. "His carriage will be here soon enough. Or perhaps he waits beneath the arches below us. He is my faithful servant. He will come for me."

"But what if something has happened to him?" Fiametta said. "You would be safer here with me, I think. I leave the city this night, with my uncle. He is a good man. He can protect us both."

Vittoria shook her head. "My story ends here," she said. "It requires only a final line." She held up a bundle of letters, tied up with black ribbon. "I meant to burn these with the others, but I made the mistake of opening one and when I started to read it, I..." She trailed off. "Not everything I regret."

"I have heard great poets talk of your letters in the salons," Fiametta said, impulsively. "With admiration and jealousy in equal measure. The poems you sent to seamstresses and fishermen are as prized as others' odes to popes and kings."

"The great poets, did you say?" Vittoria smiled. "And what of the lesser poets?"

"They said how beautiful you were."

She was rewarded with an unexpected laugh.

"I have been called worse things," said Vittoria.

"As have I."

The ink maid stared up at her. Fiametta shrank back slightly, her cheeks growing hot under the scrutiny. Vittoria stepped towards the carriage and held out the bundle of letters, with a deference that bordered on shyness.

"Would you take these for me?"

Fiametta hesitated. Finally, she nodded, and reached out through the window.

"I will guard them faithfully," she declared. "Should you ever wish their return, you need but write to me."

"It will be enough to know that they are in safe hands. Do you even know where you are headed?"

Fiametta shook her head.

Vittoria smiled. "Then Godspeed," she said softly. "And farewell."

The coachman lashed his whip, goading the horses into action before Fiametta could stop him. As the carriage lurched away, she looked down at the letters in her hand, aware that her heart was galloping in her chest. In her mind's eye, she saw a gate opening, a page turning—uncertainty and possibility, a future as yet unwritten. Fiametta laughed as the carriage picked up speed, brushing a stray lock of hair from her eyes. Only when the carriage alighted upon the Verso did she think to turn around, but when she looked back towards the statue of Fredino di Rossi, there was no sign of Vittoria upon the bridge.

XI. *The Strangest Thing*

MADDELINA SPENT AN hour combing the crumbling tombs of San Felice before reluctantly accepting that her sister had left her. She slumped upon the bench beside the grave of Ginevra di Lecce, too angry to cry. Vittoria had disappeared without a word of farewell or a final embrace, her chamber—where Maddelina had tended to her as she thrashed about the bed, screaming incoherently and dripping with sweat—standing pointedly empty. The chest of letters lay open and empty, not even a parting note.

As she watched the lettering on the ink maid's headstone slip into shadow, Maddelina resolved upon one thing: she would not allow herself to be packed up like fine linens and carted back to her father's estates, not while Vittoria embraced darkness and Carlo courted danger like some fool gallant. Maddelina had come to Cadenza to be part of its history, to insert herself in its pages—she would not be rendered a footnote. She hurried through the gathering darkness back to the church, where she changed into a doublet and hose from Ercole's stash of acquired keepsakes and tied her hair back into a short ponytail. It would be easier if she could pass for a man at a glance, a subterfuge improved by the addition of a large black cloak. She nodded with approval at her appearance in the looking-glass and, after a moment's deliberation, slipped a dagger into her boot.

As she walked down through the Verso, her hood up and cloak wrapped tightly around her, across the river Maddelina could see the flames glimmering above the rooftops across the river. Citizens were streaming by torchlight towards the Piazza della Rosa. The city had become ugly and unrecognizable—crossing the twilit Ponte Nuovo, Maddelina was grateful for the reassurance of the blade in her boot. At the Old Market, she parted from the crowds and headed east. To her surprise, she felt safer descending through the Printing Quarter, flitting like a shadow down the steps. The Salamanders had no interest here: the alleys were silent, taverns standing empty and dark. A stray hound eyed Maddelina from behind a well. Once before, she had come this way in search of Vittoria, and she remembered enough of the journey to find her way back to the printer's shop. The moon had risen by the time she arrived, which was to her advantage as no torches burned in the sconces outside, nor were there candles visible within the building's gloomy interior.

Pushing open the door, Maddelina was hit by a stench that seemed to churn out in waves from the silent presses. She pulled a face. The floorboards winced as she crept across them; in the backroom, a candle was burning low. A body was visible upon the floor through the open door. Maddelina reached down into her boot and slowly pulled out the knife. Edging forwards into the chamber, she stepped around the corpse of a huge man, the jagged remnants of a bottle's neck protruding from his own. Maddelina paled. It was Isidore, her fellow Plagiarist. Flies nested upon his face and around the pools of dried blood.

The door creaked behind Maddelina. She whirled around, lashing out with her knife as a figure sprang towards her. He stumbled backwards with a scream, crumpling into a heap on the floor.

"Please!" he begged, holding up his hands. "Don't hurt me!"

She had seen him before, in this very room, with Vittoria. Somehow the old man had sunk into an even greater state of wretchedness, dried blood matted in his hair and on his soiled clothing, a wild, incomprehensible look in his eyes. Maddelina took a steadying breath. She pointed her dagger at the corpse.

"What happened here?"

"It is a dark and sorry tale," he quavered. "I should never have left this place, but they left me no choice—they were going to make me Artifex and have me sit upon a throne inside the Palazzo Nero. You look at me as though I were a madman, but it is true. I heard them, you see, during the plague, planning Cosimo's death. Whispers through a golden mask. I fled the presses and sought out new quarters in the city, but I could not bear to be without the black water. When I returned here, my keeper flew into a rage. I begged him to leave me be, but he raised his hand against me; I picked up the bottle, and... I do not remember; I did not mean to..."

The old man gulped and drew his arms around his chest.

"What is your name?"

"I am Rinaldi," he said. "The poet."

"I seek my sister, Vittoria," Maddelina told him. "You were with her when I came here last."

"The veiled angel? She will not come here."

"How can you be so sure? What about the black water?"

"Look about you! There is no more black water."

"So where is she?"

"Do not look to me for answers, child. I was lost long before your sister."

"Yet here you sit before me, and Vittoria is gone," Maddelina said coldly. "How do I know that she did not suffer the same fate as Isidore?"

Rinaldi's eyes widened indignantly. "I would never have hurt her!" he whispered. "I loved her. And if you do also, you must let her go."

"She is my sister!"

"She walks a path of her own choosing."

Maddelina was struggling to keep her temper. She would not have this stranger, lost in his own madness and filth, claim such knowledge of Vittoria's mind. The oppressive squalor of the back room was making it hard for her breathe; she could not bear to stay here a moment longer.

"Very well," she declared. "You should know that the city has turned upon itself and torches its own buildings. It is not wise to stay here."

The old man beckoned her closer, glancing conspiratorially around the corners of the room.

"It is the strangest thing," Rinaldi whispered. "For so many years, I have been unable even to hold a pen in my hands, let alone guide it across the page. Yet since my keeper has gone quiet I have felt something change inside of me—a *click*, simple and glorious. See, now, the words return to me!"

Scrambling to his feet, Rinaldi went to his desk and

rummaged through his papers. He snatched up a sheet with a triumphant cry and pressed it into Maddelina's hands.

"Take this," he urged. "There was a time when my verses were much sought-after in this city. Perhaps they will be so again."

Maddelina stared at the parchment. Aware of the poet's hopeful gaze upon her, she looked up and smiled.

"Thank you, sir," she said. "A generous gift, truly."

Rinaldi nodded gravely and scuttled back to his desk, muttering to himself as he dipped his pen into the inkpot. Maddelina left him there, in the dingy back room with a crown of flies and the printer's bloated corpse for company, utterly absorbed in his work: pages and pages of frantic nonsense, indecipherable scrawls and meaningless marks. Emerging into the street, she closed the door behind her and took several deep breaths of air. Her hand was trembling as she returned the knife to her boot. The Printing Quarter was utterly still. To the west, there was fire in the sky.

XII. *A Thunderous Broadside*

It took gall, nobody could deny that. Even among the poets of Venice, there were few who dared take to the stage of the White Lion, for fear of earning the disapproval of the tavern's notoriously rowdy patrons. And by his dress and by his accent, the young man standing before them now—a mere spitting distance from the Arsenale!—was a Cadenzan. He acknowledged the hisses and boos with a placatory wave of his palms. His flushed cheeks suggested that he had sought courage in wine; perhaps understandably, given the circumstances.

"Hear me out, noble citizens of Venice!" he urged, above the rumbles of dissent. "I know well the bad blood that runs between our two cities, and that history would have us enemies. But believe me when I say that no one in this room has more reason than I to look unfavourably upon my birthplace, which fancies itself the City of Words."

"A bold boast!" a gruff voice replied.

"Let us see you prove it," barked another. "What verse do you offer us, Cadenzan?"

His hands shaking, the poet unfurled his parchment.

"Why, a *Denunciation*!" he declared. "My thunderous broadside against the late and unlamented Artifex of Cadenza, Cosimo Petrucci."

The crowd inside the White Lion stirred. Now here was something unexpected. Flashing them a nervous smile, Raffaele cleared his throat.

XIII. *The Wrath of Nero*

DRAGONS HAD BEEN let loose upon the Piazza della Rosa, three monstrous beings of flame clawing at the night sky, gorging on charred mouthfuls of parchment. One-by-one, the crowd stepped forward to feed them, clutching volumes looted from reading rooms and the shelves of household libraries. The stone benches stood empty; no speeches would decorate the square that night. Hoarse cries denounced Venice, the Council of Seven and the Folio in turn. At the doors to the Accademia, a thin line of guildsmen had mounted a last, desperate defence of the library; across the piazza, the Palazzo Nero was lost in darkness.

Carlo had spent hours battling through the seething masses in search of Ercole. Everywhere he looked, there were maddening glimpses of someone who might have been the gravedigger: a shock of white hair, a wizened grin, the gleam of a silver helm. But Ercole himself remained out of reach. How could he hope to find one man, in a city that had lost its mind?

The crowd swelled around Carlo, an angry, surging sea that threatened to lift him off his feet. As he was carried past the Well of Calliope, he grabbed the fountain's stone rim and pulled himself free. Wading through the ink, he climbed up beside the muse's statue. Fires were burning uncontrolled across the rooftops. Yet the people seemed not to care, swept up in a macabre dance around the blazing pyramids. Carlo had never imagined that there could be such revelry in hatred, nor glee in destruction—Ptolemy's star catalogues winked out and the maps of Hecataeus shrouded in fog.

From the midst of the tumult, a cry reached his ear. Peering into the throng, Carlo spotted a cloaked figure struggling against the tide, their arm reaching out despairingly towards him. A hood fell down to reveal Maddelina's face. Carlo jumped down into the ink and reached out from the fountain—their hands locked together, and he pulled her free. She was breathing heavily, a bruise reddening upon her temple.

"What are you doing here?" he shouted, above the din. "Where is Vittoria?"

"Gone!" she called back. "I came into the city to search

for her, but..." She faltered. "Wherever she is, she does not wish to be found."

"I am sorry, Maddelina," said Carlo. "Truly."

She nodded quickly. "And Ercole?"

"He could be stood right next to me and I would be none the wiser," he said. "It was a mistake coming here."

They stood together, knee-deep in ink, as heat billowed off the bonfires and the ragged banners of the Salamanders rippled proudly. The mood in the square was growing uglier, the defenders of the Accademia pressed back into the library doorway. Maddelina pulled her hood back up. Gripping hands tightly, she and Carlo jumped down from the fountain. The crowd enveloped them in a suffocating musk of sweat and ash. As they skirted around one of the bonfires, Carlo felt as though the breath was being physically pummelled from his chest. Through the flames, he spotted an alley leading off the square. He dragged Madelina towards it.

"You there!" a voice rang out.

The crowds stopped around them. By the alley's mouth, a group of Salamanders were passing a wineskin around a cairn of abandoned volumes, their cudgels resting easily upon their shoulders. Silently cursing, Carlo could only watch as one of their number, a youth, swaggered over.

"Are you leaving us, brothers?" he inquired archly. "Carnival is not yet done. Gasparo would know where you head in such haste."

"The hour grows late," Carlo said shortly. "And I grow weary."

Gasparo lifted his cudgel to toy with Maddelina's hood, snickering as she flinched and brushed it away.

"Three times now, you have passed this way," he said, "without once taking a book for the fires. Do you not admire our work here?"

"I seek a man named Ercole," Carlo tried. "An old man with white hair and a strange way of speech, who talks of transformations and the arts of alchemy. I was told he had joined your cause."

The Salamanders exchanged glances.

"Why, every one of us here is an alchemist!" Gasparo exclaimed, with a sweep of his arm. "Take a look around you—even a child can take dead parchment and transform it into vital fire. The barriers that separate us have been torn down, the library cabinets drained of their poison. A new future lies in the heart of these flames."

He picked up a volume from the pile and pressed it into Carlo's hands.

"Come, friend," he said, with a dangerous smile. "Make an offering in the name of your city."

A huge roar went up around the square—Carlo whirled around to see a ball of fire hurtling across the flagstones. For a moment, he thought that the great pyres had started to collapse in on themselves, but as the fireball writhed he realized, to his horror, that there was a man at the heart of the flames.

"The great Lorenzo Sardi!" Gasparo crowed. "Behold, the poet marches for our pleasure!"

Carlo did not even think. He swung the book square into the youth's face, felt Gasparo's nose crumple as its connected. Red sashes converged upon them—Maddelina grabbed hold of Carlo's arm and dragged him away, shouts of "Halt!" swallowed up by the flames. Across the piazza, Lorenzo reeled and staggered, a dying star jeered from the heavens as he collapsed to earth. His charred limbs twitched as fire pawed at his remains.

Carlo was belatedly aware of Maddelina pushing him through the screaming crowds; the shadow of the Accademia fell over them. A pitched battle had broken out at the library gates, members of the Folio standing side-by-side with the guards as they tried to repel the mob. An official leapt forward to block Carlo's path—he tossed the bloodied volume towards him, and the man instinctively caught it. Carlo charged past him, Maddelina a pace behind; the official turned to grab them, only to be felled by a blow from a Salamander. The remaining guards were lost to the melee as Carlo and Maddelina sprinted through the archway.

After the pandemonium of the Piazza della Rosa, the hush inside the library throbbed and thundered in the ears. The halls stood dark and pensive. As Carlo and Maddelina slowed to catch their breath, he realized that they were still holding hands, and hurriedly let go. Inside the main reading room, malevolent light danced in the windows of the Mezzanino. Volumes slumped in despair on the shelves. Carlo turned and looked back at the deserted hallway. He frowned.

"No one has come after us," he said.

Maddelina laughed nervously. "You would prefer an angry mob on our heels?"

"I would know what gives them pause. I'm not sure this was a wise move."

"What choice did you leave us?" she exclaimed, jabbing an indignant finger in his chest. "Would you wage war against the Salamanders on your own?"

"I hadn't thought that far ahead," Carlo muttered. He looked around the reading room. "The Salamanders had the numbers to take the Accademia hours ago. What are they waiting for?"

He moved through the bookcases, peering down aisles and scanning the upper tiers. Maddelina sighed and took a perch upon the circular counter in the middle of the hall. At the end of an aisle, a spiral staircase wound up to the Mezzanino: as Carlo climbed, his footsteps ringing out on the iron steps, the shelves fell away below him. Outside, the flames grew in the windows.

Upon reaching the gallery, Carlo let out a gasp. Hessian sacks filled with black powder had been piled up across the floor, the air alive with the sharp tang of nitre and saltpetre. The entire Mezzanino had been ringed with explosives. On the far side of the gallery, a figure sat slumped on a sack with his back against a column.

"Ercole!"

The gravedigger raised his head. His eyes widened at the sight of Carlo scrambling over the sacks towards him.

"What are you doing here?" he hissed.

"You ask that of *me*?" retorted Carlo, incredulously. "With you, sat upon an arsenal, set to blow us all sky-high!"

"Do you think I made myself the King of the Carnival of Ash of my own accord?"

Ercole twisted around. His hands had been tied behind him, anchoring him to the column. Carlo dropped to his knees and began picking at the knots.

"What happened here?" he said.

"To that, I must own to an error in calculation," Ercole

replied, "and the gauging of the relative influences of brain and brawn. When I learnt of the Salamanders and their dabbling with explosives, I sought to earn their confidence— the elements do not exist to be harnessed by the forces of idiocy and ignorance. But when I refused to fit the Accademia for a crown of fire, they elected to throw me on the bonfire instead."

"An error in calculation," Carlo repeated, with a shake of the head.

Maddelina appeared on the gallery steps, a question on her lips. The colour drained from her face as she apprehended the situation on the Mezzanino.

"The rose of San Felice?" Ercole offered Carlo an accusatory glare. "Have you lost your mind? What were you thinking, bringing her here?"

"I came of my own accord, sir," Maddelina called out. "I do not need Carlo's help to put one foot before the other. And if those ropes are the problem, I have the means to cut you free."

Reaching down inside her boot, she paused.

"What is it?" said Carlo.

"My knife!" she exclaimed despairingly. "It must have been knocked loose in the square!"

"Then our fingers must suffice," he said. "Come, help me."

She ran to his side. Hard as their fingers worked, they could not free Ercole—it was as though the ropes had been soaked in water, so tightly were they knotted. A deafening cheer went up from the Piazza della Rosa.

"It is too late," Ercole told them faintly, his gazed fixed on the gallery windows. "The fuse has been lit, the transformation begun."

"Confound these knots!" Carlo cried.

"Too many to unpick, and too little time. A question of arithmetic. It is time for you to go," he added meaningfully.

"We cannot just abandon you!" Maddelina exclaimed.

"Do not condemn each other to death in my name," he said. "I would not wish that upon my conscience, whichever destination awaits me. An old man's foolishness has led me here, the consequences of which are mine alone to face. I do so without fear."

His eyes met Carlo's. Ercole's weathered face broke into a smile.

"Farewell," he said.

Throwing down the rope, Carlo pulled the protesting Maddelina away and ran stumbling along the Mezzanino, unable to bring himself to look back at Ercole. As they raced down the stairs and past the counter in the centre of the hall, a fizzing sound sparked into life along the aisles. The windows brightened. It was, Carlo realized, too late.

He was reaching out for Maddelina's hand when the Accademia exploded.

XIV. *City of Flames*

FIRE ENGULFED THE hallways, cherubs exploding into flames upon the walls, the floor strewn with the alabaster limbs of philosophers and poets. Maddelina sat up with a groan. The force of the blast had lifted her off her feet, her head throbbing where she had banged it on the tiles. Carlo was crouched beside her, his mouth moving urgently, but she couldn't hear him above the deafening ringing in her ears. He helped her to her feet, and together they scrambled into a nearby alcove, taking shelter behind a statue teetering upon its plinth.

The explosion had rocked the Accademia to its foundations, the Mezzanino lost in smoke and chunks of stone hurtling down through the levels. Fire feasted on the bookshelves. The heat was a blacksmith's hammer, bludgeoning and relentless. Maddelina stared dumbly at Carlo as he shouted at her. To step back into the inferno seemed madness, but she knew that they could not hide in the alcove forever—somewhere in the smoke there must lie a door or a window, a way to safety. At a questioning glance from Carlo, she took a deep breath and nodded.

They burst from the alcove and ran through an archway into the nearest reading room. Lecterns blazed, books writhing upon the shelves. The windows were obscured by a curtain of fire. Carlo threw up his hands in despair. A portion of ceiling came down on the bookcase behind him, sending it teetering upon its base—screaming a warning, Maddelina ran forward and charged into his back. The ground shivered as the shelves crashed down upon the tiles. Maddelina's hearing returned to her in a sudden flood, plunging her into the heart of the inferno, the roaring flames and the groan of wood, the violent crack of falling masonry. Carlo had frozen on his hands and knees, examining the floor.

"What are you doing?" Maddelina cried. "We have to find a way out!"

"We have," he said.

Peering over his shoulder, she saw that the fallen bookcase

had punched a hole in the mosaic. Tiles crumbled and cascaded into darkness. Through the layers of rock beneath the library floor, Maddelina caught a glimpse of another level of solid ground.

"Have you lost your mind?" she shouted. "We'll be buried alive!"

"Then by all means, stay here!" Carlo shouted back.

Lying on his belly, he slid himself backwards into the hole, sounding out the rockface with his feet for purchase.

"Come on!" he yelled.

A huge stone smashed into the floor at Maddelina's feet. She took one look at the blazing reading room and went after Carlo, disappearing down through the broken mosaic.

INSIDE THE DOGE'S Apartments in Venice, shadows danced across the ornate wooden ceiling of the Scarlet Chamber. A fire was burning merrily, to the delight of the carved cherubs who nestled among the acanthus leaves entwined around the hearth. Andrea Gritti sat at his desk, his pen scratching briskly across the parchment. He cleared his throat. Dipping his pen in the inkpot, the Doge paused, as though hearing a noise. He shook his head and resumed writing.

Outside the palace, the moon's reflection rippled in the lagoon.

DOWN THEY WENT into the earth, one careful handhold after another, through swirling clouds of ash and scraps of burning parchment. The Accademia was a blood-red eye, gazing balefully over them. Carlo concentrated on the rockface, seeking out the ledges and niches that could support him. He could hear Maddelina's breaths as she came after him, the tsks of irritation as she struggled for grip. The floor reared up in a jagged wave of stone. When he judged the distance safe enough, Carlo let himself drop, landing in a crouch on the ground. He went back to help Maddelina but she waved him away, scrambling down from the rocks with a triumphant exclamation. Her face was covered in sooty streaks and there was dried blood on her temple, but her eyes were bright. Brushing down their clothes, they peered into the gloom, trying to piece together their surroundings.

They were standing in an underground chamber, which at some point in time had suffered a great act of violence, buckling the floor and crushing toppled pillars between jaws of earth. Bookcases leaned at odd angles; dusty scrolls lay scattered across the ground. The passage of years hung heavy in the cool air.

Maddelina blew out her cheeks. "Are we safe, do you think?"

"I have no idea," replied Carlo. "We are alive for now, at least." He stared down at his bloodied fingers. "I could not save Ercole."

"Had we waited a moment longer, we would all be dead," she told him. "Ercole's blood is on the hands of the Salamanders, not yours."

A loud boom from the surface reverberated down through the chamber. Carlo stepped back as a book came plummeting down from the Accademia, bouncing off the rocks and landing in a shower of sparks and charred parchment. They retreated into the bookshelves, the only illumination the glowing embers spiralling down from the burning library. Carlo carefully slid a scroll free from the shelf. The parchment threatened to crumble to dust in his hands as he unrolled it to reveal pages of cramped Latin text, painstakingly rendered in a scribe's delicate hand. At the end of the aisle, Maddelina reached out to trace her hand around a crushed window frame looking out directly into the earth.

"Light came through this window once," she murmured. "What sort of library *is* this?"

As Carlo looked down at the decaying parchment, a strange expression crossed his face. His hands began to tremble. Swallowing, he looked up at Maddelina.

"It is not a library," he said hoarsely. "It is *the* library. The first. This is the House of Uccello."

IN THE AFTERMATH of the Great Fire of Cadenza, a popular myth arose that it had been the vengeful spirit of Lorenzo Sardi who had caused the blaze to spread from the Piazza della Rosa to the wider city, hot sparks carrying on the spectral poet's breath to the neighbouring palaces. Other witnesses attested, more soberly, that it had been the flames engulfing the Bibliotheca Niccoló that had burned out of control, setting the district alight. Did it matter, in the final reckoning? Fire raged through the streets of Cadenza, indiscriminate and furious, consuming the churches and the printing houses, the taverns and the trees and the workshops. The Accademia shone brightest of all, a blazing lighthouse announcing the end of the world. As the Salamanders' pyres shuddered and collapsed in upon themselves, the throngs upon the Piazza della Rosa suddenly realized the peril of their situation: a mass exodus from the square ensued, bodies trampled beneath the crush. There were fistfights on the clogged bridges, screams as bodies toppled over the parapets and into the river.

Standing alone atop the East Gate, Poggio watched the city burn. His shift was supposed to have ended hours ago, but there was no sign of his commander nor any of his fellow guards. Poggio would happily have abandoned his post, if only he could work out the safest direction in which to flee— into the fire-ravaged city, or out into the pitch-black fields, where he saw Venetians behind the silhouette of every hedge and tree. Frozen with indecision, he remained marooned at his post, clutching his pike with white-knuckled hands.

As the Accademia dissolved into flames, Poggio spotted a strange figure upon the Via Maggio. An old man came tottering towards the gate, reeling as though drunk, his wild hair singed and standing upon end, his clothes hanging in charred rags from his arms and legs.

"Halt!" Poggio cried.

"You will have to shout!" the old man hollered back. "I see your lips move but there is a great buzzing in my ears, as though a swarm of bees have taken residence in the canals of my brain."

"You have come from the Accademia?" Poggio bellowed down.

He nodded emphatically. "That I have, at pace and showered in soot and sparks, as though fired direct from a Spanish cannon. By all known logic, the laws of man, I should be dead—and yet, is the aether not beyond logic and law? If it can direct a tortoiseshell toward a philosopher's head, why not deliver an old man to safety from an exploding inferno?"

Poggio stared down at him, bewildered.

"The gate is closed!" he called down. "Come back when it is light!"

The old man gestured behind him. "You would maintain the curfew? How can you call it night, when the sky burns brighter than morning?"

"Fire or no, this gate stays closed," Poggio shouted, pleased at the firmness in his voice. "I have my orders."

"From whom? You would seem to be all alone up there. Where is your captain of the guard? Halfway on the road to Ferrara, I'll wager."

That thought had not occurred to Poggio—yet, as he considered it, it seemed exactly the sought of thing that Federigo might do.

"Where are you headed?" he cried.

"That, the road will determine," came the reply. "I am a wayfarer, possessed of a restless temper, who cannot remain in any one place for long. There is nothing left in this city for me. I must continue on alone."

"All the more reason to remain here until dawn," Poggio told him. "Better that, than risk the road at night."

"This city will not *be* here by dawn," he countered. "Better to open the gates now by choice, than be here when the fire takes it by force. Come, my valiant watchman, raise your barrier, and we can walk to safety together."

Poggio hesitated. Mad though the old man might be, there was sense in his suggestion, and the notion of company upon the road made the flight into the night a more palatable prospect. Leaning his pike against the wall, Poggio hurriedly began to turn the winch. Cogs bit; chains turned. As the gate jerked open, the old man clapped his hands together and tottered forward, whistling a tuneless melody to himself.

MADDELINA STARED AT Carlo in disbelief. "The House of Uccello?" she said. "But how?"

"After the earthquake struck, the Folio must have built the Accademia right on top of it," Carlo said slowly. "Like a gravestone."

"And when the Salamanders set off their explosion..."

"...it reopened a path down to it," he finished. He rubbed his face in amazement. "My family possesses a scroll said to have once rested upon these shelves," he murmured. "*De Incendio Urbis*, by the poet Lucan. It is the pride of the Mazzoni family, just a single volume. And here..."

Carlo gestured around the shelves, overwhelmed.

"Not everything need be destroyed," Maddelina told him, her eyes shining. "We can bring these volumes back to the surface so that they can be read once again."

"And where shall we put them?" Carlo said, with a bitter laugh. "There are no more libraries to house them!" He kicked out angrily at a smouldering page. "I still cannot believe what has happened here—what has been destroyed, in the name of the people."

"They did not fight to stop it."

"Then they are fools."

"They are frightened, Carlo! Cosimo, the plague, the threat of Venice..."

"They have killed their own city."

At that moment, he was aware, there might have been no one else in the world save the two of them, surrounded by the wisdoms of the ancient world, their truths undimmed by the darkness—the angle of the midday sun in the sky, the moon's pull upon the tides; a crown lowered into a brimming bathtub.

The earth shivered once more, burning wooden spars and fragments of mosaic raining down inside the cavern. Carlo looked up dubiously. "I do not know if we shall be able to escape this place."

"Didn't you tell me that all the great writers of Cadenza were buried beneath the Accademia?"

He smiled ruefully. "I had hoped to live a little first before joining them," he said. "To write something worthy of their company."

Maddelina brushed a sooty mark from his cheek with her thumb. "Do not despair," she said affectionately. "The fire cannot last forever."

"And until the flames die out?"

Laughter echoed around the House of Uccello. "Why, poet, need you ask?" she declared, with a sweeping gesture towards the dusty shelves. "Tell me a story!"

Acknowledgements

The Carnival of Ash is a work of fantasy, with only the loosest mooring in past reality. That said, it owes a huge debt of inspiration to certain histories of the Italian Rennaissance and beyond. I am particularly grateful for the following volumes:

Venice: Pure City, by Peter Ackroyd; *A Universal History of the Destruction of Books*, by Fernando Baez; *The Devil's Doctor*, by Philip Ball; *Books in Chains*, by William Blades; *Kalllimachos: The Alexandrian Library and the Origins of Bibliography*, by Rudolf Blum; *The Civilization of the Renaissance in Italy*, by Jacob Burckhardt; *Fighting the Plague in Seventeenth Century Italy*, by Carlo Cipolla; *April Blood* and *Fire in the City: Savonarola and the Struggle for the Soul of Renaissance Florence*, by Lauro Martines; *Ancient and Medieval Siege Weapons*, by Konstantin Nossov; *Murano: A History of Glass*, by Gianfranco Toso.

Needless to say, they share no blame for any anachronisms or infelicities you may find in these pages: like Apellicon of Teos, I take full responsibility.

Building a city—even one of the imagination—is no small task. A decade has passed since the idea of Cadenza first came to me, and for much of that time I never dreamed that it might find its way into print. Huge thanks to everyone at Rebellion Publishing; to Chris Bryans and Neil Coffey, for their wise words of advice; and to RCW's Sam Copeland, for his heroic championing of Cadenza's cause. My thanks and my love in equal measure go to Lindsay and Ezra. This book is for them.

FIND US ONLINE!

www.rebellionpublishing.com

/rebellionpub   /rebellionpublishing /rebellionpublishing

SIGN UP TO OUR NEWSLETTER!

rebellionpublishing.com/newsletter

YOUR REVIEWS MATTER!

Enjoy this book? Got something to say?

Leave a review on Amazon, GoodReads or with your
favourite bookseller and let the world know!